AERIE

By

Anne Riley

Aerie is a work of fiction. The names, characters, and events included in this work are products of the author's imagination. Where real places or entity names are used, they are done so with fictitious intent. Any resemblance to actual persons or events is entirely coincidental. The Internet is real, though. I swear.

Thank you

Celeste Riley Brennecka - Editor

CreateSpace Independent Publishing Platform

ISBN: 978-1499534801

AERIE

According to Mike Taylor, Computer Genius

"That, my friend, is the great Oz."

"The rumors are flying. It's a fricking zoo upstairs."

"Dammit, Liam. Do you hear me? Cara is gone. Missing. I can't find her anywhere."

"Two minutes, twenty-five seconds, Lauren. What took you so long?"

"Rumor had it Peter's head almost exploded."

"Liam is a good guy, but he's not going to cut it as the poster boy for Technology World."

Roger, one-niner, target is approaching north by northwest of our present location …"

I'm just hot, right now. I'm sexy too, but that's another story altogether."

"The cherry wood version. Very sophisticated."

"Authorized breaking and entering? This will be fun!"

"Ha, I know that look. Watch out, Liam. She's in negotiating mode."

"You are such an incredibly bad liar, Cara. What are you planning?"

"I've told you before. It's only a felony if you get caught."

AERIE

Is dedicated to:

Jim, Celeste, and Erin

How lucky I was to get to know you first.

The world is a better place because you are here.

Love, love, love.

AERIE

TABLE OF CONTENTS

AERIE

By

Anne Riley

To Josh Henry —
Enjoy!

[signature] 7/24/14

June 1991

Chapter 1

PRINT. Cara Larson pressed the Enter key and glanced at her watch. The data model would take at least a half hour to print. She walked to the window where the clouds hung so low they obscured the houses nestled in the West Hills. It could be January judging by the leaden cast of the sky. But it wasn't. It was June. The third day of June. She had been back in Portland exactly four weeks. She soaked in the view. The cooling rains and the thousand hues of gray were familiar and precious, but not comforting. Not today.

Three months ago her life had been humming along. She had been working on an important computer project for Pyramid Corporation in suburban Chicago when the announcement came over e-mail. Fleet, a large sportswear maker headquartered in Portland, planned to build a new system called FIT. FIT. Fleet Information Technology. Fleet didn't do things in a small way. The company wanted to create a single integrated business system to replace the mass of overlapping systems that had mushroomed as it grew into the largest sportswear producer in the country. Consistent with its prominent status, Fleet wanted Pyramid, the most prestigious technology firm in the country, to bid on its flagship project.

FIT was Cara's chance to return home. She needed about three and a half seconds to send her request to serve on the proposal team to Charlie Schmidt, the managing partner of the Chicago office. The irony didn't escape her. All her friends were moving east, trying to get promotions in New

York, the home of Pyramid's headquarters. Here she was going as far west as possible. She was a salmon swimming upstream.

As a Portland native, Cara had an edge when Pyramid's management selected the team. Plus, she practically fell down on her knees and begged Charlie for the chance.

She worked tirelessly on the proposal. She and Peter Whittington, the hard charging project manager, flew between Chicago and Portland so often they were on a first-name basis with the flight attendants on the 7:00 a.m. nonstop. They submitted so many preliminary data models and network architectures and implementation plans, she thought they would all drown in a sea of documentation. They pulled so many all-nighters she was no longer able to tell the difference between a sunrise and a sunset.

Amidst the blizzard of paper and promises and four-star dinners, Fleet agreed to a nine-month, $10 million contract that made the managers at Pyramid glow with anticipation and Cara dizzy with relief. She didn't give a hoot about relevant market position or upside profitability or any of the other pretentious terms they threw around like confetti during the negotiations. All that mattered was that she was going back to the rain. Back to the green. Back to Mama.

She stared at the busy sidewalks below and felt the familiar squeeze in her stomach, the tense worry. She should have seen the signs, should have known something was wrong, should have come back sooner, should have ... should have ... *should have!* Those words tormented her.

She eyed her computer. She excelled at her job. She could make information come alive. She enabled companies to get data at the push of a button, penetrate new markets, and sell to customers all over the world. She could make that box sing. But she hadn't been able to see the simple truth in the one face she loved.

She glanced at her watch. The half hour had flown by. She hurried from her office and weaved through the forest of cubicles to the copy room.

The four-by-six foot data model was just rolling off the printer. Carefully she tore off the printout, furled it into a long tube, and secured it with two rubber bands. She stopped at the project administrator's desk as she returned to her office. "Anna, I'm transferring my calls to you for the day. I don't want to be disturbed except for an absolute emergency. I'm determined to review this model today."

"No problem, Cara." Anna peered up from her keyboard and straightened her oversized striped sweater as it slipped over her shoulder. She noted the size of the paper tube. "Will one day be enough?"

Cara gave her a wry smile. "Still fifteen hours left. I have a fighting chance."

Anna waved her on as she adjusted her sweater again. "I'll make sure you're not interrupted."

Cara unrolled the printout and taped it to the wall. She pushed the Transfer button on her phone, removed several colored pens from her desk drawer, and set to work reviewing the data structure for the purchasing segment of Fleet's proposed system. She managed the Purchasing team. Her job was to unite the myriad ways Fleet purchased products and materials. Joe Martin headed the order entry team, which needed to be reconstructed to accommodate orders from all over the world. Bob Tillson led the manufacturing system, which required a complete overhaul now that Fleet was experiencing rapid growth in its athletic apparel and footwear lines.

Cara started into the model, verifying the data tables. She laid out her notes and interview transcripts across the desk. Then on the chairs in front of the desk. Then over the floor. The once-pristine printout took on the colors of a rainbow as she highlighted each table according to its status: Green meant go; everything was correct. Yellow meant redesign; the concepts were correct, but the table structure was either flawed or inefficient. Red meant stop; more research was required. By the time she marked all the tables and sketched out several alternatives near the yellow and red ones, her frustration had disappeared, but so had her energy. Three o'clock! Where had the day gone?

Mike Taylor strolled along the row of nondescript cubicles toward Cara's office, chatting amiably with his visitor. His bleached hair spiked upward and glistened with an unnatural sheen. "I think you have a terrific idea, Liam, but we should run it by my boss. If anyone can crush inspiration, it's Larson."

"That's what I need, Mike." Liam Scofield settled his hands in his pockets and matched the stride of the blond young man beside him. "I've been running Windwear for seven years now, and I've developed a simple way to test an idea. Find an expert in the field, like your boss, Larson is it? and explain the concept. The key is in the reaction. I can always tell within a minute or two if it's time to revisit the idea department for a few modifications."

"Well you're in the right place. Larson is legendary for finding a computer system's weak points and beating them unmercifully until they either die an agonizing death or survive as a workable design."

Mike paused in front of Cara's office. "Before we go in, I think I should warn you about my boss. Larson is … intense. A real hard driver. You know the type. Demanding. Relentless. Chews people up and spits them out if they don't have their facts together. Destroys, on average, three new ideas before lunch."

"Hmm, sounds like a winner. Tell me, does this Larson guy have some factual basis for rejecting ideas, or is he an equal opportunity idea hater?"

"Don't get your knickers in a twist. I just wanted to warn you."

"Fair enough. Warning duly noted. I am officially prepared to meet Genghis Khan."

"Good." Mike smiled, opened the door to Cara's office, and motioned Liam to proceed. Liam took two steps inside and stopped in surprise as he met a bitter memory. Of golden hair, violet eyes, and a sparkling diamond. He blinked once, and the image cleared. Strange to have such a flashback, especially when the woman standing at the far end of the room looked nothing like his ex-wife. She was not blonde like Jennifer. Fiery hair somewhere between russet and red struggled from an unkempt knot at her neck. She didn't share Jennifer's violet eyes. This woman had large green ones that were so focused on her work she had no idea anyone else was even in the room. And she wore no ring on her finger. He whispered to Mike, "This is ... Larson? Your boss?"

Mike sighed. "Yeah, I'm afraid so. Don't say I didn't warn you." He crashed the door handle into the wall. "Cara what have you been doing in here all day? I need you to meet someone." He stopped. "Uh-oh." He took a few steps backward and leaned his head outside. "Anna, did you give Cara crayons? She's been in here coloring! Do you realize what her billing rate is?" A crumpled paper wad came flying back at him. Mike dodged the lumpy missile as it fell harmlessly to the floor. "It's dangerous out there. We'd better keep going."

Cara was redrawing a set of three tables for handling material receipts. She did not even look up as the two men approached.

"Hey Cara, you're coloring outside the lines." Mike surveyed the disheveled office. "You are such a slob, boss."

The only response was the raspy scratch of pen on paper as Cara continued to mark up the model.

"Look at this place. What would Peter think? I tell you, boss, he is going to fire your butt one of these days." Liam glanced at Mike in surprise.

Cara was unaware of Mike's commentary. After a few minutes, she capped the pen. "Done." She rubbed her eyes and turned toward her desk. Had a hurricane swept through? Open binders filled with flow diagrams and interview transcripts covered the desk and spilled over the chairs and across the floor. She looked up at the two men standing in the middle of the room. Mike stifled a laugh. The other man seemed more than a little confused. "Mike, you didn't tell me we had a visitor."

"Actually I did, but as usual, you ignored me." He turned to Liam and shivered dramatically." Didn't I tell you? Intense." He smiled at his boss. "Cara, meet Liam Scofield, president and CEO of Windwear Corporation."

Cara approached them, studying Liam as she walked across the room. He was tall, his face a study in browns. Waves of thick hair, the color of fresh coffee, careened about his head, even though it was cut short at the sides. His face was tan and rough from the sun. A dimple shadowed his left cheek, and his wide thin mouth was drawn into a measured frown. What drew her attention were his eyes. Intense and deep and serious. Compelling eyes. She extended her hand as she reached him. "Cara Larson, manager of the purchasing team. It's a pleasure to meet you."

Still frowning, he took her hand. "Likewise, Ms. Larson."

Cara was puzzled. Had she slipped up someplace? Forgotten an appointment? Missed a meeting? She slanted a look at Mike. "Is there a problem, Mike?"

"No, not at all," Mike said innocently. "Liam has some ideas that might affect FIT, and I thought you would want to hear them before you did your review." Mike tilted his head at the colorful diagram. "Guess I'm a little late, huh?"

Cara sighed in resignation. At twenty-one, Mike was blond, brash, and brilliant. Okay, a bleach blond with an ever changing spiked hair-architecture, but that was the style these days. He was the quintessential whiz kid. An authentic genius just two years out of Stanford, Mike served as the lead designer for her team and the technical expert for the entire thirty-five-member project. He had the easy confidence that came with genius, and his cleverness was matched only by his irreverence to any and all authority. She couldn't control him. And didn't try.

"Please take a seat. Tell me what's on your mind." An embarrassed tinge crept up her face. "Sorry. Let me make some room first." She picked up the notebooks from one of the two wooden chairs and placed them in the corner. Without a word, the men moved the remaining documents next to the newly formed pile.

"Thank you." She walked to her desk, and Liam and Mike settled in the uncomfortable seats.

Mike eyed the piles. "Been busy, eh, boss?"

Cara nodded. "I just finished."

Mike studied his watch with exaggerated care. "I know. I timed our entrance perfectly."

Cara let the ghost of a smile sneak through. "What do you have, Mike?"

Mike's transformation was sudden and complete. Laughter gone, he leaned over, his face serious. "Remember last week when Rick Penner asked us to interview Liam and a few of Fleet's other major suppliers to learn about issues with Fleet's purchasing system?" Cara nodded. "Well, Liam brought up an awesome idea to streamline operations. I'm talking innovative, elegant, cutting-edge stuff. More complicated than your basic vanilla system, but if we encrypt security codes and come up with a time-stamping technique to prevent unauthorized access and—"

Cara put her two hands together in the form of a T. "Time out, Mike. Take a deep breath." She glanced at her visitor's serious face. "Before we start, would you mind rustling up something from the cafeteria?"

"No sweat. The usual?"

She nodded. "Thanks."

Mike slammed the door exuberantly on his exit, and Liam turned to her with a wary expression. "He's very ... enthusiastic about his work."

Cara raised an eyebrow. "Mike's enthusiastic about everything." She studied him thoughtfully. "Is something the matter, Mr. Scofield?"

"Why do you ask?"

She sighed. "Mike did it, didn't he?"

"I'm not sure I know what you're talking about."

"Did he give you the Attila speech? Let me see, what colorful adjectives did he use today? Relentless? Ambitious? Over-zealous? He likes that one in particular." Her smile didn't quite reach her eyes. "By the time he shows visitors in, they expect to find Ms. Attila the Hun waiting to eat them alive. Am I right, Mr. Scofield?"

A faint glint of humor escaped from his eyes. "Well, you're not exactly what I expected. I'm afraid I had you pegged as a six-foot-four, 300-pound ex-football player who eats nails for breakfast."

"I see. I thought I cured Mike of this particular habit." She sighed again. "He can be … unconventional."

"I can see that, Ms. Larson. However, I've already been to junior high and have no desire to repeat the experience."

Cara took in the man's annoyed expression. "I apologize for Mike's behavior, Mr. Scofield. He *is* young and sometimes misjudges a situation. Mike was actually paying you a compliment. I believe he thought you shared his sense of humor."

"Are you saying I don't have a sense of humor, Ms. Larson?"

Cara barely kept herself from rolling her eyes. "Of course not. Just not Mike's sense of humor. Believe me, it's not a criticism."

"Does anyone share his sense of humor?"

She smiled. "Well, you would have been the first."

"I guess that's something."

Cara caught the hint of a smile at one corner of his mouth. "Indeed. I'm not sure I could handle a world with two Mikes." She paused. "Shall we start over, Mr. Scofield?"

"Fair enough, Ms. Larson."

"Please, call me Cara."

"All right … Cara." Her name came off his lips like warm honey on a cold night. Cara felt an unfamiliar twinge at the sound. Strange.

"I'm confused," Liam was saying as she dragged her attention back to his words. "I came here today at Mike's request. I thought he was serious about my idea having potential. Now, I'm not so sure. I don't know whether his invitation was just a junior high prank, or he actually thinks the idea has merit."

"Let's back up if we can, Mr. Scofield. Tell me about your initial discussion with Mike. Barring his 'junior high behavior,' did he understand your operational issues?"

"Yes, he did."

"Did he identify the technical concerns related to your idea?"

"Yes."

"And did he provide you with alternative implementation scenarios?"

"Yes."

"Are you satisfied he is competent and capable of dealing with your issues?"

"Yes, I am." Liam shifted slightly in his seat.

"Well, Mr. Scofield, I would say you're in luck. Your ideas have just passed test number two."

"Nice recovery, Cara. I can tell you've had practice cleaning up after your young colleague, but I'm pretty busy these days. I don't have patience for some convoluted pseudo-psychological Rorschach test that is intended to secretly qualify me as a customer. If I decide to retain Pyramid for this work, I expect you to be honest and direct and keep my company's best interests in mind at all times. I'm not sure Mike inspires that level of confidence."

Cara dropped her elbows to her desk, crossed her arms over them, and faced him squarely. "Mr. Scofield, I understand what you're saying, and you have every right to be annoyed. But I would like you to understand the situation a little more clearly. Mike Taylor is a genius. He is, without question, the best designer at Pyramid. I wouldn't trade him for a whole army of designers. Now, Mike didn't walk in here and say your idea was good or okay. He walked in here and said your idea was awesome. I don't hear that very often. That is the only reason we're talking right now.

"If you want to get upset about whether Mike's approach is unprofessional or immature, or his sense of humor is twisted off center, or we do not portray the perfect picture of professionalism, all of which are true to some extent, feel free to walk out the door and share your ideas with someone else. I won't stop you. On the other hand, if you want to stay for a few minutes and discuss your ideas with us, well, that's all right too." She paused, tapping her fingers on the desk as if waiting. "It's your choice, Mr. Scofield."

Tense silence filled the office as they stared at each other. "Well, I can see why you're not in sales," he said at last.

"And I can see why you're not in personnel."

"Mike wasn't lying about all those adjectives, was he?"

"Only the part about being six-foot-four and 300 pounds."

He paused, considering his options. "I guess you'd better call me Liam."

Cara suppressed her sigh of relief. She hated playing the role of hard-nosed businesswoman. The man sitting in front of her was correct on every point he made. She didn't like pushing a potential client's back to the wall from the start. It didn't bode well for the future. Delivering a system was difficult enough when everyone got along. It could be a disaster if they were sniping at each other from the outset. She was really going to have to rein Mike in.

As if on cue, there was a knock on the door. "Can I come in now? Are you finished, Cara?"

"Finished with what?"

"You know, the apology thing." Mike walked over to Liam and handed him an icy bottle of water. "Every time I bring a new client to meet her, she sends me to get refreshments. So she can apologize for my 'junior high behavior'." Mike mimicked Cara's voice when he said the last few words.

Liam and Cara exchanged a look. She shook her head in silent defeat.

"Did she grovel, Liam? I've been trying to get her to grovel for the longest time, but so far no go. Did she do it this time?" Mike's eyes were hopeful.

Liam couldn't help his smile. "Afraid not, Mike."

"That's quite enough, Mike," Cara cut in. "Mr. Scofield is not amused."

Mike glanced sideways at Liam. "No, Cara, you're wrong. There is definitely a flicker of amusement. That's good news. It was touch and go for a while there. I thought for sure we'd lost him."

Liam laughed aloud. "He must be very good, Cara."

She raised one eyebrow. "Why don't we proceed? Where would you two like to start?"

Mike turned to his visitor. "Go ahead, Liam."

"I started Windwear seven years ago, making hiking boots. The company has grown quickly and now produces a full line of outdoor footwear and outerwear. We're planning to expand into the camping gear market within the year.

"Right now, we use an over-the-counter accounting program with a mishmash of spreadsheets and loose forms to manage our production. It will be woefully inadequate for the growth we are expecting in the next few years."

As Liam spoke, Cara turned her chair sideways, crossed one leg over the other, and stared into space. Liam looked uncertainly at Mike who grinned and shrugged his shoulders.

"Windwear supplies many companies, Fleet being the largest, with hiking boots and outerwear. Manufacturing these large orders causes huge swings in our production capability. Because the purchase orders cover such sizeable quantities, our customers spend several weeks or even months preparing them. By the time we get a PO, the timeframe is often tight and the volumes are so large, it's difficult to meet the schedule. We are forced to either delay the order or work people overtime, which sends our costs out of control.

"The flip side presents problems as well. When no large orders are in the pipeline, the manufacturing facility sits idle soaking up costs and producing nothing."

Cara turned to Mike. "We addressed this in FIT, right? Aren't we're adding the capability for Fleet to issue blanket POs?"

"Yeah, instead of issuing POs on a random basis, Windwear and Fleet would agree to terms of a blanket PO covering certain products for a fixed price and a specific period. When Fleet wants to place an order, they offset it against the open quantities on the blanket PO, thus avoiding the approval process altogether and cutting response time."

Liam nodded. "That's definitely part of the solution, but I want to go a step further."

"Listen to this, Cara," Mike said. "It's awesome. Tell her, Liam."

"I want to link Fleet and Windwear's inventory systems together."

Cara looked up sharply. "Link them together? How?"

"Well, I assume Windwear is like a lot of companies. We use a local network for our in-house systems to enable everyone in the company to communicate. We also subscribe to Compuserve to connect with organizations outside the company. It made me think. If the infrastructure exists to allow companies to interact over a network, shouldn't two companies be able to interact for a specific reason? That's what I want to do. I want to set up an electronic link between Fleet and Windwear to enable us to share production information.

"The arrangement benefits both sides. Windwear would obtain access to Fleet's inventory information. We could then schedule production at our discretion and use our capacity more efficiently. In return, Fleet can check product availability at any time."

"Isn't it brilliant, Cara?" Mike jumped in. "Windwear would kill its competition with a system like this. They'd be begging for mercy. It would be awesome!"

"Well, that's the plan. If it works with Fleet, we would want to expand the capability to other large customers." Liam stopped and waited for the reaction. This was the key moment. Time to read in this woman's face the strength of his idea.

Cara sat still, staring into space, head angled, eyes focused. Not one flicker of emotion. Not a smile, not a frown, not a quiver of an eyebrow. Not a clue to validate the concept. All she did was listen, with those big green eyes furrowed in concentration, her opinions hiding beneath a prim mask. Perhaps he was wrong. Maybe this was a bad idea. He'd had some of those before.

Mike burst into the silence. "Of course, we would need to determine the type of operating data to be transmitted and how to store—"

Cara put up her hand to stop Mike. She faced the two men in front of her. "Mike, you were right. It is elegant. And innovative." She brushed her fingers along her jaw, choosing her words carefully. "And quite possibly, illegal."

Chapter 2

Liam and Mike both lurched forward. "Illegal?" they shouted in unison.

"I told you," Mike sighed grimly. "Relentless."

"What do you mean, illegal?" Liam said, ignoring Mike. Damn, he thought. Bad idea.

"I'm not a lawyer, and we'll definitely need a legal opinion, but there may be some antitrust implications to a setup like this."

"Antitrust? You're going to have to explain." Damn, he thought again. Really bad idea.

"Let's say you create an agreement with Fleet fixing prices over a set period of time, and then implement this system your competitors do not have. If these two things cause Fleet to purchase from you rather than your competitors, you could be sued on grounds of inhibiting competition. That is, by definition, an antitrust case. You may not actually be inhibiting competition, but you can be sued if you merely create the conditions that make a significant reduction in competition probable."

Liam ran his thumb and forefinger across his chin. "Wait a second. You mean to tell me we can be penalized for being better at business? That if we work hard to provide pricing advantages and efficient product delivery, we can be sued?"

She nodded. "This is an ambiguous area. An invisible line defines a fair playing field between competitors. The problem is, no one knows where the line is anymore. Technology is changing the way businesses operate in a fundamental way, and the feds haven't been able to keep pace with regulations. Sometimes the only way for companies to affect change—or prevent it—is through lawsuits.

"From what I've seen on this project, sportswear is a highly profitable, extremely competitive business. If Windwear gains too much of an advantage, your competitors may sue to prevent you from operating your new system. At least until they can figure out how to keep up with you."

"This is crazy. We want to use a system like this *because* we're in a competitive industry. We want a competitive edge."

"I thought you wanted to cut costs and make your operations more efficient."

"Of course we do, but if we can reduce competition at the same time, all the better."

"Reduce competition yes, but not eliminate it. Finding the proper line between those two conditions is the critical issue." For a moment, silence filled the room. Then Cara snapped her fingers. "Which, of course, is exactly what you do."

"What?" Liam was puzzled.

"Walk the line. If you made the system generic enough to be accessible to other businesses at a reasonable price, your antitrust problem would disappear."

Liam met her smile with a frown. "You mean generic enough so my competitors can use it? Why would I want to do that? I'm not interested in giving my competitors an advantage."

"Actually I was thinking along the lines of you selling them that advantage." Cara studied him thoughtfully. "This kind of information would help a lot of businesses. Why not create a saleable product? It might prove to be profitable."

Mike's eyebrows shot up in surprise. "Ooh, Cara. An entrepreneurial idea! Don't let Oz hear you. Your reputation will be toast."

"Hush, Mike."

She turned back to Liam. "If you design the software correctly, you could sell it to everyone, not just your competitors. Can you imagine the revenue stream you would generate?"

"Revenue stream! This is serious." He stood up and closed the door. "We can't let Oz hear you."

"Mike," she warned.

Liam shook his head. "I'm not in the software business. I wouldn't know the first thing about building or marketing a program like this."

"You wouldn't need to. That's where the joy of partnership comes in. You provide the idea, and Pyramid provides the technical expertise. We design and test, and you implement and market. You profit from selling the software, Pyramid profits by installing it for your customers. By the time your competitors acquire the system, you'd be way ahead, setting the pace for the rest of the industry."

"I understand what you're saying. Can you even make a system like this generic? And affordable? I hadn't considered any issues beyond linking Fleet and Windwear. How would you build it?"

Mike jumped in. "We would need at least two pieces, a data transfer module and a gateway to provide security and limit access."

Cara nodded. "The big problem in cross organizational systems is extracting data from one platform for use by companies on different platforms. Liam is right. We eliminate the problem if we use an online provider like Compuserve or UUNET. We would still need to create a version of the software for each platform, but once data is uploaded to the server, a common format would be used, and data exchange would freely occur." She looked at Mike." Can you imagine, Mike, installing and customizing this program for every one of Fleet's customers and suppliers? And for every one of their customers and suppliers? We would enjoy the steadiest pipeline in the business. Peter would be in heaven."

"That's true. What do you think, Cara? Windwear is already on Compuserve. Should we stay with that?"

"I don't think so; the network is too closed. I was thinking CIX, via UUNET or PSINET. Or ANSCORE, even though it's new. NSF supports ANSCORE, so we should consider it. Both use TCP/IP. We're probably safer going with the NSF—"

"Whoa," Liam said. "You lost me. I have no idea what you just said, or if you were even speaking English. What are ... UUNET and CIX and NSFNET and ANS—"

"Sorry, you pushed our geek buttons." Cara smiled. "UUNET is a provider of commercial online services. It, along with several other networks, has joined together to form CIX, which stands for Commercial Internet Exchange. CIX provides most of the commercial internetworking capability in the country. ANSCORE, which is actually spelled 'A N S space C O plus sign R E,' is the latest competitor in the commercial arena."

"I see, and ANSCORE is better because it is supported by NSFNET. What is NSFNET?"

"NSFNET is the network owned and operated by NSF, the National Science Foundation. NSF operates the biggest backbone in the world and carries the majority of network traffic in the country." Cara paused again. "Have you heard of the Internet, Liam?"

"Yes, but if you forced me to give you a definition, I couldn't."

Cara smiled. "I'm not surprised. It's an evolving term. The Internet is the collective name given for all the computers and servers and communication mechanisms that work together to transmit information between institutions. The NSF, funded by the federal government, is by far the largest player in the game. Currently, the NSF allows its network to be used only for research and education purposes. It's becoming a problem because businesses want to use the network for commercial purposes, like the one you're now suggesting. A host of independent networks, like CIX, are filling the need, but there is a push to open the NSF backbone to commercial use. So far, NSF has refused. ANSCORE is the current compromise. ANSCORE is a new commercial network authorized to use NSFNET under strict rules. We'll have to research those rules to make sure Windwear can live with them."

Cara faced Liam. "We might be able to work together on development, Liam, but we would need to consider several issues. Who would finance the development? How do we divide ownership rights? How would profits from future business be split?" She stopped. "I can picture a whole troop of lawyers working on this one. We would need some time to draw up a contract to specify all the rights and responsibilities in such a system."

"Hold on. We've gone pretty far afield from my original concept. I walked in here with a plan to smooth out operations between Fleet and Windwear, and in a matter of minutes, you've turned it into the latest software offering for the entire industrial world."

Mike laughed. "It's Pyramid's motto, Liam. 'Sell, sell, sell.' Our products don't even have to exist for us to sell them. At a healthy profit too!"

Liam slid a glance at Mike, and then turned to Cara. "I understand, basically, what you are describing. In normal circumstances, I might consider pursuing the idea, but these are not normal circumstances for Windwear. My company is in the midst of several changes. I need this system to be the foundation for Windwear's expansion plans. My time frame is short. I don't have time to wait for lawyers who want to produce software to be sold all over the world later, when I need it right now. Maybe Pyramid isn't the company to work with."

"You make a good point. This could get awfully complicated, awfully quickly." She thought for a moment. "Mike, take a look at the contract. Do you think we can er ... slide this in under the present terms of the FIT purchasing system?"

"Cara, are you completely nuts? Oz will have your head in a New York minute."

"Who's Oz?" Liam shifted his gaze from one to the other. "You've mentioned him ... or her ... several times."

Mike furrowed his eyebrows, cleared his throat, and said in his best radio announcer voice, "Peter Whittington, FIT project manager." His tone switched back to normal. "Known around here as the Great Oz."

"Have you met Peter, Liam?" Cara asked.

"No, why?"

"I ... never mind. It's not important." She turned to Mike. "What does the contract say?"

Mike grabbed the dog-eared contract and started leafing through the pages until he reached the section titled "Fleet Information Technology System." He straightened himself to his fullest height, cleared his throat, and recited in a rarefied Boston accent, "The third party supplier of Technology Services, herein known as Pyramid Corporation, will deliver to the first party receiver of Technology Services, herein known as the customer, aka Fleet Incorporated, aka endorser of celebrity athletes, aka leading athletic supporter in the industry, etcetera, etcetera, etcetera, a Fleet Information Technology System, also known as FITS, which, true to its name, will send the party of the first party into fits and will be incapable of being used, understood, or afforded. This will in turn, require the party of the third party to rewrite the entire system to the tune of several million dollars in additional costs, so, in the end, the party of the first party will end up with a new-and-improved system known as FIT, which will still be incapable of being used, understood, or afforded, but will at least result in an acceptable acronym." With a supercilious nod of his head, Mike paused. "All that effort just to cover their *S*." Liam closed his eyes and shook his head.

Cara was taking notes and did not look up when he finished. "You can't fool me, Mike. That's much too straightforward to be from the legal department." Now, from the top. Please."

Mike heaved a long-suffering sigh. "Okay, okay. If you insist." He leafed through the pages. "Here we go. 'System Functionality: Purchasing'." He droned on for five minutes, reciting the terms of the contract.

"That's more like it. Maximum verbiage, minimum responsibility for delivery, and zero technical direction. Another perfect contract from Pyramid." She glanced up at Liam. "And to your advantage, Mr. Scofield. There is nothing to prevent us from putting your system in place as part of FIT."

"You'll never get it past Ozzie," Mike said.

"Now who's being relentless?" Cara arched a brow at Mike. "Let's assume, for the sake of argument, Peter has a good day, and we convince him of the wisdom of this idea. The question is, Liam, are you sure you want to do this?"

"Why wouldn't I?" Liam asked.

"Three issues. First, are you sure you want to provide Fleet, or any of your customers, with this kind of access? You would be handing them a lot of power. If Fleet can determine that your stock is low, nothing would prevent them from going elsewhere. You might lose business without ever knowing you had a chance at it."

Liam nodded. "Yes, that is a concern. The blanket purchase orders will help. They establish fixed production quantities which would enable us to build inventory so Fleet can obtain products as they are needed. Holding inventory can be expensive, but if I know it will be sold within the PO date, those dollars are relatively risk free, especially compared to the cost of sitting idle. We are actually in a similar situation now. If we can't produce by a given date, Fleet is forced to go elsewhere. We would only improve our chances under the new system."

"Good point. Now, let's switch the perspective. What if Fleet doesn't want you to access its inventory levels? Perhaps they're ordering from someone else. It wouldn't take a genius for you to call up an inventory part and realize it's being purchased elsewhere."

"Awkward moment alert," Mike announced.

"On the contrary," Liam countered, "Fleet would love to be in that position. The system will foster competition among suppliers, which will only benefit Fleet. The blanket PO protects us in the short term, but in the long term, we'll need to cut prices and improve service if we want to keep their business. Fleet can only win in that environment."

"But life might be more difficult for Windwear."

"I'm not worried. Windwear has excellent products and even better people making them. I'll take on anyone as long as I have a system providing me with the right information to make decisions."

"Other companies may not share your level of confidence."

"They don't have to use the system."

"Then you'll really kill them in the marketplace," Mike cackled.

Cara eyed Mike thoughtfully. "You're right, Mike. A system like this changes the entire game; companies will need to use it just to keep up." She let out a long, slow whistle. "You could be sitting on a gold mine, Liam."

"Maybe, but that's of secondary concern. I must focus on what's good for Windwear. Now, you said you had three reservations. What's the third?"

"Right." Cara paused, choosing her words carefully. "Have you thought about how this information will affect your employees?"

"I don't understand."

She leaned forward. "May I be frank, Liam?"

"You haven't been up to this point?" he asked warily. Mike snickered.

"The customer information available in this system would be powerful. A lot of Fleet's competitors would pay good money to get their hands on it."

"Are you implying my employees can be bought, Ms. Larson?"

"No, that isn't what I meant. You're in an extremely competitive industry. Corporate espionage is not uncommon. This kind of information in the hands of a competitor would be like gold. Security would have to be tight, even more robust than what we're building in FIT. With multiple parties involved and such valuable information ... I don't doubt we can do it, but we should be extra careful here." She looked at Mike. "What do you think?"

"Yup, I agree. I'm thinking of a ton of technical issues, not to mention the secur—"

At that moment the door flew open and Peter Whittington, face purple and eyes fierce, stood framed in the doorway. "CARA!" he bellowed. "In my office, RIGHT NOW!"

Cara had seen him come in, but Mike and Liam, with their backs to the door, started at Peter's roar. Mike cringed. Liam watched the woman in front of him. Without a word, she rose from her chair and slipped on a cool gaze. She picked up her notebook and leaned toward Mike. "Work on those technical issues and come up with three possible scenarios for development. I'll be back in fifteen minutes." She walked out of the room. Peter slammed the door as she went through, and the papers on Cara's desk bristled in the wake.

Mike shook his head, a troubled frown on his face. "That, my friend, is the great Oz."

Chapter 3

Peter preceded Cara into his office. He did not even wait for her to close the door before beginning his tirade. Peter Whittington, a portly, balding man of forty-five, was beside himself with frustration over this woman. She did not listen to him. She did not follow his instructions. She did not cower when he yelled at her. Why had he allowed Charlie Schmidt to talk him into giving her a management position? He studied the list of transgressions in his hand as she sat across from his powerfully appointed teak desk. And began to yell.

Cara sat calmly through the barrage. "Why did you schedule your people for fifty-four hours of work per week instead of sixty, as I instructed?" Peter yelled.

"They need some time each day to organize themselves," she said quietly. They need a life, she thought angrily.

"I want a new schedule on my desk by 8:00 a.m. tomorrow," he roared.

"Why are you including unnecessary functionality in the system? Don't you know Pyramid suffers every time you give in to Fleet's demands?" he shouted.

"Those changes reflect Fleet's essential business activities," she answered quietly. I won't guild your path to a partnership with a system that earns Pyramid a profit but doesn't meet Fleet's needs, she thought angrily.

He exploded in the face of her calm responses. Cara knew Mike and Liam could hear the tongue-lashing from her office. Hell, Pyramid's Tokyo office could probably hear. "As a manager, you must make sure Pyramid comes first. Profit comes first, second, and third. Understood? I knew you couldn't hack this job. You're too soft. You need to stand up to Penner and say no."

Cara sighed. Well, it couldn't get any worse. "I understand, Peter. I know this isn't the best time to bring this up, but Mike has the president of Windwear in my office, and he floated an interesting idea by us." She explained Liam's proposal in a few quick words.

Peter's face turned purple. "Are you deaf or just STUPID? Haven't you listened to one word I said about excess functionality? Now you want to add a subsystem to FIT without changing the price?"

"Please listen for five minutes and let me explain the advantages. If you still think the idea has no merit, I'll tell Mr. Scofield no deal." Peter paused, and Cara pressed on. She explained how Pyramid could leverage a modest investment into access to the biggest companies in the West. How access could lead to a steady stream of new business. How revenues would rise from multiple customized installations. How the Portland office would be the most profitable in the country. How it could lead to a partnership in New York. She was thorough. She was persuasive. She was shameless. And she was done in less than five minutes.

Her boss appeared subdued by the time she finished. He almost appeared to be listening. That was a first. "What's the impact on the current system design?"

"Of course, we haven't done the research yet," she said cautiously, "but it is more like a separate system placed on top of FIT. The FIT data structure will need some minor changes, maybe an additional table or two to hold data for transfer, but not much else."

"How much would it cost to build?"

Again, Cara shook her head. "It's hard to say without research—"

"Off the top of your head," his voice rose warningly.

"I'm not sure. Two hundred, maybe three hundred thousand."

"Okay, I'm not promising anything, but go ahead and do the preliminary design work. I want a full report next week on feasibility, cost, and manpower before I agree to a damned thing. Understood?" Cara hid her surprise and nodded. "And no extra time for this. Your namby pamby team already has the cushiest schedule on the project." She nodded again. "That will be all." Cara practically ran from his office. She was afraid he might change his mind.

Mike looked at his watch. "Sixteen minutes. You're late. Who won this round?"

Cara walked through the door shaking her head, a bemused expression on her face. "Well, Liam," she said as she sat down at her desk. "Peter just gave us the green light to model your system."

Mike's eyes widened. "You asked him? When he was in that state? Cara, do you have a death wish?" He looked at her in disbelief. "And he agreed?"

"He did."

"All right!" Mike leaned over Cara's desk and slapped her hand with an ecstatic high five she vaguely returned. "Tell us everything."

Cara relayed the conversation. As she finished, she closed her eyes and rubbed her fingers across her forehead.

"What's wrong, Cara?" Liam asked.

"It's not like Peter to expand functionality so easily. I can't shake the idea that ..."

"That what?"

She shook her head. "I'm not sure. I'm just surprised at his reaction."

"Maybe we should get started before he changes his mind," Mike said.

"You're probably right." Cara agreed.

"This is going to make a huge difference for my company," Liam said. "This approach solves my timing problem and will work with my other expansion plans. I can't tell you how much I appreciate your help."

"That's why we're here," Mike piped up. "We like to please our customers, don't we, Cara?" Cara rolled her eyes.

"What's the first step?" Liam asked.

"Well, first we—"

"I'll take it from here, Mike," Cara cut in. "Peter will not give an inch on the schedule, so we'll need to hustle. Mike, you get to fly. I want you to hop on a flight to Los Angeles tomorrow and talk to Fleet's three largest customers. I want to know their take on this idea. I want information on hardware, operating systems, and accounting systems at the very least, plus any procedures that would create a problem for an interface like this. I'll do the same with Artemis and Windwear. I'll have Anna put together a questionnaire for Fleet's other top suppliers and customers. That should give us a solid basis for a preliminary design."

"Why do I have to fly?" Mike whined.

"Because I'm your boss and I said so." She turned to Liam. "Do you think your development team can fit me in tomorrow afternoon? I'll try to get to Artemis in the morning."

Liam pulled out his calendar. "How about two o'clock?"

"Let's plan for then. You'll need time beforehand to prep your people."

"Yes. I want to brief both my development and legal teams on the security issues before you arrive."

"Good." She turned to Mike. "Can you think of anything else, right now?"

Mike shook his head. "I think we're good."

Cara walked around the desk to stand in front of Liam. "I'll see you tomorrow, then."

He took her hand. "I look forward to it."

She smiled and held on to his hand a bit longer than was professional. "I'm sorry about the confusion earlier ..."

"No problem. I appreciate you taking the time to meet with me. I know you're busy."

"Liam," she said quietly, "this was worth my time. It's a good idea. A very good idea. You should be proud."

"Thank you, Cara. I consider that high praise. And thank you again for pitching the idea to your boss. You didn't have to, and I can tell it wasn't easy. I'm grateful." He smiled at her then. A wide smile that made his eyes dance. No man should have eyes like that, she thought. Absolutely dangerous. She released his hand abruptly.

Liam noted her action with puzzlement, and then turned toward Mike. "Mike would you walk out with me? I'd like to discuss some of the options you mentioned involving the Internet."

Mike's eyes lit with enthusiasm. "You bet! Cara, I'll call you before I leave for La-La Land." The two men left, leaving her office quiet and empty.

Cara glanced at her watch. Five fifteen. Another day gone in a flash. She walked to the window and stood for a moment, thinking about that meeting. More work to squeeze into an already impossible schedule.

The clouds hung so low she could almost touch them. The trees bent eastward. A storm was coming in from the Pacific. Cara closed her eyes and wished she could feel the rain on her face right now. It always seemed to wash away her worries and leave her refreshed. If she hurried, she could squeeze a run in and still get to Mama's by seven. She crossed the office and reached for her beat-up nylon bag.

In minutes she changed into a baggy pair of running shorts and a tie-dyed T-shirt whose sleeves were torn off at the shoulders. She braided her hair and let it fall down her back. She ran down the stairs and out through a side door. Outside, she leaned against the smooth granite of the building and stretched her calf muscles. The rain began to fall as she turned toward the sidewalk. Pedestrians pulled hoods over their heads and began to scurry to their destinations.

Liam and Mike stood on the corner of the street discussing the future of the Internet when they saw Cara emerge from the building. They both stopped and watched her. As the rain fell in earnest, she straightened, angled her face to the sky, and wrapped her arms around the back of her head. On her face was a smile of pure joy. Then she was off, skipping through the city streets, a spiral of color dancing amidst a torrent of hooded figures. Liam turned to Mike with a question in his eyes. "Don't look at me," Mike shrugged. "I can't figure her out either."

Liam ignored the heavy rain and headed to his car parked in a garage three blocks away. He had a million things to think about today. This system that suddenly seemed like a reality. The new research and development department. Windwear's facilities expansion. The initial public stock offering that would fund the company's growth. Any of these issues could consume hours of his time. So why was it that all he could think about was the woman whose office he had been in for half the afternoon? God, she was beautiful. And smart. Maybe that's why she reminded him of Jennifer the first instant he saw her.

Until the flashback today, he hadn't thought of Jennifer in years. He hardly remembered her face now, but he remembered there were days after she left when he hurt so badly he didn't think he'd survive. Somehow he forged pain into victory. In a twisted way, Jennifer was the cause of Windwear's success. He had worked day and night to prove her wrong.

He remembered when he first met his ex-wife. Her intelligence and beauty impressed him so much he fell in love overnight. He recognized her talent right away. He also recognized that even though women had made huge strides in the business world by the 1980s, Jennifer still had to work twice as hard as a man to succeed.

Liam had been happy to help his wife. He pored over his contact lists and introduced her to CEOs and financiers and business leaders. He may have opened the doors, but Jennifer walked through them all by herself. She worked hard. She earned every ounce of success that came her way. Every one of her victories brought Liam a sense of satisfaction. He celebrated when she landed her first big job at Bank of Portland. He cheered every accomplishment and promotion, even the last one, the one sending her to Metropolis Bank in New York. He hadn't understood why she needed to go so far away, but he accepted without question her explanation that it was necessary for her career. Yes, he cheered Jennifer's every victory with enthusiasm. Right up to the day he was served with divorce papers.

He remembered how he staggered in shock when he opened the envelope. He called her right away, thinking it was a mistake. It was no mistake, she told him. He asked her to reconsider. They could work things out, he told her. He would move Windwear to New York. She refused. Refused every suggestion he made to save their marriage. He realized then he was no longer of any use to his wife. She made the point abundantly clear a short time later. Windwear was a joke, she told him the last time they had ever spoken. And so was he. Besides, she had met someone else. Would he just sign the papers so she could move on?

He hadn't dated much after the divorce. Windwear took all his time. He soon learned his company was a demanding mistress, which wasn't such a bad discovery. He had at least a fighting chance of understanding Windwear. He would never understand his ex-wife.

He reached the parking garage and started up the five flights of stairs to his car. What brought all these memories back today, he thought? It must be Cara Larson. She set off an alarm somewhere deep inside him. An alarm telling him he ought to be careful when faced with a woman who was smart and beautiful and clever and forthright and ... Whoa, Liam, he caught himself. Careful.

He unlocked the car door, swung his briefcase in the back, and folded his long frame into the driver's seat. He started the engine and left the garage. His fingers drummed rhythmically on the steering wheel. He couldn't stop the smile that came unbidden to his face.

Chapter 4

"Right this way, Ms. Larson." Staci Manning led Cara down a wide sunlit hallway on the third story of the Windwear building. The building was probably a hundred years old but had been restored to pristine condition. The double-hung windows stretched from floor to ceiling, letting in the afternoon sun, so different from yesterday's thick rain. High ceilings, brick walls, and cornices wore a fresh coat of ivory paint giving the whole place an airy feel. The wooden floors reflected the tap of Staci's heels as they approached the conference room. To her left were large double doors leading into the manufacturing facility. Cara smiled. Somehow, she wasn't surprised Liam's office was so close to the manufacturing line. Staci turned right and opened the doors to the conference room. "Liam, Ms. Larson from Pyramid is here."

The meeting had just broken up. People were milling around, stretching their legs, and visiting with one another. Liam stood at the far end of the room, his back to the windows, reviewing a document with a woman Cara could only describe as stunning. Her raven black hair was thick and straight, and her blue eyes were vivid and beautiful as she leaned toward Liam. At Staci's words, Liam's head shot up, and his face crinkled into a smile. He hurried across the room with his hand out. "Cara, I'm glad you're here. How did your meeting at Artemis go, this morning?"

Cara's eyes widened in surprise. He actually seemed happy to see her. Perhaps she did have a future in management. "Hello, Liam. It went well. Mitch Keenan was interested in the new subsystem. In fact, he wants you to call him and fill him in on more details."

His grin held as much surprise as pride. "Well, what do you know? Come in, I'll introduce you to everyone." She met Paul Davis, Liam's oldest and closest friend, and Windwear's first employee. He was tall and thin, with a receding hairline and wire-rimmed glasses. Paul was in charge of information systems at Windwear, Liam explained, and he would head up work on the new subsystem. In quick succession, she met the three specialists assigned to build Windwear's operations system and the two accountants responsible for selecting and installing the new accounting system.

Liam continued to guide her around the room. "This is Lauren Janelle, our legal counsel. She has only been with us a few months, but is already involved with many of the changes going on at Windwear. She holds a law degree from Harvard and was at Bergman and Stein in New York for the past three years. We were lucky to lure her away." As they approached, Lauren flashed Liam a smile and placed a hand on his arm as she extended her other to Cara. "Ms. Larson."

Hair black as ebony, skin white as snow, lips red as blood. The words from the fairy tale leapt into Cara's head. Lauren Janelle was truly striking. Cara eyed the hand clutching Liam's arm. But maybe not as sweet and innocent as our friend Snow White. She took in Lauren's designer outfit, a close-fitting suit of mint green that emphasized her dark hair and long legs, and found herself sighing at her own navy trousers and simple silk blouse. She snapped on her most professional smile. "It's a pleasure to meet you Ms. Janelle. Please, call me Cara."

"Liam told me all about the new system," Lauren said. "I made a cursory review and found several issues I'd like to discuss with you—"

"Issues?" Liam interrupted. "You didn't tell me about any issues, Lauren."

"Liam, you only announced the existence of this system this morning. I haven't had time to perform a detailed evaluation, but now that Ms. Larson is here, I don't want to let her leave without expressing my initial concerns."

"What concerns?" Liam frowned.

"Liam, I know you would like to discuss this now, but we have a call with Richard Bancroft in about two minutes. We should—"

"Two minutes? Our call isn't until three-thirty."

"No, Richard pushed it up this morning."

Liam turned to Cara. "I'm sorry. I didn't realize I had a conflict."

Cara tried to hide her disappointment. "Oh, maybe we should reschedule."

"Is it important I attend?"

"Actually, yes. The chances of a project's success increase dramatically when top management shows its commitment to the project."

"That makes sense." Liam turned to his lawyer. "Lauren, let's postpone the call with Richard until—"

"No!" Lauren's voice came out with an edge. "This is a critical call. We need to nail down the details for the IPO broker agreement today."

Cara surveyed the room. "Your meeting sounds important, Liam. I'm sure we can manage with a good substitute. Do you think Paul would—"

"Yes," Lauren cut in. "Paul can fill that role. Plus, Liam has already briefed the staff."

"Cara, I'll stay if you think I should," Liam said.

"We'll be fine." Cara smiled. "May I tour the manufacturing facilities after the briefing? I'd like to learn firsthand how the capacity planning and scheduling systems work."

"Paul can be your guide," Lauren interjected.

Liam nodded. "Whatever you need, ask Paul. I'll stop in later when I'm done with my call."

"Thank you."

"We'd better hurry." Lauren took Liam's arm. "Richard is on a tight schedule."

Cara tried to contain her surprise as they left. If she behaved like that with a boss at Pyramid, she would have been written up in fifteen seconds. She smiled. Of course, if she behaved like that with Peter she would need to have her head examined. Oh well, Windwear wasn't her company. She had more important things on her mind than the personnel policies of a company that was not even an official client. Like how she was going to build a whole new system for that unofficial client, when the schedule barely had room for her official one.

The afternoon passed quickly. Before the tour, she explained the rationale behind the new subsystem and the approach she and Mike worked out this morning before he left for L.A. The team, in turn, described how the new company-wide operations system would handle their expected growth. She was impressed by their analysis.

Paul proved to be an informative tour guide. Cara groaned at the complex spreadsheets the line supervisors used. Each shift needed at least two hours to schedule production. If an unexpected change occurred, they had no time to recompile the information. They just made their best guess and adjusted on the fly. Cara understood how the new subsystem, coupled with the new operations system, would improve Windwear's ability to manage production. By 5:30 p.m., she had seen the entire facility, and Paul accompanied her back to the conference room.

"Do you mind if I stay for a few minutes and record my notes, Paul? I like to write everything down as quickly as possible."

"Of course. Go right ahead, but I need to leave. Liam and Lauren are still locked in his office. I'll let the security guard know you're here. Do you know your way out?"

Cara nodded and held out her hand to Paul. "Thank you for showing me around, Paul. You were most helpful."

"Anytime. I think this project is going to be great for Windwear."

"Yes, I do too. I'll let you know when the prototype is ready. Plan on a week to ten days."

"I'll look forward to it. Good-bye, now."

Cara sat down and opened her laptop. She quickly became engrossed in her notes. After several minutes, she jumped up. "Damn." She spotted the telephone sitting on the desk at the far end of the room, hurried over, picked up the receiver, and pressed nine to get an outside line. "Mama! I'm sorry I'm calling so late. How have you been today?"

Liam stopped just inside the conference room. Cara was on the phone, her profile visible from his vantage point. He smiled. No danger of her noticing him. She wore the same faraway gaze he had seen yesterday. "We've finished *Tales of the Alhambra*. What should we start next?" she was saying. "Cooper? Hawthorne? What's your pleasure?" Cara paused, listening, a half smile hovering on her lips. "Perfect. It's one of my favorites too. I'll pick a copy up on my way over." She waited and listened once more. "I love you too."

Liam frowned. He was just about to leave the room when he heard her say, "Bye Mama, I'll see you soon." Surprised, he glanced up as she cradled the phone against her cheek. She was staring into space, an expression of utter sadness in her eyes. Quietly he backed out of the room, counted to ten, and then knocked on the door. "Hey, Cara, how did the meeting go today?"

Cara turned her head and brushed at her eyes before facing him. "It went well. Paul was quite helpful. How about you? Did your get your agreement figured out?"

"I did. I think we concluded all the steps involved in talking about raising money. Soon I'll be able to take an extended trip to the East Coast to start actually raising money."

"Oh? That's progress. Isn't it?" She smiled and leaned on the desk as he stood by the door.

"I believe it is." He paused for a moment. "Cara, I have something for you."

Her eyes widened in surprise. "Something for me?"

"Yes, for you. I saw you out running yesterday, and I thought you might be able to use this." He walked over, placed a small box in her hand, and edged back against the conference table, watching her.

She stared at him uncertainly as she opened the box. Inside lay a small oval flashlight connected to elastic straps.

The contraption wrapped around the palm, leaving the wearer's hands free. A smile lit her face. "This is ingenious."

One look was all it ever took to assess the quality of a new idea. His smile opened into a grin. "Actually it's a prototype. With a little work, we may be able to introduce it as a genuine product."

"A prototype?" She strapped the light onto her palm and pumped her arms to simulate the swinging movements of running. "It's so light. I hate to carry anything while I run. This solves the problem perfectly." She paused, looked at the light and the pleased grin on his face. "You designed this, didn't you?"

He colored slightly. "Well …"

"I thought so. You are so creative."

"Thank you, Cara."

She tested the light, turned the switch on and off, broadened and narrowed the beam. "This is so practical. I bet you'll sell a million of these."

"Well, that's the plan."

She gazed at the flashlight for a long moment, and then removed it from her hand. She replaced the light in the box and handed it back to him. "Unfortunately, I can't accept this."

He held the box and stared at her in confusion. "I don't understand."

"I'm sorry, but Pyramid has strict rules about accepting gifts from clients. It might be misconstrued as contributing to, you know … what's the term … 'undue influence'."

"Surely, a big company like Pyramid wouldn't mind a small thing like this. It's just a prototype."

"Just a prototype? Are you kidding? This should be locked in a safe and marked top secret. Pyramid would have my head over something like this."

"Is Pyramid really that strict?"

"Not always, but in this one area, I assure you, they mean every word of their policy."

"Do you always do everything Pyramid tells you to do?"

"I try." Cara seemed almost shy as she spoke, and a tinge of pink crept up her face. "This is my first experience as a manager, and I don't want to make any mistakes. Or at least any colossal ones. I'm afraid I'm not ..." she struggled with her words, " ... very good as it is, and—"

"What do you mean? You're extremely bright, and Mike seems to—"

"Don't bother being polite. I'm sure you noticed the effect I have on my boss. That lively tête-à-tête you and half the country overheard yesterday is almost an everyday occurrence." Her tone was light, but she frowned as she spoke.

"Okay, okay. I'll let you off the hook. I only gave it to you because I don't like the idea of you running alone in the dark. Portland may not be Chicago, but it's still not safe to run alone at night."

"You are so kind, Liam. It's been a long time since anyone has ..." she paused as if not sure she wanted to finish what she started to say.

"Since anyone has what?"

"Nothing. It's not important."

There was a small space of time when both of them were quiet. Liam was still leaning against the conference table a few feet from her. "Cara, would it break all Pyramid's rules if I kissed you?" Her eyes widened in surprise. He shrugged. "Well, what would happen? Would the Pyramid police arrest you? Would the sky fall in?"

Cara tried to think. She was not sure how to respond to the man smiling down at her. It wasn't like she hadn't been in this situation before. She could wither a man with a few cutting words. She had done it more than once. Unfortunately, the man in front of her did not look particularly witherable. She took in his innocent smile and dark eyes. He would probably take anything she threw at him as encouragement.

She lowered her head, trying to appear nonchalant while her heart beat like a trip-hammer. She had to admit he was clever. Did he have any idea how seductive he was, standing there, asking permission to make a pass at her?

Aha, she thought. She knew what to do to put him off. She would talk. And she would keep talking until he changed his mind. Or lost interest. Or fell asleep. If nothing else, she would bore him to death. It wouldn't be hard to do; she was a boring person. She looked into those smiling eyes and shook her head somberly. "I'm ... I'm afraid it would be much worse than the mere sky falling in."

"Oh? Do tell."

"Mmm. A complete disaster." She flattened her voice into an official sounding monotone. "First the powers at Pyramid will delve into my past. They'll interview anyone who's ever known me. My friends, relatives, acquaintances. They'll talk to my third-grade teacher, my third-grade teacher's second cousin, my third-grade teacher's second cousin's dog." She gave an exaggerated sigh. "They'll find out Joey Parker held my hand on the playground when I was eight."

"Lucky Joey Parker," Liam said softly.

She ignored him. "Then they will find out how Ryan Myerson kissed me in the seventh grade. But they will conveniently omit any record of how I slapped him upside the head afterward."

"I'm sure Ryan thought it was worthwhile."

"Then they will find out about the incident in my junior year of high school ... ooh, I hope they don't find out about that." She looked at him through half-closed eyes, waiting for his reaction.

"Hmmmm," was all he said.

"Once they've pieced together my sordid past, they'll talk to all my colleagues at Pyramid. They will get Mike to admit I brought you into my office and filled your head with enticing promises. Of course, he'll forget to tell them they were systems promises, not ... not other types of promises."

He looked almost sympathetic. "I bet he'll say you treat all men the same way."

"Finally, they'll come to you, and in order not to lose the big deal, you'll tell them I chased you until you were practically forced into kissing me."

"Probably the only way it would ever happen between us, Cara."

"After all that research, the board of directors will meet in New York, crack a few crude jokes at my expense, have some drinks, and file out of the room with serious, sorrowful expressions. And banish me to the Fairbanks office."

Casually, too casually, Liam stood up. He was standing so close to her she could smell the scent of his skin, could feel his warm breath on her face. His hands were still lodged in his pockets, but his eyes were dancing. "Fairbanks, eh?" He tilted his head to one side. "I've heard Fairbanks is nice this time of year."

Cara's lips parted as she let out a laugh. It was then he leaned down, hands still in his pockets, and gently touched his lips to hers. Nothing touched Cara but those warm lips, but it seemed as if he imprisoned her in concrete. Unfamiliar sensations roared through her. Fire and ice. Storm and calm. Daylight and darkness. She had never felt anything like this before. And he was barely touching her. She returned his kiss softly. After several long moments, he lifted his head and stared into her eyes. She could only stare back at him in hazy silence. He took a deep breath, his eyes never leaving her face. Then, as if finding an answer to a question that had long eluded him, he whispered, "You're quite beautiful, Cara. You'll look great in a parka."

She rolled her eyes unsteadily. "I think you are quite dangerous." She placed a trembling finger on his chest. "You will be the death of my career."

He glanced around the room. Then he grinned, slid the back of his hand across his forehead in mock relief. "I think we're safe."

"You never can tell. Pyramid has spies everywhere."

"Do you want to live dangerously?" He placed his hands on her shoulders and drew her to him. His hands moved down her back, and he pressed her close against his length. She wrapped her arms around his waist and let her fingers travel along his back. He lowered his head and kissed her deeply.

"Cara, are you still here? I want to talk to you about those lega—" Lauren stopped at the door. Her voice brought Cara back to reality. She jumped and tried to pull away, but Liam was not ready to let her go. He kissed her leisurely for another moment. As he released her, Cara caught a look of unbridled fury etched on Lauren's face. Liam winked at Cara, then turned, his arm resting on her shoulders. "Hello, Lauren."

"Hello, Liam," Lauren said so calmly that Cara wondered if she imagined that look. "I didn't realize you were still here."

Cara slid from Liam's arms. "I need to go." She placed the box in his hands. "Thank you," she whispered.

" I'll call you," Liam said. "Soon."

She gave him a slight smile as she picked up her laptop and purse. She hurried past Lauren and out of the room.

Cara tapped on the back door of her mother's house. Jeanine Walker, her mother's companion and nurse, answered the door and gave Cara a warm hug. "Good evenin' child." Jeanine, a native of Arkansas, had lost neither her southern accent nor her old world manners.

"Hi, Jeanine. How's Mama today?" They stood in the cramped familiar kitchen of her childhood, and Cara soaked up comfort from the old space.

The older woman shook her head. "She's had better days, child."

Cara sighed. "Did you talk to Dr. Weaver? Did he say anything?"

"No, hon, but the chemo will make her sick for a day or so."

"When is she scheduled for the next round of tests?"

"Next Thursday. Dr. Weaver said he won't be able to tell how well the chemo's workin' until she finishes the last treatment on Wednesday."

"Did he say anything else?"

"Nothin' more."

"I know. I pester his office three times a day, and they always say the same thing." Cara gave the nurse a hug. "Thank you. I don't how we'd get along without you."

Cara tiptoed into the living room. Mary Larson was settled in an overstuffed chair, nestled in a blanket, dozing quietly. A small lamp shed a pool of light over her thin, snowy white hair and pale drawn features. She had lost some of her hair these past few weeks, but surprisingly, not all of it. That was good. Although she never said so, Mama took a lot of pride in it.

Cara stared at her mother, fighting down her guilt. Why had she waited so long to come home? Why hadn't she seen the signs sooner? Over and over again, she asked these questions, but they never helped. Not Mama, not her daughter. Nothing changed in the asking.

"Hi, angel." Mary Larson smiled at her daughter. "Did you have a good day?"

Cara banished her frown. "I did, Mama. How about you? Your hair looks great. Did Jeanine take you over to the Cut and Comb?"

"Yes, she did. Isn't that Jeanine a doll?"

"Sure is." She pulled a chair up close. "Tonight, a treat for you. James Fennimore Cooper's *The Last of the Mohicans*. The adventures of brave Natty Bumppo."

"One of my favorites." Mary settled back to listen. It was true. Her mother loved the American classics. That was how she learned about this country, she once told Cara. America introduced itself to her through the works of Whitman and Irving and Thoreau and so many others. That was so long ago, Cara mused. When her mother was brand new to this country. When Mary was young and newly married. Before Cara's father died, and life turned difficult ... Cara pushed the thoughts away.

"Would you like to go outside, Mama? It's a beautiful evening."

"I'd like that." Cara eased her up, guided her slowly to the back porch, and seated her in the old Adirondack chair. Gloomy thoughts encroached. How long would she be able to do this? What would the coming weeks be like? She read for nearly an hour before Jeanine came outside. "Child, it's time for Mary to retire for the evenin'."

Cara laid the book aside. Jeanine would need to give Mama a shot and several pills. "I'll join you in a few minutes."

"Thank you for reading, Cara Mia." Her mother's voice sounded tired but happy.

"Anytime, Mama." She gave her gray cheek a kiss. "I'll come and say goodnight in a minute."

Jeanine helped her mother into the house, as Cara sat back and tried to make sense of the past few days. Her mind kept traveling to Liam. And that kiss. And how, for the first time in a long time, she felt, for one small moment, wonderful.

Cara went to her mother's room and found her settled in bed. "How about another chapter?"

"That would be nice."

Cara read, knowing they would need to reread this chapter tomorrow. She knew Mama just liked to listen to the sound of her voice. Within minutes, her mother dozed off. Cara kissed her forehead and turned out the lamp. She walked to the living room, picked up her old gym bag, and headed to the spare bedroom.

"Jeanine, the sun hasn't set yet. I'm going for a quick run."

Jeanine poked her head from the kitchen where she was preparing tomorrow's meals. She studied Cara's face and nodded. "Be careful, ya hear?" Cara remembered Liam's words. *"I don't like the idea of you running alone in the dark."* She pushed the image away.

Cara flew out the front door and down the three wooden steps leading from the porch. She didn't bother to stretch. She didn't bother to think. She raced down the stairs, her fiery braid swinging behind her, the evening breeze brushing her face. If only she could outrun her anger and frustration and fear. It was wishful thinking, as it was every night. There was no hope of finding peace in the silent well of misery that was her heart.

Chapter 5

The phone on Cara's desk rang at 8:01 the next morning. "Yes, Anna."

"Ms. Lauren Janelle on line two."

"Thanks." Cara stifled her surprise and punched the blinking button. "Cara Larson speaking."

"Cara, I didn't get a chance to speak to you yesterday." Lauren's voice was brisk and businesslike.

"No. I had another engagement."

"I saw you were otherwise engaged, yes."

"I didn't mean ..." Cara sighed. "How can I help you, Lauren?"

I told you I had concerns about this new computer system."

"I'm happy to answer your questions."

"This project is not a good idea. Too many changes are happening at Windwear right now, and we can't afford another one. I want to cancel it."

"Cancel it? I don't understand. Is this request coming from Liam?"

"I've discussed the matter with Liam. He realizes the timing isn't right."

"I must be missing something, Lauren. Based on the meeting yesterday and my own conversations with Liam, I would say the opposite is true. I think Liam prefers this project be completed as soon as possible, and I agree with him. The company's current systems are inefficient. Both the new subsystem and Windwear's other system upgrades are absolutely necessary if the company plans to grow."

"Don't sell me, Cara. I know about Windwear's systems."

"Then you know that even if Windwear doesn't go forward with any expansion plans and only uses the new systems to improve operations, it's profits will increase dramatically within a few months."

Lauren hesitated. "Well, even if that is true, this whole arrangement is suspect. Liam wants me to prepare an agreement to purchase the subsystem from Fleet. Fleet? It's too indirect. If we're going to develop a system, we should work directly with Pyramid and not get involved with Fleet. There's too much potential for mischief."

"That is an unfortunate situation, but from a timing standpoint, Liam needs to go this route. Negotiating a new contract with Pyramid would take months, and from what Liam has said, time is of the essence. Windwear is going public soon. He needs the subsystem to be in place to handle the company's expected growth. He has no choice but to work within the framework of the FIT project. Do you have a problem writing up the agreement, Lauren?"

"Of course not. You're missing the point. This is an inefficient model. We're paying Fleet too much for this system."

"I'm not privy to all the financial details, but in this case, whatever deal Liam made with Rick Penner over at Fleet, it seems to be working. The collaboration is excellent, even with the tight schedule. Liam may be paying a little more than necessary, but if he is, I don't think it's such a bad idea."

"Cara, you don't understand. Fleet's involvement makes this whole thing too complicated. Windwear doesn't need such an extravagant system. We should pare back and meet just our requirements. I don't want to pay for Fleet's requirements."

"Now, you're into my area of expertise, Lauren, and I disagree. The system has some complex parts, but they are related to infrastructure and security. The actual concept is brilliant in its simplicity. In fact, Mike and I commented about how head-slapping obvious Liam's ideas were once he described them. I can't believe no one ever thought of this before. The potential is huge."

"Potential?" Lauren's voice was suddenly laced with interest. "What potential?"

Cara noted the abrupt change in tone. "Has Liam told you about his plans for the new subsystem, Lauren?"

"Of ... of course, but I want your opinion. If you want me to support this waste of time and money, I have the right to know why."

Something in Lauren's tone made Cara wary. "I told you my reasons. I think you need to talk to Liam. I realize you've only worked with him for a few months, but you should trust him. He understands his business, and he understands what's good for it."

"Don't lecture me on Liam, Cara. You've only known him for two days."

"True, but I've had several years of systems experience. You're way off base on this issue, Lauren. I can't speak for Liam, but I think you should talk to him before you go behind his back and try to shoot his plans down. Liam knows what he's doing. He's thought through every detail of this subsystem."

The silence on the other end of the line lengthened. "What's your game, Cara?" Lauren finally asked, her voice low and suspicious.

"My game? I don't understand what you mean."

"I saw you and Liam last night. I couldn't exactly miss the two of you. He was practically swallowing you whole. Usually when a woman seduces her customer, she has no confidence in her product. But you strike me as a little more clever than the average sleazy sales rep trying to close a deal—"

"I beg your pardon?" Cara interrupted sharply.

"Now I understand where all these ideas Liam's been spouting are coming from."

"Hold on, Lauren. I told you, this system was Liam's idea from the outset. Though I only met Liam two days ago, I can already tell he is perfectly capable of filling his head with ideas without help from anyone else."

"And you have no trouble goading him on, even if it goes against the best interest of his company."

"I am doing no such thing. This system will do nothing but help Windwear."

"Along with your career prospects, no doubt."

"There's no harm when both sides benefit in a business transaction. I'm not sure why that should be a foreign concept to you."

"I want you to stop this thing with Liam. In fact, I want you to remove yourself from the project altogether."

"What?"

"You heard me. I want you off the project."

"Now, why would I do that?"

"Perhaps you don't want your boss to hear about your … what shall we call them … sleazy sales tactics?"

"Are you threatening me, Lauren?"

"I'm doing nothing of the sort, but I am telling you I don't appreciate your interference."

"I'm not interfering. I'm doing my job."

"Your job?" Lauren laughed. "What precisely is your job? Exactly what part of the development project were you working on last night?"

"I'm not even going to dignify that statement with a response."

"That's because there's no defense for the indefensible. Do as I ask. Withdraw from the project and let—"

"And let the project fail?" Cara interrupted. "Is that what you want? Because that's what will happen if Windwear proceeds without assistance. It's too complicated for the company to handle alone."

"You heard what I said. Withdraw, or I talk to Peter."

Cara was silent for several moments. "Fine," she said at last. "Let's talk to Peter. Should I set up the meeting? When are you free?"

There was a sharp silence on the other end of the line. "I'm just offering you some friendly advice, Cara. I want to make sure we're clear on how this project will move forward."

"Oh, I'm perfectly clear," Cara said, unable to hide her annoyance. "Now, let me offer a little friendly advice of my own. I can tell you didn't talk to Liam about the system's potential, or what you witnessed last night. My guess is you're the one who's worried he might ask you to take a step back. So I'll tell you instead. Step back, Lauren. I'm not sure what *your* game is, but I'll say this: this new subsystem will be a huge benefit to Windwear. If you care about the company, don't obstruct this project. Let me do my job."

"As long as you confine yourself to your job. I mean what I say. If I catch you and Liam in any more compromising positions, I won't hesitate to talk to Peter Whittington. And I will make my concerns quite clear." The line went silent.

Cara replaced the receiver in stunned surprise. In all her years at Pyramid, this was a first. Of course, last night was the first time she had ever kissed a client and put herself in this position. She closed her eyes in frustration. It was ironic after such a vile conversation, that she found herself actually agreeing with Lauren Janelle, but that was the strange truth. Not about Lauren's concerns for the project. The attorney had been wrong on every point she made. But she was right about Liam. Or at least that Cara should stay away from him.

She sat back, deep in thought. Despite her bravado, she would be foolish to ignore Lauren's warning. She had seen one too many promising careers destroyed for this very reason. She thought of Tami, her best friend in Chicago. How well she remembered the day the president of Varner Corp. walked into the admin center and interrupted his CFO going at it with Tami on top of the copy machine. The story spread through the office like match to kindling. The copier lights blinking madly. The neon lamp along the platen rolling repeatedly underneath them. The papers flying out the exit tray in every direction. Tami naked and screaming. The CFO, pants draped around his ankles, lost in passionate oblivion.

Cara shook her head. The CFO managed to save his marriage and keep his job. He even cultivated a reputation among his peers as some sort of "real man." Tami wasn't so lucky. She lost her job. The last Cara heard her friend had fled back home to Wyoming, hoping her past wouldn't follow.

Cara couldn't take any chances right now. She'd been only half kidding when she told Liam about Pyramid's fraternization policies. If Peter found out, she'd be toast. He would have all the ammunition he would need to fire her. She couldn't lose this job. Mama needed her now more than ever. And yet ... she thought of that kiss. Of Liam. Of how she felt. As if she were lost in a world without worries. Calm down, she told herself for the hundredth time. Get hold of yourself. It was just a kiss. A simple little kiss. A simple little heart-stopping, nerve-shattering, soul-wrenching kiss she would never forget.

It wasn't just the kiss, and Cara knew it. She liked Liam. What wasn't to like? She could name a hundred things that attracted her. It would be far too easy to fall in love with a man like Liam Scofield. That was one thing she didn't want to do. Could not afford to do. Lauren's blunt warning merely added emphasis to the point.

She punched the intercom button. "Anna, I need to change the schedule. I'm going to put Mike on the supplier interface. He'll go to Windwear this week. I'll stay here and work with Fleet on the customer interface. Would you please adjust the schedule?"

"Will do," Anna's voice crackled across the intercom.

A few minutes later, Mike leaned his head into her office. "You want me to go to Windwear? But you've done all the prelim—"

"I can't meet the schedule any other way, Mike. I have too many issues here at Fleet to deal with. Come on in and let me give you my notes from yesterday."

Mike walked in, a frown on his face.

Chapter 6

"No, Cara, you can't do that. The plan can't support these new tasks." The rhinestones on Anna's denim jacket glinted as she pointed to the screen. "You need to add more hours to the schedule or cut some of the work."

Cara knelt at Anna's desk, studying the schedule on the screen. It was Thursday. Exactly one week since Liam Scofield walked into her office and blew her project plan to pieces. Along with her composure.

The team was already pushing hard. Still, Cara felt pressured to accelerate the schedule after Lauren's unsettling phone call. Anna had cajoled business requirements from Fleet's top customers and suppliers. The team had completed the system architecture, designed the supporting data structure, and constructed event diagrams. Cara had mocked up a rudimentary customer interface, which a customer would use to dial into a supplier's system to access scheduling and inventory data. The customer would enter an inventory code, and the supplier's system would display quantities on hand and in production. Mike wrote the supplier interface which mirrored her work on the customer side.

So far they were on time and within budget, but issues remained. Major issues. Like communication infrastructure. Like ultra-complex security. They hadn't determined which online provider to use. And security would be a nightmare. They would need to encrypt data on each end-use computer as well as on the server. System management would be sticky. Who was responsible for what in this type of distributed system? How would it be maintained? Monitored Updated? Cara could envision a gnarled web of agreements that would make a law firm salivate but would kill a system's effectiveness faster than any technical glitch. She and Mike would tackle those issues soon, when they developed the management module.

Despite the challenges, they had advanced far enough to conduct a demonstration for Fleet's key customers and suppliers tomorrow. The demo would give them a concrete, if not entirely complete, view of the new subsystem. If the attendees voted for approval, Cara would then submit a proposal to Peter to officially add the subsystem to the FIT project.

She still wasn't sure Peter would agree. He was so intent on minimizing cash flow and protecting profits he might not be willing to incur short-term costs in exchange for long-term revenue. Of course, the whole question would be moot if the group rejected the subsystem.

It was Liam who named the new subsystem. Mike came back from Windwear, indecent with excitement. He was giving the Windwear team a preview of the supplier interface when Liam said, "I feel like an eagle, perched on the highest tree in the forest, looking down at every detail below. That's it. We'll call the system Aerie." Cara wished she had seen Liam's face at that moment. Don't, she told herself. Do not think about Liam Scofield.

"Okay, Anna. You're right. Let's add six hours to everyone's schedule for the next four weeks and change the productivity rate from 65 to 75 percent."

Anna adjusted the numbers on the project plan. "You can make it, Cara, but you won't have much room for rework."

"Okay, we'll go with this. Would you please print two copies and send one to Peter? And email everyone with the change in hours. I'm sure they'll be thrilled."

"Sure thing."

"Hey Cara, where've you been? You weren't in your office coloring." Mike rushed toward her. "Are you busy? I've run into a problem testing the supplier interface."

Cara stood up. "Mike, thirty people are coming in at 9:00 a.m. tomorrow. How bad is it?"

"Something even I can't handle. I know you can help. I'm set up in the south conference room."

"Okay, let's go." Cara picked up her notebook.

"I need to pull my report off the printer. You go ahead. I'll catch up."

Cara walked to the conference room, notebook in hand, studying her list of still unresolved problems. She stopped abruptly at the entrance. Mike is not going to live to see his twenty-second birthday, she thought. "Hello, Liam. You look nice. Important meeting today?"

He was dressed in a dark suit and snowy white shirt, looking drop dead handsome as he sat in the chair, long legs crossed, elbow resting on the table, hand swinging nonchalantly over the edge. "You could say that. How are you, Cara?"

"Busy." She turned toward the door. "Let me get Mike."

"Actually, I'd like to speak to you for a minute."

"All right." She walked in and perched in the seat nearest the door. "How can I help you?"

"Is something wrong, Cara? I phoned several times this week. You haven't returned my calls."

"I received your calls, Liam, and I transferred them to Mike. He's assigned to Windwear this week."

"Yes, I know Mike is assigned to Windwear this week. I work there. I even know how to get hold of him if I want to speak to him. Which is more than I can say for you. I haven't had much luck getting hold of you." He shifted in his chair and faced her. "Are you avoiding me, Cara?"

Cara studied his face. He had no idea about Lauren's phone call, she realized. "I told you. I've been busy."

"Too busy to answer a phone call? Do you always ignore your business associates? You strike me as being more professional than that."

Cara opened her notebook with an exaggerated flourish. "Of course, you're right. I've been sitting here all week just thinking of ways to ignore you, Liam. Let's see. Fleet's swimwear division is fighting with the footwear division about which material inspection data should be stored in FIT. No agreement is in sight, but talks are continuing. Hmm, here's another way to ignore you. Corporate can't decide how the buyers' transactions are to be authorized in the new system. Or what the authorization levels are. Or who will authorize the authorizations. And how they will appear in FIT." She paused. "Oh, and here's another one. Every single division in Fleet uses a different policy for returning goods, which makes it a tad difficult to write one coherent return system. At least not without resulting in a major power struggle." She smiled. "Shall I go on? The purchase order—"

He held up his hand but a smile glimmered in his eyes. "Okay, okay, you made your point. So where am I on your list?"

She ran her finger deliberately down the page as if looking for his name. She turned the page and ran her finger down again. Then turned another page. "Oh. Here you are. Number 121."

He laughed out loud. "That low. Really! Even *after* our kiss?"

It took effort, but she managed to keep her voice even. "That did move you down a bit. You *were* in the top twenty."

"You're doing that thing again, Cara."

"What thing?"

"That thing you did the other night before I kissed you. Blather a lot of nonsense. Joey Parker and Ryan Whosists and your junior year in high school. It didn't work then."

"What do you mean?"

"I mean it didn't put me off."

"Liam—"

"Let's not play games, Cara." His face became serious. "Talk to me. Are you upset about that kiss?"

"Why would you ask such a question, Liam?"

"Well, you sent Mike to Windwear this week when you made the original visit—"

"Mike is our best designer. You should be pleased. Besides, I'm a manager. My responsibilities are here."

"Isn't Windwear one of your responsibilities now?"

"Yes, that's why I sent you my best designer."

"Cara, I haven't known you long, but I've already figured out you're a straight shooter. But right now, I'm getting the

distinct impression you're being less than candid with me."
She flushed slightly. "So, I did upset you."

Cara sighed. "Let's just say it wasn't the ideal way to
start a business relationship."

"I see. I misunderstood the situation." He gave her a thin
smile. "I apologize, Cara."

The silence lengthened between them. "All right, Liam.
Is this the reason you wanted to talk to me?"

"Partially." She waited, and he let out a short sigh. "This
new system is critical to Windwear's future. I can't afford to
jeopardize my company's chances for success over a simple
kiss gone wrong."

"What are you implying?" she asked sharply. "Do you
think because I didn't return your calls I'm going to renege
on my agreement to write Aerie?"

"No, that's not what I meant at all. I just don't want any
misunderstandings between us. I spent a lot of time with
Mike this week, and I like what you two are doing. But this
system is complex, especially if we make it a standalone
product. I need access to you ... to your time and expertise. I
need to be kept in the loop regarding Aerie's progress."

"You don't think I understand that? Do you know how
many systems I've built?"

"I didn't mean to imply anything of the sort. I just don't
want to lose access to your technical expertise because I
overstepped my bounds ... elsewhere."

She studied his face for a moment. "All right, Liam. I
accept your apology. So tell me, what technical expertise do
you need so urgently?"

"Well, I need to discuss our security operations at
Windwear and some legal issues Lauren brought up. I'd
prefer not to speak here at Pyramid. How about if we go to
lunch—"

"No."

Liam raised an eyebrow. "Cara, it's just lunch. A
business lunch."

"Then if it's business, let's talk here. Or at Windwear."

"Cara, what's wrong?"

"Why do you think something's wrong, Liam? Because I prefer to conduct business at a business site?"

"No, because you're acting strangely. I realize I stepped over the line by kissing you. I didn't intend to upset you. I apologize. All I want to do now is arrange a simple business meeting to discuss Aerie."

"Fine. I've provided several acceptable locations for your simple business meeting."

"What's going on, Cara? You're not usually so touchy."

"You just called my professionalism into question, Liam, and now you're accusing me of being dishonest. That might have something to do with it."

Liam closed his eyes. "I'm not doing anything of the sort. I'm trying to figure out how to have a confidential discussion about Aerie, and it's proving surprisingly difficult."

"That's my fault?" she snapped. "I didn't start this. You were the one who behaved unprofessionally. I'm not usually manhandled by my business associates."

"Come on, Cara," he snapped back. "I've apologized. A couple of times now. Though why I don't know. You didn't exactly seem to be suffering when I kissed you. In fact, if anyone was doing the *man*handling, I would say it was you. It was quite pleasant, I might add."

She shook her head in exasperation. "I can see now how heartfelt and sincere your apology was, and I have the perfect solution for you. I'll ask Peter to take me off Aerie. Now, if you'll excuse me, I really do have a hectic schedule."

"Cara ... wait ..."

Cara did not wait. She turned to leave and walked straight into Mike. She glared at him. "I trust everything is under control for tomorrow."

Mike looked sheepish but not quite apologetic. "Uh ... well ... yes. I—"

"Good. I'll be out for the rest of the day."

"But—"

Cara was already halfway down the hall before Mike could react. He watched her retreating form, and then turned to Liam with a puzzled expression.

"Damn," said the man in the dark suit.

Chapter 7

Five minutes later, Cara hit the pavement at a dead run. Uninvited thoughts raced through her head, and she could not control them. Maybe she could outrun them.

Her cold body protested at being pushed so suddenly. Her breathing was labored, her feet burned, and her stomach whirled in a knot; but they felt like nothing compared with the frustration boiling within. It was one thing to decide not to pursue a relationship with a man. It was another thing altogether to be misunderstood by that man. It was even worse when that man called her out for acting exactly the way she had been acting. Unreasonable and touchy.

She hated this sense of weakness. She hated having to bow to Lauren's wishes. She hated being pushed in directions she did not want to go. Worst of all, she hated that she didn't feel free to explore a ... what exactly was she looking for with Liam? ... A friendship? A relationship? She didn't even know what name to give it. She only knew she wanted it. Even as she knew it was a mistake to want it.

She raced through the sun-swept streets at a quick pace, the heat on her face and sweat in her eyes. Her thoughts refused to obey her. He looked so good, sitting in the conference room. His dark hair curled at the collar of his shirt, his deep eyes fenced in by small wrinkles, his wide mouth drawn into a wry smile. For a moment she wanted to cast aside all her worries, throw herself into his arms, and kiss him again.

She moved through a shaded lane populated on both sides by tall oak trees, their crowns meeting over the middle of the street. The coolness of the lane was refreshing after the warmth of the sun. She would have to catch her breath before starting the hills.

To her surprise, she found herself calming down. Her pace was still too fast, but her head was clearing. Okay, aside from a case of wounded pride, what had she lost? Nothing. This would all work out. Aerie was in good shape. Mike could manage from here. She had stayed away from Liam all week, so Lauren had no basis for further complaint. Other than the fact Liam considered her a starry-eyed schoolgirl who couldn't handle a kiss, nothing was wrong.

She forced other thoughts into her head. She went over how the return process would work in FIT. Which reminded her about the problem of recording inventory in Aerie. Which reminded her of Liam. Which put that handsome devil right back in her thoughts. Next subject.

Next subject, Mama. She needed to meet Mama and Jeanine at the hospital later this afternoon for the tests. Her stomach tightened. Her speed picked up again. Next subject.

The hills loomed. Thank God. This was the first time she ever welcomed this part of the run. Now she had no more time to think, no more time to do anything but struggle up the steep rise in front of her. Her lungs burned, her face glistened with sweat, and her chest heaved with the effort of breathing. Breathing became all that mattered. Her only goal was to get enough oxygen into her lungs to take another breath. And another. And another. All thought passed from her mind. This was the reason she loved to run. For this moment right here, when life dissolved into its most basic feature. To breathe. She devoted every ounce of energy to that one purpose. Out of the struggle, her mind and body came together in a peace she had come to treasure.

From then on, she ran as if in a trance, her body maintaining its rapid pace. She topped the hill, recovered her wind, and moved into a hazy state of semi-consciousness. The zone. The spectacular colors of late spring, the deep pink of rhododendron, the cobalt blue of delphinium, and the bold red of geraniums assaulted her vision, but did not register in her mind. The scent of pine enveloped her as she passed through the old neighborhoods, but she ran by without noticing. All that existed were the cadence of her steps and the rhythm of her breath.

Three blocks from the office, she knew she had a terrible problem. The speed and distance of her run had pressed her body beyond its limit. Her skin was icy, her stomach cramped, and spasms of pain came rapidly. She felt faint and knew she was dehydrated. Every step taught her a painful lesson in stupidity. She usually avoided the alley between her office and the neighboring bank building, but she needed privacy right now. When she finally staggered to the end of her run, she slowed to a walk and dragged herself to the alley. The air was cool in here, and shady. She found a patch of tall weeds and hunched over, resting her hands on her thighs. Then she fell to her knees, her body balking at the brutal, self-inflicted assault. The tears streamed down her face as she retched.

Liam waited at the corner of the street, holding a fluffy white towel and a cold water bottle, not sure from which direction she would come. Damn, if she weren't one of the most perplexing women he'd ever met. He was so sure after that kiss she was at least ... interested. He had seen the look in her eyes. Something important passed between them. It wasn't just the way she gazed up at him, or the way she folded herself against him as if she belonged there, it was something more, something deep. He had not been able to get her out of his mind. He sighed. Well, something had shifted between then and now. The "ice queen" act she threw at him this morning emphasized the point. The change not only unsettled him; it could cause problems for Windwear.

He shook his head in frustration. Congratulations, Liam, you've outdone yourself this time. You disregard the fact this woman is building the most critical system in Windwear's history and instead, charge forward and kiss her with more brass than brains. Clever business strategy. Then you insult her while you apologize. Very nice touch. You're surprised she wants off the project? Idiot.

There she was. He would talk to her and straighten everything out. If he had learned one thing about Cara Larson in the short time he'd known her, it was that he could talk to her. She slowed to a walk. She didn't look good. The sleeveless T-shirt accentuated her slender arms, and the baggy shorts made her long legs seem too thin. She was pale, sweat was running down her face, and she was grimacing in … pain? She was walking now, dodging the afternoon lunch crowd. He watched as she turned into a nearby alley.

Troubled, he strode across the sidewalk. He entered the shadowy alley. She was nearly hidden by the weeds, knees tucked under her body, head resting on her arms, rocking back and forth, moaning quietly. He knelt down and touched her back. It was soaked with sweat. "Cara, are you all right?"

She flinched at his touch, and her head snapped up in fear. She could muster no more energy to act. When she saw him, she laid her head back down. "Go away, Liam."

He didn't go. Instead he unscrewed the water bottle and with a hand around her waist, lifted her toward him. "Cara, you're dehydrated. You need to drink something."

Cara glanced at the bottle, then twisted from his grasp and retched again. Exhausted, head down on her arms, she practically begged him, "Go away. This is bad enough. Don't embarrass me by staying. Please …" she stammered and retched again.

He caressed her back gently as she convulsed. "It's all right. Everything is going to be all right." He repeated the words until her body relaxed. He held the towel around her shoulders. "Cara, does this happen often?"

Cara sat up on her heels and pulled the towel around her. She was spent, utterly exhausted, and could dredge up no more anger for the man by her side. She shook her head. "No, I went out too fast. I couldn't adjust my pace."

He wanted to ask why she ran so fast, but he didn't. He knew why. "Do you want to drink something?"

She nodded and took a swallow. She closed her eyes, willing herself not to gag.

"Can you stand up? Come on, up we go." He grasped her hands and helped her up. She shivered, and he wrapped the towel more tightly around her.

She nestled into the towel. "Where did you get this?"

"Mike is a resourceful young man. He handed them to me on my way out. He thought I needed a peace offering."

She nodded, too weak to fight with him. She didn't want to anyway. "You're freezing," he said. "Come on, we need to get you out in the sunshine and warm you up." Placing his arm around her, he walked with her out of the alley and away from the building. In a few minutes, they found themselves in the South Park Blocks, a long narrow strip of greenery meandering through the west side of the city. Stately elms, pristine gardens, and copper-encrusted statues filled the greenway. They must have looked like a pair: he, tall and handsome in his dark suit, and she, slender and pale in her beat-up running clothes. "Better now?"

"Yes. Thank you, Liam. You're very kind. Especially after I behaved so badly earlier. I owe you an apology ... I was being unreasonable."

"I think we both could have handled things differently." They walked in the sunshine for a few minutes. "Cara, I am sorry. About the kiss, about upsetting you. That wasn't my intention. You were right. I overstepped my bounds in about fifty different directions."

She smiled. "Only fifty?"

"I stopped counting after that." He grinned down at her.

They walked quietly for a few more minutes. "Liam?"

"Yes?"

"It wasn't a simple kiss."

He halted in midstride. "What do you mean?"

"Earlier, in my office, you said it was a simple kiss. It wasn't. It was ..."

"Spectacular?" he offered.

She rolled her eyes as they resumed walking. "Maybe more on that end of the scale than simple. And it wasn't one kiss, it was three."

"Hmm. I see you've thought a lot about this."

"Actually, I've thought a lot about how complicated things can get. I have a lot on my plate these days. My job is busy, and I'm taking care of ..." Her voice trailed off.

"Taking care of what?"

"Nothing. A lot of things."

"And you don't want to get involved with anyone."

She didn't say anything, and Liam turned her to face him, his hand resting lightly on her elbow. After a moment, he nodded. "Enough said. Or not said, in this case."

"Liam, I—"

"No explanations are required, Cara. I understand. I learned a long time ago not to go where I'm not welcome. It usually doesn't end well." He paused. "But I told you the truth about Aerie. I don't want to lose your expertise. Would you reconsider staying on the project if I promise to behave like a perfect professional?"

She nodded with what seemed like genuine relief. She held out her hand as if to seal a business deal. "I think we can start over. We're too close, anyway. This would be the worst time for a management change."

He took her outstretched hand. "Good. I meant what I said earlier. I like what you've done so far."

"Wait until the demonstration tomorrow. Mike is a genius. I swear, he won't leave anyone in doubt Aerie is the next best thing to hit the business world since compression software." She glanced at her watch as she drew her hand back. "Oh, Liam, I need to go. I have an appointment. I can't be late." She started toward the office.

He walked beside her. "You sure you're feeling okay?"

"I'll be fine."

She stopped in front of the building's glass doors. "Thank you for your help."

He took her hand in exaggerated formality. "Ms. Larson. The pleasure has been mine. I look forward to our meeting tomorrow."

"Ooh, I'm impressed." She laughed as she glanced at her watch again. "I need to go, Liam. Thank you again." She waved as she disappeared through the door. "See you tomorrow."

Liam watched her go. How did she do that, he thought. Blend steel and silk so completely he couldn't tell he'd been bested until after the fact. What a fascinating mix of contradictions was Cara Larson. Beautiful and untouchable. And somehow, despite his efforts to start something between them, she had managed to send him back to square one. Damn.

Chapter 8

Friday morning was filled with last-minute preparations for the demonstration. Maintenance workers installed two phone lines in the north conference room. Mike set up presentation equipment to display the image from his workstation onto a large screen fixed on the wall. The team members rehearsed their parts of the presentation until they were exhausted and Mike was satisfied.

Fleet's top customers and suppliers began streaming in at 8:30 a.m., but Cara barely had time to greet them before continuing her preparations. Liam arrived with Lauren and Paul, and after a professional handshake, ignored her. As agreed, Cara thought. So why was she so annoyed? It didn't help that Liam placed his hand at Lauren's back and introduced her to everyone in the room. And Lauren, with her beautiful black hair and flashing eyes, was smiling up at Liam with such adoration Cara thought she would puke. Lauren Janelle could use a dose of professionalism.

The meeting proceeded smoothly. She introduced the history of the Aerie project and outlined its purpose. Mike demonstrated the system. Even without the security features in place, and knowing the appearance would vary according to each company's platform, the attendees were able to grasp Aerie's benefits. Halfway through the demonstration, Anna slipped into the room.

"Cara, I'm sorry to bother you. You have a phone call, and the caller insists he speak with you right away."

"Who is it, Anna?"

"A Dr. Weaver, I believe."

Ice clutched Cara's heart. Oh God. Mama's doctor. The tests yesterday. The results. "Thank you." She hurried out behind Anna. Liam's eyes followed her as she left.

"Dr. Weaver," Cara spoke into the phone as she sat down at her desk.

"Cara, the results are back from your mother's blood tests. Can you come in today and talk with me?"

"Of course. Now?"

"No, I reserved a time at 11:30." She glanced at her watch. An hour and a half.

"All right. Dr. Weaver, can you tell me—"

"Why don't we talk when you get here," he said gently.

Cara fumbled with the phone as she hung up, a sick, hollow feeling growing inside. If the news was good, he would have told her. She lay her head down on the desk, the pain in her stomach threatening to make her ill.

She let herself back into the conference room and sat down. What happened during the next hour was forever lost to her. She must have stood up as planned and explained about the time frames, resource needs, and programming elements Aerie would require for implementation. She must have answered the attendees' questions with some semblance of logic. She must have asked for the vote to approve Aerie. And she must have received it, because before long, everyone was milling around, shaking hands, discussing a myriad of details, and generally looking like this thing was going to work. But she didn't remember any of it.

Mike approached as she packed papers into her briefcase. "Hey, we did it, boss. Why don't we go to lunch to celebrate with Liam, Lauren, and Paul?"

"I ... I ... don't think so. I have an appointment."

"Cara, did you get the memo? This thing is a smashing success." He peered at her closely. "Hey, are you okay?"

"Actually, no, Mike. I need to take care of something. You go ahead to lunch." She snapped her briefcase shut and left the room.

She was halfway down the hall when Liam fell into step beside her. "Hey, Ms. Larson. Nice work today."

Cara didn't look up. "Thank you."

"What's going on?"

"Nothing."

"Cara, please stop." She halted, head bent, avoiding his gaze. "Pardon my saying this—it probably violates Rule 1, Paragraph A of your professionalism handbook—but you look terrible. What's wrong?"

"Nothing. It … it's a personal matter. I need to go. I have an appointment at 11:30." She dropped her keys as she tried to open her office door. "Damn."

Liam bent over, picked them up, and handed them to her. "You seem upset. Can I help? How about if I drive you to your appointment?"

"No, that's all right. I don't want to trouble you."

"It wouldn't be any trouble."

"I'm fine, thanks." She fumbled with the keys as she tried to unlock the door.

Liam took the keys from her fingers, unlocked the door, and held it open for her. "Where are you going?"

She didn't answer, but her eyes glistened with tears as she walked toward her desk. She pulled her purse from the drawer and groped for her car keys. When she couldn't find them right away, she slammed the purse down in exasperation. "Damn." She closed her eyes and took a deep breath.

"Cara," Liam said gently, "Let me help."

She stared at him, her face troubled. Then, making an effort to calm herself, she again reached into her purse and found the keys. "Maybe I could use a steadier hand than mine at the wheel." She placed them in his hand. "Thank you, Liam."

"Where am I taking you?"

"Good Samaritan Hospital."

"Cara, are you ill? From yesterday? Did you—"

"Please, Liam. No questions. Not right now."

He studied her face for a long moment. "Fair enough."

Dr. Weaver was waiting when she arrived. She took a seat, trying to glean hope from his expression. There was none to see. The doctor looked at her with compassion. "I'm sorry, Cara. There is no easy way to tell you this, but as your mother's medical power of attorney, you should understand the situation. Mary's cancer has not responded to chemotherapy."

"But she's been doing better." Cara wanted him to look down at his notes and tell her he had made a mistake, that everything was going to be all right, that a miracle had occurred, that her mother would be fine.

"Your mother is a remarkably strong woman, but this is an aggressive form of pancreatic cancer. We've confirmed it as an adenocarcinoma. We did a CA19-9 test—"

"What is that? CA19-9?"

"Carbohydrate antigen 19-9. It's a tumor marker for several types of cancer, including pancreatic. The blood test shows a high level. In fact, the count has risen despite the chemo. We verified those levels with a CEA test—"

"What is—"

"The carcinoembryonic antigen test. The results are the same. The X-rays confirm our findings." He held the slide over a small light tray on the side of his desk. Gray masses covered large regions of the visible area of the X-ray. They were everywhere. "The tumors have spread beyond the pancreas to several organs. Liver, spleen, stomach, lungs."

"Oh, God." It was all she could say. He was going on, talking about increasing the dosage of chemotherapy, exploring alternative treatments, outlining the chances of success for each option. She couldn't think, couldn't digest anything he was saying. In that moment, that awful moment of realization, she wanted to die herself.

"Did you hear me, Cara?"

She stared blankly at the doctor. "You and your mother must decide how to proceed." His voice was kind. "We have counselors here. If you prefer, I can talk to Mary. One way or the other, she needs to know her options." He didn't need to tell her there wasn't much time.

"I understand. I'm … I'm not sure what to do. I should talk with Mama. May I call you tomorrow and let you know?"

"Of course."

She stood. "Thank you, Dr. Weaver. For everything ..." She couldn't finish the sentence.

He stood up and walked her to the waiting room. "Are you going to be all right? Can someone drive you home?"

Liam was up in an instant. "I'm here. Cara? How are you doing?" He turned questioning eyes toward the doctor.

"You're with Cara?"

"Yes."

"Good." The doctor lowered his voice. "Will you be able to stay with her for a few hours? I don't think she should be alone, right now."

Liam nodded and placed his arm around her waist. Together they left the office. She seemed to be in shock. They walked to the parking lot. "Where should I take you?"

"My apartment is only three blocks from here." She gave him the directions, then leaned back in the seat and closed her eyes.

Chapter 9

Cara's apartment was on the top floor of an old Victorian house. Slanted ceilings, pale walls, and long narrow windows dressed in airy wisps of blue gauze filled the space. She loved this apartment. She had crammed the living room with overstuffed furniture, warm lamps, and a wall of books. Several boxes lay in the corner, waiting to be unpacked.

Liam stopped at a pastel love seat. "You sit here. I'll make some tea." He set off toward the blue and white tiled kitchen. Cara sat still for nearly thirty seconds before she stood up and paced the room. She walked to the bookcase and studied the volumes jumbled haphazardly on the shelves. She began rearranging them in alphabetical order. A few minutes later, she heard the sharp whistle of the teakettle.

She wandered to the kitchen and leaned against the doorway, studying Liam. He poured steaming water into two mugs and wiped the counter by the sink. He must have felt her eyes on him, because he turned to find her staring at him. He smiled, hung the towel on its hook, picked up the mugs, and placed one in her hands. "Come on, let's go in here." He nodded to the living room.

She sat in the love seat once more, and Liam settled into a chair facing her. "Do you want to tell me what's going on?"

She stared down at the steaming mug for a long time. "Liam," she finally said, "my mother is going to die."

"Your mother?" He took a deep breath. "Tell me."

She closed her eyes. "My mother is dying of cancer. That's why I met with Dr. Weaver. He told me it has spread ..." she gestured helplessly, "everywhere."

"I'm sorry, Cara."

She stood up and paced tensely around the room. "If only I had come home earlier. I should have realized something was wrong. I remember how tired she was at Christmas. I should have seen it then, should have made her go to the doctor then."

"Cara, do you think this is your fault?"

Suddenly the words came tumbling out so fast she couldn't stop them. "This *is* my fault, Liam. At least partly. I wasn't home enough. I was in Chicago, working. Coming home for a three-day visit every six months. I thought I was doing everything right. Working all those hours, sending her money so she could retire. I was all wrong. Completely wrong. I missed the most important thing of all. Now it's too late to undo the damage. I had no idea she was sick until I came home for good last month. By then ... I think it was too late, even then."

"Hold on, Cara, you're losing me. Please slow down and start from the beginning."

She sat down and drew a long breath. She sighed. Looked away. Stared at the man sitting across from her. Sighed again. Then told him the story she had never told anyone else.

Her parents met while her father, Frank Larson, was stationed with the Air Force in Aviano, Italy. In 1963, her mother, Maria, married Frank and left her home and family in Aviano. They moved to Portland after he was discharged from the military and settled in the tiny North Portland house where her mother now lay dying. Cara was born in February of 1964. She took after her father, with her red hair and green eyes, but inherited her mother's thoughtful nature.

In 1966, Frank Larson was killed in a freak auto accident. Her mother didn't talk much about that time. She never talked about much at all. She carried a quiet old world reserve Cara learned to respect, if not always understand. Over the years, Cara learned that Mary, Americanized from its original Maria, chose to stay in the United States because of the opportunities available to her daughter. Her mother made the choice despite her dislike of what she called the *frenesia*, the "frenzy," the hectic pace of life that defined her adopted country.

For as long as Cara could remember, she and her mother struggled together to form a life. And for as long as she could remember, her mother had worked hard so they could live in the house on Dekum Street, and Cara could attend the private school only a few blocks away.

In her early years, Cara enjoyed every moment of life with the sweet innocence of youth. Everything changed in the seventh grade. The first day of school that year, as a matter of fact. She came home, proud in her crisp uniform, chatting excitedly about her new friends and new classes. Mama stirred spaghetti and hummed softly. Cara sat contentedly at the kitchen table, the light from the hanging lamp spilling on her red hair. She closed her textbook, placed her completed homework in her folder, and produced a large stack of important-looking papers.

"You can tell it's the first week of school by the number of papers. Shall I read them to you, Mama?"

"Of course, Cara Mia." Cara read aloud every word on every paper. She worked through the syllabus from each class, procedures for after-school activities, and the list of rules and regulations. Her mother listened to every word of every paper.

"Oh Mama, this is so exciting. Here's a letter from the office." She ripped it open and started to read. "Invoice. Tuition for the academic year ..." Cara's voice trailed off, and then her eyes widened in alarm. "Three thousand dollars! Mama! We can't afford this! There must be a mistake ..."

Mary turned off the stove, walked across the kitchen, and took the letter from Cara's hands. She glanced briefly at the bill and placed it in her apron pocket. She sat down next to her daughter. "Of course we can afford this, Cara Mia."

"But Mama, three thousand dollars!" In that moment, Cara learned the meaning of sacrifice. Events that had been confusing suddenly became clear. How many nights had she woken to find, not Mama sitting at the kitchen table, but Mrs. Li from next-door? Mama told her she liked to take late night walks, but Cara realized she had taken a second job. How many weekends had Mama taken in extra sewing when she was exhausted? She said she liked to make beautiful things, but Cara saw the dark circles under her eyes as she read to her during those long evenings. How many family heirlooms had Mama gazed at and held gingerly? She said she put them away for safekeeping, but Cara knew now she had sold them. Cara's eyes brimmed with tears. "No, Mama. No more. You work too hard. School is not that important. I can go to Clarendon, like everyone else in the neighborhood."

Her mother, who rarely interrupted, did so then. "No, Cara Mia, listen to me. You must understand. Life is about opportunities. Education is the way to create opportunities. With education you can dream, you can be free, you can choose your life. If you do not choose your life, others will choose it for you." Her mother smiled. "You are intelligent and inquisitive. You can become anything you want. I want to give you the best possible chance to do so."

"Mama, the neighbors are intelligent and inquisitive too," Cara argued, tripping over the unfamiliar words. "Do you mean to say they won't have opportunities? Please Mama, I'll work hard. I'll make opportunities for myself."

Her mother patted her cheek. "With arguments like those, you will probably become a lawyer. We all make choices. This is my choice for you, and I will hear no further discussion on the subject."

Cara had learned not to argue with that tone. "Okay, Mama, but I'm going to help. When I get out of college, I'm going to get the best job in the world, and you'll be able to quit your job and live like a queen. I'll buy you your dreams, Mama. I'll buy you your freedom."

Mary Larson studied her daughter for a long moment. "Cara Mia, some things you cannot buy ..." She stopped, leaned down, and wrapped her daughter in a hug. "Yes, I believe you will, Cara Mia."

From then on, Cara had a focus in life. She went out the next day and found a job running errands at the grocery store a few blocks away. She began babysitting three times a week for the neighbors with the curly haired twins. She did yard work in the spring and summer and delivered flyers for neighborhood businesses. Anything she could do, she did. She was determined to earn enough to allow Mama to quit some of her extra jobs.

She and Mama never discussed the subject again. Every Saturday, Cara bundled her earnings into an envelope and set it on the table before she went off to one of her various jobs. Every time she returned, the envelope had disappeared. Mama never said what she did with it, and Cara never asked. But over time, Cara noticed Mama took in less sewing, and now and again they went to a real restaurant for lunch.

She could never change her mother's mind about college. Mama insisted she attend Lewis & Clark, a prestigious and expensive private school on Portland's west side. So Cara helped to defray the costs. She worked all through high school and was awarded not one, but two scholarships. In college, she took extra class loads each term to save on tuition. She graduated in three and a half years with a major in computer science and a minor in business. Four weeks before graduation, she received a job offer from Pyramid.

She did not want to refuse the job. The country's premier technology company offered excellent pay, great benefits, and unlimited opportunities. It had only one significant drawback. She would have to move to Chicago. She decided to turn the offer down, but Mama would hear none of her arguments. "Is it a good company, Cara Mia?"

"The best, Mama."

"Then you will go to Chicago." It was that tone again. So Cara went.

She worked like a demon in Chicago. Pyramid provided extensive training courses, and she took advantage of every one. She designed databases and accounting systems. She wrote code and conducted systems tests. She documented systems, wrote manuals, and trained customers. She set up networks and electronic mail systems and learned to debug all types of computer code. She worked at multimillion-dollar organizations as well as one-person offices. She logged long hours and traveled extensively to glamorous cities like Des Moines, Iowa and Bloomington, Illinois, where she lived out of a suitcase for weeks at a time. When she wasn't working, she longed to go home, where the only snow lay up in the mountains and where the summer air wasn't heavy, except with the scent of roses and pine.

She sent every other paycheck home to her mother, and within months, Mama retired. Well, Mama never actually retired. She volunteered at the hospital, joined the garden club, and did things she never had the chance to do before. And Cara kept working. The weeks slipped into months, the months slipped into years, and she rarely returned home for more than a long weekend. She called at least once a week, of course, and made it home for Thanksgiving and Christmas every year, but the visits were always too brief.

Even when she worked on the Fleet proposal, she had rushed in and out of town so fast she never took time for more than a quick visit. How she wished she had slowed down long enough to look—really look—at her mother. Like she did once she moved back. She realized immediately her mother was unwell. Cara insisted she see the doctor right away. And right away they found the cancer. At the time, the doctors thought the tumors were mucinous neoplasms, precursors to a more serious form of pancreatic cancer. The chances for a cure were good, they had said. It wasn't until today that Dr. Weaver confirmed Mama's cancer had morphed into the more virulent, and often fatal, adenocarcinoma.

Liam remained quiet when she finished. She was spent from the telling, but she seemed calmer now, as if somehow saying the words aloud made it easier for her to face them. "If only I had taken more time," she said quietly. "If only I had spent a few extra minutes to recognize what was happening. I would have taken her to the doctor earlier, and they would have caught it earlier. And maybe my mother wouldn't be facing any of this now."

She sighed. "I can't go back. I can't undo this. I know I can't, but that's all I want to do. Instead, I need to face her somehow, and ask how she wants to spend her last months of life. I know my mother. I know what she's going to say when she sees the X-ray. As much as I want her to fight, she's going to do things her own way." Cara stood up, fighting back tears. She paced restlessly around the room. "I ... I'm not sure what to do. I want to help her, but all I've done is make things worse."

Liam stood up and faced her. "Cara, look at me." She stood in front of him, and he held her hands in his. "I'm not going to try to talk you out of how you feel or what you believe. It's not my place, and it's not a fair thing to do. I haven't walked in your shoes, but from what you've told me, I don't agree with you. I don't think your mother could have a better daughter in a hundred lifetimes." She tried to respond but he shushed her quietly. "Maybe you're right. Maybe you're wrong. If there's one thing I've learned it's that no one can change the past. Not you, not me, not God himself. Sometimes, it can help to set your worries aside. Let them be what they're going to be. Focus instead on the challenges ahead. You're going to be plenty busy helping your mother. Do you think you can do that? Set aside your guilt, for now? Focus only on your mother and reserve judgment on everything else until later?"

"I don't know." She closed her eyes. "Everything is such a mess."

"Do you want to tell your mother how you feel? About how ... responsible you feel?"

She shook her head sadly. "There is nothing I would like more in the world, Liam. I want to get down on my knees and beg for her forgiveness, but that would be so wrong, so selfish. She has so much suffering to endure. I won't make her take on my guilt too."

That was the moment Liam fell in love with Cara Larson. Fell hard. As if he tumbled out of an airplane without a parachute. He realized he had only known her for a few short weeks. He recognized the parallels with Jennifer and remembered how disastrous his marriage had been. Yet none of that mattered now, because he knew ... her. He had seen so many facets of her already, as if they were the myriad faces of a shimmering diamond. A professional at Pyramid. A subordinate of Peter Whittington. A mentor to Mike Taylor.

A dancer disguised as a runner. Now, a daughter faced with the loss of her mother. What he saw was not a reflection of Jennifer, but a woman of intelligence, integrity, and empathy. He realized with utter conviction she was the one person he wanted to stand beside for the rest of his life. What was the quote his mother gave him so long ago? The one she gave him when he started Windwear? The embroidered square, now tattered and faded, that still hung in his office? The one from Dario Fo, the playwright? *Know how to live the time that is given to you.* In a flash of blinding certainty, Liam knew how he wanted to live the time that was given to him. He wanted to marry Cara Larson.

"Liam, what's wrong?" Cara was looking up at him, concern etched on her face. "I ... I'm so sorry. I should never have imposed on you this way. I—"

"No, Cara. You didn't impose. I was just thinking about something."

"You had such a strange expression on your face. Like you'd been hit by a truck."

"That's probably true." He smiled down at her. "Cara, I'd like to meet your mother. Would that be all right?"

Chapter 10

Mary Larson glanced up from her book and then at the clock. "Cara Mia, you're early. How did you get the afternoon off?"

"I finished work early, today." She led Liam into the room. "Mama, I ... I brought someone to meet you." Liam knelt down next to Cara. "This is Liam Scofield. He's ... a friend of mine."

Liam held out his hand and covered Mary's frail one. "I'm honored to meet you, Mrs. Larson. Cara has told me a lot about you."

Mary looked at Liam, then at her daughter. "Cara Mia, you never mentioned this young man before. How do you know him?"

Cara sighed. Ever the mother. "I met him at the office. Liam and I are working on a project together."

"Oh. Are you a ... Cara, what do you do again?"

"I'm a systems analyst, Mama."

"That's it. Are you a systems analyst, too, Mr. Scofield?"

"Please, call me Liam. No, I run a company that makes hiking boots. Cara is helping us with a new software program. She is very bright, Mrs. Larson."

Mary Larson beamed. "Call me Mary. She is bright, my Cara Mia." She smiled and reached for her daughter's hand. "So, Liam, you like my Cara Mia?"

"Mama," Cara groaned.

Liam smiled. "Yes, I like her."

For two hours, they kept Mary Larson company. As Mary started to tire, Cara read poetry from the collections of

Emily Dickinson. When Mary dozed off, she stopped reading and handed the book to Liam. "Liam, would you mind reading to Mama if she wakes up? I ... I need to get her some juice."

"You bet."

Jeanine stood at the island in the kitchen, preparing dinners for the weekend. Cara sat on the stool, tucked her knees up to her chest, and wrapped her arms around them. She used to sit just like this and watch Mama cook when she was young. She let out a sigh. The nurse looked up with concern.

"Jeanine," Cara began, but she was unable to continue.

"What is it, child?"

"I ... I talked to Dr. Weaver today."

Jeanine's face fell, and she nodded gravely. Putting down her spoon, she came over and hugged Cara. "Oh, child. I'm so sorry."

It was too much. All of it. Cara couldn't take any more. She could not endure one more minute without releasing this heavy sorrow weighing on her. She settled in Jeanine's ample arms and her body shook with heaving gasps, but the relief of tears did not come. "Shh, shh. It's all right, child. It's all right." The older woman held her tightly.

"Cara—" Liam stopped as he entered the kitchen. "I'm ... I'm sorry," he stammered, and started to back out the door.

Jeanine looked up from where she held Cara. "No need to apologize, young man."

Cara quickly released herself from Jeanine's embrace and slid from the stool. She turned away from Liam as she brushed at her eyes. "I'm sorry. I forgot about the juice." She walked to the refrigerator and removed the carton of apple juice.

By the time they returned from the kitchen, Cara had pulled herself together. She handed the juice to Mary while Liam dragged a chair close. "You sit, Cara. I'll read to both of you for a while." Cara made sure her mother was comfortable, before sitting down. For the rest of the evening, Liam read to the two women. His voice was rich and deep and soothing. Cara curled up in the chair and closed her eyes. Liam darted a quick glance at her as he read. He continued until both Mrs. Larson and her daughter slipped into exhausted sleep.

It was Sunday when Cara felt composed enough to talk to her mother about the choices that lay ahead. She and Jeanine took Mama to church in her best Sunday dress, a blue floral crepe that made her look lovely and regal despite her fragility. It was a beautiful afternoon, the late June sun was bright, and the flowers bloomed profusely in the yard. The scent of roses wafted on the breeze as Mama leaned back in the deck chair and breathed in the smells of summer. Life, beautiful life, all around them. The irony struck too deeply. Cara struggled to form words of hope while her heart filled with despair. She had done nothing over the last few days but think about the right words to say, and now that the moment had come, the words fled from her tongue. "Mama …" Mary smiled gently at her daughter. Cara didn't trust herself to speak. "Mama …" she tried again, but her courage failed her.

In the end, her mother was the strong one. Her mother showed her how grace behaved in the face of adversity. She set Cara at her feet, stroked her hair, and explained in her quiet way that her time on this earth was nearly over. It would soon be time to bid the sweet song of life good-bye. She was at peace, she said, and did not want Cara to worry. And she did not want her to try too hard to keep her body alive when her spirit was already moving on. Cara protested and asked that she at least talk to Dr. Weaver about the alternative treatments that might save her life. Mama shook her head and said something about not fighting too hard against the ways of nature.

Cara did not want to accept her mother's wishes. It was against all her instincts not to fight. "Cara Mia, struggles come in all shapes and sizes. I have just exchanged one type for another." For the first time, Cara understood how difficult it must have been for Mary Larson to go down so much of this road already.

She held Mary's hand in hers. "Are ... are you afraid, Mama?"

"Yes, Cara, I am, but not so much when you are with me."

Cara couldn't think of anyone in the whole world who was as strong as her mother at that moment. She leaned over and hugged her. "I'll be with you, Mama. I won't let you walk this road alone."

Liam visited frequently. He was busy at Windwear, and he often seemed exhausted by the time he rang the bell at the little house on Dekum Street. He charmed Mary and made her smile. He brought roses at every visit. Not store-bought bits of perfection in red and yellow, but rare types, grown—Cara was sure—in local gardens. Lavenders of the most delicate shade. Peaches tinged with deep fuchsia petals. Whites that opened to reveal soft cores of gold.

Mary looked forward to the evenings he visited. Cara and Liam took turns reading. It seemed as if they returned to American Literature class. They became reacquainted with Whitman and Hawthorne, Lincoln and Irving. Cara marveled at how she had forgotten such writings. But Mama, introduced to these works so much later in life, never forgot them or lost her love for them. She reveled in the idea that words could outlast a life, that part of a person could be immortal.

Each day brought steady deterioration in Mary Larson's health. Within a week of Cara's visit with Dr. Weaver, Jeanine revised Mama's diet down to only the blandest of foods. Cara frowned with undisguised revulsion, but Mama never complained. By the second week, Mary was no longer able to walk on her own. Cara bought a comfortable wheelchair, and Mama enjoyed the long lazy walks Cara took with her around the neighborhood. By the fourth week, Mama's health deteriorated, and she became all but confined to bed. Her pain and discomfort grew steadily worse. Cara and Jeanine set up a hospital bed in the living room so she would be in the middle of all the action. But Mama became less and less aware of her surroundings, as if the battle had turned inward, to a place Cara could not go.

Cara accepted each aspect of her mother's failing health with no outward emotion. She focused every ounce of energy on being cheerful as she made her mother as comfortable as possible. But when she was away from Mary, her sadness was almost too heavy to bear. She had trouble eating and sleeping and dragged listlessly through each day.

She went to work each day, visited Mary during her lunch break, and left promptly at 4:00 p.m. each evening. Often she returned to the office after her mother fell asleep and worked until the early morning hours. It wasn't a burden; she wouldn't have slept anyway. At work, she became increasingly quiet, dealing with issues with as little drama as possible. She didn't mention her mother's illness or Liam's involvement in her personal life. She didn't want to invite any questions outside of the FIT or Aerie systems, especially from Lauren.

Liam was shocked at the deterioration in both mother and daughter. He noted with dismay as Cara seemed to wither before his eyes. After Mary fell asleep, he watched Cara's shoulders sag as the pretense of cheerfulness faded to despair. He did his best to cheer her up. He took her on long walks, holding her cold hand in his. He told her amusing stories about growing up with three brothers, or of the early, difficult days of Windwear's existence. He would run with her on dark summer evenings, adjusting his long stride to her shorter one. He tried to chase the sadness from her eyes, but she seemed like a ghost, a pale shadow of the woman he had known only weeks before.

Tonight he was particularly troubled. Even Cara, in her preoccupied state, noticed. "Liam, are you all right? Is something the matter?" They were returning from a walk, heading up the steps to the front porch.

"Cara, I need to go away for a while."

"Away?"

He nodded. "I've mentioned how busy things are at Windwear. Well, we've reached a critical stage. I need to go back East and talk to the investment community. It's time to put together the deals to finance all this growth we've been planning. Lauren has been after me for weeks to take this trip, but I've been delaying. She came unglued today when I told her I wanted to wait a few more weeks."

Cara hardly heard him. Away? Her heart began to fill with an ache that surprised her. She felt as if she were awakening from a long sleep. Where had she been all these weeks? What was this strange sensation? When had Liam become so important to her? When had he become so entwined in her life she no longer thought of life without him? When had she begun to care about this man?

"Cara?"

"Of course you should go. You haven't been delaying your trip because of Mama, have you?"

He hesitated. "This isn't an easy thing you're dealing with. I want to be here, to help where I can."

"You have." She smiled. "You've been wonderful, Liam. I ... I don't know how we could have made it this far without you. You made this whole unbearable situation manageable somehow. I don't know how you did it, and I can't ever thank you enough, but Windwear is important. You need to take care of your business."

"I don't want to go right now, but I don't think I can avoid it. So much hinges on this trip. If things go according to plan, Windwear will grow faster than I ever imagined."

"You know I wish you the best of luck. How long will you be gone?"

"Two weeks."

"Two weeks!" It seemed like a lifetime. "You'll miss the review, but I suppose Lauren and Paul will be there."

"Paul will. Lauren will be with me."

"Oh. She will." There was that strange, hollow ache again.

"Absolutely. I wouldn't try to work these complex financial deals without my expert legal counsel. She's sharp, I tell you. She's been the driving force behind all these changes at Windwear. We couldn't undertake this expansion without her. In the short time she's been at Windwear, she's become indispensable."

Sharp, indispensable. Yes, Lauren was all those things. Not to mention beautiful and sophisticated and glamorous. Lauren. With Liam. For two weeks. Two whole weeks.

"I'd better go, Cara. Lauren is waiting. We still need to review a few issues, and our flight leaves early tomorrow." He leaned down, tilted her face up to his, and kissed her cheek. "I'll call you. Soon."

"I promise to return your calls this time."

He smiled. "You're learning."

"Liam?"

"Yes?"

"Would you do something for me? Would you say goodbye to Mama before you leave?"

Liam stared at her for a long moment. "You bet." He turned and headed into the house.

The sadness in Cara's heart threatened to overwhelm her. She ran down the porch steps and wandered slowly along the sidewalk. All around was a fairyland, dappled in starlight and shadows and summer warmth. In the silvery moonlight, she could almost pretend the rest of the world didn't exist.

She returned fifteen minutes later, opened the front door, and went to check on her mother. Mary was sleeping peacefully. Liam was gone.

Chapter 11

Cara knocked on Peter's door at 2:59 p.m. He had scheduled their meeting for three o'clock, and she knew not to be late. When he didn't answer, she poked her head inside. The office was empty. She settled in one of the two striped wing chairs situated in front of his desk. A leather-bound calendar covered almost the entire surface of the huge teak desk. Gleaming gold pens were lined up meticulously in a row on one side. A gold-framed picture of his two children stood alone in the corner. Bold watercolors hung from the walls in perfect symmetrical composition.

Cara thought of her own office. The walnut veneer desk and old wooden chairs had seen better days. The only item resembling decor was a coffee mug a friend from the University of Washington had given her. "How 'bout them DAWGS?" it boasted in purple and gold. A sad thing when something from UW qualified as art.

How nice to let her mind wander over such frivolous matters. She hadn't had much time to think these past few weeks. The days had been passing in a blur of nerveless activity, and all she could do was hang on through each one.

She and Mike had completed the design of Aerie's management module. She compiled a list of ancillary services that would be needed to set up and link a system to Aerie. Pyramid would be rolling in money. So many billable hours would come from the Portland office even the bigwigs in New York would sit up and take notice. She was willing to bet Peter made partner within a year.

The project team had completed the concept phase for FIT. The data tables were verified and normalized, and the activity diagrams had been double and triple checked by Fleet's team. They hammered out the problems that seemed insurmountable only a few weeks earlier. The fight between swimwear and footwear concerning material inspection was resolved with—surprise!— a compromise. And the company finally created a single policy for returning defective goods. She still needed an answer from Fleet's top management regarding buyer authorization. No one ever seemed to agree when control over the purse strings was up for discussion. She wasn't surprised, but it didn't make designing the system any easier.

Overall, FIT's design was solid. Only a few minor issues remained. This meeting with Peter would serve as the final update before the Concept Phase Review next Monday. She looked forward to hear him say, *Good job, Larson. I knew you would make a good manager.*

The Concept Phase Review would stand out as one of the defining points of the project. The purchasing team would be first to present, followed by the manufacturing team, and then the order entry team. During the review, each team would present the proposed data model, activity diagrams, and system architecture to Fleet's management team for approval. That approval was critical. Approval set the design in contractual stone. Once approved, the functionality included in the design, termed the project scope, remained fixed for the rest of the project. If Fleet wanted to modify FIT after the Concept Phase Review, it would need to go through a formal process to incorporate the modification, and the cost of making the change would be added to Pyramid's fee.

Cara learned long ago to conduct aggressive analysis in the concept phase to limit future changes. A project could absorb a few adjustments to scope, but too many would kill a project. She'd been involved on one project with an incomplete concept design. The whole thing fell apart in programming. The client was angry. Pyramid was angry. Lawsuits flew. And the system was never built.

Peter walked into his office. "Oh, hello, Cara."

"Hello, Peter. You wanted to see me?"

"Yes, I wanted to talk to you about Monday's review." He opened a thin file folder. "About this Aerie system ..."

"Yes?" Cara eyed him guardedly. This was not the Peter she knew. She'd been in his office for over fifteen seconds, and he hadn't even raised his voice.

"I've talked to our attorneys. Since the original proposal didn't include any mention of Aerie, they don't want to refer to it during the Concept Review."

"What exactly does that mean?"

He waved his hand vaguely. "Well, I'm not sure. It sounds like a lot of legal mumbo jumbo to me, but I agreed."

"Peter, the purpose of the review is to finalize the scope at the end of the concept phase. Of course Aerie didn't come up at the time we wrote the proposal; no one had thought of it then. That's not a valid reason to throw it out now."

"Well, the lawyers don't agree. They see Aerie as part of the programming phase, and they prefer to keep the review strictly to conceptual issues."

Cara shook her head. "That doesn't make sense. We've done a concept phase for Aerie just as we have for FIT. If we don't include Aerie in the review, how do we establish it as part of scope?"

"Look, I don't want to get the legal boys in a snit. If I piss them off, they'll call in the internal auditors, and then we'll really lose time. Just do as I've asked."

"Okay, but I want to make sure I understand what you're asking. Should we discuss Aerie's functionality during the review?"

"No. Leave Aerie out completely."

"Oh." She frowned. "Peter, Aerie is integrated into the rest of FIT. Are you sure—"

"Dammit, Cara. Would you for once do what I ask without any backtalk?"

"But Peter, this is a huge change. I'll need time to reorganize the presentation. I want to make sure I know how to proceed." She paused, and Peter glared at her. "So, Aerie is out of the FIT review. Will we conduct a separate review?"

Peter nodded and began shuffling papers on his desk, his signature sign of dismissal. "Uh ... yes ... we'll probably do something like that. Later. Not now."

Probably? Later? Cara was growing very uncomfortable about this discussion. She opened her planner. "When should we schedule it?"

"I'm not sure yet."

"Peter, I need to know the timeline if I need to create a special presenta—"

"Goddammit, Cara!" Peter slammed his fist on his desk and made the picture of his children rock wildly back and forth. "I didn't say when. I'm not sure yet. I'll tell you when I decide. Just make sure Aerie is out of Monday's review. Understood?"

His yelling didn't surprise her, but his vagueness did. Peter was a man of precision. As he returned to his paper shuffling, the true purpose of the meeting hit her. "Yes," Cara said slowly, "I believe I do understand."

"Good. That will be all."

"There isn't going to be a review for Aerie, is there, Peter?"

He looked at her sharply. "What do you mean?"

"The review is too close to make a major change like this. You're throwing it out of scope. You're excluding Aerie from the contract."

"Don't jump to any wild conclusions. We'll do the review."

"When? Later? After Fleet approves FIT's concept design without Aerie included?"

Peter gave her a hard look. "That's right, Cara. I am not required to include Aerie in FIT. I'm throwing it out."

"Why? You approved Aerie after the demonstration. Everyone has been working under that assumption. Fleet's customers and suppliers have spent a lot of time and money preparing their systems to handle it."

"I didn't approve anything. There is nothing in writing about Aerie."

"Peter—"

"They took a risk. I can't help the decisions they made.
The attorneys are adamant, and the schedule can't handle the
additional work. We can't meet our time and profit targets if
we include Aerie. It's out."

"What do you mean, 'the schedule can't handle the
additional work?' We're way ahead with Aerie. We've
worked overtime to design this thing. We're nearly done with
the prototype. We haven't missed one deadline on the
schedule."

"Enough, Cara. End of discussion."

"Well, Rick Penner will be furious at this news."

"No, he won't." Peter gave her another hard look. "We're
not going to tell him."

"What!?"

"He doesn't need to know."

"You must be kidding. You can't do that."

Peter glared at her as if she were stupid. "Haven't you
learned anything over these last few months, Cara? If we tell
Fleet now, they'll go ballistic, and the entire project will be in
jeopardy. We will end up spending precious time arguing
over scope instead of building the system. Both sides will
lose. Pyramid's reputation will suffer, and Fleet will get a
substandard system. I have experience in these matters. After
the scope of FIT is set, and everything is running smoothly,
we can bring up Aerie without any of the emotional turmoil
that will occur if we bring the issue up now."

She sat back. "And charge them a hefty price to add it
back to scope. I understand. This is about profit. Forget about
our agreement. Forget about customer service. Forget about
our goddamned word—"

"Watch yourself, Cara."

She fell silent, opened her mouth to say more, fell silent
again.

"Now, here are your instructions. You will conduct the
review of FIT. You will not mention Aerie. If anyone brings
up the subject, you will put them off."

"I'm not going to be able to put everyone off."

"That's where I am counting on you to do your job."

"What do you mean?" she asked warily.

"You, my dear, will do the tap dance."

"I beg your pardon?"

"You know exactly what I mean. You will do the tap dance. You are going to make everyone believe Aerie is in scope even though it isn't."

She stared at him in disbelief. "I can't believe you're asking me to do this."

"Believe it." He leaned over, piercing her with another hard glare. "Your job next Monday is to do your best to confuse the hell out of every person in the room. You will toss out so much technical jargon they'll sink in it. They won't understand a word you're saying, but they won't want to seem stupid, so they'll nod their heads and agree. You will slide the design past them with their eyes wide open. With some skillful maneuvering on your part, they'll walk out of the room thinking Aerie is still in scope."

Cara sat back, unable to say a word.

"That's better. No backtalk. I like that." She could only stare at her boss in shock. "Oh, and one more thing, Cara. I want you to listen carefully and do exactly as I say. I want you to deliver the Aerie prototype, along with all its documentation, to me. I want one copy and one copy only to exist. Then I want you to purge everything related to Aerie from the network, including all the tape backups."

Cara shook her head. "I don't understand—"

"I'm not surprised; you still have a lot to learn." He smiled and shuffled his papers. "That will be all."

She had reached the door when he spoke again. "Cara?" She turned to face him. "Don't go against me on this. Don't even try. I can make life difficult for you."

She stared at him in silence, unable to hide her sudden sense of apprehension.

"Ah, I see I've made myself clear."

She stood at the door a moment longer, unsure how to respond. "Go," he said. "Don't forget what I've told you."

The shock began to wear off as Cara drove to her mother's house. How should she respond to this unexpected turn of events? She had dealt with some unscrupulous managers before, but never one willing to cheat a high-profile client for such a self-serving purpose. Maybe cheating wasn't the right word. Unbelievably, Peter was correct regarding his obligations. The contract wasn't specific. In legal terms, Peter had every right to set the scope of the project. If Fleet disagreed, it was up to Fleet to push back.

That was the rub. The technology was complex. A gap existed between what the people at Fleet knew and what they needed to know to implement the new system. That was the reason Fleet hired Pyramid in the first place, to provide the guidance and expertise the company itself didn't have. Instead of plugging the knowledge gap, Peter was exploiting it. And he was using Cara to help him do the job. Tap dance, he told her. Obfuscate, in other words. Conceal. Confuse. Muddy the waters. Cloud the air. Make the client believe the scope contained all the functionality the company expected, when in reality it fell short.

Peter's actions were legal, Cara supposed, as long as Fleet's management could be persuaded to sign on the dotted line. She knew what would happen once the ink dried. Pyramid would slowly begin to explain what the company had actually approved. And the additional fees would flood in as Fleet was forced to pay for functionality it thought it had already purchased. Oh, Peter had the right, Cara thought, but it was so damned wrong.

Think, Cara, think! She could consult a lawyer. No good, she sighed. Nothing illegal is happening. She could talk to Rick Penner. Right. And watch the lawsuits rain down on her like a storm in winter. She would end up with no job, no career, and no reputation. Not a brilliant strategic move. She wished Liam were here. He was creative. He'd be able to think of a way out of this mess.

No, she did not want to think of Liam. Every time she did, she pictured him with Lauren, gallivanting around glamorous East Coast cities. He phoned exactly one time. Last night. She had been running and missed the call. He left a number, but when she called back, the desk clerk told her Mr. Scofield requested he not be disturbed for the remainder of the night. She hung up, the hollow ache deep in her gut once more an unwelcome companion.

Cara realized something was wrong as soon as she turned into the driveway. Dreadfully wrong. All of the sudden the world began to turn in slow motion. Her car, slowing to a stop in the driveway. Jeanine running from the door, arms flying, face streaked with tears. The sudden sick feeling she had been dreading for weeks. "Jeanine, what is it? What's wrong?" she shouted as the nurse hurried toward her. "Tell me!" She heard the panic in her own voice as if it were far away.

"Hurry, Cara. Hurry. It's your Mama. She's collapsed." Thoughts of Peter and Aerie and Liam fled from her mind as she ran frantically into the house.

"Mama! Mama!"

Chapter 12

Dr. Weaver stood at the edge of the bed as Cara ran into the living room. He straightened as she approached. Cara searched his face for any sign of hope, but saw only resignation. "I'm afraid this isn't good news, Cara. It's a matter of time, now. A few days, a week at the most." He adjusted an intravenous tube containing the medicine to ease her mother's pain and checked to make sure the catheter was secure in her frail arm.

Cara nodded silently, absorbing every detail of his actions. She sat down by the bed and held Mary's hand. Then this is where she would stay until Mama completed her journey. She would remain with her as long as she could, accompany her on this road as far as she was able. She was surprised at how calm she was, now the moment was at hand.

She called Anna and explained she had a family emergency and would be unable to attend work for several days. Peter called back and told her he postponed the review one week. This way she would have more time to purge Aerie from the network, he added. She called Mike and told him she wouldn't be in, informed him of the change in schedule, and reminded him of the few open issues they still needed to resolve before the review. She tried to call Liam but the desk clerk said he and Lauren had checked out. God, why did everything hurt so much?

Mama fell into a fitful coma. Occasionally she would awaken and look around with hazy, unfocused vision. At times, she would catch sight of Cara, smile gently, and hold her hand. Every once in a while, they would exchange a few words. Cara hardly left her side. The last few moments they shared were private ones between mother and daughter. Cara held onto them with a burning intensity she would never forget. In those last hours, she grew to love her mother more than she ever thought possible.

It was in the early hours of a Monday morning, on a velvet midsummer night, that Mary Larson drew her last breath. Cara knew the moment it happened. In her mother's face, conflict ceased and peace prevailed. Silence pervaded the night.

For Cara, peace was nowhere in sight. Anguish and relief warred within her as she faced the finality of the moment. She held her mother's hand and laid her head down on the edge of the bed.

She woke with a start. Five o'clock. Mama's cold hand had slipped from her grasp. Cara stared again at the peaceful face, reliving the last moments of her mother's life. Emptiness welled within her, more frightening than any emotion.

She called Dr. Weaver's office first. His answering service took her message. She contacted the funeral home to remove her mother's body. It was awful and difficult, but not as bad as she imagined. She knew her mother's body was just a physical memory, that Mary's spirit had already found a new home. Somehow, that thought made the cold details of death easier to bear. She called Peter. And a few of Mama's close friends. But she didn't call Liam. She didn't have his number, didn't even know what city he was in.

At 6:15 a.m., the phone rang. "Hello?"

"Cara? Is that you?"

"Liam. Hello."

"I'm glad I caught you. We've been busy, and I've hardly had two minutes to put together to give you a call. I wanted to catch you before your review. To wish you luck."

"Thank you, but, we've ... we've been pushed back a week. We're scheduled for next Monday, now."

"Oh. Well, that will work out. I'll be able to come." She didn't say anything. "Cara, how are you doing?"

"I'm fine."

"And your mother. How is she feeling?" Cara was silent, could not find any words to say. "Cara, are you there? I asked how Mary is."

"I heard you. I … I …" She paused and took a small breath. "Liam, Mama died early this morning."

There was a muffled gasp on the line. "Oh, Cara, I'm so sorry. Are you all right? Is there anything I can do—"

"Everything is fine. Jeanine will help me handle the details."

"I'll come home. I'll get the first flight out."

"No, there's no need. We can manage. Stay and finish your business."

"I'll be there as soon as I can." He hung up before she could say another word.

Liam replaced the receiver and reached for the phone book. Ten minutes later, he was booked on a one o'clock flight leaving La Guardia. He grabbed his wallet and room key and knocked on the door of the room next to his.

"Good morning, Liam." Lauren opened the door and glanced at her watch. "You're early. I thought we weren't meeting until 9:45." She stopped. "Is something wrong?"

"There's been a change of plans, Lauren. I need to get back to Portland. Will you drive me out to La Guardia?"

"Why? What happened?"

"It's a family emergency."

"You don't have any family in Portland. What's going on?"

"Cara's mother died this morning. I need to get back to Portland."

Lauren's lips tightened. "I'm sorry about that, but I don't think this is a good time for you to leave. We are close on these negotiations."

Liam shook his head. "I wish we were close on these negotiations. You know as well as I do every single investment group we've talked to has rejected our proposal as being too risky."

"No, that's not true. Every single investment group has rejected our proposal because it's not profitable. Liam, I wish you would consider using my projections."

"Don't start with that again, Lauren. I told you, your projections are unacceptable."

"But—"

"No buts. Still, I take your point. After our meetings with the Hegelman Team and the Traxel Group last week, I realize my projections might be too conservative. I spent all night working up new numbers."

"You did?" she asked in surprise. "Let me see them."

"They're in my room. I'll show them to you in the car—"

"At least give me the details."

He nodded. "Fair enough. I've formulated three different outsourcing options. None of them are as drastic as yours, but all are well within my range of acceptability. I added some revenue from Aerie to make the numbers work. I was conservative because I can't predict how well Aerie will perform, but I was still able to move the payback period from five years to three."

Frustration was written all over her face. "Three years? Are you still projecting flat growth during that time frame?"

"Yes, that's the most realistic scenario. However, after three years, our profits will rise dramatically, especially if we take the first few conservatively."

"You're still offering 45 percent of the nonvoting stock"?

"Yes, with conversion to voting status after five years."

"And you'll still hold all the voting stock yourself?"

"Absolutely. I need to retain control of the company while we go through all these changes. After five years, the common shares convert, and the company will be subject to more extensive board oversight. By then our operations will be more predictable, and I'll reconsider management control." He looked at his watch. "Lauren, I have to go. Will you drive me? We can talk more in the car. Or should I call a cab?"

She smiled suddenly. "Of course, I'll drive you. When should I be ready?"

"Forty-five minutes. An hour. No later."

"I'll be ready. Just knock on my door."

"Thanks, Lauren."

Lauren double-parked the rental car near the departure terminal causing the driver of the late model Buick behind her to lay on his horn and swerve sharply. "You'd better hurry, Liam, or this compact is going to be a subcompact."

He leaned back in the passenger seat, a sheaf of papers on his lap. "We should have done this at the hotel."

"You're the one running late, not me. I'm just here doing your bidding. Besides, I didn't know you were leaving so suddenly. I didn't have a lot of time to prepare these documents."

"Sorry, Lauren." He pulled his pen from his pocket. "What do I need to sign?"

Lauren picked up a document fastened with a binder clip, turned to the last page and handed it back. "Right here."

"What's this?" *Nondisclosure Agreement.* He thumbed through it.

"The Agreement to keep our discussions with Cyclops private. You usually sign it at the start of the investor meeting, but since you won't be attending ..."

He briefly read the document. On the last page, he spotted the space for his name as the president of Windwear and the space for Carl Streeter, the representative of the Cyclops Consortium. "All right. This seems to be in order." He scrawled his signature on the line, added the date, and handed it back. She handed him another multi-page document.

"God, the paperwork doesn't end. You probably own a tree farm in southern Oregon and are getting rich as we speak."

She laughed. "How did you guess?"

He held up the document. "What's this one?"

"A second copy of the NDA. In case Cyclops insists on having an original." Liam leafed through the pages. It was exactly the same as the first. "Also looks good." He again signed his name, but before he could add the date, Lauren thrust a dark blue, soft-covered notebook at him. "Last thing. My notary book." She took the document from him.

He reached for the notebook. "I didn't know the NDA needed to be notarized."

"Usually it doesn't. Then again, you're usually at the meeting. I don't want to risk giving Cyclops the opportunity to void the NDA and then talk freely to our competitors about our strategy. That's also why I want to make sure both parties have originals in hand."

"Good thinking." He scrawled his name on the next blank notary line.

"Sign on two lines. We have two NDAs." She took back the notary book. "I'll fill in the rest of the information later."

"Anything else?"

"No. That's all."

He opened his briefcase and handed her a file folder. "Here are my new business projections. Please review them. Attach this document as Exhibit A when you talk to Cyclops. I've included a script in the front. I don't want you to deviate from it."

"Liam, I am not five years old."

No, you're not, but you are my employee, and this is important. I want you to do exactly as I say. Present the proposal and stall. Do not promise anything other than what is written here. Do you understand? And don't agree to anything. Just find out where their comfort zone is and stop."

"What if Cyclops says yes to the proposal?"

He gave her a wry smile. "That's not going to happen. Still, I want to get their reaction. Once they say no, I want you to go back to Hegelman and Traxel and pitch the revised proposal. I think one or both will be receptive, especially after our initial meetings. They are more likely to say yes than Cyclops, but don't say yes to them either. That's all I want you to do. I'll call you in a couple days to find out where we are." He handed the file to her.

He didn't notice the angry look she threw at him because at that moment they were interrupted by a sharp squeal of wheels and a stream of colorful adjectives delivered by a red-faced Russian cabby. "Damn. You better go, Liam, or we'll both end up in the obituary column instead of the business news."

Liam opened the door, stepped out, and turned back to Lauren. He handed her one of his business cards with a phone number scrawled on the back. "This is Cara's number in case you need to get hold of me." He smiled as he closed the door. "Thanks again for the ride. I'll talk to you in a few days."

Lauren grasped the card and waved him off as he hurried away. "Ride?" she sneered. "You want a ride, Liam Scofield? Well hang on, my friend, because you just started the ride of your life." She picked up the folder, scanned the contents, and tossed it on the passenger seat. "Thank you, Liam. You just gave me the opening I've been looking for."

Chapter 13

"I'm sorry, Ms. Janelle. Windwear's proposal is just too risky. The price-earnings ratio is too high, and the payback period is too long." Richard Bancroft, vice president of Boston First Bank and Windwear's principal banker, pulled off his glasses and rubbed his eyes as he spoke.

Lauren sighed and crossed her legs. She looked around the table at the members of the Cyclops consortium. "Windwear is a young company, gentlemen, but rock solid. Mr. Scofield himself put these figures together and asked me to present them to you." She sifted through the folders in front of her. On top was the new proposal Liam had handed her this morning. She slid the folder to the bottom of the stack and instead picked up the one containing his original proposal, the one rejected by Hegelman and Traxel last week.

She rose from her chair and approached the overhead projector. "Our quality and customer care programs are Windwear's greatest assets. Though our costs aren't the lowest in the business, our strong reputation enables us to attain premium prices for our products. Our customer return prog—"

"Pardon me, Ms. Janelle, but I don't give a rat's ass about Windwear's quality program or customer service program or any other weak-kneed, wishy-washy, New Age program you want to talk about." The words belonged to Carl Streeter, vice president of Marshall, Longham and Fray Investment Bankers. "I'm concerned about one thing and one thing only. Profit. And frankly, there's not enough of it in this proposal to generate even a fleeting interest from me."

Lauren cleared her throat. "If you'll let me finish—"

"No, Ms. Janelle, you listen to me." Carl pushed his chair back, leaned over, and stared imperiously at her. "You may think Windwear is a hotshot company from the wilds of Or-ee-gone, but out here, you're like a wino on the street, a nameless face holding your hand out for a free lunch. I have a hundred more deserving proposals sitting on my desk this minute. Most of us are here as a favor to Bancroft. He's taken time out of his schedule to fly down from Boston to meet with us. He seems to think your little company shows some promise. Promise means profits and growth, and I don't see anything like that for five years." He pointed to the image projected on the screen. "There's only one number on that slide that makes any difference at all, and it's a non-starter. You want me to wait five years for a decent return? Five years! That's a lifetime in this business. Too long for me. If you can't give me better projections within two years, you're wasting my time."

Richard looked at Lauren, expecting her to respond, but she remained silent. He raised an eyebrow in surprise, then cleared his throat. "Now settle down a minute, Carl. Before you walk out on the deal, let's review Windwear's history. Scofield built this company from nothing. With almost no investment money, he's made Windwear into one of the fastest growing companies in the West. They enjoy a strong customer base, and are a major supplier to Fleet. I agree, his numbers are on the conservative side, but I've been doing business with him for three years, and I can tell you this: Scofield doesn't make promises he can't keep. If he says he'll bring in a single-digit return, you can count on it, and he will probably bring in more. But he won't put himself in a position where he is forced to make excuses for not meeting a commitment he never should have made in the first place. He's walking into a major three-way expansion. I can't blame him for being conservative. We might be able to talk him into slowing down his expansion, maybe take on only one major project at a time—"

"Hell, no!" Carl banged his fist on the table. "That's the only thing I like about this company. I like big risks. Big risks mean big profits. You pull Windwear's expansion plan from the deal, and I'll walk!"

"Big risks can also mean big losses."

"Which is why I want to make sure Scofield can guarantee higher profits. With this expansion plan, he can manipulate resources to cut costs." Carl paused, his eyes lighting up. "That's what I want to do. I want to make Scofield listen to reason." He drummed his fingers on the table. "I want majority ownership in the voting stock. Then we can show this new-age prick how to play ball like a man and not a boy. God, I can't stand these young upstarts who think they understand business when all they can do is manufacture a few widgets. I'll teach him how to be fiscally responsible."

Richard shook his head. "I'm afraid not, Carl. Scofield is firm on this point. He retains majority ownership and management control of Windwear."

Carl stood up. Several consortium members followed suit. "Then this discussion is over. You've wasted my time, Bancroft."

He stood for a moment, glaring hard at Richard Bancroft, waiting for him to change his mind. Richard tilted his graying head and shrugged his shoulders. "It's your loss, Streeter."

Carl gathered his papers. He was nearly out the door when Lauren, still standing at the front of the room, almost shouted, "Wait Mr. Streeter. Mr. Scofield has another proposal. Please sit down and let me explain."

Carl turned around. "Another proposal? So, Ms. Janelle, you've been holding out on us."

Lauren smoothed her skirt under the podium. "Of course not, Mr. Streeter. I just haven't been able to get a word in edgewise while you two engage in what might prove to be an unnecessary battle of wills." Her flashing smile took the edge off her words.

Carl walked back and sat down. "By all means, Ms. Janelle, proceed."

Lauren returned to the table and picked up the next folder in the stack. She removed a second set of transparencies from the file, and once again walked to the front of the room. She placed a slide on the projector, this one displaying a line graph showing double-digit growth and soaring profitability. The group stirred with interest. "I agree with Mr. Streeter. There is no reason why Windwear cannot achieve dramatic growth rates within two years." She replaced the graph with a bulleted list of actions.

"The first thing we do is change how Windwear enters the camping gear market. By investing in a joint venture or entering into a production agreement with a manufacturer in Southeast Asia, where labor rates are low and the exchange rate is favorable, we can cut costs by 30 percent. We will be able to lower prices and garner a huge market share in a short time. With Windwear's reputation for quality, our sales will increase rapidly."

"I'm not sure I understand," Richard said. "I thought Liam wanted to expand the manufacturing facilities in Portland."

"Well that was one option, and I'll be honest, Liam's first choice. Once we reviewed the financial impact, he changed his mind. This is a much more cost effective approach." Lauren addressed the consortium. "Of course, we'll use Aerie to assure we maintain tight control on costs."

"Aerie? What the hell is Aerie?" Carl was looking more interested by the minute.

"Aerie is a new software program under development. Without going into too many details, I can say Aerie will enable Windwear to monitor the production status of any inventory item along its supply chain. We're planning to install this system for all our major suppliers and customers as soon as development is complete. As you can imagine, a system like this would dramatically reduce the risk of manufacturing in the Asian market."

"When will it be finished?" Carl's eyes were practically glowing.

"I'm not sure, Mr. Streeter."

The air became charged with excitement. Questions rolled off the tongues of the investors who minutes ago were ready to take their money and go home. Who was developing it? How did it work? Was it for sale? Who thought of the idea? Did they need any investment capital? Lauren tried to hide her surprise at the sudden interest. She held up her hand in protest. "Gentleman, if I knew you would be this interested in Aerie, I would have come more prepared to discuss it. Unfortunately, I cannot answer all your questions at this time. We are still too early in development. However, you can rest assured this is the type of innovation and forward thinking you will get from a company like Windwear, even if it is located west of the Mississippi." There were a few snickers, but the good-natured smile she added to her comment made Carl's eyes light with appreciation. Even Richard Bancroft seemed impressed.

"Now, if I may continue. I calculate we can cut an additional 20 to 25 percent from our cost estimates by altering our plans to upgrade the manufacturing facilities in Portland. Mr. Scofield plans to introduce several modifications that would be unnecessary if we outsource to Asia. For instance, he's added a complex system to measure product quality at every step in the process. It's an innovative touch, but excessive, considering our profit targets."

Richard narrowed his eyes and leaned back in his chair. Lauren cast a quick glance his way and waited for him to speak, but it was Carl, not Richard, who broke the silence. "This is great! With these changes, Windwear could hit a 12 to 14 percent margin the first year. Not bad. Not bad at all."

"What do the numbers look like five years out, Ms. Janelle?" Richard asked.

"I apologize. Those figures are not available, Mr. Bancroft. We spent all weekend putting this proposal together with a two-year window. If you'd like, I will—"

"Never mind, Ms. Janelle. I'll talk to Liam myself."

Lauren hesitated. "Of course." She turned to the rest of the group. "These changes will not come without cost, gentlemen. Increased potential for profits and growth increases the value of Windwear. The price per share rises under this scenario from twelve to sixteen dollars."

"Sixteen!" one consortium member nearly exploded. A restless buzz erupted in the room. Lauren caught snippets through the clamor. "That's a 25 percent increase over the original proposal!" "Robbery!" "The increase is worth it just to get our hands on that Aerie thing." "With these figures, the P/E ratio is still in line."

Carl Streeter stilled the noise with an impatient gesture. "An interesting offer, Ms. Janelle, but insufficient. Under your scenario, Scofield is not required to make these changes. Since you are only offering nonvoting common stock for our investment, shareholders will have no say in how Windwear is run."

"Liam and I worked on these figures together, Mr. Streeter. He's committed to them." She softened her sharp tone. "The stock remains nonvoting for only five years. After that, the shares convert and assume all voting rights."

"Five years! Might as well be a lifetime. Scofield could destroy Windwear in five years. In the meantime, the company and the stockholders are at the mercy of this guy who is a cross between a hippie and a new-age environmentalist. I wouldn't pay five cents a share for Windwear, Ms. Janelle. Not five cents. I'm not in the market for nonvoting stock. I will only consider investing in voting stock."

"I'm sorry, Mr. Streeter. Liam owns all one thousand shares of preferred voting stock and intends to keep them."

"Fine, then he won't get any money from this group." He shook his head. "Or from anyone else in the investment community. Not even with those revised figures."

Lauren flicked off the overhead machine and gathered up her papers. "I'm sorry we couldn't come to an agreement gentleman. Of course, I'll discuss your concerns with Mr. Scofield. Perhaps we can meet again Wednesday or Thursday?"

A low rumble ensued as chairs scraped across the floor and the members rose. Richard spoke over the din. "Let's plan for ten o'clock on Wednesday, everyone."

Lauren heard the quiet murmurs and stifled expletives as she turned to leave. She sighed, picked up her briefcase, and left the conference room.

"You know, Ms. Janelle, you may be on to something with your revised proposal."

She glanced up to find Carl Streeter entering the elevator with her. "Obviously not something attractive enough to secure your investment."

"Well, not under the terms you specified."

"You made *that* clear, Mr. Streeter." The elevator stopped and the doors opened. "Now, if you'll excuse me ..."

As she stepped off the elevator, Carl took Lauren's arm and guided her to a quiet corner of the lobby. "Ms. Janelle, don't tell me you buy all that New Age garbage Scofield was spouting last Friday as if it were the next major religion. I could tell by looking at you during his presentation you thought it was a bunch of hogwash."

Her voice was flat as she responded. "Of course I don't. Liam is the president of Windwear. He chooses the direction of the organization. I'm merely his attorney."

"Right. I read your bio in the proposal. A bachelor's in finance from Cornell. Law degree from Harvard. Three years of corporate law at Bergman and Stein. You know as well as I do he's going to kill his growth opportunities if he takes Windwear public with his projections. The stock price will never rise to double digits." Lauren's lips tightened, but she didn't respond. "Do you think you can convince him to implement the changes you outlined?"

"Why do you ask?"

He tipped back his head and laughed. "Because Windwear would be a goddamned good investment if your proposal were implemented. I'd be the first one to put money down, but not without some safeguards."

"What do you mean, safeguards?" she asked warily.

"Assurances. Written assurances Scofield will follow the steps outlined in your proposal."

Lauren shook her head. "Liam would never sign a contract specifying detailed operational commitments. He's too ... too skittish for that. He likes to keep his options open. It can be damned irritating, but no one can deny he's been successful."

"What about the voting stock? Would Scofield be willing to part with any voting shares and a seat on the board in exchange for more funds?"

"To what purpose? As long as Liam holds the majority of the voting stock, he retains control of Windwear."

"At least I would have a say. You would be amazed at how much influence I can wield by being loud and obnoxious."

She shook her head. "I don't believe that would amaze me."

"I'm serious. I could do great things with Windwear if I had the chance. I don't like seeing a promising company behave so foolishly in front of the investment community. You realize they will laugh him out the door with his proposal, don't you? He won't get another chance, either. Word will go out from the consortium that he's one of those idealistic Left Coasters, and the doors will shut before they even open." His eyes narrowed. "I can personally make sure the word goes out. Investment funds are far too scarce for anyone to waste their time after Scofield's attempt here."

"You can't do that. We signed a Nondisclosure Agreement."

"People talk. You can say a lot without naming names."

"Go ahead. I have several appointments with other investment groups if our negotiations with Cyclops fail. They seem quite interested."

"Have they seen Scofield's proposal?" Lauren remained silent. "Just as I suspected. A snowball has a better chance in hell than Windwear has of getting any money once they discover management control isn't part of the deal."

Lauren took a breath and tried to still her growing panic.

"What about you, Ms. Janelle? I can't understand why you made the jump to little Windwear after such a high-powered start with Bergman and Stein. Unless you saw the potential too. You must have thought Windwear would strike gold, and you would reap the benefits."

"These things take time. I've already pushed Liam hard on these changes. I need to be careful, go slow—"

"You're going to lose everything if you go too slow. Opportunities don't last forever. When this one is gone, your chance for success may disappear, too. Along with your stellar reputation. You're taking an interesting risk, Ms. Janelle."

Lauren closed her eyes. "Damn," she whispered in frustration.

"Too bad." He began to walk away.

Lauren hesitated. "Wait." It was the second time today she'd had to beg. She hated to beg. "Wait, Mr. Streeter. I have another idea."

Carl turned and didn't even try to hide his interest. "Oh?"

"It will cost you."

"What will cost me?"

"A seat on the board."

"Ms. Janelle," he drawled, "I'm not interested in a seat on the board." Her eyes widened in surprise. "No, Ms. Janelle. I want control. Do you hear me? I want at least 51 percent of Windwear's voting stock, or you can ride into oblivion with Scofield and all his new-age hiking boots."

It hit her quite unexpectedly. The half-formed ideas that had been growing out of frustration and delay suddenly clicked together with blinding clarity. It could work, she thought. With help from the man in front of her.

She studied Carl Streeter. He was more right than he knew. From the start her plan had been a simple one. Take Windwear public. Turn the company into a low cost producer. Force the stock price up with quick profits. Sell at the top. Then move on.

Her simple plan was proving far more difficult to implement than she expected. What had Carl called Liam? A New-Age prick? She had thought so, too. A quick target. An easy mark. Unfortunately, Liam Scofield was not as easy to manipulate as his easy manner suggested.

Ever since she arrived at Windwear, she had carefully cultivated Liam's trust. She outwardly encouraged his wild and costly ideas while finding subtle legal obstacles to block them. Her efforts had been nothing but frustrating so far. Every time she complicated an issue, Liam simplified it. She remembered how she slapped down the thick stack of environmental regulations related to the new materials he proposed to use in the coming outerwear line. They would need months to study the regs, she told him. They should halt work on the new Research and Development department and redirect efforts to this more immediate problem. But Liam didn't halt anything. Within a week, he dropped a slim report on her desk with his decisions about which materials to use. When she asked about the source of the report, he smiled and told her he had made a call. He had a friend who ran an environmental consulting company. She reviewed the regulations and Windwear's requirements and made a list of recommendations. All Liam needed to do was sort through the report details and choose the materials that best suited the company's needs.

The same thing happened with Aerie. Lauren had done her best to stop that money-sink of a project. But Liam, with the help of that bitch, Cara Larson, rolled over every objection and kept throwing money at the project. She might need to rethink her opinion of Aerie, though. The interest the consortium showed in the software had caught her by surprise. Maybe Aerie wasn't a complete loser of an idea.

At least she'd been able to convince Liam to take the company public. It was the only way to fund his ideas, she told him. Then he insisted on terms no sane investor would accept. She had produced the projections the company would need to entice interest from the investment community, but Liam had rejected them out of hand. He surprised her today with his revised numbers. They were actually quite reasonable, if one was willing to accept moderate profitability and an average stock price. She shook her head. Moderate and average were not part of her plan.

She'd been searching for an opportunity to force Liam's hand, and she had been growing increasingly frustrated when she had found none. Until today. Suddenly, today, opportunity fell into her lap with the oh-so timely death of that bitch Cara's mother.

She gazed at Carl Streeter thoughtfully. She had miscalculated. She thought the consortium would accept her figures even without control of the voting stock. They should have. They were strong numbers. She even threw Aerie in as an added enticement. But Carl was greedy. Too greedy for his own good. Well, she could use that. She eyed the polished, urbane investment banker, who practically salivated every time the word Aerie was mentioned, and saw in him the opportunity to rescue her plan. "I understand what you're saying, Mr. Streeter, but the real question is, do you understand what you're asking?"

"What do you mean?"

"You want control of Windwear? It's not on the table."

He looked surprised. "How much to put it on the table?"

"Of course, that's up to Liam." She seemed bored now, almost disinterested.

"Can you convince him?"

"It would be difficult. And very expensive."

"How much?"

"Oh, I don't know, but I will say the price goes beyond money. Far beyond mere money."

She stood in front of him, elegant, hard, and beautiful. A smile crept slowly over his face. "How incredibly intriguing you are, Ms. Janelle. I can't help but be interested. How would you like to explore the possibilities over dinner tonight?"

She tipped her head in assent. "Seven o'clock. Aureole." He nodded. With a smile, she turned and walked away.

Carl studied her retreating form. "What could there possibly be beyond money?" he asked himself.

Chapter 14

The midafternoon sun streamed through the living room windows. Cara stood in the center of the room, holding an old shoebox, preparing to dispose of her mother's medications. She cringed when she looked at them, recalling Mama's pain, remembering her suffering. She shook her head. She didn't care. She wanted her mother back, pain or no pain. She wanted her back so she wouldn't have to face this awful loneliness. Immediately, she felt ashamed. It was a relief Mama was gone, she chided. A relief Mama didn't have to suffer any more.

All at once her mental battle receded, and the enormity of her mother's death engulfed her. For the first time, she understood—really understood—that she would never see her mother again. Never see her smile or hear her words of encouragement or feel the soft warmth of her touch. The box dropped from her hands. She heard footsteps behind her. "Jeanine, what am I going to do? How do you stop missing someone you love so much?" She turned around with troubled eyes, and there stood Liam. Tall, kind, wonderful, Liam. With hair careening around his head and shadows underlining his tired eyes. Right here in front of her. Not in New York or Boston, but right here, close enough to touch.

He moved to her in a few long strides and wrapped her in his arms. "Cara." He held her close. "I'm so sorry."

"How am I going to get through this, Liam?"

"There's not much you can do, except gather up all your memories and hold them tight. After a while, when they don't hurt so much, those memories will comfort you." He rocked her quietly. "And you can hold tight to me, Cara. I'm here."

"Thank you for coming." She closed her eyes, leaned against him, soaking in his warmth. "I miss her. I miss her so much."

"I know, and you will for a long time."

After several moments, she pulled away and gazed up at his tired face. "You shouldn't have come, Liam. I'm so happy you did, but I know you had—"

Just then, Jeanine walked into the living room. "Oh, Mr. Scofield. How kind of you to come."

"Hello, Jeanine. I'm sorry about Mary." He released Cara and went over to embrace the older woman.

"Thank you, Mr. Scofield. You helped make her last few weeks very happy, you know." She reached into her apron pocket and fished out a wrinkled envelope. "This is from Mary. She asked me to give it to you."

Liam stared at the envelope, his name written in a shaky scrawl. "Thank you, Jeanine."

She nodded and left the room. Cara studied Liam and then the envelope. "She loved you very much, Liam. I'll leave you alone for a few minutes."

He was staring out the picture window when Cara returned to the living room. She'd left him a half hour ago, and he had not come to find her. She was beginning to worry. "Liam?" He didn't turn around, but she saw that his shoulders sagged in private grief. She laid her face against his back and slipped her arms around his waist. He curled his hands over hers and brought them to his lips. She felt his hot tears on her fingertips. "You aren't alone either, Liam," she whispered softly.

Lauren inserted her room key into the hotel's office center and opened the door. The fluorescent lights reflected off the computers and fax machines. Her eyes lit up as she spied the laser printer connected to the computer. "Perfect." She powered up the computer, removed a disk from her briefcase, and inserted it into the drive. She scanned the files. There it was. She clicked on the document. *Underwriter's*

Agreement: Sale of Windwear Common Stock. This was the template agreement outlining the terms Windwear would accept when selecting an investment group to spearhead the company's initial public offering. She and Liam had created the agreement several weeks ago. The only information missing was the name of the underwriter. *Cyclops Consortium*, Lauren typed into the blank space for the underwriter name.

She scrolled to the last page of the agreement. She opened her briefcase and removed the Nondisclosure Agreement Liam signed earlier that day. All she needed to do was make sure the final pages of these two documents were identical.

When preparing legal documents, she often placed standard legal verbiage at the end; document amendment requirements, for example, or the provision for payment of attorney's fees. The two documents in front of her contained almost identical boilerplate language. She adjusted the wording on the final page of the broker agreement to match exactly that of the NDA. After few minor adjustments to the margins, she achieved her goal; two identical signature pages, one signed, and one unsigned.

She filled the paper tray with Windwear letterhead and printed the agreement. She attached Liam's revised projections. Exhibit A. Voilà. She was looking at a pristine, unsigned version of the proposal Liam had instructed her to present to Cyclops this morning, which of course, she had not done. She placed the document in a file folder and stored it in her briefcase. "I'll need that later."

She returned to the computer and saved the file. *Cyclops Underwriter Agreement-Version 1*, she typed. Then she set to work revising the agreement, this time changing its provisions to match the ones she presented to the consortium this morning. It was a little more challenging to get the new wording in and still keep the signature page unchanged. She worked carefully for a half hour, replacing words here, altering phrases there, and adjusting the margins until she was satisfied. She saved the file. *Cyclops Underwriter Agreement-Version 2.*

She printed the new agreement. She lifted the document off the printer, removed the last page, and shoved it through the shredder sitting beside the desk. She picked up the final page of the NDA Liam had signed that morning.

She thought of that moment at the airport. She had been holding her breath, hoping he wouldn't notice how nervous she was. She wasn't sure he would buy her cock and bull story about needing two originals of the NDA. She knew he would ask, and she knew he would inspect both agreements. He was always so damned careful.

But she managed to slide the lie by him, after all. She had the cramped quarters of the rental car to thank for that. If Liam had just unfastened the binder clip and spread the pages out, he would have seen that the number of the page he signed was far out of sequence from the other pages of the NDA. It was a four-page document, but the final page displayed the number fifteen, the same number as the final page of the underwriting agreement. But the binder clip hid the number, and Liam hadn't spotted the discrepancy.

Lauren reached for her notary stamp, affixed the seal, and signed her name. She initialed each page of the agreement with a well-practiced *LS* in the lower right corner. Long ago she mastered how the bottom of the *L* swept into the top of the *S* and how the *S* never seemed to close all the way, making it look more like a snake than a letter of the alphabet. Some skills a lawyer needed to learn early in the game. Perfect. She examined the entire document once more. Only one thing was missing. The date. She would have to wait for Carl Streeter before she could add that last bit of information.

Satisfied, she clipped the pages together. She attached her detailed projections to the agreement. Exhibit A. "Voilà," she said aloud, "a perfectly executed agreement." An agreement Liam had never seen but had nevertheless "signed." Well, if she played her cards right, he would never see this document, at least not until it was too late for him to do anything about.

She placed the executed document in a separate file folder and laid it on top of the one holding the unsigned agreement. She stood up and stretched like a languid cat.

Now, she needed to do some shopping. She would need something special to wear tonight. Something sparkling and shimmery. This was going to be a very important dinner.

Lauren settled seductively into her seat and stared at the steam swirling from her coffee as she waited for Carl to begin. All evening they'd been like two boxers, dancing around each other, each waiting for the other to throw the first punch, hoping to find weakness in the act of aggression. So far, neither one had made a move. She raised the steaming cup to her lips and took a sip. She would wait all night if she had to. Success depended on patience.

Carl broke first. "Well, did you talk to Scofield? Is he willing to deal?"

She gave an elegant shake of her head as she returned the cup to the saucer. "No."

He rustled impatiently in his seat. "You're wasting my time. If Scofield won't deal, I'm not interested."

"It's not an insurmountable obstacle. I believe I can still deliver those 510 voting shares you want so badly."

Carl almost choked on his coffee. "Without Scofield's approval? How do you propose to do that?"

"I've spent all afternoon working out the details."

"Ms. Janelle, are you planning to break the law?"

"Of course not."

"Selling shares without an owner's approval seems like breaking the law to me."

"Then, you aren't a lawyer, are you, Mr. Streeter?"

"How would you do it?" The words came out involuntarily. "Even if you slid this by Scofield, you wouldn't be able to get by the authorities. Not unless you plan to perpetrate mass fraud on the SEC and thousands of investors across the country. And get your pretty ass sued in at least a hundred different courts when the truth comes out."

"I have no interest in being sued. I assure you, it can be done perfectly legally."

Carl stared at her, and she returned his look steadily. "You sound convincing. I'd like to believe you, but I'm afraid I can't. There are too many obstacles."

"Oh?" Her voice was calm, but her eyes were hard.

"You won't be able to get around the disclosure laws. You know as well as I do you must disclose every material detail when you take a company public. Selling controlling ownership of the voting stock qualifies as a tad bit more than 'material,' wouldn't you say? If you don't fully disclose, a single shareholder can sue to void the offering." He scowled. "Not to mention Scofield himself. It would probably be the first time in the annals of American financial history a CEO sued to void his own offering, but if anyone would do it, it would be that prick, Scofield." Lauren remained silent. "If you do disclose, Scofield won't hesitate to kill the offering."

Lauren's words were cautious when she spoke at last. "I agree. The strategy is not risk free, but with careful handling, it can be done. I would need your help as the managing underwriter of the offering."

"What kind of help?"

"If you want to continue this discussion any further, I will need some assurances from you."

"What sort of assurances?"

"Of your cooperation. Or of your silence, depending on your decision."

Carl couldn't help but smile. She was like a cat. Subtle, quiet, careful. Taking a step and assessing its impact before taking another. She was so goddamned intriguing. He was practically hanging on every word she said. "What do you want, Lauren?"

Her voice didn't even change cadence. "A million dollars. Deposited into a numbered Swiss bank account. By noon tomorrow." She handed him a slip of paper. "If you're interested, leave a note at this address for Lydia MacVey. If I'm satisfied with the deposit, I'll let you know when we'll meet next. If you don't hear from me, the deal is off." She stood up and gathered her handbag and wrap. "Good evening, Mr. Streeter."

Liam became Cara's strength in the following days. Things she never could have faced alone, they faced together. He helped her organize the details of the funeral. He boxed up Mama's belongings for charity when she couldn't bear to do it. He stood by her side during the funeral and at the reception afterward. He stayed at the house and kept her company as the empty darkness fell.

That first night, she asked him to stay, as much for his sake as for hers. "Please. You can stay in guest room. I'll sleep on the couch."

"Absolutely not. I'll take the couch."

She laughed then, the first genuine smile either of them had shared in a long time. She peered at the couch, and then at him, head cocked, one eye closed. "Well, all six-feet-three of you should fit nicely. No, Liam, I'll take the couch."

He relented, and she heaved a sigh of relief. That night, she snuggled into the cushions while Liam pressed a soft blanket under her chin. As he'd done for her mother, he sat by her side and read. Cara asked him to read not Whitman or Longfellow, or the American writers, but the English masters. She wanted to hear Keats and Shelly and Wordsworth. She fell asleep to his deep resonant voice and dreamed of lush green countrysides and fields of daffodils.

Liam stopped reading when he was sure she was asleep. He stared at her for a long time. How was it that he, Liam Scofield, who hadn't read a poem since ninth grade English class, had just read several of the most starry-eyed, sentimental poems ever written, and somehow, didn't even mind? He leaned over to straighten the blanket around Cara's shoulders and felt something hard underneath. "What the hell?" He carefully opened the blanket and found her hand clutched around a hard object. Gently he pried her fingers away. It was a picture. Taken last Christmas. Of the two of them. Mother and daughter. Smiling happily, arms around each other, love and devotion shining from their eyes.

He stared at the picture for a long time before placing it on the table. How long, he thought, until she looked at him that way? He leaned down and kissed her cheek. "You do not play fair, Cara Larson. A man doesn't stand half a chance against the likes of you." He flicked off the light and went to bed.

Chapter 15

"The time is … 10:02 p.m. The temperature is … seventy-four degrees Fahrenheit, twenty-three degrees Celsius. Winds from the northwest at six miles per hour. To complete your call, press nine, then hang up. Or stay on the line for this information to repeat." Lauren stood at the pay phone in the dark entryway of the seedy bar, letting the message repeat for the fifteenth time. She kept her eyes on the door. Her blonde wig was only slightly less itchy than the stiff blue jeans and tight polyester sweater she poured herself into less than an hour ago. Her skin crawled with disgust. It would only be for a few hours. She didn't care that New York was the biggest city in the country. She had worked here for three years; she couldn't risk being recognized. She glanced at her watch. He would be here soon.

Up until an hour ago, she wasn't sure she would even go through with this meeting. Leave it to Carl Streeter to confuse the issue. A measly $250,000. This afternoon she paid a sweet young teenager to pick up an envelope left at the hotel desk for one Lydia MacVey and place it in a locker at La Guardia Airport. Two hours later, from a pay phone in the drenching rain, she verified that account number 1104-7312-9106 had indeed been opened, and the card containing the user identification code and password were valid. However, the account didn't contain one million American dollars, as she anticipated, but a quarter of that.

So, Mr. Streeter knew how to play the game too. She shouldn't have expected him to make this easy. After reviewing her plans and squeezing her anger into cold reason, she decided to go ahead after all. From yet another pay phone, she called his direct line and gave him instructions for the meeting.

Carl walked in, sat at the bar, and ordered a beer. He wore a checked Western-cut shirt, and his paunch hung over a wide buckled belt. She could smell his cologne from here. And the leather of his new boots. The hairpiece was perfect. He was a walking midlife crisis out to prove he was still a stud with the ladies. She waited another ten minutes before moving. No one else came in. Good. She strolled from the entryway into the bar. Swinging her hips, she sauntered toward a booth. As she passed him, she gave him a nudge with her tight-fitting jeans. He leaned back in surprise. "Oops. Sorry, honey." She raised an eyebrow in coy invitation as she continued on.

Carl turned back toward the bar and let out a slow whistle as his eyes met those of the bartender. The look that passed between them required no words. Carl licked his lips in anticipation. "Make that two beers, buddy. I think I got me some action." The bartender leered at the older man and began to pour two beers from the tap. Some guys had all the luck.

Carl swaggered to the back booth and towered over her. "Mind if I join you, sweetheart?"

Lauren's eyes dripped invitation. She took the beer and let her hand linger in his. "For me? Why, what a surprise." She slid over, arching her back, her top stretching suggestively over her breasts. "Have a seat, cowboy."

The bartender watched the pair in amusement. He had been in the business a while, and he was good at picking out a likely match. This one surprised him. She was too young and pretty. He was too old and fat. Never can tell in this business, he shrugged. Some guys had all the luck. He moved on to the next customer.

Between sexy glances and flirtatious laughter, Lauren and Carl were all business. "I'm here, Lauren. I've played your silly games and followed your cloak and dagger instructions. Tell me how you plan to pull this thing off."

She let out a high-pitched giggle and placed a hand on his arm. "I'm not going to provide full disclosure at all, big boy."

He would have jumped from his seat if she hadn't been digging her fingernails into his arm. "What the hell? I thought you said you were—"

She leaned in and brushed his cheek with her lips. "Calm down and play the part, Carl, or the deal is off. And you can kiss the quarter million good-bye. Do you understand?"

Carl forced himself to relax and put his arm around her shoulder, pulling her close. "Tell me."

With her head bent toward his, she started again. "I estimate it will take ten weeks from the time we first file with the SEC until the shares go on the market. Except for the underwriter's agreement, I have the entire registration packet ready to go. After I meet with the consortium tomorrow and we sign the agreement, I'll send the whole thing to the printer. On Friday morning, thirty copies of the registration statement will be delivered to me in Washington, D.C. On Friday afternoon, Liam and I will walk into the SEC and make a big production of our filing. We'll play the story up, little company taking the big step into the real world. We'll tour the offices, meet several bureaucrats, and introduce Liam around. I'll make sure everyone understands I'm the attorney of record, and that any and all communication is to go through me."

Carl stroked her cheek and gazed into her eyes. "So you're the gate for information at Windwear. That won't prevent Scofield from reading the S-1 and discovering you sold his company out from under him."

Lauren brushed her breasts against his elbow. "There will be just one slight problem. The S-1 will not include any details about the sale of the voting stock. Not a single detail."

His hand tightened on her chin. "You said—"

"Behave, Carl. As I said, the S-1 will not include one word about the sale of the voting stock. However, the statement will include a copy of the underwriting agreement signed by Liam Scofield himself. When the SEC does its mandatory review, the discrepancy will be so obvious they'll call me immediately to resolve the issue." She widened her eyes and softened her voice. "Of course, I will be shocked such a lapse was made under my purview, then appalled, then embarrassed." Her eyes grew even wider and more innocent. "I will explain it was all just a dreadful error on the part of the printer. I will apologize profusely for the trouble we've caused, and I'll proceed to respectfully drag my feet in providing them an updated S-1."

"The feds will never believe you. They'll be suspicious from the word go."

"You underestimate me. Who said the biggest, most incredible lies are the ones most likely to be believed? Machiavelli?"

"Hitler, I think."

She shrugged. "Well, whoever. He was right. Why shouldn't they believe me? I provided the underwriter's agreement with the correct information. Would I do such a thing if I were trying to pull the wool over their eyes? Not likely. I'll make sure they know it was nothing more than an embarrassing oversight." She curved into his arm again. "Anyway, we're protected. The S-1 is just a red herring. Until the prospectus is approved by the SEC and becomes effective, a potential investor cannot rely on the information inside. We are protected by the very disclaimer the SEC requires on every S-1 while we wait for approval."

"What happens when you're forced to provide full disclosure? Once Scofield reads the S-1, he won't hesitate to kill the deal."

"Don't worry about Liam. I'll take care of him."

Carl's eyes narrowed. "Scofield may be an arrogant prick, but he isn't stupid. How do you think you're going to float this by him?"

"You don't need to know how I do it, only that I do it."

"Like hell. I want every detail, or I'm not playing this game."

"Actually, Liam is less of a concern to me than the consortium. That's where I'll need your help."

"What kind of help?"

"After the agreement is signed, only three parties will be privy to the sale of the voting stock. Myself as the attorney for Windwear, you as the managing underwriter, and the members of the consortium. I can trust you and I won't say anything about the deal while the filing goes forward. I need the same assurance from the consortium. I've included a gag order in the underwriting agreement specifying no one is to talk about the deal until the filing becomes effective. I need you to enforce the order, especially for one Richard Bancroft, friend and mentor to Liam Scofield."

He nodded. "You're in luck. It's standard practice for underwriting activities to be kept confidential until federal approval. In addition, the consortium members will do no selling of Windwear securities. As the managing underwriter, I field my own sales team and build the book under my terms."

Lauren let out a quick sigh of relief. "You do like to have control, don't you?"

"This isn't about control, it's about money. By controlling the book, I keep the discount fees. Speaking of which, I want 10 percent."

Lauren sat up sharply. "Ten percent?" With effort, she snuggled back under his arm. "Ridiculous. The best I can do is eight."

He shook his head. "At a price of sixteen dollars per share? That's low for the industry, and the consortium is taking a risk, especially if they can't do their own selling. I need to give them more incentive to participate."

She considered for a moment. "If you can get a firm buy commitment from the consortium, I'll go to 9 percent. Otherwise, eight is the best I can offer."

"How firm is firm?"

Lauren stared at the man beside her. Of course he would want every detail pinned down. She liked that. No surprises. "Three million shares are being offered at sixteen dollars, which amounts to $48 million. I want Cyclops to commit to purchase two million of them."

He raised his eyebrows in surprise. "Thirty two million dollars is a lot of money."

"Not to mention an extra $10 million for the voting shares. That makes $42 million. You have some rich members in your consortium. You can sell this deal. Besides, the firm buy only comes into play if the market can't bear the opening price."

"Nine percent?" he asked. She nodded. "Deal."

She smiled and leaned into him. "Carl, we're both going to be very rich, very soon." She gathered her belongings as if she were preparing to leave.

He grabbed her wrist. "Not so fast. I want to know how you'll keep Scofield quiet."

She stared at the hand squeezing her wrist. "I told you. I'll handle him."

"And I told you the deal is off unless I get every detail."

Lauren sat silent for a moment as she studied Carl. "All right. I suppose you've earned the right to know." She opened her purse and removed a sheet of paper. "When the SEC comes back and asks us for the amendment to the S-1, this is what I'll give them."

Carl unfolded the paper. It was filled with legalese, including the following paragraph:

Under the terms and subject to the conditions contained in the underwriting agreement dated the date hereof, a consortium of underwriters named below, including Marshall, Longham and Fray as managing underwriter, named below have agreed to purchase severally, and the company has agreed to sell to them severally, the respective number of shares of the Company's common stock as recorded adjacent to the names of the consortium members listed below.

This was followed by a list of the consortium members and the number of common nonvoting shares each would commit to purchase. Below the list was an additional paragraph:

Each consortium member has agreed to purchase jointly, and the company has agreed to sell to them, the respective number of shares of the Company's

*preferred stock whose rights are specified in the
section of the registration statement entitled
'Preferred Stock', resulting in ownership of the
stock as recorded adjacent to the names of the
persons listed below.*

This was again followed by a list, this time of preferred
stock owners and their ownership percentage. At the top of
the list was Liam's name, with 490 shares and an ownership
percentage of 49 percent; followed by Carl Streeter,
managing underwriter, with 306 shares and 30.6 percent; and
then Richard Bancroft, vice president of Boston First Bank,
with 102 shares and 10.2 percent. Several other names were
listed with smaller ownership percentages. Carl looked up
from the document, a frown darkening his eyes. "I don't like
this at all."

She stared at him passively. "Don't like what?"

"This agreement. I told you I wanted 51 percent of
Windwear."

"No. You said the consortium wanted 51 percent of
Windwear. Under these terms, the consortium owns 51
percent of the voting stock."

His eyes narrowed. "You know what I meant, Lauren. I
want control of Windwear. Complete and unfettered. *I* want
51 percent. The deal is off."

She shrugged. "And what do you think Liam will do
when he sees that in print? Your name above his as the
majority owner? He would kill the deal in less than a
heartbeat."

"So what? All I have here is a seat on the board and a 30
percent vote. Scofield and Bancroft together hold 59
percent."

"All right, Carl. Whatever you say." She took the paper
from him. "I'm sure I can find other investors who will be
interested in my proposition."

Carl barely contained his anger. "Stop. I want the quarter
million back. Every penny." She shook her head. He
tightened his hold on her arm. "How in God's name did you
think you would get this past me? I wouldn't buy into this

deal for forty-two cents, much less $42 million. 30 percent! I should have known better than to think you could pull this off."

That's when Lauren laughed. Laughed with relief and pleasure. And triumph. "Carl Streeter, you just made my day."

"What the hell are you talking about? If this is some kind of joke, I don't find it funny."

She laughed again. "Not a joke, Carl. A test. You passed. Or rather, you failed. With flying colors."

He grabbed her wrist again. "What the hell are you talking about Lauren? You tell me or I'll—"

Lauren snapped her arm away and impaled him with a venomous glare. "You threaten me, Carl, and the deal *is* off. And you will never know what you missed." For a long moment, they glared at each other.

At the bar, the bartender watched the scene with amusement. Trouble in paradise, he thought. I knew the guy was too old and fat.

With effort, Carl contained his anger. When Lauren realized he had calmed down, she unfolded the paper and handed it back to him. "Read the document again, Carl. Go ahead. Take your time. Take as much time as you want."

Carl read the paper several times. He couldn't find a goddamned thing out of the ordinary. All he kept seeing was that 30 percent figure jumping out at him like a party girl popping out of a cake. He shook his head in exasperation but was careful to keep his voice calm. "I don't know what I'm supposed to be looking for. Why don't you just tell me?"

Lauren snuggled in next to him. "You don't see it?" She didn't wait for an answer. "Excellent. That is exactly what Liam will see. Or won't see. Now, if we can get it by Bancroft tomorrow, we'll be home free."

Again, Carl made an effort to keep calm. "There won't be any meeting unless you explain this."

Lauren smiled indulgently, as if he were a child. "All right, Carl." She leaned closer and began to explain.

Carl sat back. "This is quite clever, Ms. Janelle. You just might get away with this."

"With your help, I think we can."

"How do you plan to handle the news about Aerie? Do you disclose now or at the time you provide this?" He waved the paper in the air.

"No. I think we should use Aerie as a chit to calm your consortium members if they don't like the details of the ownership arrangement. Which brings up another important issue."

"Yes?"

"I need you to keep everyone in the consortium quiet on the existence of Aerie. I don't want that getting out. It could force the stock price up too early."

"You're right. If we wait to announce Aerie until after the IPO, we will get the benefit of the increase in stock price that will come with it. "

"Exactly."

"That will take all the risk out of the firm buy."

"Yes. As long as your people stay quiet about Aerie."

"This really is quite clever."

"So, Carl, now you know the plan. Are you in?"

"What do you think?"

"What I think doesn't matter, but if you want to go forward, I expect an additional $750,000 in that numbered Swiss bank account by noon tomorrow."

"If I don't?"

"Well, look at it this way, Carl. You just bought me a very expensive beer." She tipped the glass and drained its contents.

Chapter 16

Richard Bancroft looked up from the document. He flipped to the last page to examine the signature. It was Liam's all right. As his primary banker for the past three years, and with the amount of IPO paperwork he'd seen in the past few weeks, he recognized it. He just didn't understand it. "Well I'll be damned. I must say I'm surprised, Lauren. I can't believe Liam agreed to this."

Lauren smiled. After a day of shopping in New York at real stores, who wouldn't be happy? She had returned from her shopping spree to find an additional $750,000 had been deposited in her shiny new bank account. As she expected. Carl knew a good deal when he saw one. She stared at the only obstacle left between herself and her goals and tried not to betray any sign of nerves. If she could slip this agreement by Richard, she would have clear sailing the rest of the way. "Liam understands the game is played by different rules in the public arena. He just needed some time to think things through.

He still owns 49 percent of the voting stock, and he will remain president and CEO of Windwear. Actually, I think selling majority ownership to the consortium will raise the confidence level of the entire investment community. The price of the common shares will be much stronger this way. Windwear will have no trouble funding its growth strategy."

Richard still looked troubled. "Even so, I'd like to talk to him before I agree. I haven't been able to reach him at his office. Do you know where he is?"

"I wish I did. He left suddenly, and he hasn't called. He had a family emergency. I express mailed the agreement to his home because I wasn't sure he would even get to the office. Staci didn't say where he was?"

The older man shook his head. "No. She said he called her from the airport and told her about the emergency and that he would be unavailable for a few days. He asked her to direct all calls to you. I tried him at all the numbers she gave me."

"Leave another message at the office. I'll make sure to tell him to call you when I talk to him next. I know he'll check in sooner or later." She paused, striving for the right balance between sincerity and regret. "He did sign this agreement. I would hate to return to Portland and tell him we couldn't make it happen. On top of everything else he's had to deal with this week ..." Lauren stopped. She didn't want to overplay the sympathy angle.

Richard rubbed his fingers along his jaw and examined the signature again. "I suppose you're right. He still holds a majority of the voting stock in his possession. What are the resale restrictions?"

"The agreement is clear on this point. The voting shares held by the consortium can only be sold by majority approval of the consortium itself. This guarantees the consortium members determine the makeup of their management team." She smiled. "Of course, Liam preferred approval be based on a majority of the entire voting share distribution and not just that of the consortium, but that wouldn't be fair. Membership in the consortium is not Liam's choice as much as an internal Cyclops decision."

Richard nodded. "So that means that Carl, as majority holder of consortium shares, controls the membership."

Lauren held her breath. Damn, she thought. He was getting too close. She dared not look at Carl, whose searing glare was boring into her as if it were a tangible thing. "Carl doesn't control the actual membership. He only controls changes from the original membership. No one is required to sell his shares, Richard."

"True. And both Carl and I hold seats on the board?"

"Yes. In addition, all the consortium members who own voting stock are eligible to attend the management meetings, which will prove unwieldy, I'm sure. I expect one of the first orders of business will be the creation of an executive board to oversee operations."

Richard let out a slow whistle. "This is so different from what Liam envisioned. I can hardly believe he agreed to this."

Lauren nodded. "Expectations and reality often differ, especially when a company enters the public arena. I can assure you, Liam understands the compromise he's making. After all, he is getting sixteen dollars a share. Windwear is going to walk away from the table with almost $50 million. All the same, I wish he were here to tell you himself. This has been quite an education for all of us." Carl let out a strangled cough, but Lauren ignored him and kept her gaze focused on Richard.

Richard leafed through the document one more time. He reread the key sections. The firm buy commitment was a coup for Liam. He wouldn't need to worry about last-minute market hiccups or business downturns that could frighten the consortium members and allow them to pull out, leaving the offering high and dry. And the buy was at a fixed price, no less. That alone might be worth giving up a few seats on the board and a well-distributed majority of the voting stock. Especially when Richard would hold one of the new seats and 10 percent of the management vote. He sighed. He might not always agree with Liam, but he would always give his ideas a fair hearing. That would be important with Carl Streeter sharing the board. Maybe this wasn't such a bad deal.

Lauren wanted to stand up and scream at Richard to sign, but she clenched her hands and maintained her reassuring smile. Richard turned to her. "Let me try Liam again."

"Of course. If you harbor any doubts at all, you should alleviate them now." She felt sweat break on her forehead as Richard dialed the number. She wiped it away as unobtrusively as possible.

"Staci, Richard Bancroft again. I am sorry to bother you, but I need to speak to Liam. Has he called? Left another number where he can be reached? I tried to reach him using the cellular and pager numbers you gave me, but no luck." Richard paused, listening, his face growing somber. "Funeral? Today? All right. Let him know I called, if he does report in. Please ask him to call me as soon as possible."

Richard hung up, deep in thought. He looked at the signature again. "I'm sure he knows what he's doing," he said almost to himself. He turned to Lauren. "All right, let's sign. Let's give Liam one thing to be happy about this week."

Lauren slid into the booth of the coffee shop and set her briefcase beside her. She pulled her cellular from her purse, raised the antenna, and punched in the phone number of Windwear's main offices. She waited impatiently while it rang. "Staci Manning please, Debra. I'll wait."

"Liam Scofield's office."

"Staci? This is Lauren." The attorney's voice came out brisk and cool. "Have you heard from Liam, today?"

"Oh hello, Lauren. Once, a few minutes ago. He said he would be in the office late tomorrow morning."

"Damn."

"Is everything all right? Can I help you with anything? You sound worried."

"Yes, you can. Did Richard Bancroft phone the office today?"

"Why yes, twice. The last time a couple hours ago. He wanted to talk to Liam. Rather urgently I gathered, from the tone of his voice."

"Did you tell him Richard called?"

"Well," Staci hesitated, "he didn't give me a chance. He couldn't talk long. He was at the funeral. He just said he'd be in tomorrow."

Lauren breathed a sudden sigh of relief. "Good. I just came from a meeting with Richard and managed to answer his questions. You don't need to bother telling Liam that Richard even called. That will be one less worry he has to deal with this week."

"Oh. How nice of you, Lauren." The surprise in Staci's voice irritated her.

"In fact, please forward all Richard's calls to me from now on, Staci. I will be his direct contact for the next few months."

"What?" Staci sounded puzzled. "Liam didn't mention anything like that to me."

"He has a lot on his mind, with the funeral and all." Lauren dropped her voice to a low pitch. "Staci, what I am about to tell you is confidential. I don't want you to discuss the matter with anyone but Liam. Do you understand?"

"Yes, of course."

"I'm in the midst of some sensitive financial negotiations. In a few minutes I will express mail an important document to Liam. An extremely important document, Staci. Eyes only important. You should receive it by noon tomorrow. Liam needs to sign it and express mail it back to arrive here by ten a.m. on Friday. Do you understand?"

"Yes. I'll make sure to tell him."

"One more thing, Staci. These financial negotiations are delicate. This is a critical period. Until further notice, all activity related to Windwear's financial proceedings must go through me. I'll sit down and explain everything to Liam when I talk to him next. Until I direct otherwise, you are not to mention a word to anyone about Windwear's financial activities."

"Of course, Lauren."

"That's all for now. Good-bye, Staci." She hung up before the secretary asked any questions. She put her phone away, snapped open her briefcase, and removed the folder containing the unsigned agreement. She placed the folder in the express mail envelope, sealed it, and attached the waybill she had filled out earlier. She double-checked the account number. She wanted to make sure there was a clear paper trail for this particular envelope. Satisfied, she picked up her belongings and left the café.

As she walked to the express mail drop box, Lauren found she was nervous. Surprisingly so. Rarely did she doubt the merits of a plan once she set it in motion. Of course, rarely did she commit outright fraud as part of the plan. She was poised at the brink of indecision and felt keenly the discomfort of her position. The envelope in her hand contained the original agreement Liam asked her to present to the consortium. Once she dropped the envelope in the box, it would go to Liam's office. He would sign it, have it notarized, and mail it back. And when she received the executed document back from him, she would promptly destroy it.

The alternate agreement she created using her own rosy projections was now signed, dated, and fully executed. She could now begin the registration process to make Windwear a publicly traded company. Or, she could stop the whole effort right now. She need only call Carl Streeter to void the deal. Of course, he would make her return the million dollars. That would be a disappointment. Still, she could change course; she could abort her plans, which were more gel than concrete at this point, anyway. She was rapidly arriving at the point of no return. Once she put the letter in the box, she would be committed. Once the letter was on its way, she knew she would see her plan through to the end.

Damn Liam Scofield for putting her in this position. He had never given her the free hand she needed to do her job. The one valuable thing she learned about the law was that it was malleable. Sometimes the law didn't permit a person to do what needed to be done. Sometimes the law needed to be bent. Occasionally the law needed to be broken. Like today. This wasn't really fraud, she told herself. Oh, technically it was. Forging her boss's name on a document with intent to deceive was definitely fraud. But the crime was a temporary one. Once she convinced Liam she was actually furthering his goals, her actions would be magically transformed from criminal to creative.

She could have been more straightforward with Liam, she thought, as she walked among the crowds on the wide city pavement. She could have explained that relinquishing 51 percent ownership of Windwear was in his best interest. The problem with Liam Scofield was that he had no appreciation of how much $50 million actually was, how such an amount could change a man's life. He was stubborn. He focused on people and products, not profits. She figured the odds of getting him to agree with her way of thinking were fifty-fifty, at best. Given his past behavior, even that estimate might be too optimistic. She dared not risk his rejection with so much money at stake. So, she opted for the lie instead. This was only temporary, she told herself. A temporary lie. A temporary crime. He would thank her later. He would appreciate all her efforts once he found himself rolling in money. It wouldn't hurt that she would be rolling in money, too.

She came to a stop at the express mail box. There's nothing to worry about, she told herself. Nothing at all. She would be able to convince Liam. She was sure of it. As she told Carl Streeter, she could be persuasive. She took a deep breath. Then dropped the envelope down the slot.

Chapter 17

"Okay, Mike. I'll be in tomorrow." Cara hung up the phone. It was Thursday, three days since her mother's death. Already, the business of living was encroaching on the timelessness of the past few days. Tomorrow she would be back at Pyramid, preparing for the review, trying to figure out how to deal with the bombshell Peter dropped the night Mama collapsed. Strange how she'd completely forgotten about Peter.

Tomorrow, Liam would be back in New York or Boston or some such city, working complicated financial deals that would take Windwear to new heights. He told her he would stop by before he went to the office. He wanted to say good-bye before he once more immersed himself in the world of Windwear. Then he would be gone. Again.

She paced the room restlessly. She felt strange. Uneasy, unsettled, unhappy. As if something important were slipping away. As if she were searching for a word at the tip of her tongue, tantalizing in its closeness, elusive in its distance. What was making her so edgy?

"Everything all right, Cara?" Liam stood in the doorway, watching her.

"Yes. No." She shook her head and continued to pace distractedly, rubbing her hands together, letting them fall to her sides, and then rubbing them together again.

"You don't pace very often, Cara. Do you want to talk?"

She stopped. "I think I'm ..." Without thinking, she started to pace again. He smiled, still leaning against the door. "I think I'm worried about going on. About picking up the

pieces of my life where I left them, before Mama got sick."
She stopped, embarrassed at her words.

"Go on."

"I worry I'll forget Mama, Liam. That I'm going to be
caught up in the everyday business of living and not
remember her. She's always been a part of my purpose, a
reason for me to exist in the world. Now that she's gone I feel
so ... cut loose. As if I'm drifting along without any idea how
to go forward. I'm afraid ... I know how life is, how my job
is, how *I* am ... I'm afraid I am going to get caught up in the
swirl of living, that I'm going to get tossed in every direction
and lose my way." She shook her head in frustration. "I'm not
sure what I'm trying to say."

"Cara, moving on isn't a bad thing. You're right to
realize your life will be different going forward, but you don't
need to hurry. You are wise to take your time and go your
own speed."

"The problem is I don't have a clue what that speed is.
Even the first step seems too hard. I want to move forward,
but I don't want to forget."

"I don't believe you'll ever forget your mother. She is
and will always be a part of you. You carry her with you just
by being you." He walked across the room and put his arms
around her. "It's too soon, Cara. You've been through a lot.
Don't force things. You'll find your way in time."

She looked up at him. "How can you be sure, Liam?"

"I have a bit of experience in this area. Some of it was
pretty bleak, but I assure you, time does blur the hard edges.
You'll be happy again, someday."

"Thank you, Liam. For being here. For being a true
friend to me." She gazed up at him from the circle of his
arms. "I have something for you."

"For me? What?"

"A little something. A gift. Don't go away, I'll be right
back."

She dashed down the hall to the spare bedroom and came
back a few moments later, holding a small box in her hand.
"This is for you. I want to thank you for helping me."

"You didn't need to get me anything, Cara. You know I'm happy to be here."

"I know, but I want you to have it. Open it, I want to see if you like it."

He opened the box. Inside were a pair of cufflinks and a tie clip. They were solid gold, shaped like diving dolphins. "Cara, these are amazing."

"I realize you don't dress up much, but they remind me of you. Wild and smart and ... free." She stopped, once more embarrassed by her words.

He looked at her sharply, with an expression she couldn't read on his face. "These are incredible, Cara. They will definitely raise the standard of my current wardrobe. Thank you." He smiled. "Now, it's your turn. My gift isn't wrapped, so you'll need to close your eyes." Her eyes widened in surprise. "Closed, not opened, Ms. Larson. Come on, I don't have all day." Obediently she closed her eyes. "And no peeking," he called as he left the room.

She knew what the gift was before she opened her eyes. The delicate scent of lilacs wafted across the room and around her like a heady perfume. "Liam!" she said with her eyes still closed. "Where did you manage to get lilacs in the middle of summer?" Her eyes flew open and he stood in front of her, tall and handsome, smiling almost shyly, holding a huge bouquet of lavender lilacs. He remembered. Once, when he brought roses to her mother, he asked about her favorite flower. And she had told him that though she loved roses, they would never match the sweet scent of lilacs in spring.

He walked over and put them in her arms. "Uh-uh. You must never ask a man to divulge his floral procurement secrets."

She giggled and rolled her eyes. "Oh, sorry." She bent her head and took in the luscious fragrance. "They're beautiful." She found a vase, trimmed the stems, and put them in water. She knew they would only last a few days. That fact made the gift even more precious.

She placed the vase on the table and turned to find Liam watching her. He had such a strange expression on his face. "Cara ..." He put his hand in his pocket and seemed to be struggling with something. "I have something else ..." His voice trailed off, and all at once he appeared totally unsure of himself. As she watched him, her heart became so full she could hardly breathe. She walked over to him, placed her hands lightly on his chest, reached up on her tiptoes, and kissed his cheek. "Thank you, Liam. For everything."

He tensed at her words, and she wondered if she'd done the wrong thing. She tried to step back, but Liam pulled his hand from his pocket and wrapped his arms around her. Then he was kissing her. Kissing her with such emotion it surprised her. He pressed her close, and she wilted under his strength. She returned his kisses as he gave them to her, passionately and with utter abandon. Desire rushed over her like a storm. She could not taste him enough, could not steal enough of his warmth, could not get close enough to him. "Cara," he whispered, and she knew he was feeling what she was feeling. He lifted her effortlessly into his arms. And just as he began to carry her down the hallway to the bedroom, reality crashed into the haze with the sharp ring of the telephone.

Cara blinked, dazed at the sound. Liam, too, seemed to be struggling to orient himself. The ringing kept coming, and finally, he put her down with an unsteady kiss. "You'd better answer that. It might be important." She nodded and stumbled to the phone. "Hello?"

"Cara, I must congratulate you. The dying mother routine was brilliant. I wish I'd thought of that."

"Lauren," she said dully.

"But I'm tired of the game. It's time Liam came back. After all, he hasn't been in my bed for three long days. He's probably getting, how should I say this ... restless."

Cara froze. She had forgotten all about Lauren. She closed her eyes. Oh God, she was going to be sick. She dropped the phone. The receiver crashed down between them and banged hard against the cupboard.

"Cara?" Liam said with concern. "What's wrong?"

"It's for you." She stared at him, then at the receiver hanging from the cord, almost touching the floor.

He picked up the phone, his eyes still on her. "Hello?" A string of noise came bursting from the phone, but Cara couldn't make out any of the words. "Lauren! Wait a second. Hold on. Calm down. Take a breath and tell me what's going on. You did! They went for the revised plan? The whole thing? How did you convince them? Did they like the outsourcing information? The Aerie revenue? Lauren, you're brilliant. Tell me all the details." His eyes glowed, and he gave Cara a brief thumbs up before he turned away to talk to Lauren. Then Cara no longer heard what he said. Just as well.

She went to the bedroom and closed the door. She walked to the adjoining bathroom, knelt down by the basin, and threw up. She rinsed her face and mouth and sat on the edge of the bed, dazed and nauseous.

A few minutes later, Liam knocked on the door. "Cara, may I come in?"

"It's open."

"Are ... are you all right?"

"I'm fine."

He sat beside her on the bed. "I need to leave. That was Lauren. Seems she closed the deal I thought had no chance, whatsoever. I still don't know how. Anyway, she express mailed the agreement to the office. I need to review it, sign it, and send it back by 4:00 p.m. Then I have to get on a plane tonight—"

"Tonight? Back to New York?"

"No, D.C. I'm going to send the agreement to Lauren in New York. She'll have the consortium sign in the morning and then catch a train down to D.C. We're going to file the registration forms with the SEC tomorrow afternoon."

"Congratulations." Her voice sounded tired, even to her.

"Are you okay?" He turned to face her. "I ... I shouldn't have let that happen earlier. You told me before you didn't want to get involved with anyone. I ... I need to respect your wishes. I'm sorry—"

She held up her hand to cut off his words. She didn't want to hear his apologies or explanations or denials. She didn't want to hear anything at all. That way she could pretend she wasn't a substitute, a stand-in for someone more beautiful and more desirable, a convenient alternate to satisfy his *restlessness*. "You don't need to explain, Liam." She forced a smile. "You're right. I think you should go."

He nodded. "I'm not sure how long this will take, but I'll do my best to get back Monday for the review. I'd like to talk to you then, when we have more time. Would that be all right?"

"Sure, we can talk then." She stood up. "Good-bye, Liam."

Chapter 18

Liam had been gone six hours, but it seemed like six years. Cara was organizing her mother's files, trying to distract herself from the man consuming her thoughts. She pushed the memory of Liam's kisses from her mind, and tried not to think how he aroused in her feelings she never felt before. She tried not to think how he'd flown back to Lauren with scarcely a backward glance.

She opened the desk drawer and removed the files. Old tax returns. Insurance documents. Bank statements. As she pulled them from the drawer, a small passbook dropped to the floor. She picked it up, opened it, and felt the world shift beneath her.

The account had been opened in the fall of 1976. The deposits were made once a week, maybe every other week. Always on a Monday. Odd sums. She browsed through the entries in her mother's neat handwriting. September 20, 1976: $32.78. October 3, 1977: $45.95. February 13, 1978: $56.53. On and on. She recognized the entries at once; the money she placed on the table every Saturday morning for so many years. She riffled through the pages. No withdrawals. Ever. Why hadn't Mama spent the money? She quickly flipped to the last entry. The last deposit was made in December of 1985, the month she graduated from college. Her eyes widened when she read the number on the last page. The passbook showed a balance of over $60,000.

Cara pulled the plastic sheath from the passbook, and a neatly folded sheet of paper fell to the desk. She opened the page with trembling fingers.

September 20, 1976

Sweet Cara Mia,

Today, you have given me a gift that warms my heart. A gift from your own selfless effort. Because your spirit matches the fire in your hair, I know there will be many more such gifts to come. With them you intend to purchase my freedom from the everyday labor of life. You have a good heart, my child, and my pride and love for you are boundless.

You know I hold myself quietly in my own heart. This is my nature, but also my choice. There are many things a mother must tell her daughter to prepare her for life. Sometimes, too many, I venture you would say. It is my solemn duty, Cara Mia, to fulfill this responsibility. As important a duty, perhaps even more so, is to give you the freedom to decide for yourself those things that are important to you. I cannot, and will not, stamp upon you the tenets by which I live. You cannot sing another's song. It is your responsibility to learn your own personal truth in order to live a life meaningful to you. This gift you gave me, this generous gift, is evidence you have started on this path. You are forming the values that will form you and will enable you to find your own happiness.

As for me, my sweet Cara, this gift, as generous as it is, is not required for my happiness. I have all I need in this life. I have all I need because I have you. There will come a day when you will go out in the world and be far away from me, but you will never be far from my heart.

I will violate my rule this one and only time, my Cara Mia, and tell you of my dreams for you. What I wish for you, my daughter, is that as you grow, you will find what I have already found, the one thing in life that gives you peace, that gives you joy every day. When you find it, keep it close, and do not let it go.

This is not as easy a task as it seems. We try many things and make many choices before we learn what is right for us. Rare is the person who chooses wisely the first time. The world will bring many opportunities your way. Look for the things that match your heart, that satisfy your mind, that fill your soul. Find them and keep them, for they are the things that will bring you peace and happiness.

Someday, I will return this precious gift to you. Not because I do not appreciate it, but because I appreciate more the one who gives it to me. I hope you may use it, if necessary, to find your peace, as I have found mine.

Mama

Cara slowly folded the letter. Oh, God. If she had doubts before, she had none now. Her mother didn't need the money Cara had so diligently earned all those years. Mama's words tormented her. *This gift, as generous as it is, is not required for my happiness.*

Cara sat back, the meaning of Mama's words flooding through her. Oh God, her life was nothing more than a series of well-intentioned misdeeds. She had vowed to save her mother from poverty, but instead had taken away the one thing her mother valued. Herself. She rode off like a knight on a white horse to save her mother from a danger that didn't exist. *I have all I need because I have you.* Oh God. How could she have been so blind? Mama never wanted the money. Never needed it. She needed her daughter, and her daughter had been far away when her health began to fail. Now, it was too late; she could not right the wrongs she had committed.

She sat numbly as the harsh truth hit her. In all the weeks her mother lay sick and dying, Cara had not allowed herself the weakness of tears. In these past few days when she faced Mama's death, she had not cried. Now, she could not stop the tears from coming. They flooded from her eyes as if they would never stop. They soaked her face and clouded her mind, but they brought no relief, only sorrow and regret. And her regret ran so deep she thought if a person could die from heartbreak, she would not survive the night.

Cara awoke with a start at half past two, pulling herself from the depths of a frightening dream. She was falling, falling, falling into blackness. Her heart beat rapidly, and her mother's words chased each other over and over in her head. She hadn't remembered them until now. *Match your heart. Satisfy your mind. Fill your soul.* She turned over impatiently and crunched her pillow closer to her face. The words would not go away.

At three o'clock she gave up the battle for sleep, put a warm sweatshirt over her nightgown, and went to sit in the back yard. The sky glittered with stars. Even as the city lights cast a bronze glow to the south, the northern sky dripped with brilliant crystalline sparks. She stared at them, reviewing all the moments of her life she could have lived differently, moments that would have brought her to this night with anything but this oppressive sadness.

She pulled out the letter, flipped on the porch light, and read Mama's words again. And again. The letter contained so many more messages than she had grasped from her first reading. Yes, Cara's efforts had been misguided, even wrongheaded. But her efforts hadn't disappointed Mama. Or made her angry. Mama understood, even appreciated them. Cara sighed. What Mary Larson really wanted, what she always wanted, was for her daughter to find happiness. Her hopes lay right in front of Cara, in faded blue ink and yellowing paper. *What I wish for you, Cara Mia, is that as you grow, you will find what I have already found, the one thing in life that gives you peace, that gives you joy every day.*

She flicked off the porch light and sat quietly as the eastern sky brightened. The cool crispness of the dawn brought cold rationality. She realized, as she gazed at the fading stars, that she was lost, that she was as far away from the peace her mother talked about as those stars were from Earth. How do I go forward when I don't even know who I am, she thought? The whisper of past comfort drifted across her mind. Liam's words. *"No one can change the past. Not*

*you, not me, not God himself. Sometimes, it can help to set
your worries aside. Let them be what they're going to be.
Focus instead on the challenges ahead."* She shook her head.
Focus on the challenges ahead. How could she? She spent
her whole life living a mistake. She had no clue how to move
ahead.

She gazed around as if seeing the world for the first time.
The flowers still bloomed as they had yesterday. The birds
still broke the morning stillness with their song. The breeze
still lifted her hair with indifference. *What are you going to
do? What are you going to do? What are you going to do?*
The words fluttered all around her. The birds sang them, the
breeze whispered them. They echoed inside her head, over
and over and over. *What are you going to do?* "I don't
know," she whispered to the iridescent sky. "I don't know,
dammit. Tell me what I'm supposed to do." But the sky
remained unmoved, save for the deepening pink in the east.

She stood abruptly, knocking the chair sideways. "Tell
me what I am supposed to do!" she shouted at the dawn.
There were no answers in the sunrise. There were no answers
in her heart. There were no answers anywhere. Frustrated, she
shoved the fallen chair aside and flew into the house,
slamming the door with a vicious bang. She could not wait
for answers. She could not wait for something that might
never come. The world was rushing in again. She couldn't
hold it back. She needed to face the challenges ahead,
whether she wanted to or not.

The burning spray of water punished her skin as she
showered. Steam swirled around her, mirroring the turmoil
within her heart. She had to think. She had to get hold of
herself. How could she move forward when she was so
utterly lost? She concentrated on Mama's letter. The letter
contained the only wisdom she possessed right now. What
did Mama tell her? *Look for the things that match your heart,
that satisfy your mind, that fill your soul.* Right. How was she
supposed to find the things that matched her heart when she
didn't understand her heart?

She took a deep breath and let the water wash over her. Calm down, she told herself. Think. Okay, she was lost. But maybe not totally lost. Ninety-nine percent lost, but still, not totally lost. Think. Just because she didn't know what Mama knew, just because she didn't know the secret to her own happiness, did not mean she knew nothing at all. She needed to start with what she did know. She needed to start with that one percent.

Her thoughts turned to Liam. What did she know about him? At this moment, she could not honestly answer that question. She had been so immersed in caring for her mother these past weeks, she hadn't thought of anything else. Now, with some space to ponder the question, she realized she did know a few things about Liam Scofield. He was kind and patient and generous. He had kissed her as if they shared something special. But ... he was seeing Lauren. Or was he? Lauren said she and Liam were involved, were sleeping together. The thought dismayed Cara, but didn't surprise her. She had seen the two of them together, had observed their easy rapport, had heard the appreciation in Liam's voice when he spoke of her. Liam respected Lauren, even admired her. Did they share something more? Was Liam the kind of man to play the field? Was he the kind of man to sleep with Lauren one night and kiss Cara breathless a few days later? Even if he were, what right did she have to pass judgment? She told Liam she didn't want a relationship. Why shouldn't he do as he pleased? What did she want from him, anyway? She couldn't answer that question either. But she did know one thing. She knew, above all, that she and Liam Scofield were friends. Whatever else existed between them she did not know and could not name. For now, their friendship was enough, an anchor in the uncertain sea of her life.

She rinsed the shampoo from her hair and squeezed conditioner into her hand. One question addressed, she told herself as she worked the thick white substance through her hair. On to question two. Peter. She needed to decide how to respond to Peter's orders. Indecision tore at her. Peter had ordered her to do something not only unusual, but unethical. Her actions would have serious consequences for Windwear, especially now that Liam planned to push ahead with the IPO. Defying Peter would risk her career. She had worked hard these past five years. She had been successful. Did she want to risk her future to fight Windwear's battles? On the other hand, obeying Peter would risk something else, something important ...

She stopped abruptly as the steaming water washed over her. She may not know all the answers, she thought. She may not fully know who Cara Larson was, but she definitely knew who Cara Larson wasn't. Cara Larson was not a liar. Cara Larson was not a cheat. Suddenly, she smiled, and the heaviness lifted from her heart. She raised her arms, and the water coursed down her body like a spring rain. That was the moment Cara Larson decided what battle she was willing to fight. "Peace," she whispered quietly into the steaming swirl, "peace is going to require a few changes." She switched off the water and hurried to get dressed.

She put on her new suit carefully. The soft gold skirt and short jacket were set off with a black silk blouse that emphasized her large eyes and delicate skin. She clipped her hair back from her face and let it fall loosely down her back. She examined herself in the mirror. Quite a difference from the old Cara, she thought. It wasn't the only change the people at Pyramid were going to see.

Mike dropped all the files he was carrying when he saw her. "C ... C ... Cara? Is that you? Are you all right?"

She gave him a warm hug. "I'm fine, Mike. Thank you for the flowers you sent for my mother. They were beautiful."

For a moment, Mike wasn't sure where to put his hands. This is Cara, he said to himself. Ms. Professional, Ms. Strictly Business, Ms. Stressed Out, Uptight, No Nonsense, Cold-as-Ice, Cara Larson. He shrugged. Oh well. Miracles do happen. He took her in his arms and whirled her around. "It's great to see you."

"Come into my office and catch me up. We have a review next Monday, and I feel like I've been away for a lifetime."

Chapter 19

Sunday evening found Cara exhausted. She had worked straight through the weekend, double and triple checking to make sure she was ready for the review. She had purged all the files related to Aerie from every computer on site. She had deleted the program files from the network. She had found and removed all the documentation related to Aerie, and even collected the surveys Anna had done. It had taken hours to locate and delete the files from the nightly backup tapes. She was sure she'd found everything. Even if some miscellaneous documents were still lying around, they wouldn't amount to much. It was as if Aerie never existed.

She stared at the pile in front of her. Six disks and a three-inch-thick stack of papers. Not nearly imposing enough considering the trouble they would cause tomorrow. She wondered how things would turn out. She had no idea. She placed the items in a manila envelope, scrawled Peter's name across the front, and sealed the flap.

The sick sensation squeezed in on her again. It had been a constant companion all weekend. She studied the envelope for a long time. Then, surrendering to her misgivings, she opened her desk drawer and removed six blank disks. She walked over to the recycling bin and removed a thick pile of discarded papers. She placed the papers and blank disks inside a second manila envelope. She sealed the flap, wrote Peter's name across the front, and circled his name with a thick red pen. She placed both envelopes in her desk and locked them in. In all her years at Pyramid, this was the first time she had ever locked her desk. She flipped off the office light and threaded her way along the dark corridor to the elevator.

It was strange not having to be anywhere, not having to watch the clock and squeeze in another task before leaving to visit Mama. No responsibilities awaited her. Strange not to be needed. She'd often been alone in her life, but this was the first time she felt lonely. Cheerful thought, she chided, as the elevator descended. Come on, Cara. It's still light enough for a long, relaxing run.

By eight o'clock Monday morning, Cara stood at the podium in the meeting room, finalizing her presentation. Arms crossed, remote control pointer in hand, she clicked through her slides to make sure all vestiges of Aerie were gone. She didn't hear the door open or the sound of footsteps across the carpeted room. She did feel the warm hand on her shoulder, smelled a familiar tangy scent, and heard his soft words. "Hello, Cara," Liam whispered in her ear.

She started at his touch. "Hello, Liam." Her eyes flitted over his face and back to her computer. She turned the machine off and gathered her notes.

Liam's hand dropped to his side. "How are you?" She was wearing a navy suit with a bold jade stripe running down the right side and a matching blouse of jade silk. Her hair fell down her back and was held back by a jade headband. Her eyes were wide and green. And troubled.

"Fine. Busy. I have a review in a half hour, and I still have to do some preparation. If you'll excuse me—"

"I understand. Can we talk later? After the review?"

"For goodness sake, Liam, let the poor woman do her job." Lauren approached Liam, wearing a triumphant grin. Her long, scarlet tipped fingers clawed his arm. "All ready for the review, Cara? Would you mind if I borrowed Liam for a minute? I need to go over a few matters with him."

"He's all yours." She picked up her notes and headed out the door.

Two minutes later Cara was in her office, seated at her desk, staring at the single page in her hand, slowly rereading each word. She shook her head. She hoped she had the courage for this.

Liam didn't knock. He stood at the door and waited for her to notice him. She was staring at a piece of paper with a strange expression on her face. He wondered why she was acting so cool toward him. Was she upset because he kissed her? Or because he left so abruptly? Or was something else worrying her? All at once, the answer to the question seemed vitally important. He waited almost a minute before she glanced up. She slipped the paper into a folder. "Come in, Liam. Please, sit down."

"Well I must say, you definitely look busy." She didn't even smile at his teasing. "Cara, is everything all right? You seem worried."

"Everything is fine. I have a review in ten minutes. I always worry about reviews."

"Are you ready?"

"Mmm, as I'll ever be." She forced her eyes to his. "How was your trip?"

Liam brightened and sat in the chair opposite her desk. "Excellent. Windwear is going public. We managed to get every single term we wanted, once we revised our numbers a bit."

"Congratulations. Very impressive."

"I didn't think we stood a chance, but Lauren managed to say the right words at the right time to get the investors to sign. She's brilliant. I don't know what we'd do without her."

Cara kept her voice even. "I'm glad it worked out for you. How did you structure the deal?"

"Well, we plan to sell three million shares. Probably around the beginning of October. The Cyclops consortium will purchase up to two million shares at sixteen dollars per share. The other million shares will go on the open market. I can hardly believe little Windwear will be worth almost $100 million."

"One hundred million dollars!" Cara let out a long whistle. "How much cash will you raise in the offering?"

Liam smiled nervously. "I hope we're not being too greedy. We're selling as many shares as I feel comfortable with. Forty-five percent. Which will net us over $40 million after the investor fees are paid. I'll hold the remaining 55 percent of the common stock as well as all the voting shares."

"What will you do with all that money?"

"I'm going to do things right, Cara. I'm going to grow the company the way it ought to be grown. First, I'll create a new research and development department."

"Good. Then you'll find a home for those creative ideas that are always flying out of you."

He shot a look at her, but she seemed to be a million miles away. She probably didn't even realize what she'd said. Or that her words made him feel like $100 million. "Next, we'll expand our manufacturing facilities here. We're up against our limits, and the demand keeps growing. We need to double our capacity, at least. Last, we'll enter the camping gear market, which will be a perfect complement to our current product lines."

"Will you have enough manufacturing capacity for all that growth?"

"I'm not sure." Liam's face clouded for a moment. "If we manufacture everything in the US, we might have to triple our capacity. Lauren thinks the camping gear business requires a different cost structure. In fact, we're flying to Taiwan later today to arrange a joint venture or manufacturing agreement. If we make an overseas deal, we'll only need to double the Portland facilities."

Taiwan. So soon. With Lauren. Again. "Oh."

"I wanted you to be the first to hear our good news. You helped make this happen, you know."

Cara raised an eyebrow. "Me? What do you mean?"

"This all happened because of Aerie. The news about Aerie made all the difference. When Lauren mentioned the development project—"

"Lauren mentioned Aerie? I thought she opposed the development effort."

"She had her reservations, but after the meeting with Cyclops, she changed her view. She said the investors were falling all over themselves to get in on the ground floor. They practically opened their checkbooks on the spot."

Cara closed her eyes. "You told your investors about Aerie?"

"Sure. Lauren did." He looked at her closely. "Is that all right? Please tell me it's all right, because I included revenue from Aerie to make the numbers work."

Cara was staring into space. She hadn't even heard his question. "Cara? Is there a problem with Aerie?"

His worried tone brought her back to the present. "Why did you do that, Liam?"

"Do what?"

"Tell your investors about Aerie? You know this isn't a done deal. This review is the first time Aerie will be considered as part of the project. Until it's officially included in the contract, its status is subject to uncertainty. You know how risky it is to make deals without having everything lined up."

Liam breathed a sigh of relief. "But the review is just a formality. Peter approved Aerie weeks ago."

"Yes, but only informally. Aerie won't go into the contract until after the review—"

"I understand, but I don't see the problem. Everyone is on board. Rick Penner loves it. Paul is ecstatic. Fleet's customers and suppliers have thrown in their support. What could get in the way, at this point?"

"Liam," Cara said, "it's not that simple—"

Just then the door opened, and Peter Whittington filled the doorway. "I need to speak with you, Cara." He glared through Liam as if he didn't exist. "Now."

She stood up abruptly, knocking over the ceramic mug holding her pens. They clattered on the desk in the sudden silence of the room. "I'm busy at the moment, Peter. I'll come to your office in five minutes."

Liam raised an eyebrow. He had never seen Cara defy her boss.

Peter's face began to turn a telltale shade of purple. "Now, Cara."

Cara opened her mouth to reply, but Liam stood up. "No problem, Cara. I'll catch up with you later. Remember, you promised me a talk." He walked to the door. "Hello, Peter." Liam winked at her as he left the office.

Peter shut the door quickly. "Did you tell him? About Aerie?"

"Of course not."

"Good." He skewered her with a hard glare. "Where is the software? I want it before you start the review."

Cara's mind whirled. Liam's information changed everything. She needed time to think, but she had no time for that now. Peter would be suspicious if she tried to stall. She unlocked the desk drawer and removed the manila envelope. "Here you go."

Peter grasped the sealed envelope and noted his name circled in red ink. "Did you get everything?"

"I did." Eagerly, he started to rip the envelope open. "I'd be careful, Peter. If you're smart, you'll take that home and review it privately where no one will interrupt you or ask questions." She glanced at her watch. "We have a review in a few minutes. I would say this is not the right time. Mike and Anna often burst into my office unannounc—"

Just then the door flew open and Mike leaned into the office. "Cara, are you ready? Come on, we're going to be late ... oh, sorry."

Peter clutched the sealed envelope. "Point taken. I'll look later." He glowered at Mike. "Leave. She'll be down in a minute."

Peter paused as he waited for Mike to leave. "You know, Cara. I expected you to give me a lot more trouble over this." He waved the envelope in the air. "You've given me nothing but trouble over every little thing on this project so far. Why so cooperative all of the sudden?"

"You didn't give me much choice, Peter."

He chuckled. "Well, I didn't realize how effective a few simple ... instructions could be. I should have done this months ago. It would have saved me a hell of a lot of trouble."

She swallowed hard and tried to appear submissive. God, it was a stretch. "I'm sorry if I've been a source of irritation for you. I had a chance to think about things these last few days, and I realize I have a lot to learn. Everything is much clearer now that you ... explained the situation."

"Am I hearing right? Do I detect a glimmer of reality getting through that Pollyanna head of yours?"

Cara lowered her head so he would not detect her revulsion. Peter laughed. "I never thought I'd see the day when that rock of idealism you stand on would start to crumble." He nodded his head in mock sympathy and patted her arm. "Well, don't worry. You won't regret it. I'll see what I can do about getting you a promotion."

She swallowed. "That ... would be nice."

Peter laughed again. "Ooh, how the righteous do fall." He sauntered out of her office. She heard him chortle as he entered the corridor, "God, I love this business."

Cara slumped at her desk, fighting down the nausea threatening to dislodge her breakfast. "Slug," she grimaced at the door. "You slippery, slimy, sleazy, scuzzy SLUG!"

Chapter 20

The Concept Review had been in progress for an hour. Everything was going as planned. Cara was presenting the purchase order form. A mock-up of the form lit the screen on the wall, and the attendees were asking the expected questions. Was there a field for country on the address line? How many characters did the type-of-shipment field contain? Would the field length accommodate express mail account numbers? Then someone asked a question not directly related to the subject at hand, and Cara knew the moment had come.

"How do we determine the quantity to order?" His nametag identified him as George. She'd never met him, didn't know where he worked or what his job was. He asked the question so innocently no one had any idea the bomb was about to drop. Except Cara. She took a deep breath. "You will determine the order quantity the same way you do right now, by phone or by fax."

The questioner seemed puzzled. "Hold on a minute. What's this new system I've been hearing about? Arctic ... Egret ... Armor ... something like that?"

Rick Penner took over. "You mean Aerie, George. Why don't you explain about the Aerie system, Cara?"

It was a moment out of time. Cara gazed around, fixing the image in her mind, because in less than ten words, she would blow it apart, and Humpty Dumpty would have a better chance at reconstruction than the pieces she would leave behind. Peter looked smug. Rick proud. Liam expectant. Lauren, sitting between Paul and Liam, still hadn't wiped the triumphant smile off her face. Then there was

Mike; he just looked bored. "There's not going to be an Aerie system, Rick."

Pandemonium. Rick, Liam, and Peter all stood, talking at once. She put up a hand for silence, and Rick spoke, shouting everyone else down. "Quiet down, everyone. Quiet down, and let Cara explain. I'm sure she has a perfectly reasonable explanation for this." The volume of the room lowered to a murmur and finally dropped off altogether. "Now," Rick said, "explain."

"There's not going to be an Aerie system, Rick."

The uproar started again, but Rick quickly quelled it. "What do you mean?"

"I mean exactly what I said. Aerie was never specifically mentioned in the proposal between Pyramid and Fleet. It has been removed as a subject for review."

"Cara, this is not the assumption we've been working under these last several weeks."

"You're right. It's not."

"You told us we received the go-ahead to include Aerie in this project."

"That's correct."

"What happened? Did you lie to us?"

She felt like she was in a courtroom drama. "No, Rick. At the time, I told you the truth."

"But it's not the truth now." She nodded. "So when was this decision made, and by whom?" Cara kept her eyes on Rick, but she saw several heads turn toward Peter.

Peter stood up, his face almost purple, his eyes livid. "Cara, I want you to stop this review, right now."

With effort, she kept her gaze fixed on Rick. "I was not privy to that information. I only know the decision was made."

"CARA!" Peter raised his voice in warning.

"Do you mean to say," Rick abruptly cut Peter off, "that after many weeks of work, several hundred man-hours spent by this team, and significant financial commitments made by some of Fleet's most important customers and suppliers, you plan to drop Aerie?"

"Yes."

"Why didn't you tell us of this decision earlier?"

"That wasn't a choice I was given."

Rick's voice was beginning to rise as the impact of her words sunk in. "What are we supposed to do with the work put in by the team, Cara? What about the new procedures we've adopted so we can utilize the system? How am I supposed to explain to Fleet's management Aerie is now excluded from FIT?"

"Rick, it's not a completely closed book. There is a possibility—a good one, I've been told—that after this review is complete, Pyramid will open negotiations for the design and construction of Aerie."

"You mean as a separate development project?"

"Yes."

"What will that cost?"

"Again, I am not privy to that information, but my guess is a minimum of two million dollars."

The uproar started again. Peter jumped up, rushed over to Cara, and grabbed her arm. "ENOUGH, Cara! In my office. RIGHT NOW!"

At once Liam was up. He strode across the room and towered in front of Cara and Peter. "Calm down, Peter." He removed Peter's hand from Cara's arm.

"I will not calm down," Peter snarled. "Cara just made a grave mistake. I will not sit by and let her destroy this project." He grabbed her arm again, and Cara stumbled. Liam reached out and grasped her other arm, barely keeping her upright.

"Let her go, Whittington. Now." Liam's voice came out low and dangerous. Cara forced herself to stand perfectly still while the two men squared off. "Are you okay, Cara?" Liam asked, his eyes never leaving Peter's face.

"Yes, I'm okay."

Slowly, Peter released Cara's arm. With as much dignity as she could muster, she walked to the table, picked up her briefcase, and left the room. It was deathly quiet for several moments. After she left, Liam stood aside. Peter hurried from the room.

Liam walked over to where Rick was still standing in shocked surprise. "Rick, do you know what the hell is going on?"

Rick shook his head. "Damned if I do, but any way you cut it, it's not good." Liam nodded, his lips pressed together in tight concern.

Peter followed Cara into his office and slammed the door. "You fool! You stupid IDIOT! Why did you do such a damned foolish thing?"

Cara fought to keep her composure. "You really have to ask, Peter? I told you the other day. It's dishonest. You made an agreement with our client. I admit, it wasn't well documented, but it was clearly understood by all parties. You changed the agreement and did not notify your client. It's legal, I suppose, in the strictest sense of the word, but it's certainly not ethical. I chose not to participate in your deception."

Peter screwed up his face in indignant disbelief. "You CHOSE not to PARTICIPATE? Well, aren't we self-righteous? You, with all your naïve talk about 'serving the customer' and 'open communication.' You don't understand the first thing about business, about what it takes to succeed. I wonder how self-righteous you'd be if you were out of a job?"

Here it comes, she thought. The ax. Quick and easy. Might as well speak her mind while she had the chance. "Is this what's required to succeed, Peter? Ethics of convenience? Do you spend all your time lying and cheating and doing whatever you can to get the next promotion? Do you ignore your own agreements for a few more dollars on the income statement, and justify your actions because Pyramid demands a healthy cash flow? Does your ambition have any limits? What will you do next time? Theft? Larceny? You're right about one thing. If that is what's required to succeed, I'm in the wrong place."

"Great sermon, Cara. Such high-minded morality. I can't wait to report to my superiors how your do-gooder actions managed to lose Pyramid a two-million-dollar contract."

She looked at him incredulously. "Me? I lost Pyramid a two-million-dollar contract? Not me, Peter. You, and your dirty little scam will end up costing Pyramid at least $10 million."

"How do you figure?"

"Easy. You just destroyed your credibility with Fleet. We count on referrals for future business, and Fleet has a lot of influence in the Northwest. They'll never trust you again. How many referrals do you think you'll get now?"

"You forget, Cara, I wasn't telling them the bad news. You were."

"Don't fool yourself, Peter. It was clear by both your behavior and my implication who was giving the orders. They may be angry, but they're not stupid. After a while, they'll realize I was telling the truth. But not you. They will never trust you again."

He paused. "You might be right, Cara. If I were the one negotiating Aerie." He scraped his fingers across his jaw. "No, Ms. Larson, I will give that honor to you. You will face Fleet. You will explain how wrong you were, how you tangled the Aerie project up and confused everyone so completely, that Pyramid is now forced to start over just to clear up the mess you made." He smiled a slow, dangerous smile. Cara could almost see the wheels turning in his head. "You will make clear this debacle was *your* fault. You will repair the damage by negotiating a new contract for Aerie."

Cara's mouth dropped open in surprise. He planned to keep her on as the scapegoat? The slug. He would keep his hands clean and still end up with a new, two-million-dollar contract. "So, you're not firing me?"

"Hell, no." He laughed, suddenly enjoying the game immensely. "I expect you to twist the screws nice and tight, too. Maybe you can even get three million for Aerie. "

"You are despicable. What if I refuse?"

"You can't. Remember what I told you the other day? I can make life difficult for you. Dismissal would only be the start. Investigations, lawsuits, even jail time. I can add to the list if necessary."

Cara wanted to throw up. What an offensive, rotten, sneaky, slimy slug. She could hardly stand to be in the same room with him. He wouldn't know integrity if it jumped up and bit him. But she did. Mama had given her the clue. And Mama had given her the means. Now, Mama was gone. There was nothing to hold her back.

She pulled the sheet of paper from her briefcase, walked over to the desk, and took a pen from the middle of the gleaming row. She signed the paper. "I guess you'd better set that fine legal team to work, Peter. Get someone else to do your dirty work. My resignation is effective today." She walked from his office without a backward glance.

Cara's hands shook as she entered her office. She closed her eyes and leaned her forehead against the door.

"You want to tell me what's going on, Cara?"

She whipped around to find Liam leaning against the edge of the desk. "What are you doing here?"

"I'm here for some answers. What the hell happened downstairs?"

"I thought the discussion was more than clear. Aerie is out of scope. Pyramid wants to negotiate a separate contract for it."

"That much is obvious. But how did this happen? When did this happen? And why didn't you tell me?"

"When exactly was I supposed to tell you, Liam? You haven't been around much. And how was I supposed to tell you? I would have a dozen lawsuits filed against me in no time if I went around spilling confidential information to a person who is not my client."

"Fleet is your client. You didn't tell them, either."

"I told the truth in the review. I was instructed not to tell Fleet."

"Peter instructed you not to tell Fleet about dropping Aerie?"

"Yes." She looked at him, her eyes troubled. "I did the only thing I could, Liam, which was to say, in public, that Aerie was out of scope. Now, it's up to you and Fleet to do your best to negotiate it back in."

"What the hell kind of a company is Pyramid, anyway?"

"I've been asking myself that very question for the last ten days."

"Ten days?! You've known about this for ten days?" He closed his eyes. "Cara, I need Aerie. Now. My investors expect it, and my revenue projections require it. Windwear's whole future depends on Aerie. The IPO. My expansion plans. Everything."

"I understand, Liam. I do—"

"No, Cara, you don't understand. Without Aerie, Windwear is fucked." He ran his fingers through his hair in agitation. "Well and truly fucked."

"I'm so sorry, Liam. I didn't understand how Aerie fit into your plans until you told me this morning—"

"Will you talk to Peter, Cara? Tell him we'll pay his price. We're willing to negotiate a new contract as long as we can continue with the current development effort. We'll meet his terms. We'll even give him a premium on the contract price. We just can't stop work on Aerie."

"I don't think so, Liam."

"Please, Cara. You're the head of the team. You understand the system better than anyone. God knows, you're the only one Peter even listens to—"

"No. You don't understand. After today, Peter won't listen to anything I say. But he will listen to you. Aerie was your idea, after all. You have the best chance of convincing him to keep Aerie in scope."

"You're probably right." Liam paused, trying to rein in his frustration. "How should I approach him?"

"Focus on the money, Liam. Peter always responds to the profit argument. Remind him how much Pyramid can make from all the customization projects that will come with Aerie."

"You're right, that's good advice." He shook his head. "God, this is what I can't understand. There is so much money to be made here. For Pyramid. For Windwear. This is such a no-brainer, win-win prospect. I don't understand why Peter wants to delay." He stopped, uneasiness darkening his eyes. "Something not's right here, Cara. Nothing adds up. Do you know what's going on? Is there something you're not telling me?"

Cara didn't hear his questions. She was trying to make sense of an idea that suddenly popped into her head along with Liam's words. What did Liam just say? *So much money to be made.* All at once, the whole sorry picture clicked into place. Of course. Peter Whittington was a dirty, rotten, double-crossing, sneaky, slimy slug. He had no intention of negotiating a new contract for Aerie. He intended to take the software for his own purposes.

Cara drew in a sharp breath as the truth hit her. Peter planned to take Aerie and have Pyramid build it. But to do so, he needed to head off the obstacles in his path. First, he needed to remove Aerie from the project scope. If Aerie remained in scope, the software would be part of FIT, and therefore owned by Fleet and Windwear. But if Aerie were removed from scope, Fleet and Windwear would have no rights to it. Pyramid could then step in and take it. Second, Peter needed to prevent Fleet and Windwear from demanding Aerie, regardless of the scope question. Now, she understood why Peter instructed her to purge Aerie from the network and backup tapes. As of this minute, there was no evidence Aerie even existed. Perfect. Pyramid would not be forced to give up something that didn't exist. And if Fleet and Windwear took matters further and sued Pyramid for stealing Aerie? Pyramid could easily dispute the claim. There would be no evidence of wrongdoing if there were no evidence of Aerie. How can someone steal something that doesn't exist?

Oh, that slug, Peter. Cara could picture how the scenario would play out. Peter would create a team to build Aerie. In six months or so, when development was complete, Pyramid would announce a new service offering that would take the technology world by storm. Pyramid would make a killing. Peter would end up with a fat promotion in New York. And where would Windwear be? On the outside looking in, of course. The company would need to wait in line like everyone else to buy the software it had invented. In the meantime, Windwear's IPO would go down in flames.

Cara closed her eyes. Why hadn't she seen this before? Because Peter had manipulated her, too. He implied Pyramid would negotiate a new contract for Aerie. If she had understood the truth, she never would have played along, even this far. Such manipulation for a measly two-million-dollar contract didn't make much sense. But for tens of millions. For that amount of money, it made perfect sense.

"Oh my God. Liam, you have no idea how right you—"

Just then two burly security guards entered her office without invitation. "Excuse me, sir," one of the guards said to Liam. "You need to leave now. We've been instructed to escort Ms. Larson from the building."

"Cara?" Liam looked at the guards and then at Cara.

"Liam," she said urgently, "listen to me. You can't let Peter take—"

One of the guards stepped in front of her, blocking her view of Liam. "Miss, I am instructed to tell you that you are to speak to no one and leave the premises immediately."

The other guard put one hand on Liam's arm, and with the other, opened his jacket wide enough for Liam to see the holster at his side. The guard pushed him toward the door. "You too, sir. You need to leave. Right now."

Chapter 21

Cara packed her things slowly. Think, she screamed to herself. Think! She still had Aerie hidden in her drawer. Right now, Peter had nothing. After a moment, she snapped her head up and said to the guards, "I'm going to need another box. May I call my assistant?" They nodded.

She picked up the phone and punched the intercom button. "Anna, would you ask Mike to bring me a box, please? Maybe two, just in case. Thanks." She replaced the receiver and sat down. She scratched some words on a sticky note. "Design Manuals." She slapped the note on a box. She wrote another and pasted it on the desk, as if awaiting a box Mike would bring. Then another.

She pulled out her empty nylon workout bag and unzipped it. Reaching into the drawer, Cara removed her running shoes. Ooh. They were ripe. The guards took a few steps back. She opened another drawer and took out a jacket, some T-shirts, and a pair of shorts. She stacked them in a pile next to the shoes. The guards stepped further back. She opened the middle drawer and slid out the envelope containing Aerie. She slipped the envelope into the bag, followed quickly by the stinky pile and reeking shoes.

Mike burst into the office. "Hey Cara, here you go. *Little boxes, little boxes*— Whoa." He stopped in mid-melody when he saw the guards. "What's going on?"

Cara walked over to him, took the boxes from his hands, and pasted a sticky note on the back of his palm. "What's going on, Cara?"

The boxes blocked the guards' view. "I've been relieved of duty. These ... gentlemen will be escorting me from the building once I pack. Thanks for the boxes."

He stared at her, then at the note on his palm. She rarely saw Mike at a loss for words. "I should get going, Mike. I promise to call you soon and explain."

"What happened? What did Peter do?" Mike finally asked, as he slipped the note into his pocket.

"I'll call you later." She took the boxes from his hands. "I need to take care of this now."

"But—"

One of the guards approached Mike. "You delivered the boxes, son. Now, go."

Mike turned on him angrily. "Well, *Dad*, thanks for the advice—"

"Mike," Cara shook her head. "It's okay."

The guard grasped Mike's arm and steered him out. When the door closed behind him, Mike reached into his pocket for the note. It contained seven words. *Lauren. 23rd Floor. Ladies Room. One hour.* "What the hell?" He crumpled up the note.

Peter checked his watch when he heard the knock on his office door. Right on time. Liam Scofield just betrayed how valuable Aerie was to him. Excellent. "Enter."

Peter looked up from his desk as the two men filed in. As if it were an execution, he thought gleefully. He forced himself to appear somber. "Liam, Paul, come in. Can I get you some coffee, water?"

The two men took a seat. "No, thank you. We're fine," Liam said.

Peter settled back in his plush leather chair, folded his hands behind his head, and let out a deep breath. He was the picture of composure. He studied the two men in front of him through half-closed eyes. He had seen Liam leave Cara's office not five minutes ago. The young man's expression was evidence the conversation had not gone well. This was going to be fun. He had to admit, he'd been thrown off track when Cara pulled that stunt downstairs. It was an unexpected wrinkle for sure, but with a few minutes to think, he realized it was a wrinkle he could exploit. Cara Larson's defiance had given him a plausible reason for delay.

Yes, he was going to enjoy this. He was going to put this arrogant boy in his place. No one tangled with Peter Whittington and came out ahead. Not Pollyanna redheads with more mouth than sense, and not arrogant young studs who tried to cheat him out of profits that belonged to him.

He itched to rub his hands together, but it wouldn't do at the moment. Instead, he shook his head in apology. "I can't tell you boys how sorry I am about this mix-up. I assure you, I'm taking care of it without delay." Peter let the words hang in the air as he observed the puzzlement on their faces. They were such boys in a man's world. "I should have known better than to give that girl so much freedom. She's young and inexperienced. Still, nothing can excuse her behavior. I fired her, effective immediately. I've notified Pyramid's legal department of the situation. We'll press charges if necessary. This kind of behavior is intolerable for an organization of Pyramid's caliber. We pride ourselves on the highest ethical standards in the industry." Peter straightened a little taller in his chair. Oh this was so much fun. This was as good as sex!

"I'm not sure what you're talking about," Liam said. "What did Cara do to … warrant prosecution?"

"Well, as far as I can tell, the trouble started after the demonstration back in June. I realize Aerie was a technical success, and all the suppliers and customers gave their approval." He lowered his voice. "But I rejected Cara's proposal. I told her the software wasn't needed, that we could handle all the functionality covered by Aerie in our current scope."

"What?" the two men cried in unison.

"Gee boys, in a way, this is my fault, too. I feel responsible for your problems. I should have kept tighter control on that little phony. She's always been a handful, but I chose to trust her. Against my better judgment, clearly. If I had known she lied to you, I would have stepped in right away and corrected the situation." He shook his head in regret. "This isn't easy for me, either."

"I find this hard to believe," Liam said. "Everyone on the project knew about Aerie. Are you saying you had no idea your people were working on it?"

Peter smiled apologetically. "I'm a busy man. I'm not on the floor as much as I want to be. Do you have any idea what's involved in running a project of this size? Besides, I make a point to trust my people. It's an important aspect of my management style. Building trust and responsibility is part of my job when I teach young managers." He tried to turn the snicker on his lips into a sincere smile. This was perfect. A page right from Cara's goody two-shoes management book. Oh, this was *much* better than sex!

"Obviously, I made a mistake with Cara," Peter continued, "but she lied to me, too. Let me show you." He pulled a file from the rack on his table. It contained a brand new set of weekly progress reports Cara had revised, as he had instructed, to exclude any mention of Aerie. He had printed them off just this morning. "Here they are. Cara's progress reports. No mention—not one, single, solitary mention—of Aerie anywhere. She purposely hid her unauthorized work on Aerie from me." He let the words sink in. "She fooled me just like she fooled you."

Liam leaned forward. "Why would she do this? It doesn't make any sense."

"I wish I knew the answer. I'm hoping she made an honest mistake. If not … well, you can understand why I feel the need to investigate."

"What are you getting at, Peter?"

Peter bestowed a fatherly smile on Liam. "I hope this was a judgment error based on inexperience. She was excited about Aerie, but when I explained about cash flow and the constraints of the FIT schedule, she wouldn't take 'no' for an answer. She brought the subject up at least ten times, and I rejected it every time. She begged and pleaded for me to include Aerie in scope—"

"That doesn't sound like, Cara," Liam said. "She's never been anything but professional."

"Well, that's good, son. Glad to know she treats our customers with respect. I think this time she played the odds and lost. She continued development in the hopes of winning my approval during the design phase. When I told her to remove Aerie from the review, well, she threw a tantrum. She complied, but only because I ... insisted."

Peter eyed Liam closely. This was almost too easy. He would exact his revenge on the little bitch and this bloodsucking leech, and be partner, all in one fell swoop. Oh, he was good at this game. Very good. "I hate to even think about the other reason, boys, but I'm afraid I must face facts."

"What other reason?" Liam asked.

"Well, I hate to think one of my employees would do such a thing, especially one as young and promising as Cara Larson. You can never tell about people, how ambition can get the best of them. I'm disappointed to learn how grasping and self-serving she turned out to be."

Paul, who had been sitting quietly during the entire conversation, saw Liam's grip tighten on the arm of his chair. "What's your point?" he cut in before Liam could respond.

"Cara believed Aerie had commercial possibilities," Peter explained. "She believed that, with some modification, Aerie could become a stand-alone product. I'm afraid she was carried away by her own ambition. When I told her once and for all Aerie would not be part of FIT, she took matters into her own hands."

"What do you mean?" Liam asked.

"I mean," Peter said, with as much chagrin as he could muster, "that Cara Larson stole Aerie."

A tense silence filled the room as Liam and Paul absorbed Peter's words. "I don't believe you," Liam finally said.

"Well, young man, of course, you're free to believe what you want. I can only rely on the evidence in front of me. Cara developed Aerie without my permission. I demanded she delete it from the system. She did. That's when I think anger got the best of her. She blamed me for removing Aerie from scope at the review today, and then she stole it. Luckily, we make backups of all our work. She only has a copy. She won't get away with this."

"Peter," Paul protested, "I don't believe Cara would—"

Liam stopped Paul with a hand on his arm. "Let Peter finish," Liam said. "I want to hear what he has to say."

Peter was surprised at how calmly Liam was taking the news. "I don't believe Cara's actions, as serious as they are, pose a threat to the project, but she was wrong about Aerie's potential."

"What do you mean? Aerie is—" Paul stopped abruptly when he saw Liam's expression.

"Aerie has some potential for Fleet and its supply chain, but as a stand-alone product, it would be far too difficult to implement. There are too many obstacles. Aerie has no commercial possibilities at all. Even so, now that she has stolen the software, I'll be forced to investigate and possibly prosecute. Pyramid can't tolerate an employee who breaks the law and compromises client relationships. We need to make an example of her."

"So, what happens to Aerie, now?" Liam cut into the silence.

Peter glanced at the manila envelope perched on the corner of his desk. So nondescript for an item worth so much money. These young studs had no clue of the potential treasure sitting right in front of them. He peered at the two men. "My plans haven't changed, gentlemen. My job right now is to build FIT as planned. This is Pyramid's flagship project in the West, and my management insists I give it my full attention. We are on a tight schedule, and we have a lot of complex functionality to deal with. I need to give my customers the best possible service I can. I'll let the attorneys decide how to handle Cara."

"What about Aerie?" Paul asked.

"Well, I'll talk to my managers in New York and try to convince them to open negotiations on a separate contract for Aerie. It's the least I can do, boys. Maybe we can put together a new team, headed by Mike Taylor, to continue the work. Since I feel responsible for Cara's failings, I promise I'll make the effort."

Liam and Paul glanced at each other. "We appreciate your help, Peter," Liam said. "We understand what an awkward situation this is for you, but regardless of Cara's actions, Windwear and Fleet made a good faith effort to produce Aerie. We have expended significant resources in that effort. Your problem is unfortunate, but frankly, it's *your* problem, not ours. We should not be required to pay for your internal management issues. Cara led us to believe Aerie was to be included in FIT. She was our contact, and as far as we're concerned, Pyramid is bound by her word. We expect Aerie to be in scope."

Peter raised his eyebrows and barely held onto his fatherly voice. "I see your point, boys, but the matter isn't quite so simple. Cara was not the project manager. She had no authority concerning FIT or Aerie. The contract clearly states the project manager makes all decisions. Regardless of what she told you, my word is the only one that counts."

"That leaves it pretty wide open for you, doesn't it?" Liam said.

"At the beginning of a project, yes, but once the scope document is signed, the boundaries are set. The scope becomes an extension of the contract and provides checks and balances for the project manager." He shook his head. "I'm sorry, boys. I can't put Aerie in scope. My first responsibility is to FIT."

Liam nodded. "Understood, Peter. We appreciate your frankness, and we understand your time constraints. Perhaps we can ease the situation by offering to take Aerie off your hands. We're willing to buy the software from Pyramid. That way, neither you nor Fleet will be diverted from FIT."

Peter looked sharply at Liam while he digested this information. Damn. The boy had walked him right down the path. He'd let Peter go on and on about why he had no need for Aerie. How could he justify keeping it? He scratched his chin. "You have a point, son, the software is probably better off with you than me. But before I consider selling, I should get a ruling from our legal department. They're going to investigate, you understand. I probably shouldn't get rid of the evidence before they have a chance to examine it."

"You can investigate and sell the software to us at the same time," Liam said. "Those are not mutually exclusive activities."

"Well, you may presume as much, but I'm not a lawyer. I'll need approval from my attorneys. If they give me the go-ahead, I'm sure we can work out a deal."

"How long will that take?" Liam asked.

Peter shrugged. "Hard to say. Pyramid is a large company. I can request top priority, but I can't tell the attorneys how to do their jobs."

"Days, weeks, months ...?" Liam pressed.

"I would expect sometime in the next couple weeks. I'll make a few calls and let you know."

Liam nodded. "I'll be in Taiwan for the next few weeks. I'll contact you as soon as I return. In the meantime, my attorney will draw up terms of sale."

Peter rose to his feet and extended his hand. "Great. Great. I'll let you know as soon as I receive word from legal. I'm sure we can work this out, boys." He couldn't resist a final jab. "Even if Cara does go to jail."

Liam hesitated for a moment, and then shook Peter's hand. "Thanks for your time, Peter. I agree with your approach. I'll have my attorneys review the FIT contract, too. Maybe they can find a simple way to shake Aerie loose from FIT. I'll have them call your attorneys in the morning."

Peter struggled to keep his smile intact. "Er ... I'm not sure that's necessary, young man—"

"Not at all, Peter," Liam cut in. He smiled, but his eyes were ice cold. "Happy to help."

Chapter 22

The guards stood in the lobby, towering over Cara. "We'll need your card key and office keys, Miss Larson."

"Oh." Cara set down the boxes, placed her nylon bag on top, and opened her purse.

"And your cellular."

Cara sighed. She could feel people's eyes on her as they walked by. Security guards. Boxes. She knew what they were thinking. They would be right. She handed over the keys and her mobile phone. The cellular had been issued by Pyramid, and the company had a right to have it back, but still, she felt unexpectedly nervous without it. She picked up her belongings, and the two men watched as she left the building.

Cara walked to her car and placed the boxes in the trunk. She picked up her bag and purse and hurried to a coffee shop less than a block away. "May I use your phone?" she asked the clerk as she ordered a cup of coffee.

"Sure." He pointed behind him to a small office. "In the back."

"Thanks." She dashed into the office and dialed the number. "Mike, did you get my note?"

Yes, Ca—"

"Don't say my name, just listen. Meet me at the Sixth Street fire escape in five minutes."

"But—"

"Please, Mike. It's important."

"All right, but—"

"Thanks."

"Cara, what the hell?" Mike exclaimed as he opened the fire escape door. "What happened? The rumors are flying. It's a fricking zoo upstairs."

"I quit, that's what happened."

"That's not what Peter said. He said he fired you. He said you stole Aerie."

"What?" Cara closed her eyes. So, that was Peter's story. Tell the world she stole the software, and then go underground with the development effort. A perfect cover. Until he discovered he didn't have the software. "You're better off not knowing anything, Mike, especially if Peter starts asking questions." She pulled her bag closer. "Did you talk to Lauren? Did she agree to meet me?"

"Yeah, she did. She'll be there." He gave an exaggerated shiver. "What is it about Lauren Janelle that is so disgustingly cringe worthy?"

Cara rolled her eyes and smiled despite the fact that everything was going to hell around her. "Come with me, Mike. I need your help."

They headed up the stairs. "Geez, Cara, if I knew we'd be walking up twenty-three flights of stairs, I would have insisted we meet on the fourth floor."

"You're young. Walk."

Lauren entered the women's restroom seven minutes later. Cara was waiting at the far end of the sitting room. Lauren hurried over with an angry stride. "What do you want, you bitch? Do you realize what you've done to Windwear?"

Cara held up her hand. "Save the lecture, and listen up, Lauren. I'm probably the only person in the world right now who can help Windwear."

Lauren's eyes narrowed in suspicion. "Why should I believe you? You just cheated your own company. And Windwear. You're no better than—"

"I don't care what you believe," Cara cut in. "I need your help. If you want to take the chance I'm lying, go ahead and walk out the door. But if I'm telling the truth, you'll miss your opportunity not only to save Windwear but also to grow the company the way Liam's been planning. The stock offering. The research and development department. The manufacturing facilities. Using Aerie to finance your growth—"

"Liam told you about our plans?"

"Yes, he did."

"The fool." She looked at Cara again, this time a little less suspiciously. "What kind of help?"

"First things first, Lauren. I have a few questions, mainly legal ones." She paused, choosing her words carefully. "What is the exact legal status of Aerie?"

"What do you mean, *legal status*?"

"Well, Aerie is not fully functional. The software can't run on its own. We needed to piggyback the prototype onto other software to do the demo. It has gaping holes all over the place, no security system, no communication links. As far as I'm concerned, it doesn't even qualify as a real piece of software yet. So my question is, does Aerie legally exist? Or does it sit in some sort of legal limbo until it becomes a stand-alone product?"

Lauren shook her head. "Nothing in America is in legal limbo, Cara. Every physical thing in this country is owned by someone."

"Even a partially finished work-in-progress like Aerie?"

Lauren nodded. "From a legal standpoint, as soon as Aerie was put in tangible form, its legal rights came into existence and became vested in its creator. Even though the software may change form, the fact it can be identified on a computer or disk gives it a legal right to exist. But that isn't the key question. The key question is who created Aerie. The creator holds the ownership rights."

"All right. So, who's the creator? That's as confusing as the legal status. Pyramid, Fleet and Windwear all contributed to the creation of Aerie, but no legal agreement regarding ownership exists. And given the events of today, there's not likely to be one."

"Who do you think holds ownership?"

Cara let out an impatient sigh. "I don't know. Normally, when we write a custom system like this, the customer owns the software, which means Fleet. In this case, since Fleet agreed to sell Aerie to Windwear, Windwear would be the rightful owner. However, this is not a normal situation. Peter excluded Aerie from scope. He also ordered me to remove every trace of the software from the files. There is now no evidence Aerie was ever a part of FIT. How can Fleet or Windwear own something that isn't included in the contract and isn't in any of the project files?" She paused. "Liam can also argue Windwear is the rightful owner because he originated the idea—"

"You can't claim ownership of an idea. Windwear has no rights using that argument."

"But the prototype wouldn't exist without the idea. Liam and Paul directed our efforts. We built what they envisioned."

"The prototype is separate from the idea. You said Pyramid, Fleet and Windwear all contributed to this effort. Did either Liam or Paul do any of the actual design or programming work?"

"No, Mike and I did all the work on the prototype."

"Then Windwear would have a difficult time convincing a court the company holds any ownership rights at all. Windwear is not party to the FIT contract. If the project files are scrubbed clean, as you say, Windwear can show no proof of its involvement in FIT. Liam and Paul did no actual work on the software—"

"They have documentation showing their development efforts."

"Windwear cannot use its documentation as evidence of the work done on FIT when the FIT project itself shows no matching evidence. At best, Windwear's documentation is proof the company was working on its own system. Under these circumstances, Windwear holds even fewer rights than Fleet. If Aerie is excluded from scope as you say—"

"Wrongly excluded from scope."

"An irrelevant point. Rightly or wrongly, Aerie is now out of scope. Only two possibilities for ownership remain. Aerie belongs either to you and Mike, as the actual creators, or to Pyramid, as your employer."

"Pyramid? No way. Pyramid can't claim rights to software produced on a custom project."

"You just told me Aerie is no longer part of FIT. As long as Aerie is out of scope, Fleet is not the owner. Ownership then flows to the creators. You and Mike created the software, and you and Mike work for Pyramid. By law, anything you create as an employee in the normal course of business and at the direction of your employer, belongs to your employer."

"But that's not fair. No one, not even Pyramid, ever intended for Pyramid to own Aerie."

Lauren raised one eyebrow. "Except Peter. Perhaps this was Peter's plan all along. If he can make the case Fleet doesn't own Aerie, Pyramid is next in line as the rightful owner."

"Can we argue we built Aerie outside the 'normal course of business'? Once we received Peter's approval, he left us alone. He provided no input or direction."

"That's a weak argument. You weren't writing video games on the side. Before Aerie was removed, the software was integrated with FIT. You used Pyramid's equipment and space, Fleet's personnel, Windwear's expertise. You wouldn't stand a chance if this case landed in front of a judge. Courts don't rule against employers in these kinds of matters, especially large, wealthy, well-connected employers. Do you realize what would happen if every individual who worked on a piece of software insisted they be recognized as a creator? One person could hold up the entire show. The whole industry would grind to a halt."

Cara closed her eyes. What a slug. Peter had just been waiting for Aerie to fall into his hands once he removed it from scope.

"So Peter made you remove Aerie from the project files. What did you do with it?" Cara hesitated, and Lauren frowned at her. "You gave Aerie to Peter, didn't you? Dammit, Cara, how could you be so stupid?"

"What ... what if Peter doesn't have Aerie?"

"What do you mean, *what if Peter doesn't have Aerie*? Are you saying ..." Suddenly Lauren smiled. "Interesting, Cara. Very interesting indeed." Her words came out slowly, as if she savored the delicious possibilities forming in her mind. "That would definitely change the game. If Peter doesn't have the software, all he can do is chase after whoever does. And all those arguments you mentioned, weak though they may be, would need to be contested in a long, drawn-out legal battle."

"I see."

"That is, *if* he can even find it. It would be an awful shame if Peter couldn't find Aerie anywhere."

"What do you mean, Lauren?"

"Don't act so goddamned innocent, Cara. If Peter doesn't have the software, everything is wide open. Jungle law. Back to the old ways. When the rules were written by no one but understood by everyone. Possession is nine-tenths of the law." She paused. "So, Peter doesn't have Aerie. That must mean you do, or we wouldn't be talking right now."

"Peter thinks he has Aerie, but he doesn't. He has six blank disks and a pile of paper from the recycling bin."

"What?" Lauren's eyes widened, and she smiled at Cara with reluctant admiration. "You surprise me, Cara Larson. I didn't think you had a dishonest bone in your body."

Cara ignored her. "It won't be long before Peter figures it out. He's going to be livid when he does. He cut Aerie from scope so Pyramid could develop and market it. He never intended to sell the software back to Windwear. Ever."

"The son of a bitch! So, you figured out his plan and took Aerie. Now you have a plan, I presume. One involving Windwear?"

Suddenly they heard a commotion at the door. There was a harsh thud and the door shook. "Sorry ma'am." Mike's muffled voice came from the other side. "We have an emergency. Please use the restroom down the hall." Cara and Lauren turned to listen. "I think it has something to do with a baby, ma'am. Emergency delivery. There's a lot of blood on the floor. You don't really want to go in." The noise stopped, and they heard footsteps walking away. "I'm just trying to help where I can." Both women stifled smiles.

"Where were we?" Lauren said. "Oh yes. The plan."

"The plan." Cara nodded. "I need to know one thing before we go on, Lauren. I need to know what you'll do with Aerie if I give it to you. I need to know you won't destroy it."

"Destroy it? Why would I do that?"

"A few weeks ago, you called and demanded I kill the Aerie project. Or don't you remember our conversation?"

"That was before, Cara. Things have changed."

"Before what?"

"Before I learned its value."

"Right. The investors. Liam told me how interested they were in Aerie. So, now that you understand the value of the software, what will you do if I give it to you?"

"What do you think?"

"I'm not in the mood to play games, Lauren."

"All right, Cara." Lauren thought for a moment. "I understand Aerie is valuable, but only if it can be developed. Only Windwear and Pyramid are in a position to pursue development. If Pyramid gets the software, Windwear cannot possibly benefit. If Windwear gets the soft—"

"I cannot believe this is such a difficult question," Cara said in frustration. "My God, Lauren, the answer should be easy. You work for Windwear."

"Every problem deserves to be examined from all angles."

"Or from every angle that can benefit you." Cara peered at Lauren. "Promise me if I give you Aerie, you will give it to Liam and not to Peter."

"I just told you I would—"

"No, you didn't. You went through a self-serving thought exercise that makes me trust you even less. Promise, Lauren. Say the words, or I walk away right now."

Lauren sighed. "All right, Cara. I promise. I promise to give Aerie to Liam."

"Good." Cara sighed. "I have no choice but to trust you anyway, troubling as that thought may be."

"Spare me your moral judgment, Cara, and tell me your plan."

Cara sighed. "You have no time to waste. I think Peter plans to push forward with development, whether he has the prototype or not. You need to convince Liam of three things: first, to take the software; second, to develop Aerie as quickly as possible; and third, to keep the whole matter quiet. Make sure he understands Windwear is Aerie's rightful owner and Pyramid holds no rights at all. And don't mention that law of the jungle crap. If there is even a question in Liam's mind any other rights exist, he won't go forward until he makes sure the path is clear."

"What do you mean?"

"I mean if Liam is not sure Windwear holds ironclad rights to Aerie, he'll try to clear up any questions first. He won't develop Aerie under a cloud of suspicion. It's too important to him. He'll go to Peter in good faith, tell him he has the software, and try to work a deal. And Peter will steamroll him. He'll demand Liam give him the software in order to negotiate a new contract. He'll tell Liam Pyramid must retain custody of the software until the project is complete. Since that is the normal way projects work, Liam will turn over a copy. Then Peter will stall Liam's project and quietly develop Aerie for Pyramid. Windwear will lose big."

"If that happens, we would have a copy, too. Windwear would still be able to proceed with development."

"Are you kidding? Liam's only advantage is that Pyramid is starting at zero. Pyramid has no documentation, no organizational information, no prototype, nothing. Peter controls the best systems people in the business, but they can't write a system they don't know anything about. If Liam gives Peter a copy of the software, his advantage is gone. Plus, once Peter realizes Liam has Aerie, he'll do everything he can to prevent Windwear from going forward with its development effort. He will use every means possible to stop him. He'll sue. Or steal Windwear's copy. Or try to sabotage Windwear's efforts. Be careful of Peter. He's not trustworthy."

"You're right, that's exactly what Liam would do." Lauren closed her eyes thinking. "Let's take a step back for a minute. How do you propose I explain to Liam that I got hold of the software in the first place? In a way that won't make him go to Peter to try to clear up any questions."

"That's a good question. I've been thinking about the best way to handle that. I think you should tell him you found Aerie."

"Found it?" Lauren laughed derisively. "You think he'll believe me?"

"It's the least risky explanation. You probably haven't heard the news yet, but Peter put out the word I stole Aerie."

"What?" Lauren said in surprise.

"He plans to press charges. How do you think Liam will react if he finds out he received Aerie from Cara Larson, the soon-to-be felon? Believe me, it will be worse than how he'll react to questionable ownership rights." Cara shook her head. "No, I think you should leverage Peter's story a different way. Tell him, you came to my office. We argued. You spotted the software while I was packing my things, and you took it. Be matter of fact. Don't overdramatize. Just tell him and quickly move on to explain Peter's plans. When he understands Peter's intentions, he won't feel obligated to tell Peter anything."

"All right, Cara. I agree, that's the best approach, but it won't be easy. From what you're telling me, you have no actual proof against Peter. I'm going to have a hell of a time convincing Liam not to talk to him."

"You must, Lauren. Find a way." Lauren nodded. "Then we agree? You tell Liam you found the software. You convince him he's the rightful owner, and you make sure he understands Peter's plans."

"Agreed."

"Good. Now, I need to go through several issues. They're important, so pay attention. Possession of the prototype doesn't guarantee Windwear a victory. You hold, at best, a three-month lead over Pyramid, and Peter will work the team like mad to catch up once he realizes he doesn't have the prototype.

"The packet contains my notes about how to finish Aerie. You should connect with a technology consulting company to help you get to market. Cole Martin is the best. If you can't get them, try Sidwell Parker. I provided a complete list if you need more names." Lauren nodded.

"Next, if you want to thwart Pyramid's chances and buy yourself more time, do everything you can to hire Mike Taylor away from Pyramid. Check his noncompete clause carefully. Pyramid makes its employees sign a document saying they will not work in the same markets or product lines for nine months. Mike might not be able to work on Aerie, but he could free Paul up by taking on other development projects. And Pyramid wouldn't be able to use him on its own development effort. You wouldn't be sorry. He's one of the best."

Cara paused, catching her breath, mentally clicking through her list. "For God's sake, keep the development effort quiet. If Peter finds out Liam has Aerie, he'll go after Windwear with a vengeance."

"You've said that about fifty times Cara. I get the picture. Anything else?"

"One more thing. At some point during development, perhaps even now, you should apply for the patent to Aerie. Don't bother with copyright; the rights aren't strong enough. Being first with the patent will allow you to sue Pyramid if they come up with a product even similar to Aerie. You'd know more about that sort of thing than I would."

"Right. Patent, not copyright. Anything else?"

"No. All the instructions are in the envelope. Keep them safe. If Peter ever sues, this is your evidence Windwear is Aerie's rightful owner."

Lauren nodded and eyed Cara suspiciously. "Why are you doing this, Cara?"

"What do you suggest I do?" Cara asked impatiently. "Give Peter the software? Over my dead body. Give it to Fleet? Fleet can't develop Aerie as long as FIT is in development. No, Windwear is the only choice. Liam needs the revenue from Aerie to fund his expansion plans. Besides, it was his idea in the first place."

"You could keep Aerie for yourself."

Cara looked at Lauren in distaste. "No. I've made other plans."

"You're an idiot, Cara. You don't fool me for a minute. I can see you're in love with Liam Scofield."

"What?" Cara asked incredulously.

"Don't give me that innocent look, Cara. You think you can win him over by giving him Aerie? It won't work." Lauren laughed. "I'll play your game. I'll give Aerie to Liam. I'll tell him a convincing story and make sure he's grateful. To me. In fact, he'll be so grateful he might even make our partnership more ... er ... permanent."

"What do you mean? I haven't known Liam long, but I do know he's quite protective of Windwear. He would never share ownership of his company with anyone. Not even with brilliant lawyers who luck into getting their hands on important pieces of software."

"I wasn't talking about Windwear. At least not directly."

"What—" Cara stopped and stared at Lauren. "Oh, I understand. You mean you're going to marry him."

"Let's say I wouldn't refuse if he asked me. After all, if my plans come through as expected, he'll be worth a lot of money. And I can be ... persuasive."

"Yes, you can. Do you love him, Lauren?"

"Love him? What's love? Liam suits my needs. He'll be worth millions. He's good looking. He'll be great in bed—"

"Ooh, you're losing your touch, Lauren. You led me to believe that momentous event had already occurred."

"Well ... er ... I ..." Lauren stammered. "I mean—"

"Forget it. Don't bother to add any more lies to your list. You told me what I needed to know."

Cara reached into her nylon bag, pulled out the envelope, and handed it to Lauren. "I don't admire blind ambition, Lauren. I've seen it destroy too many people. In this case, I'm counting on yours to see this thing through." She paused, suddenly weary. "I hope you get what you want, Lauren. I hope you make Windwear a huge success. I hope you make a ton of money from the IPO. And if Liam decides the price to pay for all your efforts is to marry you, well, that's his choice." She released her hand from the packet. "Liam said you were good, Lauren. In fact, he said you were brilliant. Don't prove him wrong on this one." With those words, Cara turned and left the room.

Mike opened the door to the fire escape, and he and Cara stepped onto the sidewalk. "Please tell me what's going on."

Cara shook her head. "No. The best thing for you is to know nothing. Then you'll be able to answer Peter's questions honestly."

"What kind of questions will he be asking?"

"You heard the rumors. He's on a witch-hunt. You'd better stay out of the way or you'll be burned at the stake too. Trashing one career is enough for today. I don't want to take you down with me."

Mike couldn't hide his troubled expression. "Go talk to him, Cara. Ozzie is a jerk and a complete loser, but he listens whenever money is involved. Even your most conservative estimates on Aerie will make his eyes pop out. Hell, he'll be the big winner in this thing, but he needs us to make it work. You need to convince him. You can't just leave like this."

"I tried to. He wasn't exactly in a listening mood."

"Then I'll talk to him. Someone needs to explain to him the utter stupidity of letting you go—"

"No, Mike." Cara made an effort to steady her tone. "I'll tell you what. Maybe you're right. Maybe I'm overreacting. Give me a few days, and I'll call Peter again when things have calmed down."

Mike breathed a sigh of relief. This was the old Cara coming through. Reasonable. Tough. Relentless. "Okay, but I mean what I said. If you don't talk to him, I will. You watch. This whole thing will blow over. You'll be back at Pyramid as soon as Ozzie realizes he can't build Aerie without you."

"Of course, you're right. Everything will be fine." Cara reached up, wrapped Mike in a fierce hug, and kissed his cheek. "Thank you, Mike."

He gave her an exaggerated cringe. "Cara, you're getting mushy on me. You know I hate that."

"All right, all right. I'll talk to you later." She kissed his cheek once more before she let him go. Then she smiled and waved and hurried down the street.

Mike watched her leave. "Three days," he said to himself. "She'll be back in three days. A week at the outside."

Chapter 23

"Mike, do you have a minute?" Liam stood at the entrance to Mike's cubicle.

"Sure." Mike looked up from the paper he was studying. "This whole day is shot to hell anyway. Why not?"

"Can we talk? Somewhere … private?"

"We can go to the conference room. God knows, no one's going to need it for the rest of the day."

"What do you know about all this, Mike?" Liam asked as they walked down the corridor.

"Me? You're asking me?" Mike flipped on the light in the conference room, closed the door, and plopped into the chair at the head of the table. "You tell me. You talked to Cara. And Peter. I imagine you know more about what's going on than I do. Tell me, what did the great Oz have to say?"

"He said Cara lied. To you. To me. To everyone." A stiff silence filled the room. Cara's words flashed through Mike's head. Witch-hunt. "Peter never approved Aerie. Cara pursued its development without his permission and against his wishes. When he found out, he made her remove the software from the network. When she announced Aerie was out of scope and insinuated Peter was to blame, he had no choice but to fire her."

After the first jolt of surprise, Mike didn't even hesitate. He laughed. "That's a bunch of horse hockey, and you know it. Do you even know Cara? Obviously not. If you did, you'd understand by now she's incapable of lying. Whenever she tries to lie her face gets all red, and her tongue gets all tangled up, and she shifts her feet from side to side like a kid who's been out playing too long and needs to pee something fierce. Cara just isn't capable of lying." He held up his hand. "I know, definitely a disadvantage in this business. Besides, it makes no sense at all. There's not one reason why she would do such a thing." He stopped. "Did Ozzie give you a reason?"

Liam shook his head. "He's initiating an investigation. He'll press charges if he finds evidence of criminal behavior."

"Well, I guess that shouldn't come as a surprise."

"What do you mean?"

Mike handed Liam the sheet of paper he'd been looking at earlier. "This e-mail came over the network about an hour ago. I wondered why Peter was treating Cara like a hardened criminal. Now I understand. He's just making his case."

Liam took the paper from Mike's hand. "Relieved immediately of all duties ... Locks will be changed ... Passwords will be modified ... Anyone who has had any contact with Cara Larson in the past six weeks will be interviewed ... Further contact with her is prohibited ..."

"After a poisonous gem like this, the truth doesn't even matter. A little innuendo is enough to send tongues wagging. The rumors will be flying now. In a few days, the damage will be done. Cara will be blackballed from every position in Portland, possibly the entire industry. Not officially, of course, but effectively. And if this doesn't do the trick, the formal investigation should finish her off." Mike glared at Liam. "Do you really think Cara would have taken such a risk?"

"She's been under a lot of stress. Maybe it was too much."

"Oh, give me a break. Cara's one of the toughest people I know. Are you telling me you actually believe Peter? You believe Cara's been lying for six weeks?"

"Mike, I'm not sure what to believe. That's why I wanted to talk to you."

"Fat lot of good it's doing. You don't believe me any more than you'd believe Cara."

"Maybe I should talk to her—"

"Now, that's a brilliant strategy. Talk to the one person who actually knows what's going on. I knew you were the head honcho over at Windwear for a reason—"

"Liam! Here you are." The door to the conference room opened, and Lauren hurried in. "I've been looking everywhere for you. We'd better hurry if we're going to catch our flight."

Liam stood up. "I'm not going. I need to find Cara."

Lauren's face tightened, but her voice remained calm. "You can't do that. We can't let this opportunity slip away. I was on the phone for days arranging meetings with the Taiwanese conglomerates. You can't cancel without any notice and for no good reason."

"No good reason? I have good reason, Lauren. I can't go to Taiwan and open up negotiations for business I'm unable to pursue. Without Aerie, we can't even consider expanding operations or pursuing the IPO. And after the meeting with Peter, I don't think we have much hope of getting the software any time soon."

Lauren smiled. "Things might not be as bad as you think."

"No. They're probably worse."

"Maybe not. While you talked to Peter, I had a chance to do some research. I came up with a few ideas—"

"I bet you did," Mike said under his breath.

Lauren and Liam both whipped their heads around. "What did you say, Mike?" Liam asked.

"You don't know? Oh, that's right, you were in talking to Oz. While you were busy listening to Peter's horse poop, Cara and Lauren—"

"Mike." Lauren's voice cut in so stridently, Mike stopped in midsentence. "I understand you're upset about Cara being fired, but you can't blame me or Liam or anyone else. I read Peter's memo. She brought this on herself."

"Let him speak, Lauren. What about Cara and Lauren, Mike?"

"Well, they met in the—"

"Mike's confused," Lauren interrupted again, this time shooting Mike a murderous glance. "I did see Cara before she left, but she refused to speak to me. Just walked out the door with her nose in the air. I spent the last hour in Pyramid's library trying to come up with a legal way to get us out of this mess." She turned a radiant smile on Liam as Mike choked. "I think I found one."

"You did? What did you find?"

"Liam, we don't have time to discuss this matter right now, and even if we did, I don't think we should talk here at Pyramid."

Liam glanced between Mike and Lauren. Indecision was written in every line of his face. "Mike, do you have any idea where Cara is? I need to talk to her before I go—"

"There isn't time," Lauren cut in. "We can't miss out flight. You can call her from the airport."

Liam looked at his watch. "All right, Lauren. I'll call her from the airport." He turned once more to Mike. "If you talk to her, tell her I'll call her as soon as I can." Lauren cast a triumphant sneer at Mike as she followed Liam out the door.

Mike stared for a moment at the empty doorway. He tried desperately to understand how the last three hours fit together. Cara tossing the bombshell at the review. Then getting canned. The secret meeting between Lauren and Cara. The poison email from Peter. The investigation. The witch-hunt. The events swirled in his brain, but he couldn't piece them together. Lauren knew something, but she wasn't telling. She wasn't telling Mike. And she wasn't telling Liam. Now that didn't make sense. Big surprise. Nothing made sense. "I hope you know what you're doing, Cara," he said to himself, "because I sure don't."

Liam left for Taiwan with his world in a shambles. He half expected the earth to crack into a million pieces as the plane lifted from the runway, trapping him up in the sky, stranded forever in a flying hell, like some doomed character in a dime-store horror novel.

He called Jared Dafoe, his outside counsel, as soon as he arrived at the airport, and instructed him to review the FIT contract. Liam would learn tomorrow if they could legally wrest Aerie away from Pyramid.

He tried to call Cara, too, but he hadn't been able to reach her. Her cellular was off. The line at her mother's house was busy. Busy every single time he dialed.

They were halfway across the Pacific when Lauren touched his arm. "Liam, we should talk." He started at the sound of her voice. He glanced at his watch. They had been flying for four hours, and neither had spoken a word.

"Yes, I suppose we do. You said you had an idea to get Aerie back." His voice sounded flat, and somehow he couldn't drum up any enthusiasm for that mass of electronic instructions once so bright with promise. "Some complicated legal maneuver, you said."

Lauren smiled at him with a mixture of triumph and pity. She pulled a battered manila envelope from her briefcase. Liam saw Peter Whittington's name scrawled in Cara's distinctive hand across the front. Lauren placed the envelope in his hand. "No legal maneuver necessary, just some good old-fashioned luck. In your hands, you hold the key to Windwear's future. Behold, Aerie!"

Liam stared at Lauren, then down at the envelope. "What do you mean, Aerie?"

"You should never underestimate me, Liam. Do you think I would have let you walk out of Pyramid today if I thought Aerie was lost?" He stared at her blankly. "Everything is here to go forward with development. Data model, process flows, project plan, timeline, even Cara's notes on how to proceed. With this information, you should have no trouble developing Aerie."

He was lost in a fog. Aerie. Here. In his hands. "How the hell ...?"

The shock must have registered on his face, because Lauren smiled and kissed him on the cheek. "We legal types aim to please."

When he finally found his voice, he asked the first question he could actually capture amidst the swirling thoughts racing through his mind. "How did you get this?"

"It's not important. What's important is you have Aerie and you can continue with its development."

"Tell me how you got this, Lauren."

"You're probably better off if you don't know, Liam. Trust me."

Liam stared at her in surprise, then quietly handed the envelope back to her. "I want you to contact Peter Whittington when we land. Tell him we obtained a copy of Aerie and we want to open negotiations to purchase it. We'll include fair compensation for Pyramid's efforts to date and a provision that we will fully cooperate with his investigation, as long as we are allowed to proceed with development without delay."

Lauren's eyes widened. One point for Cara Larson, she thought. "You would be making a mistake, Liam. We can't be sure Peter will sell Aerie to us in our tight time frame. Or that he'll even sell Aerie to us at all. We can't take the risk."

"Nor can we risk keeping software that doesn't rightfully belong to us."

"But it does belong to you. Pyramid holds no ownership rights to Aerie. Pyramid has a custodial right to hold software during a project, but since Aerie is no longer part of FIT, Pyramid holds no ownership rights at all."

"Peter would disagree. He is pressing charges against Cara for stealing the software. He must think he has some rights—" Liam stopped suddenly. "Is that where you got the software? From Cara?"

"Not exactly."

"Where did you get it?"

Lauren went silent.

"Lauren? Where did you get it?"

She took a deep breath. "I found it."

"You found it? You *found* it?"

Lauren nodded. "That's right."

"Where, by chance, did you find it?"

"In Cara's office."

"In Cara's off—"

"Before you jump to any wild conclusions, Liam, let me explain. When you and Paul met with Peter, I went to talk to Cara."

"So Mike told the truth. You did see her. You spoke to her? When the security guards were in her office?"

"Er ... yes. I persuaded them to let me speak to her alone for a few minutes. Her office was a mess. She was at the bookcase, packing up her books, when I spotted the envelope on her desk. I didn't know for sure it was Aerie, but I had my suspicions. I slipped the envelope into my handbag and hoped she didn't notice."

"So, you stole it."

"Listen, Liam, this is important. Cara and I argued. She screamed and threw a fit and told me to get out of her office. When I refused, she taunted me. She told me I was a fool to think Windwear had a chance to develop Aerie." Her voice dropped lower. "Liam, Cara is planning to develop Aerie herself."

Liam sucked in his breath. "I don't believe you." It was the second time today he'd said those words.

"Why would I lie about this, Liam?"

"What happened next?"

She sighed and touched his hand. He brushed it away and stared out the window as she continued. "She told me, Liam. She told me she intended to take Aerie and double-cross both Windwear and Pyramid. She was upset. I don't think she meant to blurt her plans out so brazenly; she's too careful under normal circumstances. She tried to backtrack when she realized she said too much. Then she opened up her briefcase and began throwing her papers in. That's when I spotted the other envelope. It looked exactly like the one in my handbag. She had made two copies of Aerie." Lauren paused, as if remembering. "The security guards returned, then. I don't think they appreciated Cara's screaming. They made me leave, but before I did, she said one last thing. She said, 'I'll be in New York by tomorrow and a millionaire by the end of the summer. No one will be able to stop me.' She thought she had both copies of Aerie, Liam. I'm sure she did."

Liam's eyes narrowed. "Just a second. I thought Peter had Aerie."

"He probably does. It's possible multiple copies exist. What did Peter tell you?"

"He said he had Aerie, but he would need to complete both FIT and the investigation against Cara before he could sell it to us."

"Then they both have copies." Lauren tilted her head. "I admit Cara has played this well. Taking Aerie for her own, and tying Windwear and Pyramid up in legal knots. Not bad." She stopped and waited for Liam to say something. When he didn't, she leaned forward. "You must decide what to do, Liam. At least three copies of Aerie exist. Cara has one, Peter has one, and you have one. Peter doesn't have much room to maneuver, right now, but Cara does. If you want to help Windwear, you need to stop Cara and develop Aerie yourself." Liam stared out the window. "Did you hear me, Liam? You have several options. You can let Cara go ahead with her plans. Or you can develop Aerie yourself. Or you can—"

"Dammit, Lauren, I understand what the choices are. Give me a few minutes to think."

Lauren placed her hand on his arm, her voice sympathetic. "I'm sorry, Liam. I realize you cared for Cara, but you can never tell about people like her—"

"Not now, Lauren." He shook her hand away.

Lauren waited a long time for Liam to speak, but he never did. After several silent minutes, she shrugged her shoulders, pulled her briefcase onto her lap, and set to work on her preparations for the Taiwanese negotiations.

Liam turned out his light, stared at the evening sky, and tried to make sense of the day's events. He had walked into Pyramid this morning ready to propose to Cara Larson. Again. He had planned to ask her before he left for D.C., when he had given her the lilacs, but his plan had been blown to hell with Lauren's ill-timed phone call. The new plan was to ask her right after the review. He closed his eyes. Talk about things that had been blown to hell.

What was he supposed to believe? Or more accurately, *who* was he supposed to believe? Cara? Peter? Lauren? Mike? None of their stories meshed. One of them, maybe all of them, was lying.

He forced himself to think. Focus on the facts, he told himself, just the things he knew for sure. It was a short list. The only two facts he could absolutely rely on, were that Aerie had been thrown out of scope, and that three parties now had possession of the software. Peter had a copy. Cara had a copy. Now, he had a copy, too.

How should he proceed? Peter had no intention of selling the software to Windwear any time soon. That was clear from their meeting today. Liam thought Peter might be stalling in order to jack the price of Aerie up, but with the investigation of Cara thrown into the mix, he could not count on getting Aerie now. Was Lauren correct about the legal status of Aerie ? Was it true Pyramid had no rights to the software? If so, that meant Fleet and Windwear owned the software. And Fleet and Windwear could sue Cara if she tried to pursue its development.

What about Cara? Had she stolen Aerie for her own purposes? Peter said the software had no commercial possibilities, but Liam wasn't so sure. He had seen Cara's estimates. There was a lot of money to be made from Aerie. He could understand why she would be tempted to take Aerie. If she were that type of a person.

Liam sighed. Was she that type of a person? He would never have suspected Cara of such deceit. And not minor deceit. If Peter was telling the truth, Cara had lied from the first day they met. Was the woman he loved capable of such calculated deception?

A strange ache came with the thought. A familiar ache he remembered from a long time ago. He'd been down this road once before. He had tasted the bitterness of deceit. He remembered too well the despair of being used. It had taken a long time, but he had rebounded from the blow. Windwear had saved him once before. Windwear had been his solace when everything else crumbled around him. Now, Windwear's very survival was at stake.

He forced his mind away from questions and into resolve; away from emotion and into action. He needed to face facts. Cara Larson had taken Aerie. She had outfoxed Peter. She had lied to Liam. God, she had out-Jennifered

Jennifer, whom he considered to be the all time pro when it came to lies and deceit. He closed his eyes and leaned his head against the seat. If Peter and Lauren were right, if Cara intended to market Aerie and take the profits for herself, Windwear's future was at risk. In that case, only one path lay ahead.

He would develop Aerie. He would make it a good system. No, a great system. He would be the first to market. He would make a zillion dollars in the process. And he would save Windwear.

He would be patient and watch. If he discovered even a hint Cara was developing Aerie, he would not hesitate to attack. He would wrap her up in so many lawsuits she wouldn't know which way to turn. He would hire every expert in the industry to rip holes in her work. He would fight her over every customer and every piece of sales territory. He wouldn't stop until he won. The task wouldn't be easy; technology wasn't his strong suit. He would be playing in Cara Larson's sandbox, and she would be a formidable opponent. He didn't care. He would do what he needed to do.

He switched on the light and leaned over so his head practically touched Lauren's. "So, tell me, Lauren. How do we go about developing Aerie?"

She turned to him, a smile slowly spreading across her face. "Excellent decision, Liam."

There was one more thing he would need to do, Liam thought as Lauren opened the envelope and began her explanation.

He would need to fall out of love with Cara Larson.

Chapter 24

Liam stood on the balcony, leaned into the hot afternoon breeze, and hoped that somehow, miraculously, this eternal pounding headache would disappear. God, he was not the man he used to be. They had been in Taipei exactly four days, and he seriously doubted whether he could survive one more. Luckily, the arrival of the weekend spared him. He glanced at his watch. 4:00 p.m. Saturday.

He had been going nonstop since they arrived on Tuesday. Lauren scheduled a reception with the merger candidates that evening and individual half-day meetings each day for the rest of the week. What she failed to mention was the quaint custom the Taiwanese had of drinking themselves into the ground starting first thing in the morning. Lauren said they were "get acquainted sessions." Their hosts needed to observe Liam under many different conditions, she explained. They needed to assess his character, determine if they could trust him, and decide for themselves if they wanted to build a long-term business relationship with him. Liam suspected a different agenda. The strategy, he finally concluded, was for each company to present itself as the perfect candidate, and then get him so drunk he would be in no shape to communicate with the next candidate in line. It was effective. Other than a hazy notion of who was who, he didn't remember much any of them said. He shook his head and immediately regretted the action as the pounding began again.

His hosts hadn't talked business at all. Instead, they insisted they play golf or ride horses or drive racecars at one of the little motorways dotting the countryside. They made a point of doing "American" activities, which made Liam laugh. He had never done any of those activities in America. Especially golf. He hardly even saw the ball after the first few rounds. Funny thing, even with a score of 3,000 over par, he always managed to win. He wished he remembered more of those games. His hosts must have had to make some extremely creative shots to lose so badly. He smiled despite his aching head. Overall, he had done well. Somehow he managed to play the proper role of polite guest, drink the copious amounts of liquor offered by his hosts, and remain lucid enough to get a commitment from each host to provide the two things he wanted: certain operational information, and a free weekend to review it.

Lauren wasn't invited to the sessions. In fact, his hosts were horrified when he suggested she accompany them. For all their civility toward him, they were adamant she not be included. She was angry at first. She hated to be left out of any negotiation. However, the snub turned out to be a stroke of good luck. She volunteered to compile the operational data as it dribbled in. Yes, good luck indeed, because Liam was kept so busy he had little time to study anything in detail. Until now.

The knock on the door brought the pounding back to his head. He reentered the suite. The glaring artificial lights blotted out the brightness of the sun shining on the sparkling Keelung River and the cityscape outside. "I'm here. Four o'clock. As you requested." Lauren was wearing a striking black and white skirt topped by a silky black blouse. Her lips and fingernails were painted a bright scarlet and contrasted sharply with her dark hair.

"Come in, Lauren." He held the door open as she entered. "Everything is ready. Let's get to work. Did you bring the data?"

Her smile froze. "I thought we were going to take in the sights. We can spend tomorrow reviewing the data. You need a break. We need a break."

Liam looked up in surprise. "I can't take in the sights, Lauren. I have a ton of work to catch up on. I only have this the weekend to get though all the operational data before our meetings start in earnest on Monday." He stopped. "You're right, though. You've worked hard all week. Go ahead and take the evening off. Just leave the information with me."

She hesitated for a moment, and then sighed. "What's first on your list?"

He smiled. "Catch me up on where you are with the operational data."

"Actually, I completed the analysis." She gave him a satisfied smile.

"You did?" he asked in surprise. "How did you manage to finish so quickly?"

"I'm extremely organized."

He nodded. "Indeed. May I take a look?"

"The reports are in my room. Let me get them."

She returned to his suite a few minutes later with several file folders. "Thanks." Liam reached for the files while his computer hummed to life. "Tell me what the data revealed. Is there anyone we want to work with?"

"I compiled everything you need in a file for each company. The data is sorted, prioritized, and analyzed. My summaries are on the first page of each file." She handed him a slim folder. "Here are my final recommendations."

Liam opened the folder. He read the recommendations, and then turned to the individual file of the first company. He flipped through the detailed data. Income statement. Balance sheet. Calculated ratios covering every nuance of the company's debt and equity structure. Financial valuations over a range of investment scenarios. Liam studied the figures. He flipped through the pages in puzzlement, and then opened each file in turn. All of them held the same type of data. "Lauren, where are the operational analyses I asked for?"

"I think you'll find everything you need," she said with a reassuring smile.

Liam frowned at the documents. "Where is the operating data? I can't go forward without the operating information. Did you have trouble getting it? None of these companies gave me any indication of a problem except ..." He closed his eyes and reached through his hazy memory. "Except maybe Wangchao."

"Of course not, Liam. They made the data available, but I didn't need it. You shouldn't waste your time looking over a mountain of data when our decision is clear by looking at the financial figures alone."

"You what?" he asked in disbelief.

She smiled at him as if he were a slow student who didn't understand the lesson on the first try. She leaned an elbow on the table and removed the report from his hands. As she did, the deep V of her blouse hung low, giving Liam a thorough view of her breasts. Her hands clung to his for several seconds as she clasped the report. A tinge of color washed across his face as he lifted his eyes to stare above her shoulder. Lauren flipped the pages of the report. She stood up and came around to stand next to him, bent down, and placed the report in front of him. "It's right here. Wangchao is obviously the best candidate." She brushed her thigh against his arm as she bent lower. "Their balance sheet is strong. They are well capitalized. Their production costs are low, and they earn the highest profits. Just look at their debt-to-equity ratio."

Liam stood up abruptly and strode across the room. "I need the operational data, Lauren." He turned and caught the flash of impatience in her eyes. "You've worked hard to compile this information. I appreciate your efforts, but your analysis tells only half the story. You explained the state of each business. I need to know how a company *does* business. I need to know their return statistics, their defect rate, and their customer service ratings. I need information that tells me how they do business on a day-to-day basis."

"Liam, you're talking about a massive amount of information. I would need weeks to analyze all that data."

"No. The list I gave you contains the key information I need. It should only take a few days to analyze." He shook his head. "I thought this is what you were working on all week. Damn. Now I'm really going to be behind schedule."

Lauren bristled. "You're wrong, Liam. Look at the numbers. No one is even close to Wangchao. No amount of operating information could make up for its strengths. You would be crazy to choose anyone else."

"You're missing the point, Lauren. This isn't about financing or return on investment or debt-to-equity ratios. It's about putting my name on a product someone else will be making for me. I've never done this before, and I want to be damned sure I choose the right partner to work with. If Wangchao is the lowest-cost producer but makes defective products, Wangchao won't suffer. Windwear's name will be on the product, and Windwear will lose customers and respect in the marketplace. If I choose to pay a little extra for good quality and sacrifice some short-term profits to make Windwear stronger in the future, I will. My short-term projections were conservative precisely for this reason."

He walked back to the table and lifted the folders off the desk. He thumbed through them. "Several of these companies meet my financial criteria. The operating data will allow me to make the final decision."

Lauren stood up and faced Liam. "I think it's time you realize you'll need to run your business differently from now on. You can't make these decisions unilaterally anymore. In two months, when Windwear goes public, the decisions will no longer be yours alone. You'll still be president and CEO, but you will have to answer to your shareholders. Your investors are not paying sixteen dollars a share because you like Lu Jiating's return policy or Hsin's customer service rating. Don't fool yourself into thinking they're interested in Windwear because it makes good hiking boots or will make good camping gear. They're investing in Windwear because they want to make money. The more profitable you are, the richer they get. You want to think long term? Well, from now on, long term is defined as a three-month quarter. You make your quarterly numbers, you're rewarded. You don't make your quarterly numbers, you're history. Your stock price is all that matters now."

"Do you believe that, Lauren?"

"The point isn't whether I believe it. It's the cold, hard reality of business. And you had better get used to it."

"No, Lauren. I've been fighting that "cold hard reality of business" ever since I started Windwear. It's nothing but a myth financial whiz-bang geniuses spout to cover up the fact that it's a lot easier to sit back in their glitzy offices, look at a few numbers that are nothing more than legal sleight of hand, and pass judgment on a company's future as if they were God." He dropped the files on the desk. "I agreed to go public because it's the most efficient way to raise money for my expansion plans. I did not agree to hand over control of Windwear. If giving up control were part of the deal, I would have killed the process a long time ago. I will not give up control of Windwear, and I will not allow anyone to dictate to me how to run my business. Not a bunch of shareholders and not my attorney. Do you understand?"

Lauren stared at him in surprise. "Investors invest to make money, Liam. Their job is to maximize stock price."

"My job is to maximize the long term value of the company. If I need to sacrifice short term profits for the long term health of the company, that's what I'll do."

"That's not the way things work."

"Well, that's the way things ought to work. And that's the way they are going to work with Windwear."

"You're wrong. Your shareholders won't stand for it."

"We'll see. In the meantime, I want to look at the operational data."

She shrugged. "Okay. The files are in my room. I'll get them." She turned to leave and as she did, she murmured under her breath, "Damn. I'll have to think of something else."

"Something else?" Liam asked in puzzlement. "What are you talking about, Lauren?"

"Oh, nothing. I was just thinking about how to analyze the data." She gave him a radiant smile. "Why don't we do start on this tomorrow, Liam? You need a break. You never lectured me before. Come on. Let's go out, find a fabulous restaurant, celebrate with champagne—"

At the mention of alcohol, Liam groaned. "No way. Not for me. I have two days to get through all the data. I need to get started right away."

"All right. I suggest a compromise. Dinner first. Here. I'll call room service and order something special. Then we can get to work."

"Okay, you win. Dinner first. But no champagne."

The lights were low, and the music was playing softly when Liam came out from a long hot shower that restored his good humor, if not his clear head. "What's all this?" Lauren was standing by the room service cart pouring two tall glasses of champagne.

"I know you said you didn't want any champagne, but we should celebrate. It isn't every day you become a player on the international business scene."

"Well, until I get a look at the operational data. I'm not sure I'll become one. I'm not convinced manufacturing here is much better than manufacturing in Portland, despite the cost advantages you keep telling me about."

"Don't say that. You promised to keep an open mind."

Liam settled in his chair and poured himself a glass of water. "I promise I'll reserve judgment until I examine the operational data."

Lauren sat next to him and sipped her champagne. "You know, for all your talk about being conservative, I think you're taking a big risk."

"Oh? In what way?" Liam asked with curiosity.

"You're not willing to go with Wangchao, which enjoys the lowest costs and best profit margins. Instead, you seem bent on choosing a high cost option and bridging the funding gap with revenue from Aerie. Now that's a risky strategy. You're not in the software business. What makes you think you can build and market Aerie?"

"True, developing Aerie is a risk, but it's a calculated one. We have the prototype and the road map on how to proceed. Paul has been involved in the process from the beginning. If we hire Mike Taylor and contract with a consulting company to market Aerie, we stand an excellent chance of making Aerie a success."

"So why not hedge your bets? Why not go with Wangchao and guarantee high profits. If Aerie doesn't work out, Windwear is still protected. If Aerie does work out, well, we'll be even more profitable. Better yet, why don't you let me run Windwear while you develop Aerie? It's the perfect solution. We would increase the chance of success in both areas."

"It *is* the perfect solution, Lauren, but you have the players in the wrong place. You're right. Windwear isn't in the software business. That's not our strong suit, but Paul is an expert. He'll have no trouble leading the development effort. Paul will develop Aerie, and *I* will run Windwear. That's my strong suit."

"Where do your plans leave me?" Lauren asked, a frown on her face.

"Where you ought to be. You're Windwear's attorney, Lauren. A good one. You answer our questions. You keep us on the right track. You clear the way so we can do our jobs. That's your strong suit."

"But Liam, you aren't letting me be your attorney. You need my advice to run Windwear, especially now that we're moving into a changing financial environment, but you don't listen to me."

"Not true, Lauren. I always listen to you. It is my responsibility to listen to your advice, but I am not required to follow it without question. I have heard you loud and clear on the subject of Windwear's finances. Many times. It's fair to say we disagree profoundly on how to approach Windwear's future as a public company. You also misunderstand my position on Wangchao. I'm not opposed to Wangchao as a production partner. If the company meets my standards for quality and service, and I decide I can work with them, I may well choose them. But if the data shows they don't meet my criteria, nothing will make me choose them. I won't know which choice to make until I analyze the operational data."

Lauren frowned again. "I think something else is going on."

"Oh? What else do you think is going on?"

"I think you're letting emotion get in the way of rational decision making."

It was Liam's turn to frown. "What do you mean?"

"I think you're bent on revenge. You're determined to punish Cara Larson for taking Aerie, and you're putting Windwear at risk, as a result."

Liam stood up quickly. Her name, thrown out so carelessly when he had spent all week trying to repress it, was a jolt. He walked to the balcony, breathed deeply in the evening air, and tried to push away the thought of Cara Larson.

Lauren walked up beside him and placed a scarlet-tipped hand on his arm. "I'm sorry, Liam. I didn't mean to upset you, but you must face this. Cara betrayed you. She betrayed Windwear. You're angry. You have every right to be. But you can't put the company at risk because you want revenge."

He stared out into the steamy night. "I don't want revenge," he said tightly. "I've thought this through. Developing Aerie is the right thing to do."

"This is not just about Aerie," she said softly. "Don't you understand? You don't, do you? You're completely blinded by Cara. You don't see what's right in front of you …"

"What's right in front of me?" He turned to face her. "What are you talking about?"

"I'm talking about the fact that you've been looking at the wrong woman. I'm the one who's been on your side, Liam. I'm the one who's been here for you, not Cara. I didn't cheat you. I didn't lie to you. But you don't even notice me."

Liam stared at her in surprise. "Lauren, I … I'm not sure what to say …"

"You don't need to say anything. Just open your eyes and look. Can't you see how good we would be together?"

"Lauren, we are good together. You're a fabulous attorney. You've helped the company tremendously."

"I'm not talking about the company. I'm talking about us. You and me. You have no idea how much I care about you, Liam. She opened his arms and walked into them. "Don't you know I can be more than your attorney? Let me show you. Let me show you not all women are like Cara Larson." She wrapped her arms around his neck, lifted her face to his, and kissed him.

Liam closed his eyes. God, he wished his head would stop banging. He could feel Lauren's body pressed against his, could feel his weakness in response. Maybe Lauren was right, he thought as his head pounded. Maybe he was trying to punish Cara at the expense of Windwear. What he really needed to do was forget Cara Larson ever existed.

Lauren was kissing him, her mouth insistent and probing. God, he thought through the haze of his throbbing temples, maybe a night with another woman was what he needed to forget Cara once and for all. Maybe that's what it would take to fall out of love with the woman who would not get out of his head. Almost hesitantly he pressed his lips to Lauren's.

Lauren responded to his kiss eagerly. "Make love to me, Liam."

Dammit, Liam thought in frustration. This is what he needed. Simple. Satisfying. Uncomplicated. His kiss deepened. Yes, this was what he wanted. He did not want to remember Cara. Did not want to remember the scent of lilacs. Did not want to remember her soft smile or the way she clung to him as if she would never let him go. Did not want to remember the soft bewildered gaze she gave him after he kissed her the first time. "Lauren ..." He held her away from him and looked into her eyes.

No soft smile. No bewildered gaze. Just open invitation. And triumph. "I tried to tell you before," she whispered to him. "I asked you not to leave me in New York, but all that bitch had to do was cry a few crocodile tears when her mother died and off you ran."

Liam reacted as if he'd been hit. The images slammed into his brain with the force of a cannon. Of Cara, and the scent of lilacs. Of the crazy abandon with which she kissed him the day he gave them to her. Of the way he fumbled with the ring in his pocket. Of the way he felt when she was in his arms, like he never wanted to leave her side. He dropped his hands and took a step back. "Lauren, this is a mistake. We need to stop."

Lauren's triumphant expression cracked slightly. "Stop? Why in God's name should we stop?"

"This ... this isn't a good idea. I'm sorry, but I want you to leave. Now."

"Liam, don't you realize I'm not your enemy?" Her voice was soft. "I'm not going to betray you. You can trust me. I won't hurt you. I'm not Cara—"

"Please leave, Lauren."

She hesitated a moment, eying him intently. "All right. I'll go for now. But remember what I told you. I'm on your side. I'm the right woman for you." She reached up and kissed him softly on the cheek. "My offer remains open. You know where to find me when you change your mind." She blew him a kiss as she walked out the door.

Liam snapped the pencil and threw the pieces against the wall. They landed in a pile with the other three pencils he had hurled earlier. Damn. He could not seem to focus on the data in front of him. Here it was, one o'clock in the morning, and he had only finished the operational analysis for four companies. He opened another file, but for the life of him, he could not concentrate.

He stood up and walked to the balcony. He watched the muted traffic weave through the streets. Its distant buzz matched perfectly the turbulence in his brain. His mind careened over the events of the evening. After several minutes, he left the balcony. With a sigh, he opened the door of his suite and walked to the room next door.

His knock was soft, his words softer. "Lauren, are you awake?"

The door opened in seconds. She stood in front of him, dressed in a silky red robe, her face flushed and triumphant. "Hello, Liam."

He hesitated for a second as she held the door open. He walked in and strode across the room. He heard the swish of silk as she followed him. Heard the slight flutter as it swayed in the breeze. He turned to face her. He saw the robe at her feet, and her naked, welcoming body reaching for him. "I knew you'd come."

He closed his eyes. With a deep sigh, he reached toward her.

Chapter 25

Liam grasped Lauren's shoulders and turned her gently away from him. He reached down, picked up the robe, and covered her shoulders. "Put this on, Lauren." He heard her gasp and waited several seconds while she jerkily thrust her arms through the holes and belted the robe around her waist. Liam felt self-contempt rise in his throat. He really messed this one up. He rejected her in the worst possible way. He did not want to see the look of shame and embarrassment on her face.

When she whirled around to face him, he saw neither shame nor embarrassment, but an anger so furious he took a step back in surprise. "I'm decent, now," she hissed.

"Lauren," he said awkwardly, "I'm sorry. I didn't mean to imply..."

"What did you come here to do, Liam, if not to sleep with me?" she asked sharply. "Why did you knock on my door in the middle of the night if you didn't come to drown your sorrows or satisfy your very *evident* physical needs."

"Lauren, I'm sorry. I told you—"

"Oh, shut up. What the hell do you want?"

Liam cleared his throat. "I thought about what you said about Aerie and Windwear and taking risks. I think you're right."

"Oh?" Her eyes were suddenly alert. "Do you want to sign with Wangchao?"

Her transformation from anger to interest was so immediate Liam was once more taken by surprise. "No, but I need you to go back to Portland. A flight leaves Taoyuan Airport at 6:00 a.m. I want you on it."

"What? You're sending me home? You're punishing me? Because I kissed you? Liam, you can't do that. Windwear's future depends on the deal we make here. You need me. You can't navigate these foreign negotiations alone. You can't—"

Liam held up his hand to stem her tirade. "Calm down, Lauren. Let me explain where I'm going with this." Lauren stopped, but her eyes still blazed angrily. "I think you're right about the risks associated with Aerie. We need to complete development and get to market as quickly as possible. I want you to go back to Portland and put the plans for Aerie in place. I want everything ready so that when I say the word, we can hit the ground running. I need you to do all the things we talked about. Apply for the patent, contact Cole Martin, hire Mike, start Paul working on a new security system. I know I can trust you to start the process and keep it quiet. I'll call Jared Dafoe and tell him to drop his research into the FIT contract."

"What about the negotiations? You need me to negotiate the joint venture contract."

"I can take care of them. The operational data is enlightening, and you've given me all the financial data I need. I'll handle the negotiations."

"No, Liam, you can't do this without me. You need to understand the financial impact of your decisions."

"Lauren, you've turned those numbers every which way possible. I am more than aware of the financial impact of my decisions."

"The investors' expectations need to be considered. They—"

"Relax. I told you, I've been the head of Windwear for a long time. I know what's good for the company."

"But—"

"No buts." Liam set his jaw firmly. "Your plane leaves in four hours. I'll take you to the airport." He walked to the door, then stopped and turned around. "One more thing. I want you to make preparations to sue Cara Larson if we discover she is developing Aerie."

"What?" Lauren asked in surprise.

"You heard me. Keep that quiet, too." He turned back toward the door. "I'll be by in one hour to take you to the airport."

Liam was nervous as he settled into the seat. He buckled the seatbelt, and then unbuckled it. Turned on the air vent, and then turned it off. Flicked on the reading light, and then flicked it off. He shook his head and tried to laugh, but found he couldn't. He needed to get hold of himself. This was going to be a long flight, and he would need his wits about him when he finally returned home.

His mind tumbled over the last two weeks. He couldn't believe how quickly they passed once he sent Lauren home and put his plans into action. It was as if he had wakened from a deep sleep to find himself in the middle of a boxing match.

He swept into the next round of meetings in steamy Taipei with a passion that surprised him. He left nothing to chance. He was relentless in negotiations, while somehow maintaining the facade of courtesy expected by his hosts. He showed off his newest product lines with a quiet intensity that immediately commanded attention. He dazzled Windwear's suitors with market estimates and profit projections so attractive, even he wanted to buy a Taiwanese corporation so he could invest in Windwear. Then he dug in his heels and refused to give an inch on product breadth, quality, or production levels.

He learned how to say no like his hosts did. "Maybe," he'd say with the hint of a scowl. "I'll think about it," he'd sidestep if anyone suggested a compromise in an area he deemed important. "That may be difficult," he'd say if they refused to accept using Aerie to provide production status.

He worked on the financial figures Lauren provided until he could summon the net present value of a consolidated investment under four alternative scenarios in his sleep. He developed options to foster growth while leaving firm control with Windwear. The polite affability and blinding stupor of the first week were forgotten in the relentless exchange of proposals. In the end, he got what he wanted. Exactly what he wanted.

During those first few days after Lauren left, he didn't even stop to sleep. Clarity of vision, adrenaline, and a mountain of work made sleep unnecessary. After a while he realized even a man on a mission must succumb to the weakness of rest. And weakness it proved to be. Because in those steamy, silent, midnight hours, right before he surrendered to sleep, that is when his heart betrayed his head. In those deep hours when he was too tired to think, when all he wanted to do was turn off his mind, he found it wide-awake and drifting toward Cara. His thoughts tortured him. He was a decisive man, for God's sake, but what confronted him in the darkness was as far from certainty as night was from day.

Cara Larson had invaded every part of him. He told himself he didn't love her, couldn't love her. But the thoughts that flung themselves around his head gave lie to his protest. From the first time they met, his life had taken a sharp turn directly out of his hands. He remembered the running light he invented. The sight of her dancing down the street in the rain had set off a storm of creativity within him. He had gone home and pulled out the old sewing machine he used to make his first pair of hiking boots. He tore up old flashlights and outdoor gear. He sewed and ripped and re-sewed all night. He'd hardly slept, anticipating the expression on her face when she opened it. He hadn't been disappointed. The simple delight in her smile warmed him in a way he hadn't felt in years.

He couldn't help kissing her after that. Despite all her babble about Pyramid and its rules. Especially because of her babble about Pyramid and its rules. The more she talked, the brighter the smile glowed behind her eyes, and the less he could resist her.

Memories flashed around him. He recalled how she agonized over her mother's illness. How she read to her mother on those warm summer evenings. How she comforted him after he received Mary's letter.

He sighed into the stale air of the plane. Lodged right up against those soft memories were harsh ones. He remembered their tense exchange after the review. Cara not only confirmed she knew Peter removed Aerie from scope, but she told him bluntly she had kept the fact from him. What had Peter told him? That Cara had lied; Peter had never approved Aerie. She didn't just lie, he thought; she lied from the first moment he had met her. Then there were Lauren's accusations. Cara told Lauren she took Aerie for her own personal gain.

Was that all that existed between Cara Larson and Liam Scofield? A lie where he hoped love would be? Deceit where he hoped devotion would be? He pressed his fingers over his eyes. Nothing made any sense. The data didn't add up. He believed in data. It was another rule he'd formulated along the way. The data would point to an answer, and not always the one suggested by intuition, as he discovered in his recent dealings in Taiwan.

In this case, the data was the problem. He looked at the data, all right. He studied it, analyzed it, mulled it over, and concluded it was overwhelmingly … inconclusive. For every one of Cara's lies, he found an example of honesty. For every moment of anger, he found one of compassion. For every question, he found a multitude of possible explanations. It was exhausting to constantly fight this battle between hope and hate and not ever know the truth. Time and again, he picked up the phone to call her. Time and again, he hung up without doing so.

As the days passed, the quicksand of uncertainty that so frustrated him crystallized into a resolute plan of action. There was too much doubt, he told himself, to accept the worst accusations without at least an explanation. And there was too much hope, he sighed, to give up without seeing her at least one more time. Just one look, he decided. Just one look was all he would need to determine if Cara Larson was telling the truth.

As he walked the teeming streets of Taipei, he mapped out his strategy. When he returned home, he would find her and discover the truth. If Peter and Lauren's accusations were true, he would follow through with his plan. He would stop Cara from developing Aerie. But he would gain no satisfaction in his victory. No joy. The price was already too high. He would not back down, though. He would not allow anyone to threaten Windwear.

He brought himself back to the present with a start. The flight attendant was asking if he wanted to watch a movie. The young man held out a set of headphones, a polite smile on his face. Liam shook his head and settled back in his seat. There was only one thing he had not accomplished during this trip to Taiwan, he thought as he closed his eyes.

He had not fallen out of love with Cara Larson.

Chapter 26

Staci turned from the file cabinet. "The distant traveler returns! Welcome home, Liam."

"Thanks, Staci. How bad is it?"

She smiled. "Oh, as bad as it usually is when you've been away from the office for three weeks." She handed him a two-inch stack of messages and a pile of ominous looking folders.

He grimaced. "Well, another few minutes can't hurt. Please hold all my calls. And no visitors for a half hour."

Staci gave him a mock salute. "Yessir, boss sir."

He laughed. "Clearly, I've been away too long. You've lost all deference to authority."

"Yessir. I mean, no sir."

He walked into his office and went directly to his desk. He just finished dialing Cara's number when he heard a soft shuffle near the window. Liam looked up. "Mike! I heard you joined us. Welcome aboard."

Mike walked over and stood directly in front of Liam. "Do you know where she is?"

Liam continued to hold the phone to his ear as he responded. "Do I know where who is?"

"Cara. Cara Larson. The woman you planned to talk to before you left town? The woman who was escorted from Pyramid three weeks ago? The woman who is now nowhere to be found?"

"What are you talking about, Mike?" Something was wrong, Liam thought. Something was very wrong.

"Tell me where she is, Liam. If anyone knows, you do."

No, Liam thought. This was all wrong. Her phone was ringing, and she was going to answer. Any second, she was going to pick up the phone and he would hear her voice and she would tell him the truth.

"Dammit, Liam. Did you hear me? Cara is gone. Missing. I can't find her anywhere. She's dropped off the face of the earth."

At that moment, the mechanical three-toned bell interrupted his call. "I'm sorry," the recording droned, "the number you have dialed is no longer in service." Liam stared at the phone as he slowly returned the receiver to its cradle.

"So, you haven't seen her either. Rats. Now I'm really worried."

"When did you last see her, Mike?"

"That last day at the office. The day of the review. I was worried about her. She told me she would wait a few days before she called Peter to ask for her job back. Things were crazy after the review. We had a hell of a time repairing the damage with Fleet. When I didn't hear from her after a week, I stopped by her place." His fingers thrust outward like an exploding bomb. "Poof. Gone. Her apartment was for rent. Her Mom's house was up for sale. No one had seen her. I talked to the real estate agent who was selling the house. He refused to give me a forwarding address or phone number." He peered at Liam. "Hey, are you all right?"

Liam nodded. "Go on."

"Well, I threatened him, of course. I told him I would sue. I told him I would beat it out of him. Turns out he didn't know anything. Her forwarding address was a PO box in Northeast Portland. Her phone number was an answering service. I hung around the post office for awhile, but the postmaster threw me out after three days. He thought I was stalking somebody. Anyway, she never came to pick up her mail. Not once.

"I searched everywhere. I called the police. They looked into it. Filed a report and everything. Said it seemed to them like she left of her own free will. They never even looked for her.

"I called the airlines, too. I made up this great story about how we were long lost twins separated at birth. I told them I'd tracked her halfway across the world to Portland. It did the trick. They looked, but she wasn't on any manifest on any of the airlines."

Mike noted the expression on Liam's face. "I know. I'm worried about her too."

Liam closed his eyes and ran his fingers through his hair. "It sounds to me like she took off and doesn't want to be found."

"Or she's afraid to be found. It's not like Cara to cut and run—"

Suddenly the door crashed open. "Liam, you're back!" Lauren rushed across the office and headed straight toward Liam.

Mike glanced at his watch. "Two minutes, twenty-five seconds, Lauren. What took you so long? I had you pegged as one of those under-one-minute women."

Lauren scowled at Mike. "What are you doing here? You need to leave. I need to talk to Liam. Alone."

"I bet you do. Sorry. I had an appointment. Did you?"

Liam dragged himself back from his own thoughts. "What's going on? You two sound like a pair of dogs fighting over a bone."

Lauren turned toward Liam with a brilliant smile. "I missed you, I couldn't wait to see you."

"Do you hand out barf bags with this speech?" Mike smirked.

Lauren scowled at him again. "Get out, Mike. Liam and I have business to discuss."

"On the contrary, Liam and I weren't finished with *our* business, so I think *you* should leave."

Liam cut in impatiently, "Would you two stop acting like children? I expect it from Mike, but Lauren, I'm surprised—"

"If I'd realized he was this annoying, I wouldn't have hired him."

"Tut, tut, tut, Lauren," Mike chided. "You're a lawyer. Windwear is an equal opportunity employer. You can't discriminate against people with a sense of humor."

"You son of a—"

Mike sighed and turned toward Liam. "I'm been trying my best to help where I can. I heard lawyers were genetically incapable of humor, but I've never seen more clear evidence of it than right here at Windwear."

Lauren turned exasperated eyes at Liam. "Don't let him bother you, Lauren. He takes a little getting used to. But he's right, we need to finish our discussion."

Her eyes narrowed. "I can hardly believe anything this little twerp has to say is more important than completing the merger details—"

Liam gave Lauren a measured glance, then opened his briefcase and handed her several files. "You'll find everything you need here. Review the terms of the agreement and start on the legal documents. I'll send you back to finalize the deal when the papers are ready."

Lauren's eyes glowed, her anger forgotten, as she opened the file with eager anticipation. "Did you sign with Wangchao? What are the terms? A joint venture? A wholly owned subsidary? Did you—"

"No, I signed with Hsin. As a backup supplier for our new Portland operations."

She stared at him in stunned surprise. "But Wangchao ... they had the best financial position. You were supposed to sign with them."

"No way, Lauren. Wangchao is a shady operation that cuts corners at every possible opportunity. I can't trust Windwear's reputation to them."

"But the investors expect—"

"Believe me, I'm protecting our investors with this decision. Wangchao would be a disaster for Windwear."

"This is a big mistake. Wangchao was the only chance we had to meet the profit projections expected by the investors."

Liam shook his head. "No, that's not true. I calculated everything. With the money we're getting from the offering, we can afford to triple the manufacturing capacity here in Portland. Hsin will tide us over until we're fully operational on this side. If the arrangement proves satisfactory, we'll pursue discussions to make the relationship more permanent."

"You'll kill the bottom line!"

"No, we're still within our projections. Remember, I made them conservative on purpose. I have plenty of room to maneuver."

"Liam, you're making a huge mistake. Cyclops will never accept this."

"Don't worry about the consortium. I have a five-year window before the voting stock converts and the consortium has any actual say in Windwear's operations. By then we'll be humming along fine."

"When did you tell Hsin I would be back?"

"As soon as you get them done. A week or two. They should be no big deal. Just some fancy purchase orders with a lot of restrictions."

Lauren fingered through the papers. "I can't believe you didn't sign with Wangchao."

"They're a bunch of snakes. I don't work with snakes."

Mike jumped in. "Right, Liam. No snakes. You choose to work with other types of reptiles."

"What the hell are you talking about, Mike?" Liam was getting tired of his childish sniping.

"Or maybe you don't like reptiles at all. Maybe you prefer working with rodents. That must be it. Do you like to work with rats, Liam?"

Lauren eyed Mike over the files. "I'll get to work on these files."

"That's it, scurry away, rat." Mike called as she left.

Liam turned impatiently toward the younger man. "What's this all about, Mike? Why are you giving Lauren such a hard time?"

"A hard time? You've got to be kidding. That ... that rat has been dropping rumors about Cara since she came back from Taiwan in a complete snit. She's completely trashed Cara's professional reputation. Now she's working on her personal one. It's a dirty, underhanded thing to do, especially when Cara isn't around to defend herself. And not one word is true."

"Then why did Cara run?" Liam asked quietly. "Why did she take off without a word to anyone? Not even you?"

Mike glared at him. "So, the glamorous Ms. Rat has gotten to you, too. I thought you had more sense, Liam. I'm not sure why Cara left, but I know this. She wouldn't have left without a good reason. I'm willing to give her the benefit of the doubt. I refuse to believe all this garbage about how she took Aerie for greed and power and glory. None of those things ever mattered to Cara. If you believe that huge heap of horse hockey Lauren is dishing, you don't know Cara at all."

"Perhaps that's true, Mike. Perhaps I don't. From what I understand, they aren't rumors at all."

"So, you believe all the horse hooey." Mike stood up. "Go ahead and be a complete idiot, Liam. But let me tell you one thing, and you can tell everyone who works here, too. They can say whatever they want about Cara. *You* can say whatever you want about Cara, but if I hear one word of it, I'll quit on the spot. Right now, you need me. Lauren has asked me to build a top-secret, high-security, data transfer module for the accounting system, one that's not even remotely necessary for the intended function of the accounting system. It doesn't take a genius to figure out its real purpose. You may not have the prototype, but I think you're trying to build your own version of Aerie. If I leave Windwear, I guarantee that puppy will go with me. If you thought Cara was good at making things disappear, she's a babe in the woods compared to me. Do I make myself clear?"

Liam stared at the young man in surprise. "Cara was a fool to believe in you." Mike said as he left the room.

Liam watched the young man stride angrily from his office, then picked up the phone. "Lauren? I need you to do something for me."

After a few minutes, Liam hung up the phone and punched the intercom button. "Staci? Get Peter Whittington on the phone, please. Request a meeting with him as soon as possible. Also, would you ask Paul to come up?"

"All right. What should I tell Paul it's about?"

"Tell him we're going fishing."

Chapter 27

"Come in, come in. Take a seat." The friendly words belied the haggard face in front of Liam. Peter Whittington looked awful. His eyes were puffy, his face lined with fatigue, and the fatherly complacency so evident at their last meeting, was nowhere to be found. He and Paul settled into the seats in front of Peter's desk. "How was Taiwan, Liam? Weather still steamy? I was on a project once in Taipei for six months. Hated it. Too hot, too humid, too many people, too much traffic. Couldn't wait to get back to the States."

"Taiwan was good. Still steamy. Still a lot of people in a small space, but I enjoyed the visit." He smiled and glanced at his watch. "Before I left for Taiwan, we talked about purchasing the Aerie prototype from Pyramid. I'd like to continue our discussion, if possible."

"We did discuss that, didn't we?" Peter shifted uncomfortably in his chair. " Well, I'm afraid I have some bad news, boys. We're at a complete standstill with Aerie."

"What do you mean?" Liam asked.

"That damned woman." The older man glared angrily. "I told you, didn't I, that Cara Larson stole a copy of Aerie?"

"You did, yes."

"Well, the legal department has begun a formal investigation. As soon as they complete their work, I expect they'll obtain a warrant for her arrest. The problem is, she's disappeared. No one can find her. We're stuck in legal limbo until we can locate her and proceed with the case."

"I see, but I don't understand how your internal investigation affects the sale of the software to us."

Peter shook his head. "I'm not sure what the investigation will turn up. I can't possibly write a contract for the sale of a product subject to such uncertainty."

"What if we include a Memo of Understanding with the Sales Contract?" Liam suggested. "We will agree to renegotiate the price of Aerie based on the outcome of your investigation. That way, you can continue with your investigation, and we can proceed with development. Once things are more certain, we can hammer out a new price."

"That's a good idea, Liam, but I'm afraid I can't comply. My legal department gave me strict orders not to take any action until the investigation is complete. I have no desire to get on the wrong side of Pyramid's attorneys. "

"How long will the investigation take?" Paul asked.

"I'm not sure. Weeks. Months. It's already been three weeks, and precious little has been done. The matter is a lot more difficult when you can't find the perpetrator." He looked sharply at Liam and Paul. "You haven't seen her, have you, boys? Heard from her? Anything?"

"No. We were hoping you might know where she is," Liam said. "In fact, we were thinking if we found Cara, we might convince her to sell her copy of Aerie to us."

"Are you joking?" Peter's fist slammed down on the desk. "Do you have any idea how many laws you would be breaking if you—"

"Hold on," Liam said calmly. "We aren't trying to break any laws or take something that doesn't belong to us. What I meant was, we hoped to give her an ... incentive to cooperate."

"You mean pay her off?"

"No, I mean clear the way so you would be free to sell Aerie to us." Liam leaned toward Peter. "Peter, Aerie is critical to my company's future. I'll do what I need to do to get it. If paying Cara Larson off will allow us to buy Aerie from you more quickly, I'll gladly pay her off."

Peter unclenched his fist. "I understand how desperate your situation is, boys. Unfortunately, I couldn't sell Aerie to you now if Cara Larson walked in the door this minute and dropped it on my desk. There are just too many complications. You're right, about one thing, though. This whole process would be easier if we could find her. You sure you don't know where she is?"

They shook their heads.

He drummed his fingers on the desk. "Well, come back in a few months. Maybe by then Cara will turn up, and we can complete the investigation and come to terms."

The lines around Liam's mouth tightened. "I can't wait, Peter. I need Aerie now."

"I'm sorry, boys. My hands are tied."

"I'm sorry, too." Liam sighed. "I really hoped we could work something out."

Peter peered at them with sudden interest. "By the way, what did your attorneys say about Aerie? I recall you were going to ask your lawyers to call mine. From what I understand, my attorneys have had no discussions on the matter."

Liam's shoulders slumped slightly. "Unfortunately, my attorney wasn't much help. He said we can't make you sell something you don't want to sell."

"You know that's not the case, boys. I would sell Aerie to you if I could. This is just a bad situation, all around." Peter gave Liam another sharp look. "What will you do, now? Will you develop Aerie on your own?"

Liam's shoulders slumped more heavily. "I'm not sure. Starting over would be difficult, especially without the technical expertise of Pyramid as a partner. We're not in the software business, and the system is extremely complex." He shook his head. "I really wish we were able to work out a deal." The two mean stood up, and Liam extended his hand to Peter. "Thanks for your time today."

Peter smiled then. He put a fatherly hand on Liam's arm as he shook his hand. "Like I said, son, give me some time. Maybe we can work something out in a few months. I'm sorry I can't do more."

Silently, Liam and Paul filed from the room. They rode the elevator down to the lobby, stepped into the hot August sunshine, and walked along the busy sidewalk. When they were three blocks from Pyramid, Paul turned to Liam. "Well, that was an enlightening conversation."

Liam nodded. "Yes, very enlightening. So, Paul, what do we know?"

"Three things." Paul held up one finger. "One, Peter doesn't have Aerie."

"Right. Because if he did?"

"He would sell it to us and make an easy $2 million. Or at least open up negotiations and keep us on the hook. Instead, he's hiding behind the investigation and committing to nothing. For some reason, he doesn't want us to know he doesn't have Aerie."

"True. And two?"

Paul held up a second finger. "Two, Cara does have Aerie."

Liam nodded. "Right again, and how do we know that?"

"Because she was the last one in possession, and now she's gone dark. Peter is looking for her, but he can't find her. He's worried she's planning to develop Aerie herself. Oh, and one more thing. He's pissed."

"Right on all points. And three?"

Paul smiled as he held up a third finger. "Three, Peter is now absolutely certain we do not have Aerie. And that we're up shit creek without it."

"Indeed." Liam smiled. He held up his hand and Paul slapped it lightly. "Nice work, old friend."

Liam put down the manufacturing facility blueprints he was studying as Mike entered his office. "Hey, Mike."

Mike plopped in the seat in front of Liam's desk. "The world is an interesting place, very interesting, indeed. I tell you, it's good to have friends in technical places."

"What did you find out from your ex-colleagues at Pyramid?"

"Well, for one, Peter pulled everyone who worked on Aerie off FIT and sent them up to the Seattle office."

Liam raised an eyebrow. "He did? When?"

"Right after I left."

"Hmm. That is interesting. What else?"

Mike gave him a wide smile. "You're going to love this. You know how we do a nightly tape backup of all our computer files here at Windwear?"

"Yes."

"Well, we used to do the same on the FIT project. Standard operating procedure. Funny thing, though. All the backup tapes at FIT were erased, or at least certain files were erased. About two weeks ago, Peter brought in a bunch of hotshot technical experts from the New York office to examine the tapes. Seems he was looking really hard for something."

"Aerie."

"That would be my guess." Mike leaned over and gave Liam a conspiratorial smile. "Remember during Watergate, when the geniuses at DOJ tried to read the erased recordings off the tape machine of Nixon's secretary? What was her name, Rosemary ..."

"Woods. Were you even alive then, Mike?"

"I was four. I remember. Kind of. Well, same thing happened here. From what Anna said, all these whiz-bang experts from Pyramid's New York office were crowded in the conference room, poring over the tapes, trying to reverse the effects of the AC field and derandomize the magnetization. Man, I wish I could have seen that dog and pony show. I wonder how much those guys billed the project in that losing effort—"

"Did they find anything?" Liam cut in, his voice suddenly tense.

"A little bit here and there."

"Anything important? Was it Aerie?" Liam leaned forward in his chair.

"Nah." Mike sat back and laced his fingers behind his head. "All they found were fragments of Beethoven's Fifth. Over and over and over. 'Duh, duh, duh, duhhhhhh!' Isn't that awesome? Rumor had it Peter's head almost exploded. I have to applaud Cara. That was a nice touch."

"So, Peter doesn't have Aerie."

"Nope. Not even a whisper."

"Which leaves Cara. Cara has Aerie."

Mike frowned. "Okay, Liam, I am prepared to admit there is a distinct possibility Cara is the one person in the world most likely to have knowledge of the whereabouts of Aerie."

"You're using weasel words, young man."

"Okay." Mike frowned again. "She has it. She has Aerie."

There was a knock on the door, and Lauren walked in carrying a large box. "Thanks, Mike. That's all for now." Liam looked up. "Come in, Lauren."

"Hey Rat," Mike sneered as he left the room.

"Twerp," Lauren hissed. Liam shook his head.

"I'm glad you're here, Lauren. Is this everything on Aerie?"

"Yes. Why?"

"Just leave it here. From now on, I want you to forget about Aerie. I'm taking it over."

Lauren's eyes widened. "I don't understand."

"You don't need to. I'll take care of Aerie from now on."

"Oh no you don't, Liam," Lauren said angrily. "You can't do this. Not to me. Not again. You keep taking things away from me before I get a chance to finish them. It's not fair, and I'm not going to stand for it."

Liam raised an eyebrow. "We've had this discussion before, Lauren. You work for me, not the other way around. We have no shortage of challenges here at Windwear. You can help the company best by focusing on the Hsin agreement and the stock offering, and that's what I want you to do."

"What are you going to do with Aerie? I need to be kept informed about your plans—"

"No, you don't. I appreciate all your efforts where Aerie is concerned, but it is no longer part of your job."

"But—"

"No buts, Lauren. You're not working on Aerie anymore. Do you understand?"

Lauren gave him an angry look, then finally nodded.

"Good. Thank you, Lauren."

One hour later, Liam slid into the back booth of a trendy coffee shop in Northeast Portland and greeted Paul Davis. He slid a heavy briefcase over to his oldest friend. "Here you go, Paul. We have no choice but to take this thing underground. Form here forward, not a word to anyone. Aerie is in your hands and your hands only."

Paul placed the briefcase on the seat next to him, and nodded to his oldest friend. "I won't let you down, Liam."

Chapter 28

Staci heard their voices long before they actually appeared. "Liam, this is a disaster. Go back to Whittington. Beg, plead, do whatever it takes. You need to get Aerie back." Paul's voice rose in frustration. Paul? Staci thought. Frustration? Those two things just didn't go together.

"No, Paul. He won't deal, and I refuse to beg, plead, or anything else. If he can't accept the best offer I can put on the table, we'll have to delay." Several people stepped out of their offices to watch the history-making event. Liam and Paul never disagreed about anything. At least not in public.

"Delay? How can you say such a thing after all the work my team has put in? Aerie is critical. Those are your words, not mine. How can you shelve something so important because the guy wants a few more bucks?"

They reached the reception area, but neither man seemed to notice Staci staring at them. "Paul, be reasonable, too many things are happening, right now. The new accounting system is going to take all your time, even with Mike working on it. I need to focus on the new production lines and the stock offering—"

"The stock deal is what's causing all these problems. Nothing's been the same since Lauren came and filled your head with all this talk about money and growth."

"She's right about those things, Paul. She's convinced me the IPO is the best way to go."

"Convinced you? Since when do people convince you of things that are against your better judgment? You never believed in this financial hogwash before."

Liam sighed. "It's not hogwash, Paul. We're growing, we must change with the times."

"Don't you get what's happening, Liam? What's happening to you? Where is the guy who wanted to make the best hiking boots in the world? The guy whose dream was to make just enough money to go live deep in the forest where no one could find him?"

"Things are different now."

"Different? I'll say. You let that lawyer lead you around by the nose. You don't run this company anymore. She does. She tells you what agreements to make, what suppliers to deal with. You don't discuss these things with me anymore. Like this Taiwan deal. Why the heck didn't you tell me what you were up to? I think you're making a mistake—"

"We did discuss Taiwan."

"And I asked you not to go. At least until I had a better idea of what you wanted to accomplish."

"I couldn't. Lauren had arranged everything—"

"Lauren again. You listen to her, but not to me, and you say she isn't running things?"

Liam pulled his fingers through his hair. "She is *not* running things. I am—"

"Clearly, *I* have no say anymore. You promised we would develop Aerie. I trusted you, and now you're going back on your word. You're the one who's always talking about trusting your employees. Or is trust a one-way street with you?"

"Dammit, Paul, you're not being fair. You know I had no choice."

"You have more choices than you think. Unfortunately, you keep choosing to pursue things that will make us rich at the expense of what will make us good." Paul paused and made an effort to calm down. "Why don't we do Aerie ourselves? I can spearhead the project. I can use Mike—"

"No, you cannot use Mike. Not for eight more months. He's still subject to Pyramid's noncompete provisions. Lauren reviewed them. They're tight."

Paul sneered. Actually sneered. Staci couldn't believe what she was seeing. "Lauren again. Well, isn't that convenient? She certainly keeps you focused on all that money garbage and not on the system that will actually help us make money."

"We can't develop Aerie now, Paul. Maybe in a six months or a year, but not right now."

Six months. A year." Paul slammed his fist into the wall. Actually slammed his fist! "You can't do that. We can't wait that long."

"We have no choice. The opportunity has passed. With the prototype gone and no technical expertise available from Pyramid, the window is closed. We need to move on, focus on the things we can accomplish. We have deadlines we can't afford to miss. Like the research and development department, the facili—"

"Then it's time I focus on what I want to accomplish."

"What is that supposed to mean?"

Paul frowned. "I'm leaving Windwear."

"What?" Liam said in surprise.

"I want a leave of absence. If you can't commit to Aerie, I can't commit to Windwear. Not one minute longer. I will not work for Windwear again until you start developing Aerie."

"Paul, calm down a minute. You can't do this. We have too much at stake right now. I need you to work on the accounting sys—"

"Right. You need me! Well I needed you, or at least your word, and you had no problem bailing out on me. Aerie was at stake, now it's gone." He paused, anger evident in his face. "Find someone else. I mean what I say. I'm gone until you start work on Aerie."

"Don't back me into a corner, Paul."

"I'm not backing you anywhere. You got us into this mess. You and Lauren. You two fix it. I'm gone." He turned to Staci. "Staci, are there papers people fill out when they quit?" Staci's eyes widened as she looked first at Paul and then at Liam.

"I thought you said you wanted a leave of absence?" Liam's voice was tight.

"I changed my mind. I quit. I want out. Now. While I still have a few positive feelings about Windwear left."

"I can't believe you would quit over a little problem like this, Paul. We've been through much worse—"

"A little problem? Liam, you don't even see what you're doing. You're changing the entire nature of the company. It's becoming something I don't even know. Something I don't want to know. And definitely something I don't want to be a part of. I'll take my chances somewhere else."

"I won't beg you to stay, Paul. I'm asking once, but I won't beg."

"Just like with Whittington. Well it didn't work with him, and it won't work with me. Forget it. I quit."

Liam stood, his face hard, his jaw set. With a shrug, he dismissed his oldest friend as if he were an old boot. "All right. Staci, start the papers. I'll sign them as soon as they're ready." Without another word, he walked into his office.

Liam closed his eyes and leaned heavily against the door. Step one, complete.

September 1991

Chapter 29

The shrill ring of the telephone awakened Cara. She felt around for the receiver on the nightstand and struggled to open her eyes. "Hello?" Slowly, she dragged herself awake. The mid-September sun on this Friday morning streamed through the open windows. The sound of the ocean shushed in her ears, and the tangy salt air tickled her nose.

"Caroline, it's Lisa. I need to ask you a huge favor."

Cara blinked awake. She still wasn't used to her new name. "Oh, hi Lisa. What do you need?"

"Would you be able to help serve tonight at the Inn? Jane and Maria are out sick, and I have a company coming in from Portland for a weekend conference. Please say yes, Caroline, I'm desperate."

Cara squinted at the sunshine. "Lisa, I've never waited on tables in my life. I wouldn't even know what to do."

"You wouldn't really be waiting on tables. You'd just be serving."

"Well, I don't have any other plans." She paused for a moment. "I'll do it if you teach me how to make your peach cobbler."

"But Caroline, I gave you the recipe."

Cara laughed. "Well ... my attempt didn't turn out so well. Even the birds snubbed their beaks at the results. I think I need a personal training session."

Lisa giggled. "Girl, you're hopeless. It's a deal."

"Lisa, I've never served tables before. Are you sure you want me to—"

"No problem, Caroline. I'll partner you with Jose. He's been with me the longest. He'll give you the rundown. You'll pick it up in a snap."

"You presume too much. I'm a walking disaster anywhere near a kitchen, but if you're willing to take the risk, I'll try."

"You're a lifesaver. Plus, this will give you a chance to meet some new friends. You're far too isolated in that cottage of yours. By the way, Jose is a hunk. Tall, dark, and handsome. Dreamy dancer, shameless flirt. You need to have some fun, my girl, and he's the one to provide it. Come to think of it, I don't think I've seen you around town with much male company. You could use some excitement in your life."

"What do you mean? I spend a lot of time with Bill Martinson."

Lisa stifled a laugh. "If you like watching tomatoes grow. Okay, okay, I meant with a male *under* eighty."

"Careful, Lisa. He grows a mean tomato. I've heard tales about those tomatoes. How they've been known to swallow blonde caterers with sharp tongues."

"Ooh, you scare me, Caroline. Okay, okay, I can tell when you're avoiding the subject. Again. I bet you'll change your tune after you lay eyes on that fine piece of masculinity tonight."

Cara shook her head. The last thing she wanted to think about was men, especially tall, dark, and handsome ones. The words alone brought back an image so clear it almost hurt. She pushed the thought away out of pure habit. "What time should I be there, and what do I wear?"

Lisa chatted on, explaining the procedures and dress code. Then with a quick laugh and another round of thanks, Lisa hung up and Cara found herself sitting on the side of her bed, the phone still pressed to her ear, seeing not the green ocean in front of her, but Liam's chiseled face.

It had been eight weeks since she was unceremoniously escorted from the Pyramid offices. Eight weeks since she discarded her old life and landed squarely in limbo.

She sighed. It was not supposed to be this way. She had planned to give Aerie to Peter, resign, and go somewhere quiet to start a new life. She intended to follow Mama's advice. Find out who she was and what was important to her. But nothing went as planned.

She thought at first Peter had removed Aerie from scope in order to negotiate a fat new contract with Windwear for a fat new fee. The tactic wasn't unheard of in the industry. Slimy, but not unheard of. But purging the files as Peter demanded *was* unusual. In fact, it ran counter to all normal procedure. Peter himself made the point. Tap dance, he had said. "*Confuse the hell out of every person in the room ... toss out so much technical jargon they'll sink in it ... slide the design right past them with their eyes wide open.*" She didn't need to purge anything when she could confuse her customer with words alone. That way, when Pyramid finally agreed to a new contract, the company would lose no time restarting development.

Still, even with that giant clue, she hadn't suspected Peter planned to take Aerie. Not until Liam mentioned the senselessness of Peter's actions, how he was throwing away such an obvious moneymaking opportunity. She understood then. The truth hit her like a bolt from the blue. By then, there were too few available options and even less time to act on them. She decided on two goals: one, give Windwear a head start on Aerie; two, throw Pyramid off Windwear's trail by making it look like she had stolen the software. And to make her plan work, all she needed to do was give the software to Lauren and disappear from the face of the earth.

She tumbled out of bed, tossed the covers together, threw on a sweatshirt and a pair of sweatpants, and hurried downstairs. She frowned as she brewed a pot of coffee. She couldn't shake the past today. Lisa's phone call somehow managed to get past the barriers she had built so carefully these past eight weeks. She poured steaming coffee into her mug, stopped fighting her memories, and let them wander where they pleased.

Disappearing had been surprisingly easy. Especially with a little cash and a touch of luck. Immediately after she left

Pyramid, she found a cheap motel on the east side that accepted cash and asked no questions. She didn't waste any time shutting down her old life. Listing the house. Moving the few things she wanted to keep to a storage unit. Giving notice on her apartment. Renting a post office box. Redirecting her mail.

Some things proved more difficult than others. She had visited Jeanine to say good-bye and ask her not to tell anyone of her whereabouts. Bless her heart, dear Jeanine didn't ask any questions. "I'll be in touch," she told the older woman, as Cara embraced her one last time. They both knew she was lying.

She received several offers on the house as soon as it was listed. For cash. She smiled. Was that luck or was that just what happened when you set the price so low every sleazy opportunist from miles around came out of the woodwork to try to make a fast buck? She picked the offer promising to settle the fastest, and sure enough, the deal closed in eight days. The last thing she did before she left town was sell her car to a shady outfit on 82nd Avenue. Then she boarded a bus and headed west.

Cara took her coffee cup out to the deck and sat quietly, mesmerized by the waves. Low tide. The beach spread out for miles. She breathed deeply and let the tangy air seep into her senses.

Creating a new life was far more difficult than getting rid of an old one, she discovered. She had to admit the challenge was intriguing. She couldn't use her existing identification, not if she wanted to stay hidden. And she worried about establishing a false identity using forged documents. So, how did a person go about creating a new life without any identification? She smiled. Luck and cash, that's how.

It turned out her mother had saved more than the money Cara had earned over the years. Mary Larson managed to build quite a nest egg in her final years. Cara was shocked when she totaled up the amount. All in all, between her own savings, her mother's savings, and the proceeds from the house, she possessed a tidy sum. And all that money was in the form of cash, stored in a small safe—the first purchase she made after arriving in Cannon Beach—in the corner of her bedroom closet.

On the last day of July, 1991, Cara Larson became Caroline Martin. She picked a name similar to her real one. That way, she wouldn't completely ignore people when they called her by an unfamiliar name. She had never been a good liar, but it seemed like lying was all she did these days.

She booked a room at the cheapest motel in Cannon Beach, which wasn't all that cheap, since it was the height of tourist season. She bought a bicycle and proceeded to introduce herself around town. She was amazed how people responded when she offered to provide technical services in exchange for anything but money. How could she ask for money? She didn't have one scrap of I.D. identifying her as Caroline Martin. She couldn't fill out a W-4, or deposit a check, or even open a bank account in the name of Caroline Martin. So, she bartered instead.

She installed some publishing software on Bill Martinson's laptop so he could publish the neighborhood newsletter. In turn, Bill had been supplying her with tomatoes and vegetables ever since. She organized Sue Baker's entire office during one busy weekend, and agreed to return every few weeks to reorganize after Whirlwind Sue left her mark. In exchange, Sue, owner and proprietor of Sue's Music Shop, agreed to give Cara free violin lessons. Then there was Sam. Grizzled, old, ex-hippie Sam Hastings, who made old-fashioned surfboards from balsa wood in an old shack outside of town. She set up the accounting software that had been sitting in a box on his shelf for the past year. She even taught his son, Pike, how to do the books. For payment, Sam promised to make her a special surfboard. She sighed. There was also the added bonus of Pike's clumsy advances. Oh well, nobody ever said the barter system was perfect.

She converted her new relationships into references that resulted in a no-questions-asked lease on this cottage. The owner had scrambled to find a renter before moving his family back to Portland for the school year. Luck and cash did the trick again. Along with a good word from her new friends.

She stared at the ocean. This was only temporary, she told herself. A momentary pause before she really, truly, started over. She needed to stay hidden for a few months. She needed to make sure Peter couldn't find her. She would know when she could safely reemerge as Cara Larson. It would be in the Portland papers. Not anything obvious, of course. She giggled as she imagined the headline: OLLY OLLY OXEN FREE. CARA LARSON, YOU CAN COME OUT NOW. No, no, nothing so clear and helpful. But one day she would read about Windwear's announcement of a revolutionary new computer system that would change the way the company did business. That would be her clue. Then she would know Windwear had won the fight and Peter had lost. Only then would she be free to come out of the shadows and start her life over again.

This wasn't a waste, though, this temporary stay in limbo. Despite the difficulties, perhaps because of the difficulties, she had found, quite unexpectedly, a measure of peace. The friendships she made in a few short weeks. The trust she built by helping where she could. The satisfaction she gained from learning new skills. She was astonished how different the world looked when not driven purely by money. Of course, she couldn't live like this forever, and she didn't intend to. Still, this temporary stop had given her a new perspective, one resonating with a simple joy she had never known before. Maybe, she realized, as the days unfolded so shiny and new, maybe this was what Mama meant when she talked about happiness.

Cara stood up. Enough of the memories, already. She didn't like to dwell on the past too long, because when she did, her thoughts always seemed to wend their way back to a man with dark eyes and a smile that tilted crookedly at one corner. "Enough," she said aloud.

She went inside, ran upstairs, and changed into her running clothes. She flew down the steps and out the back door. She had tarried too long down memory lane. She would need to hustle to get her run in now. She still had several appointments to squeeze in before she went to the Inn.

Chapter 30

Cara arrived early at the Inn. She smoothed her skirt and checked her reflection in the large oval mirror in the entry hall. Her white silk blouse folded against her body and highlighted her summer tan. Her black skirt was much too short, but it was all she had. It would have to do. Her hair, streaked from the summer sun and trapped in a fiery braid, fell nearly to her waist. Good enough, she thought.

She found Lisa in the kitchen, running in three directions at once as she made final preparations for the banquet. "Oh, Caroline, I'm glad you're here." She dragged Cara to a tall dark man filling water glasses. "Jose, meet Caroline Martin. She's new and needs some training." She winked at Jose whose eyes lit up as his gaze ran over her. Cara felt uncomfortable. Jose was barely twenty, she thought, with hormones that had clearly never settled down after adolescence. Handsome he was, with dark eyes and curly black hair, but she didn't care for the way he looked at her.

She held out her hand. "I'm pleased to meet you, Jose."

Jose ignored her hand, put his arm around her, and led her to the dining room. "Come, Caroline. I will show you all you need to know."

Cara rolled her eyes and ducked out from under his arm, walking briskly ahead to a table. "Let's start with the first course. Salads, I presume?" Some things never changed. All those self-preservation techniques she learned during her years at Pyramid seemed to come in handy, even here, in tiny Cannon Beach, at the edge of the world.

Jose paused for a moment and let out an exaggerated sigh. "Ah, Cara Bella, you wound me with your indifference."

Cara started at the use of her real name. With effort, she forced a smile. She had been edgy all day. Trips down memory lane did that to her. She didn't need to snipe at Jose when he was just trying to help. "Actually, Jose, I'm trying not to make a complete fool of myself. I've never waited tables before."

His smile turned at once light and harmless. He bowed with mock bravery. "I am up to the challenge."

Cara concentrated on Jose's words, and tried to memorize the rapid-fire instructions streaming out of his mouth. She needed to calm down or she would make a complete mess of this job. Then Lisa would never teach her how to make peach cobbler. "All right, Jose. I think I understand."

They walked to the serving station as the guests began to arrive. "You will do perfectly, Cara Bella. You worry too much. You are tight like a drum. Relax." He placed his hands on her shoulders and started to massage them.

Cara ducked discreetly away. "Which table should I serve first?"

Jose lowered his hands and turned around. "We serve the head table first. Do you see that tall man? The one looking this way? That's the table." He turned back to her. "It seems as if I am not the only man who cannot take his eyes off you, Cara Bella."

Cara turned to look where he pointed. There he was, just as Jose said. A tall man. Looking at her. She let out a gasp and quickly glanced down at the floor. Calm down, she told herself. This happened all the time. For some reason, even after all the weeks she'd been here, she had not been able to push him from her mind. She had seen him in a hundred different places. At the grocery store. In the library. On the beach. Every single time she had been mistaken. It would be the same this time. She would look up and realize he was too short or too old or too bald. It was an illusion, a trick of her mind. She raised her head just enough to glance at him through her lashes. Her heart stopped. It wasn't possible. It couldn't be him. It was just an uncanny resemblance. She let the image clear, but that unforgettable face was still there, stiff as stone, unchanged from the very first glance.

Liam.

For a moment, she could only stare. He seemed thin and haggard, with shadows dusting the areas under his eyes. And those eyes! Cold. Remote. Hard.

Panic set in. She turned abruptly and reached for the edge of the serving station. Oh God, what should she do?

"Are you all right, Caroline?" Jose reached a comforting arm around her shoulders. "Tell me, Cara Bella, what is the problem?"

Cara stood for a moment, trying to compose herself. Liam! Here! But not just Liam. They were all here. Lauren, to his right, her eyes as hard and cold as Liam's. Lauren had seen her too, had seen that shock of a look pass between Cara and Liam. Staci was here … and Mike! Things were starting to make sense. Windwear was Lisa's catering customer. And Windwear must have hired Mike away from Pyramid.

Well, a string of good luck had graced her these past weeks. She supposed it was fair to have her share of bad luck, too. And this was bad. Bad for her. Bad for Liam. She glanced toward the door. Could she leave? Simply run and hope they would shrug it off as a coincidence? An eerie fluke that some woman in a short skirt in little Cannon Beach looked an awful lot like Cara Larson?

"Caroline." Lisa grasped her arm and dragged her back to the kitchen. She thrust a tray of salads into her hands. "Come on, we need to start on the salads. Jose, can you get Jill and Catalina lined up to follow with the bread baskets?"

"Lisa, wait a minute. There's a problem—"

"Can you wait, Caroline?" Lisa asked impatiently. "It's go time. Take these to the head table. Once the salads are served we can talk." She pushed Cara toward the table. "Please, Caroline. Go. Now."

Conversation halted as she approached the table. Twelve pairs of eyes stared at her. Liam broke the silence. "Hello, Cara. What a surprise to find you here." His words were polite, but they came out as if he had difficulty putting them together. There was a moment of laughter as Lauren raised her eyebrows and said something under her breath. Something about Liam being a master of understatement.

Cara flushed hotly as she tried to force a smile on her face. "Hello, everyone. Welcome to Cannon Beach." The utter banality of the words mocked her. *Hi folks. You just blew my cover and with it, Windwear's only advantage over Pyramid. That should ruin any chance you have to develop Aerie before Pyramid comes after you with a passel of lawsuits and destroys your company. But hey, nice to see you anyway.*

Lauren gave Cara a sickening sweet smile. "Cara, we wondered what happened to you. So, this is where you've been hiding. It's very good cover." She looked Cara up and down with disdain, her eyes stopping on her short skirt. "Well, maybe cover isn't the word I should use." Everyone at the table snickered. Except Liam and Mike.

Liam frowned. "Enough, Lauren." Lauren opened her mouth to protest, but stopped when she caught Liam's expression. Her mouth curled in mute contempt. Cara served the salads in tense silence. Her hands shook, but she managed to keep her face blank. She served Mike last. When she placed the plate down in front of him, he turned to her. "Ranch dressing! My favorite! Thanks, Cara." He squeezed her arm and smiled. Thank God for Mike, she thought. He turned enthusiastically back to the table. "Let's eat, everybody. I'm starved."

Cara returned to the kitchen and searched for Lisa, but she wasn't there. She spotted the caterer on the other side of the dining room, preparing the dessert trays. Cara hurried over to speak to her.

Liam studied Cara from the corner of his eye. He saw her gesture to the other woman. Saw her troubled expression as she tilted her head toward his table, toward him. Then the other woman nodded, and Cara went to switch stations with another server. Good, he thought irritably.

Suddenly weary, he excused himself and stood up. Lauren cast a furtive glance his way, but he didn't notice. He walked through the lobby, out the door, then off the verandah to the beach. No sense sitting in this stifling room, his appetite had disappeared.

He removed his shoes and socks, rolled up the trousers of his charcoal gray suit, and walked across the wet sand. She was not quite as he remembered. She was thinner now. Tanned. Rested. Fit. Beautiful as ever. He recalled how he had watched in slow motion as she turned around and spotted him. It was impossible to miss her panicked expression.

A large wave ran up the shore, caught Liam at the knees, and soaked the edge of his trousers. "Damn." He inched further from the surf and continued to stare out at the darkness.

Of all the rotten luck. The weekend conference had been his idea for kicking off Windwear's new future. A way to give his employees a slap on the back and some concrete encouragement before they tackled the barrage of changes that would come in the next few months. The last thing he expected to find was the one person capable of disrupting all his plans.

Damn. One look was all it took. One look at Cara Larson made every vivid memory come crashing back. Yes, he was surprised to see her. Yes, he was angry at the things she had done. But those feelings were nothing compared to the sense of relief that flooded through him. She was alive and safe, not sick or injured or … or dead someplace all alone. God, he had been so worried. He hadn't realized until this moment how incredibly worried he had been. For a minute all he wanted to do was take her in his arms and kiss her senseless.

He ran his fingers through his hair. Damn. He had almost convinced himself he would be able to avoid confrontation altogether. Every day he read the newspaper and didn't find her picture in the business section gave him hope he would win. He and Paul had pushed so hard. During these last two months, he actually began to believe they would win without ever having to confront her face to face.

He often imagined what it would be like when he met her again. He always pictured the scene in New York, in some huge, glass-covered skyscraper, in some fancy conference room, the two of them staring at each other across a gleaming cherry wood table, flanked by a wall of lawyers. Never in a million years did he imagine he would find her in tiny Cannon Beach, dressed in a short black skirt showing a mile of leg, with nothing between them but a tray of salads.

There was no question what needed to be done. He had his plan. He would face her. And he would finish what *she* had started.

He strolled back to the walkway, replaced his shoes and socks, and rolled down his pants. Well, he was calm now. He needed to reappear and pretend he had been on the phone wheeling and dealing with some important financier for the last fifteen minutes. And fool absolutely no one.

Chapter 31

Cara breathed a sigh of relief. After their first disastrous encounter, she managed to avoid Liam all night. She kept to her station and made it through the entire evening without spilling coffee on anyone. A miracle. Now the Windwear party filled the other half of the banquet room, where a live band played, and she just needed to clear a few more tables before she could head home.

"Cara, may I speak with you?"

Startled, Cara turned to face Liam, his eyes dark, and his hair disheveled. He looked exhausted. "No."

With a quick movement, he took the tablecloths from her arms and set them on the table. "Just a word, Cara. We have some catching up to do."

"No," she said, concern in her voice. "You, more than anyone, should realize you shouldn't be seen anywhere near me."

"Well, I'm sure you think so. That would work out nicely with your plans."

"What? Are you kidding? It's for your own good, Liam. And mine. If Peter finds me, he'll—"

"If Peter finds you, he's going to throw you in jail. He knows, like I know, like we all know, that you stole Aerie."

"What?" she asked in disbelief. "You think I stole Aerie?"

"You can drop the innocent act, Cara. Everyone knows you took Aerie. Even Mike, though I will say he is still holding out hope you have some reasonable explanation for your actions. Everyone else thinks you straight up stole it."

For a moment, she stared at Liam in shock. What was Liam saying? Didn't Lauren give him the software? If not, what had she done with it? Had she kept Aerie for herself? Given it to Peter? One thing was certain, she realized as she took in Liam's hard expression; Lauren told Liam Cara had stolen Aerie. And he believed her.

"I don't have Aerie," she said flatly.

His lips tightened into a thin line. "Really, Cara. Why should I believe you when everyone else in the entire universe says otherwise?"

"With what proof?" she demanded. "You have no proof. Do you always believe what people say when you have no facts to back it up? That's not like you, Liam."

"You're right, that isn't like me. In this case I do have facts. I admit the trail is thin; you covered your tracks well. But Peter told me, in so many words. He can't sell Aerie to me because he doesn't have it to sell. You left him high and dry. You removed Aerie from the network and erased the backup tapes."

"So, that's his story," she said, almost to herself. She looked at Liam. "Do you know if he's working on Aerie?"

Liam shook his head in exasperation. "Wouldn't you like to know? I'm not willing to help you by sharing Peter's plans. You'll have to do your own dirty work."

Cara studied his hard expression for several moments. "That's all you have? A half baked conclusion based on the words of Peter Whittington, the paragon of management virtue?"

"No, there's more. Lauren told me you took Aerie."

Cara's gaze flew to his. "Lauren did? She said I ... what exactly did she say, Liam?"

"She said you two talked."

"That much is true. We did."

"Or argued, to be more accurate. She told me you taunted her, told her you were heading to New York to develop Aerie."

"Oh my God." Cara couldn't choke back her surprise.

"What did you think when you discovered the software had disappeared? Did you worry when you realized you had only one copy of Aerie? Is that why you ran to the beach instead of New York? Did you wonder who took the second copy? Did you figure out it was Lauren?"

Cara shook her head in confusion. "What are you talking about? New York? Second copy? What ... I'm not following you at all." Suddenly, she followed Liam's words all too well. Oh my God. Lauren had twisted the story completely around. She made Cara the enemy. She told Liam that Cara, not Peter, was developing Aerie. All this time, Liam was focused on the wrong enemy. But what had Lauren done with the software? "*You* have Aerie," she said softly, taking a stab at the truth. "Lauren gave Aerie to you."

"So, now you know," Liam said quietly. "This fight is between you and me, Cara. Direct competition."

Her head snapped up. "No, you're wrong. There is no competition between us. I don't have Aerie."

"Why should I believe you? Innocent people don't run, Cara."

"You'd be surprised. Innocent people do all kinds of unexpected things. Even stupid things. Like trust people who shouldn't be trusted."

Liam shook his head. "This is getting us nowhere, Cara. What happened in the past doesn't matter. I'm willing to move on. I propose we work together."

"What? What do you mean?"

"We both know that whoever completes Aerie first will win the lion's share of the market. Why don't we work together? Or if you don't like that idea, I'm willing to buy you out of the race."

"Buy me out? Liam, I'm telling you, I don't have Aerie. I can't sell you something I don't have."

His eyes flared in exasperation. "Where have I heard those words before? You sound exactly like Peter. I guess I shouldn't be surprised. You did learn at his knee."

"Liam ... " Her voice trailed off. How could she prove the truth to him? How does one go about proving a negative? Especially given the lies Lauren and Peter had been feeding him.

"Cara," Liam broke into her thoughts. "I'm a reasonable man. I understand why you took Aerie. I wondered for weeks what would make you do such a thing. I could fathom only two reasons. One is the money. I understand why you would be tempted. Aerie will make millions. Still, I can hardly believe you would risk breaking the law, even for millions. Reason number two makes a lot more sense. Revenge. Peter wasn't the best person to work for. I can understand how angry you were when he refused to include Aerie in FIT—"

"What? He didn't—"

"Don't act shocked, Cara. You don't need to pretend any more. He told me the whole story. He told me how you pitched Aerie and he rejected it."

"But he didn't—"

"He told me how you stole the software afterward. I understand. You were under a lot of pressure. Your mother just died. You worked hard on Aerie. He rejected your efforts. He treated you badly. I understand why you felt justified in taking the software as some sort of compensation for what he—"

"You think I took Aerie out of spite?" Cara said, her voice incredulous. "You think I took Aerie because Peter is a jerk?"

"I'm not blaming you, Cara. God knows I don't hold Peter in high regard. The reasons don't matter. But justified as you think you were, Aerie wasn't yours to take. It belongs to Windwear, and I can't allow you to pursue development. If I can't buy you out, I'll sue to stop you."

Her jaw dropped in amazement. "Sue me? You'd be making a huge mistake, Liam. You'll blow everything wide open. Peter will—"

"Peter is not my problem, Cara. You are. I'll work things out with Peter, later. I need to deal with you first, and if I need to sue to stop you, I will."

"Liam, you have everything backwards. I'm not your problem—"

"Enough, Cara, I can see you aren't willing to listen to reason." He glared at her, disappointment etched in sharp lines around his face. "So, we're at war. What a waste. Like

Mike, I held out some faint hope I was wrong about you. I wanted to give you the benefit of the doubt. I tried to find reasons for your actions, something that would make sense, something to explain why you would take Aerie and run. I was fooling myself. It *is* about the money isn't it? That's all you're after. That's all you've ever been after. You're a liar and a thief, and it's no more complicated than that. God, I thought you were better than this, Cara. I thought you had more character."

Suddenly, Cara had enough. She realized she couldn't convince him of the truth. Too many lies were stacked between them. And she was having a hard time, all of a sudden, looking into his eyes and seeing such bitter anger peer back at her. She was having a hard time, too, realizing the friendship and trust they once shared was so utterly destroyed. A pain she hadn't felt in a long time emerged from somewhere deep inside her. Oh God, she thought, he hates me.

"Leave me alone." She took a step away from him. "I've heard enough, Liam. Go away."

"Come on, Cara, be smart about this." He took a step forward and closed the gap between them. "If we both go after Aerie, we'll both lose."

"Go to hell, Liam." She could feel the tears start behind her eyes, and she brushed them away. "Go to hell," she said again, but the words came out in a hoarse whisper.

"Tell me, Cara, now that I've finally found you. I've wondered about this for a long time. Did you lie from the beginning? From the first time I walked into your office? Are you that calculating? Have you been lying to everyone for months? To Peter. To Lauren. To Mike. The poor kid, you have him totally bamboozled—"

"Stop, Liam. Stop right now. You have no idea what you're talking about."

"I don't? Really? I think I do, Cara. In fact, I'm an expert in this area. Because you lied to me most of all, didn't you? Tell me, was everything a lie? Was it a lie when we were kissing? Was it a lie when we nearly went to bed together?"

Cara hit him then. She hit him as hard as she could. She raised her open hand and slapped him across the face with all her strength. At that moment the band stopped playing, and the crack of her hand as it made contact with his face charged loudly into the air. Everyone in the next room turned to stare.

The moment was suspended in time. Cara stood stiff, hand half-raised, two bright spots glowing angrily on her cheeks, her breathing heavy, her eyes on fire, glaring at Liam as if he were the devil himself. And Liam too was standing still, white faced, shocked out of his fury, his hand raised in surprise, fingers touching the mark now flooding with color, watching her coldly, his breathing almost nonexistent. The tears stung Cara's eyes, but she refused to look away from him.

"Cara, Liam. Is everything all right?" Mike had hurried across the room and now stood between them.

Cara scratched a glance at him, then turned back to face Liam. "Yes, Mike. Liam was saying how disappointing my services were this evening. We seem to have come to an understanding about the value of his comments." She tossed him a look of scathing contempt, then walked away, hoping the man she just hit couldn't see how shaken she was.

Mike cast a puzzled glance at Liam before following her. "Cara, hold up, will you? I haven't had a chance to talk to you, yet."

Cara broke into a run after she left the room. She was across the lobby and out the door before Mike caught up with her. "Hey, where's the fire? Slow down, Cara." He hurried to keep pace with her. "You're going to trip in those heels and fall on your face."

She slowed, stopped, and then turned to stare at him. He was giving her the friendly grin that always warmed her heart. She took a breath. Smiled at him. Then burst into tears. Mike hesitated for a moment, put his arms around her, and smoothed her hair self-consciously. "Hey, hey, hey, it's all right. Don't cry. Everything is will be all right. I'm glad to see you again. I've been worried about you."

Cara sniffed. "Mike, Liam thinks I stole Aerie. He hates me."

"No, Cara, the last thing Liam feels toward you is hatred. Believe me. But he doesn't know what's going on. None of us do. Rumors are flying and no one knows the truth. Please tell me what happened. Why did you leave? Why didn't you tell anyone? Why didn't you ask me for help?"

She shook her head. "No, Mike. It's ... too complicated. And ... too dangerous—"

"Dangerous?"

"Mike, I can't talk. I need to go."

He stared at her, concern carved on his face, "Okay, Cara, but please, let me come by later and talk to you. We'll be done here soon. Can I stop by in a little while?"

"That's a good idea. I ... I need your advice about something."

"Advice? From me? Awesome. I'm full of advice. I won't even charge you."

She smiled weakly. "Thanks. I'll see you soon."

"Wait. How do I get to your place?"

She pointed north. "Up the beach, five houses past the Mexican restaurant. Take the wooden steps. It's the yellow house."

"Okay. I'll be there in an hour." He patted her shoulder awkwardly. "Don't trip on those heels!"

She gave him a quick hug. Thank God for Mike. She took off her shoes and ran all the way home.

Chapter 32

The doorbell rang as Cara sipped a cup of hot tea in the living room of her cottage. It was after ten. She set her cup down and walked to the door. "Hi, Mike—" She stopped in midsentence as she was met by unruly dark hair and piercing eyes.

Liam's gaze washed unhurriedly over her before settling on her face. "Hello, Cara. I've come to apologize for my behavior this evening." He stood straight and stiff, without a hint of apology, but with the slightest trace of uncertainty, as if he were trying to determine whether she planned to slam the door in his face or hit him again.

Cara met his stare silently, her voice checked by surprise. "Where's Mike?" she finally asked.

"I'm afraid he won't be able to make it. He asked me to stand in for him."

She raised one eyebrow. "Having trouble getting your own dates, Liam?"

He pressed his lips together. "Very amusing, Cara. Believe me, this is the last place I want to be."

"Then please, don't stay on my account."

"That's exactly what I'm doing. May I come in?"

The initial shock was wearing off. She supposed the circumstances of his visit didn't matter. He was here, and angry as she was, she needed to tell him the truth. Then get the hell out of town. She opened the door and stood aside. "Come in."

She led the way to the living room, a large square room, decorated in misty grays and mauves hinting of the sea at dusk. "Please sit down. Can I get you something to drink?"

He looked uncomfortable as he sat on the softly patterned couch. "No, thank you."

She sat down in a chair opposite him. "All right, Liam. What do you want to say?"

"I'm not sure I want to say anything to you."

She rolled her eyes. "Spare me the word games. Say what you came to say or leave."

"I told you. I'm not here of my own choice. Mike made me come."

She tried hard to suppress her laughter. "Mike did? Forgive me, but I find it hard to believe anyone makes you do anything, least of all Mike. He is fairly harmless. I imagine you could beat him senseless if you wanted to."

He found no humor in her words. "I'd like to, but I can't afford the pleasure, right now. He threatened to quit if I didn't come over here and straighten things out with you."

"He what?!" She smiled at him in genuine amusement. "I told you he was unconventional."

"And I told you he was still in junior high. We were both right. I don't know what you did to the boy, Cara, but he is probably the only person in the entire state of Oregon who believes in you, right now."

Her smile faded. "And that includes you."

"That's right."

She looked at him squarely. "Then you can skip the apology, Liam. My mother used to say a person never needs to apologize for telling the truth."

He studied her for several moments, as if he were turning something over in his mind. "Cara, I would like you to come to work for Windwear."

Cara almost choked. He could have said he was flying to the moon, or he was going to take off all his clothes and dance naked on the beach; she would have had a better chance of believing him. "Excuse me?"

His face was a masterpiece of indifference. "You heard me. I'm offering you a job. Working with Mike. At Windwear."

"Just a minute, Liam. You made it clear earlier this evening you don't trust me further than you can spit. That you think I'm several steps below the lowest one-celled creature in the food chain. Forgive me if I'm having a little trouble believing you want me to work—"

"Cara, I need Aerie. I need you to stop your development effort. I'm willing to hire you to take you out of the race. I'll make you a fair deal. You can put your name on Aerie. I'll give you a percentage of the profits. Hell, you don't even need to show up at the office to draw your paycheck. In fact, I'd prefer it. I just need you to stop work on Aerie."

"Liam, I understand your situation. As usual, you've come up with a creative solution to your problem." His eyes flew up to hers in surprise. "In this case, it's not necessary. As I have said repeatedly, I don't have Aerie—"

"Let's not go through this again—"

"Stop, Liam," she cut in sharply. "I've heard enough from you this evening. You've interrupted me too many times. You've jumped to too many conclusions. You've misunderstood me and my actions. You've accused me of horrible things without facts. And you haven't given me a chance to explain. It's time you listened to me."

He started to respond, stopped, then nodded. "All right. Fair enough. I'm listening. Go ahead and explain."

She took a deep breath. "I understand why you think I have Aerie. I've put most of the story together. The truth is you've been sold a bill of goods by people you trust. Those people are lying to you, Liam. They are the ones putting Windwear at risk, not me. You shouldn't trust them."

"Oh? Who should I trust? You? Right. You were the one who disappeared for eight weeks. Eight weeks, Cara. And not a single word."

"Those eight weeks were a favor to you," she said quietly.

"A favor? How is it a favor when you steal my software and disappear?"

Cara looked away and remained silent for a long moment. When she finally raised her eyes to meet his, they were filled with a heavy sadness. "You know, Liam, one of the things I always liked about you was how you strive for the win-win in every situation. You always play fair. You find a way to make things work for everyone. You trust people. You give everyone a chance. Give everyone the benefit of the doubt." She shook her head sadly. "Everyone except me."

He hesitated for a moment, as if her words affected him in away he hadn't expected. "That's ... that's not true," he faltered. "I did give you the benefit of the doubt. I ... I—"

"No, you didn't. You found excuses for why I stole Aerie, something I wouldn't have done in a million years. That's not exactly the benefit of the doubt. Did you ever think, for even one short second, that I didn't steal it?"

Liam closed his eyes. "I did, Cara. Until I came back from Taiwan and found you had disappeared without a trace."

"And instead of finding out why I left, you believed the lies Lauren and Peter fed you."

"Lies? What lies? They didn't run and hide. They didn't disappear like you did. In fact, they've done nothing but help. Even Peter, though he can't do much with all the legal issues involved. But he's kept in touch—"

"I'm sure he has. Tell me, does he ask you where I am?"

"Yes, of course he does. He needs to find you so he can complete his investigation. Then he can sell Aerie to me."

"Right, that would be his story. And what about Lauren? I bet she was the big hero when she presented you with Aerie and all the documentation in one nice package, ripe and ready to be developed."

"So what if she was? It doesn't make her a liar."

"No, it doesn't make her a liar, but it does explain a few things. So, tell me, are you two an item, now? She always did have a thing for you. God knows, you've given her the benefit of the doubt enough times—"

"She deserves it," he snapped. "She's a damn sight more trustworthy than you, if you're asking me to make a comparison."

For some reason, those words cut Cara more deeply than any of the accusations he had thrown at her so far. The ache that started earlier was growing stronger every minute. He wasn't listening. He didn't understand. He didn't believe her. He would never believe her, she realized. She felt the tears start coming. They welled in her eyes and she couldn't hold them back. She stood abruptly and turned away from him.

Liam walked over to her. "Cara." His voice was far gentler than she expected. Somehow, that made the tears come faster. He took her arm and turned her to face him. "Cara—"

"No." She snatched her arm from his hold and moved away, furiously brushing the tears away. "Go away, Liam. I can't make you believe what you refuse to believe, and I'm not willing to listen to you make excuses for the people who are lying to you."

He took her arm again and turned her to face him. "Then tell me, Cara. Tell me your side of the story. Why did you run? Why do you think Peter and Lauren are lying to me?"

She stared at him through her tears. "No. I'm done with you, Liam. You don't believe me, fine. I give up. I'm not going to fight with you anymore. And I'm sure as hell not going to fight your battles anymore."

"What do you mean?"

"Forget it, Liam. It's too late, anyway. The game is up. Windwear is screwed."

"Cara, what are saying?" His expression was troubled. "If you know something I don't know, please tell me—"

"No! I trusted you once before, and God, what a mistake that turned out to be. I've done enough for you. I tried to help you, Liam. I laid everything on the line for you. And what did I get in return? Anger. Blame. Mistrust. I know it's not your fault for believing the lies Lauren and Peter told you. I know I should I understand, but I don't. God damn you for believing them. God damn you for believing their lies. I wish you would have trusted me the way I trusted you. Maybe then I wouldn't feel like my efforts were a complete waste."

She ignored her tears and the look of surprise on his face. "I was wrong about you, Liam. I thought you were worthy of my trust, but I was mistaken. Now I'm standing here with nothing, not even the satisfaction of doing the right thing. All because you refuse to take my word over the word of liars. What's worse is that you will end up destroying Windwear just like you've destroyed me." She removed his hand from her arm and faced him. "I want you to leave, Liam."

His face was a mass of questions. "God almighty, Cara, what are you talking about? Tell me what you did. Tell me what *I* did—"

"No, Liam. I'm done. You will never believe me. I understand that now. Find out the truth for yourself. Go back to Peter. Go back to Lauren. Ask them. You trust them. Maybe you'll believe them when they finally come clean."

"Cara, please ..."

She saw the worry in his eyes, but she didn't care any more. "No. Enough. Get out of my house." She pointed a finger toward the door, her eyes as cold and hard as his had been earlier that evening. "Go away, Liam. I never want to see you again."

Chapter 33

The waves shushed softly as Liam walked along the beach. The stars looked like giant holes in the black sky. A vision of Cara cut into his mind. Her beautiful angry eyes slashing at him. The ice-cold certainty of her conviction as she threw him out of her house. God, he was a fool. He had been so sure she stole Aerie. Her guilt had been sealed not only by the oft-repeated accusations of Lauren and Peter, but by her own actions. She had left. Disappeared without a trace.

He knew the truth now. Cara didn't steal the software. He was as certain of that as he was of his foolishness for doubting her. The relief rushing through him now was as potent as it had been earlier, when he first set eyes on her after eight long weeks. The emotions he had bottled up for so long threatened to overwhelm him and cloud his thinking. God, he wanted to turn and race back up the beach and force every secret between them out in the open. He wanted to kiss away every tear and tell her he had been wrong from the start. Stop, Liam, he told himself. You can't afford to think that way right now. If he had any chance for a future with Cara Larson, he needed to focus on the problem at hand. He needed to concentrate on Cara's words, not on every other part of Cara Larson he wanted to think about. He needed to find the answers Cara had hinted at but refused to say outright. He needed to make things right.

Her tears were the clue. It was so unlike Cara to cry. She didn't break easily, but her tears and the futility in her gaze as she faced him, stopped him short. He had believed her guilt so completely and for so long, that for a moment he was lost, hanging in space with no idea what to believe next. As he hovered between truth and lie, he realized Cara knew something he didn't know. She told him so, in so many words, then stopped and refused to explain further. He frowned. How could he blame her? He hadn't believed one word she said the entire evening.

Think, he told himself. The truth was hidden in her words. Something she said tonight didn't fit. It leapt out at the time, and then vanished in the harsh back and forth of their confrontation. What was it? What did she say? She wanted to know if Peter asked where she was. Was that it? No, it was no secret Peter was looking for her. It was something else ... He stopped, remembering what she said next. *"What about Lauren? I bet she was the big hero when she presented you with Aerie and all the documentation in one nice package, ripe and ready to be developed."*

He closed his eyes, thinking back to the night on the plane when Lauren gave him the envelope that contained Aerie. And all the documentation. Hmm. How the hell did Lauren get hold of all the documentation? She said Cara had two copies of Aerie, two identical envelopes. Two copies of the disks would make sense. It would be reasonable for Cara to make a backup of the prototype. But two copies of a three-inch stack of papers? How often did people make two copies of every shred of documentation? And how did Lauren get a package that size out of Cara's office without Cara seeing? She said she put the envelope in her handbag. God knows, he didn't notice much when it came to women, but he remembered that Lauren's handbag was a small quilted contraption that could not possibly hold a large manila envelope.

Did Lauren lie about how she found Aerie? Why? He shook his head in puzzlement. Lauren had never done anything to make him question her loyalty. He had relied on her heavily these past few months. She made the deal with the consortium to underwrite the IPO, despite her opposition to his financial projections. She handled the contract with Hsin, even though she preferred a deal with Wangchao. She forgave him for his unforgivable behavior in Taiwan. She picked up the slack when he went underground with Aerie. No, Lauren had stepped up to every challenge he had given her. He had no reason to believe she was lying, but Cara was convinced of it.

What did Cara know? He thought again to this evening when he told Cara that Lauren had taken the second copy of Aerie. He remembered how confused she looked. Confused, but not surprised. What had she said? *"New York? Second copy? What … I'm not following you at all."* Hmm. Confusion about what Lauren said, but not about Lauren herself. No, Cara accepted the news that Lauren had taken Aerie without a flicker of surprise. As if she knew Lauren had the software all along.

How could that be true? Hmm. Lauren made two claims the night she gave him the software. The first was that she stole the software without Cara's knowledge. The second was that Cara planned to develop and market Aerie for herself. If Cara was aware Lauren had taken the software, Lauren's first claim was an outright lie. And if Cara was aware Lauren had taken the software, claim number two made no sense either. If Cara planned to take Aerie for herself, she would never have allowed Lauren to leave her office with the software. In fact, she never would have let Aerie out of her sight. Nor would she have discussed her plans with Lauren or anyone else. And she certainly would not have announced the withdrawal of Aerie from scope during the review. No, if Cara wanted to take Aerie, she would have done so. Quietly. Without a word. Taken it and run like hell. But she didn't. Instead, she blurted out her plans to a woman she clearly disliked. Why would a smart girl like Cara do a stupid thing like that? Liam stopped in midstride. Unless, of course, she didn't.

So, how did Lauren get Aerie if she didn't steal it from Cara? Who did she steal it from? Who else beside Cara had possession of Aerie? Peter? He shook his head. No, if Lauren stole Aerie from Peter, the last person to know would have been Cara. By then, she was history. Persona non grata. No one at Pyramid would have risked even talking to her, much less pass on any news about Aerie.

He frowned darkly. Who else had possession of Aerie? Mike? No. Cara protected him from this mess from the beginning. Mike had no idea what happened the day of the review. Liam's mind ticked over everyone who attended the review. Who else could possibly have had possession of Aerie? Not one person came to mind. Which left ... "Hell and damnation!" he swore into the blackness. Was it true what they said about the most obvious thing being the hardest to see? Or was he just the most obtuse human being to ever walk this earth? That left ... Cara. Cara knew Lauren had the software because Cara gave it to her. And she gave Lauren all the documentation too. Then once Cara disappeared, Lauren proceeded to stab her in the back with unending rumors about her nonexistent plans to develop Aerie. Cara made no second copy. Cara never planned to develop Aerie for herself. Cara didn't have Aerie at all. Lauren had lied to Liam every step of the way. But why?

He needed to find out.

He hurried across the sand to the hotel. He ran up the stairs and tapped on the door of Room 227. "Staci?" he whispered. "Staci. Please open the door. I need a huge favor."

Chapter 34

The knock on Liam's hotel room door came at 6:30 a.m. The sun was barely rising, and gray light colored the waves. Liam opened the door, and Lauren breezed through. "Good morning, Liam. This must be important. Even God isn't up at this hour." She stretched her shoulders like a cat ready for play.

"Please sit down, Lauren. We need to talk."

She sat down on the couch and flashed a smile. "All right. What do you want to talk about?"

Liam sat in a chair opposite her. "One of the reasons I hired you, Lauren, is—"

"Is because I'm a fabulous lawyer?" she interrupted with a dazzling smile.

Liam's eyes held no answering smile. "Yes, you are, but that's not the primary reason. Good lawyers abound, Lauren. No, I hired you because your background and training make you perfectly suited to disagree with me."

"What? I don't understand."

"Let me explain. I know how I want to run Windwear, but I also know I can do things that are unconventional, and at times, unwise. I realized I needed a smart, knowledgeable person with a strong personality to push back and tell me when I'm wrong and to give me the perspective I need to make good decisions." He tilted his head and gave her a tight smile. "You haven't disappointed me. I think we can agree that we fundamentally disagree on how a business should be run."

"What are you getting at?" Her smile faded.

"What I'm getting at, is that I understand I haven't made things easy for you. I've disagreed with pretty much ever suggestion you've ever made. I don't mind, but I imagine it's not easy for you. What I do mind, and what I cannot accept, is dishonesty from my employees."

"Dishonesty?" Surprise was evident in her tone. "Are you accusing me of dishonesty?"

"No, at least not yet, but I want you to keep what I said in mind when I ask you this next question." He picked up a file from the table, and examined the contents for a few moments. "Tell me again how you found Aerie."

She looked at him with a hint of uncertainty. "I told you how I picked it up from Cara's desk. Don't you remember?"

"Yes, I remember." Silently he handed her the folder Staci had worked all night to prepare. "Here's your severance package. You will receive two weeks' pay, insurance coverage until the end of the month, a copy of the reference letter we will give to any of your prospective employers—"

"What's going on, Liam? What is the meaning of this?"

"I'm letting you go."

"What? You can't fire me. You need me. I'm probably the most important person at Windwear right now. We're going public in two weeks. Who will take care of the IPO if I'm gone?"

"You will also find in the packet a form transferring your stock options back to Windwear, and—"

Lauren's face turned crimson with rage. "What is the matter with you? You can't do this. You're firing me because I found Aerie? And saved your company, by the way?"

"No, I'm firing you because you haven't told me the truth about how you found Aerie."

She looked puzzled for a minute, and then smiled as if this were all an unfortunate misunderstanding. "I didn't do anything illegal, if that's what you're worried about."

"Good. Then you shouldn't have any trouble telling me about it."

"I don't understand where this is coming from, Liam. It doesn't matter how I found Aerie. You have it and you're developing it. End of story."

Liam nodded. "All right. Just sign here. And here. And here. I'll make sure a security guard is waiting at the office to escort you while you gather your personal things. The locks will be changed by noon."

A hint of panic showed in her eyes. "All right, Liam. I may not have told you the entire truth, but it wasn't my fault."

"Oh? Whose fault was it?'

"Whose do you think?" she asked sharply. "I saw you talking with her last night. Is that where this is coming from? Did she tell you I lied?"

Liam remained silent and Lauren made an effort to calm her tone. "All right. Cara gave Aerie to me."

Liam let out the breath he had been holding. "Why don't you start from the beginning and tell me the whole story."

"There's not much to tell. I ... I didn't find the software in Cara's office. She gave it to me. When you and Paul met with Peter, Mike called and asked me to meet Cara in the restroom on the twenty-third floor. We met, she handed me the software, and I left. I didn't see her again until last night."

"She didn't give Aerie to Peter?"

"Are you kidding?" she asked incredulously. "She had just been fired. She was angry with Peter. She told me she wanted revenge."

"I see." Liam gazed at her impassively. "Why didn't she give it to Fleet?"

"Fleet was in too tight with Pyramid because of FIT. She didn't want to risk Peter strong-arming it away from Rick Penner."

"And the documentation? Cara gave that to you, too?"

"Yes." Lauren nodded. When Liam didn't say anything for several moments, she spoke again. "This is not what you think, Liam. This was all Cara's idea. She thought you wouldn't keep Aerie if you discovered she took it from Peter. She knew Peter accused her of criminal behavior. She was afraid you would think it was tainted. So, we made up the story that I found it."

"And you added a few embellishments of your own. You created the rumors that destroyed her professional reputation." His voice was calm but his eyes were hard. "Do you think I do business this way, Lauren? That I condone such behavior? That I would willingly ruin another person's career and reputation for my own benefit? Especially when that person just took a huge risk to benefit my company?"

Lauren shook her head. "I didn't try to ruin anything, Liam. I did … say a few things, but only to encourage you to develop Aerie yourself. I thought you would be more motivated if you—"

"If I felt Cara cheated me?"

"Well, it worked, didn't it? Besides, I didn't think any harm would result. Cara planned to leave town. Pinning the blame on her was the smart thing to do. As long as she was the target of blame, no one even suspected you had Aerie."

"Did Cara tell you anything else?"

"Like what?" Suspicion laced her words.

"Cara thinks you are privy to some important information that could harm Windwear. Something you haven't told me."

"Is that what she said?" Indignation flamed in her voice, but her eyes were wary. "Forgive me, Liam, but I think Cara is trying to blame me for her mistakes. I didn't do anything wrong. Cara gave me the software. She told me to give it to you. She told me not to tell you it came from her. I did as she asked. And you benefitted from what I did."

"Did you give Aerie to anyone else?"

"What? I've practically killed myself implementing all the changes at Windwear. Do you think I would undermine my own efforts by doing something so foolish?"

Liam stood up and walked to the window. He stared out at the ocean, now covered with a heavy layer of mist. "When did you plan to tell me the truth, Lauren?"

Lauren followed him. Her voice was soft and soothing when she spoke. "Liam, everything I've done, I've done for you and Windwear. I know how you feel about trust and honesty, but this wasn't my fault. Cara worried that if you learned Aerie came from her, you'd refuse to keep it. I decided not to take any chances. I may have made a mistake by accusing her of stealing Aerie, but believe me, it was only meant to be a white lie. I didn't see the harm in pointing the finger at her as long as Windwear was protected. After all, she left, ran away." She tilted her head, put a hand on his arm, and leaned close to him. "You can understand my point of view, can't you? This was all Cara's fault. I was going to tell you, when the time was right."

He took a step away from her. "The right time was when you gave me Aerie. You should have told me the truth from the start so I could decide what to do."

"But—"

"No buts, Lauren. I can't run this company properly if my attorney is lying to me."

She looked at him, unable to keep the worry from her eyes. "So, are you going to fire me?"

He sighed. "You've been a good employee, Lauren. I realize this is an unusual situation. I understand what you did, but I can't condone your actions. This is a major lapse of judgment. I'm putting you on probation for the next three months. I want you to confine your work to the IPO only. I want you to complete the registration statement for the SEC, finish the blue sky filings for the states where we will sell stock, and oversee the latest financial review being conducted by the auditors. Nothing else until I've reviewed the situation more fully."

"Probation?" Her soothing tones from a moment earlier were now replaced with anger. "You're going to put me on probation after everything I've done for you?" She glared at him angrily. "This is because of Taiwan isn't it? You're still angry about what … happened between us."

He shook his head. "Nothing happened between us, Lauren, except I behaved badly. No, this is not about what happened in Taiwan, but I mean what I say. I can't run the company if the people I work with aren't honest with me."

"Liam, I told you, it wasn't my fault —"

"One more thing," he said, ignoring her protest. "If I find out you're not telling me the truth about anything we have discussed here this morning, there will be no third chance."

Lauren contained her anger until she reached her room. He was a bastard. A stupid bastard at that. Who did he think he was, trying to back her into a corner? He should have fired her when he had the chance, because she would make sure he lived to regret his mistake. Didn't he know lawyers always had contingency plans? She could be particularly good at revenge. She flipped through her daybook and found the number. Calming herself, she dialed. As she waited for the line to connect, she sat at the edge of her bed, rolling her head around in small, angry circles.

"Good morning, Pyramid Corporation, FIT Project."

"Yes. Peter Whittington, please."

Lauren relaxed her body and closed her eyes. In a few seconds, she heard Peter's voice on the line. "Peter, Lauren Janelle from Windwear." Her voice was husky and low. "Do you have a few minutes to talk?"

Chapter 35

Cara was just finishing mile eleven. One more mile and she would be home. As she ran over the trail, she wiped the sweat from her face with her forearm. Everything ached. Feet, legs, knees, hips. She would make it, though. Sometimes on these long runs, she wasn't always sure. That's why she did them, she thought. To test herself. To prove she could be strong when she didn't feel strong. And strong wasn't the word for her today.

It had been less than twenty-four hours since the bottom fell out of her life. Again. Less than twenty-four hours since she faced Liam's sickening accusations and stubborn disbelief. Less than twenty-four hours since he stumbled through that sorry excuse of an apology and she blew him off in complete contempt.

And in less than twenty-four hours, she would disappear. Again. She had no choice. It wouldn't be long before Peter found her. Then both she and Windwear would be in trouble. She stumbled over an exposed root. "Damn."

Everything would be all right, she told herself. She would vanish again. She'd go somewhere far away, where neither Peter nor Liam could find her. Vermont. Or Maine. She had worked out most of the plans during the run. The move would be harder this time. She would have to use her real name. She would need to be extremely careful, but she would manage. She entered the forest and welcomed the cool darkness. It was time to go, she kept telling herself. Her feet pounded out the rhythm as she slogged on. *Time to go, time to go, time to go.*

The path dead-ended at the beach, and she slowed to a walk. Her house stood a quarter mile across the sand and up the hill. A perfect cool down. She glanced at her watch. Half past two. Not bad. She would shower, pack, and be on the 7:40 p.m. bus to San Francisco. Oh, and she needed to phone Lisa and cancel the peach cobbler training session this afternoon. She sighed. Peach cobbler. Violin lessons. Surfboards. Life had been almost … normal. Not anymore. She pushed the thought away. She would get on the bus to SF, travel east, and not look back. She started up the steps to the house.

The back door swung slightly inward as she approached the house. That wasn't right. The shadows must be playing tricks. She distinctly remembered locking the door on her way out. Maybe she hadn't pulled it all the way shut. She did that sometimes when she was in a hurry. She'd been in a hurry today.

She walked in and checked the door. Unlocked. "Good job, Cara," she said aloud. "You really need to get your head in gear." As she closed the door, she noticed a slight breeze ruffle the curtain on the door. She stopped. That can't happen when the door is closed. She bent down to study it more closely and gasped in surprise. The entire lower pane above the door handle was missing, as if it had been removed with a glasscutter. She detected the faint odor of kerosene and a stubble of glass where the pane met the wooden frame.

The silence was interrupted by a loud rush as two men swept down the stairs. Startled, Cara screamed, unable to move from the spot where she stood. The two men stopped midway on the stairs, but she couldn't see their faces. They were dressed in black, with black stockings covering their heads. They carried several things in their arms. Not big things, but small ones, made of metal and plastic. "Oh, my God," she whispered to herself. My computer disks. "Stop!" she yelled without thinking. "What are you doing—"

The rest of her words were lost as the men dashed down the stairs. The tall one in front grabbed her with his free hand. His grip held her tight, and as hard as she tried, she couldn't wriggle from his grasp. All at once, he flung her through the air, and the right side of her body hit the wall with a sickening crash. The sheer force of the impact bounced her back toward the intruder. He grabbed her arm again. "Get out of my way, bitch!" He slammed her against the wall with even greater force. This time her right side hit the corner of the wall separating the living room from the kitchen. Blood spurted from her cheek as she crumpled to the floor, and blackness closed around her.

Chapter 36

Cara woke up with a pounding headache in a strange bed surrounded by strange smells. The light was fading into evening, and the room was dim and gray. A small lamp in the corner spilled light into the room. A man in a dark green shirt sat next to it, reading a book. She blinked a few times, trying to figure out where she was. Scattered memories came back to her. She sat up slowly and winced as pain shot down her right side. She placed a hand to her face. "Ouch."

The man approached and laid a restraining hand on her arm. "Well, hello ma'am. I reckon you better lay back down and rest your purty head. The doctor says you shouldn't be movin' for a spell."

The voice was deep, with a Southern drawl that reminded Cara of Jeanine. Which made her think of her mother. Which made her want to cry. Dizzy and achy, she lay back down again. "All ... all right. That appears to be my only option at the moment." She gazed up at the man. He was tall, like Liam. Unlike Liam, he had sparkling blue eyes and a thick muscular build, as if he had once been a football player. Or a boxer. He was older than Liam, probably by about ten years. He seemed to be in his early forties. She smiled weakly. "How did a Southern accent like that find its way to little Cannon Beach?"

The man let out a lazy half-grin. "Well ma'am. I suppose you never heard of the famous Dallas to Topeka to Denver to Seattle to Portland route. I don't believe it's well known in these parts, or there'd be more of us up here."

She started to laugh, then grimaced at the pain in her head. "Ouch."

His eyes clouded. "I'm sorry, ma'am. I shouldn't be makin' light when you're in this condition. I'm Officer Carson, Cannon Beach Police. I'd better get the doctor to take a look at you."

She stared at him in confusion. "Am I at the hospital? How did I get here?"

"Your friend Lisa found you. She said you missed a meetin,' and she went lookin' for you. She found you unconscious, bleedin' from your head, with your back door wide open. She called the ambulance, and the emergency crew brought you here."

"I see."

"Are you feelin' well enough to talk about what happened?"

"I'm … I'm not sure what happened. I … I think I tripped. I had just finished running. Maybe I was a little woozy."

"Does that happen often, Miss …" He glanced down at his notebook. "Miss Martin?"

At that moment the door opened, and a nurse bustled in. "Oh, Miss Martin, you're awake. How are you feeling? Let me call the doctor." As she moved around the room, taking Cara's blood pressure and temperature, Officer Carson excused himself. A few moments later, the doctor walked in. He was an older man, who poked and prodded and interspersed his ministrations with distracted mutterings about the Cubs and pennants and 1945. Cara looked askance at the well-worn Cubs hat he threw on the bedside table as he walked in, but his hands were gentle and sure, and he peered directly at her with clear gray eyes. "Well, young lady, I think you'll live, but I don't think you ought to be doing the tango with the wall anymore."

"I guess I shouldn't have tried to lead." She tried to smile.

The doctor laughed. "At least not with your head."

"May I go home? I'd like to go home."

"Well, you'd be better off staying here overnight—"

"Probably, but may I go anyway? I ... I don't have any insurance."

He sighed. "Well, let's see how you handle standing up."

"Okay." She stood, and felt her head pound, but she tightened her muscles and willed herself not to sway. "What do you think?"

"You passed, young lady, but you'll need to rest at home for a few days."

"Absolutely. I will." She touched her face. "I don't think I'm going to be invited out anytime soon."

"Well, your sense of humor is intact. That's always a good sign. I'll get the paperwork started." He held out his hand. "No more dancing with walls, young lady."

She smiled despite the pounding, and shook his hand. "Deal."

Officer Carson walked into the room as she gathered her clothes and headed to the bathroom to change. He was holding a bag of ice. "The nurse told me to make sure you put this—just a durn minute. What's goin' on here?"

She stood at the bathroom door. "I've been discharged." She closed the door quickly. She took off the hospital gown and noted the bruises trailing down her right shoulder and arm. She changed her clothes and turned to face the mirror. Yikes. Her forehead and cheek were bandaged. Her jaw was marked by a dark bruise. She sighed and wondered what shade of purple her eye would turn over the next few days. Otherwise, she was all right. Except for the screaming headache.

Officer Carson was waiting for her when the door opened. "Are you ready to go, ma'am?"

"What?" she asked warily.

"You came here in an ambulance. The least I can do is give you a ride home."

"Oh." She hadn't even thought about how she'd get home. "Thank you."

The radio crackled into the air. "... finished gathering all the evidence and checking for prints."

"Are we clear to enter?" Officer Carson asked the cackle.

"Yes. We're finished. Over."

"Thanks, Rosie. I'll catch up with you later. Out for now."

He smiled at Cara as he pulled the patrol car to a stop in her driveway. "You stay here while I check out the house."

"You don't believe I tripped into a wall?"

"Oh no, ma'am. I believe you, but walls, they can be right wicked. I want to make sure they're all standin' up straight and not causin' any more trouble." He gave her a crooked smile as he locked her in the car.

A few minutes later, he came out. "All clear. You can come in now."

She walked in. Except for a bloody mark on the wall, there was no evidence this was anything but a peaceful house in a peaceful town on a peaceful beach. "Why don't you sit down, ma'am. You might want to go slow."

It was a good idea. Suddenly she wasn't feeling very safe.

The policeman strode to the kitchen and returned a few minutes later. "I reckon we should continue where we left off at the hospital. Here's that ice pack you've been needin'." He held the ice pack to her cheek, and then guided her hand to hold it in place. "There you go. That will keep the swellin' down so you won't end up lookin' like a party balloon."

"Thank you." She blushed. "I must look awful."

"No ma'am. You're right purty. You put every party balloon I ever knew to shame." She couldn't keep her laugh from escaping. "That's better. I think you're one of those people who were made to smile."

He sat in the chair opposite Cara. "Now ma'am. Why don't you tell me what's really goin' on?" He paused. "We established you didn't trip and fall into the wall."

"We did?"

"Yup."

She sighed. "You're not going to leave until I tell you, are you?"

"Nope."

She held the pack against her cheek and felt the ice melt as it touched her skin. "All right. I came in after my run and surprised two men dressed in black. They slammed me into the wall and ... and that's all. I don't remember anything else."

"Do you have any idea who they were? Or why they were here?"

She hesitated. "Yes. They were looking for something."

"What might that be?"

"Something I don't have."

"Would you care to elaborate?"

"No. It's not important. I don't have it."

Officer Carson nodded. "Where are you from, Ms. Martin?"

"Is that important?"

"Well, ma'am, you tell me. Someone broke into your house lookin' for somethin' and beat you up purty good. Your friend Lisa says you moved here a few months ago. You seem to have made a lot of friends but haven't had enough time to make enemies. It stands to reason someone or somethin' you left behind finally caught up with you."

He pulled out his notebook and flipped a few pages. "You're quite mysterious Miss Martin. I did a little checkin' after I talked to your friend Lisa. Awful strange, if you ask me. Seems like everyone in town is acquainted with you, but there's not a whit of paperwork with your name attached. I took the liberty of searchin' for Miss Caroline Martin in a few of the databases us police folk can get our hands on." He gave her a friendly smile. "Dang, if the world isn't full of a lot of Caroline Martins, but not one seems to match you. Now, isn't that strange?"

"I think I'm more tired than I thought, Officer Carson. Can we continue this conversation tomorrow?"

"Pardon me for sayin' ma'am, but you sound like you're avoidin' the subject."

She sighed wearily. "I would say that's exactly what I'm doing. I don't want to talk about who I am, where I've been, or what I've done. So if you're going to ask me those types of questions, let's just stop now."

The policeman raised an eyebrow in surprise. "Well, ma'am, you sure don't pull any punches, do you?"

"There's no need to, Officer Carson." She closed her eyes. "Besides, it won't happen again. Once they realize I don't have what they want, they won't come back."

"So, you know who did this?"

"Yes."

"Well, I admire your surefire independence, ma'am, but the law doesn't work that way. My job is to find the persons responsible for this crime. I'm not allowed to drop a criminal case unless my boss gives me the say-so."

"I don't get a choice in the matter?"

"No ma'am. Funny thing. You get as little choice decidin' whether we prosecute as you had bein' the victim. Sometimes that isn't so good. In your case, I think you'd be smart to tell me what's goin' on."

"Why?"

"Because I think you're dead wrong about the folks who hurt you. Folks like that, folks who beat up defenseless women? If they don't find what they want the first time, they generally don't stop. No, they don't stop until they find what they're after. Sometimes, that means when their victim is dead."

His lazy eyes pierced hers with a steady stare. He studied his notebook once more. "Now, let me go over what I know. Your name is Caroline Martin. You moved here several weeks ago. You do not hold a job, but you do odd work here and there for local businesses. Accordin' to your friend Lisa, you had a confrontation with a man last night—"

"He didn't do it," Cara said quickly.

"Who is he?"

She closed her eyes and ran her fingers over the bandages on her face. "Please, Officer Carson, don't ask any more questions. You're only going to make things worse."

He closed the notebook. "You know, Miss Martin, I can find out these answers with or without your help. One way is fast, the other slow, but I'm goin' to end up in the same spot in either case. Why don't you make this easy and tell me what's goin' on?"

Cara sighed and drew her knees up to her chest, ignoring the pain shooting through her body. She put her chin on her knees and stared at the wall in front of her. "No."

He stared at her for a long moment. "Well ma'am, I don't think we're goin' to solve anythin' tonight. You look plumb tuckered out. If I've learned anythin' about women, it's they need to be well rested before they'll listen to reason."

"Okay. We can talk tomorrow." She stood up and walked to the door. "I'll show you out."

He followed, towered over her, and quietly closed the door she had just opened. "You misunderstand me. I'm not leavin' tonight. For a coupla reasons. First, I've been assigned to your case, and I need to get some answers from you. Second ..." He walked over to the window, slid the curtain open, and peered outside. He dropped the curtain into place and turned to face her. "Second, a gray sedan's been parked down the street since we drove up this evenin'. Two men inside. Out of state license plates. Not your typical tourist types."

Cara walked to the window and peeked outside. Sure enough. A gray sedan. "Damn," she whispered as she replaced the curtain.

"You still don't want to tell me what's goin' on, Miss Martin?" The policeman waited but received only silence. "All right. I'll tell you what I'm gonna do. I'm goin' to call in the suspicious vehicle and get some of my fellow officers to detain the two men inside. My guess is we can only hold them for a coupla hours."

"You will?" She brightened. "That would be great."

He studied her thoughtfully. "May I use your phone, ma'am?"

She nodded. "Sure. It's in the kitchen."

Cara counted to three before she ran up the stairs.

It didn't take long to pull down the suitcase from her closet and throw in the essentials she would need for an escape. She had thought through this scenario more than once since she left Portland. How to escape in an emergency.

She slid open the closet door, pulled the cover off the clothes hamper, and removed the safe. Her fingers twirled the knob. *Click*. She opened the door and removed several thousand dollars and her identification cards wrapped in tinfoil. She tucked wads of bills in several pairs of socks and jammed them in the suitcase. She put one large wad along with the tinfoil packet in the side pocket of her purse and zipped it closed.

There was a knock on the door. "Miss Martin? May I come in?"

She froze for a moment. "Just a second."

Immediately the door opened, and the policeman took in the sight. "Goin' somewhere, ma'am?"

She turned to face him. "Yes."

"Tonight?"

She sighed. "If I could manage it, yes."

"Without tellin' me what was goin' on?"

"If necessary, yes."

He nodded. "That's what I like about you, Miss Martin. You got a knack for hittin' the nail straight on the head." He gestured toward the door. "Where do you plan to go? There are no more buses out of town tonight. And I took the liberty of pokin' my head through your garage window. You don't even own a car."

Cara paused for several moments, considering. "Officer Carson, how would you like to make a deal?"

"Well, ma'am, that's a mighty intriguin' statement. Why don't we go downstairs and you can tell me what you mean. I want to keep an eye out and make sure our friends in the gray sedan get picked up."

She followed him downstairs. The policeman peered out the window, then turned toward her. "Well, I'll be damned. Our friends in the gray sedan are gone alright."

"Good."

"But danged if we haven't got a new set of visitors. In a black car this time. Harder to see in the evenin' light. Seems someone surely wants to keep an eye on you, Miss Martin." He looked at her intently. "Do you still want to make that deal, ma'am?"

"I don't seem to have much choice." She studied him carefully. "I'll tell you everything I know about who attacked me if you'll do something for me."

"What would that be?"

She shot a glance at the window. "You get me past whoever is outside so I can leave town on the 7:40 bus to San Francisco tomorrow night."

"On the surface, that seems like an easy deal to make. I'd need to add a condition or two."

"What type of condition?"

"Are you mixed up in anythin' illegal, ma'am? Because bein' a police officer and all, I couldn't make an agreement to let you leave if you were fleein' from a life of crime."

Cara paused for a long moment. "No, not technically."

"*Technically* is a peculiar term, ma'am."

She smiled ruefully. "Too true, Officer Carson."

The policeman sat down. "I'll tell you what. You tell me what you know, and if what you're mixed up in isn't criminal, I'll help you leave."

"And if it is?"

He gave her a lazy smile. "I get this feelin' things aren't so cut and dried with you, Miss Martin."

She closed her eyes. She might as well tell him. He was her only means of escape. And escape was necessary. She understood that all too clearly, now. She sat down and began to tell him the truth. Or as much of it as she could.

He was silent after she finished her story. "So, Officer Carson?"

"Hmm?"

"Did I break any laws when I took the software?"

"What do you think, ma'am?"

"Well, if Aerie was included in the contract, it would rightfully belong to Windwear. In which case I didn't break the law because all I did was give Aerie to its rightful owner. But Aerie wasn't in the contract. In that case, the software never officially existed. How can I break the law if the thing I took doesn't exist?"

"You have a point, ma'am, but then, somethin' does exist."

"I'm not sure what you mean."

"Well, this software, official or not, is out runnin' around, important enough for someone to break in and try to steal. People generally don't go around stealin' things that don't exist. So, since this Aerie software does exist and isn't in the contract, who do you think owns it?"

She sighed. "Technically—"

"Aha. There's our friend *technically*. I figured we'd get to it sooner or later."

She nodded. "Yes. Technically, Pyramid would own the software because Pyramid employees built it. But don't you see? Peter planned this all along. He wins on the technicality. He wrongly removes Aerie from scope, then swoops in and takes it because Fleet and Windwear can't take ownership of something not in the contract."

"I'll tell you what, Miss Martin. I think you got some danged good arguments goin' in both directions. This might be a question for someone other than a lowly sergeant recently removed from the great state of Texas."

"Does that mean you'll help me leave?"

"If that's what you want, but I'm not sure it's such a good idea. Especially since I have one more condition."

"What condition?"

"I can help you, but you need to promise to keep in touch in case I need your help with the case."

She stiffened. "How can I be sure you won't tell anyone where I am?"

"That's a durn good question, ma'am. I can give you my word. I guess I wouldn't blame you much for not trustin' me, but if you want my help, you're gonna need to decide if you can."

He stood up and walked over to the couch. "Now, if you don't mind, I'll just settle myself right down on this here divan and rest awhile. I think those men outside might be interested to see a police car in your driveway for the rest of the evenin'. We can chat more tomorrow. We'll have some time before your bus leaves."

"Officer Carson?" she asked as he closed his eyes.

"Yes ma'am?"

"Do you have a first name?"

He opened one eye. "Sure do. The name is Kit. Officer Kit Carson."

She hesitated for a moment. "You're joking, aren't you?"

"Sure am, ma'am." He gave her another lazy smile. "The name is Andrew. Officer Andrew Carson."

She laughed softly. "Goodnight, then, Officer Andrew Carson. And ... thank you for your help."

"Goodnight, Miss Martin. You're quite welcome."

"Officer Carson ... Andrew?"

"Ma'am?"

"My name isn't Caroline Martin."

"I figured as much, ma'am."

She hesitated. "It's Cara. Cara Larson."

"Mighty pleased to make your proper acquaintance, ma'am. G'night, then, Miss Cara Larson."

Chapter 37

Liam pulled his car into the gravel driveway and flipped off the windshield wipers. The rain had come down heavily all night. He glanced at his watch. 7:00 a.m. Well, it was early, but he couldn't wait anymore. He'd spent every minute since the conference ended last night formulating a plan. He had thought through every detail. Now he needed to talk to Cara.

He reached across the seat and gathered the roses in his hands. No hope of getting lilacs in September. He ran up the steps to the front porch and knocked on the door. "Cara! Cara! Are you awake?"

It seemed like forever before the door opened. But Cara didn't answer. A man did. Check that. A policeman. The man stared at the roses in Liam's hands. "For me? You shouldn't have."

"Who are you? Is Cara here? Is she all right? I need to speak with her."

"Who are *you*?"

"Liam Scofield—"

"So, you're Liam." He leaned forward and peered closely at Liam's face. "Well, it doesn't look like she left any permanent scars."

"What?" He touched his face where Cara had struck him. "Did she press charges? Is that why you're here? Let me tell you, I should be the one pressing charges. It was a direct hit."

The policeman nodded. "Well deserved, from what I gather."

"I won't contest that statement." He tilted his head with a rueful grin. "Now, is she here? I need to talk to her."

"Let me find out if she wants to talk to you."

"Great. She won't want to, but I need to talk to her anyway."

Cara watched as Andrew returned to the kitchen. "Who is it?" she asked, trying to keep the worry from her voice.

"Well, well, well. Mr. Liam Scofield is at your door."

"Liam?" she asked in surprise, then shook her head. "Tell him to go away."

He smiled. "He told me you'd say that." He held out the bouquet. "He brought these for you. He said he couldn't find any lilacs."

She reached for the flowers. Pink and yellow and white roses were massed in a huge bundle. He must have cleaned out the entire florist shop. They were beautiful. They reminded Cara of her mother. "Tell him thank you. And to go away."

Andrew nodded. "He didn't think flowers would be enough. So, he told me to tell you he talked to Lauren."

Cara snapped her head up. "He did?"

"That's what he said."

"Tell him it's too late. And to go away."

"Well, I gotta say, this Liam fella knows you purty well. He said you wouldn't go for that either. So here's his last offer. He says thank you. For savin' Windwear. He understands now—"

Cara didn't hear the rest. She was already up and hurrying toward the living room. At the kitchen entrance, she stopped abruptly and turned back to the policeman. "Andrew, is the black car still parked down the street?"

"Yup."

She sighed. She returned to the table and picked up the bouquet. She walked to the living room, opened the door, and spied the black car parked three houses away. And there was Liam, standing on the porch, his back to her, deep in thought.

"Liam?"

He turned toward her, a sudden smile lighting his face. His eyes were tired. Deep grooves were carved in his cheekbones, and fine lines were scattered around his eyes. There were even a few flecks of gray in his dark hair. It looked like he'd been in a battle of his own. Still, he was the best thing she'd seen in forever.

"Cara?" He stepped forward, a worried expression replacing his smile. "My God, what happened to you?"

She took a quick step back. "Stop, Liam." She held out the flowers as if she were warding off the devil. "Please, just listen. A car is parked down the street with Peter's men inside." She brushed her cheek. "They ... they attacked me yesterday."

"What?—"

"Please, listen to me. If Peter finds out you and I have been seen together, he is going to think you have Aerie, and we're both going to be in trouble. We need to talk, though. I need your help to divert them." He paused and nodded imperceptibly. "Pretend we're having a fight. I'm going to give you back the flowers. You're going to drive back to your hotel like you're angry. Slip out your hotel the back way and head up the beach. I'll let you in the back door. Then we can talk."

Liam silently absorbed her words. Then he nodded, and with a sharp movement, snatched the bouquet from her hands and walked briskly away.

"Liam?"

"What?" he growled as he turned.

"Would you bring the flowers back? Please?"

He forced the smile from his lips but she saw it flash in his eyes. "You're making this really hard, you know." Then he turned abruptly and strode to his car. His tires left a layer of rubber on the road as he sped away.

She walked to the kitchen. "Where is he?" Andrew asked.

Cara glanced at the clock. "He should be coming up the beach in about ten minutes." She smiled. "The guys in the black car think we had a fight."

Andrew raised one eyebrow. "Hedgin' your bets, Miss Cara?"

She smiled. "Maybe."

Chapter 38

Cara was waiting on the porch as Liam hurried up the beach, flowers in hand. He walked up the stairs, and stood for a moment, taking in the sight of her. Then without a word, he covered the space between them and wrapped her in his arms. "Cara," he whispered. "God, Cara, I'm so sorry." She circled her arms around his waist and held on as tight as she could. They stood like that for a long time, soaking each other in, holding each other as if they would never let go, with no need for any words.

"Ahem. Pardon my interruptin,' but I think you two should come inside. I wouldn't want our friends in the black sedan to get a look at the two of you canoodlin' — "

Cara jumped from Liam's arms and blushed a bright red. "Andrew ... you're right. I'm sorry, I ... I ..." She took Liam's hand. "We'd better go in."

They followed Andrew, and when they were inside, Liam shook the policeman's hand. "Liam Scofield. Good to meet you. Andrew, is it?"

"That's right. Andrew Carson. Cannon Beach police."

"Thanks for convincing Cara to see me."

"You bet." He took another mug from the cupboard, filled it with coffee, and handed it to Liam. "Have a seat, both of you. I reckon we need to chew over a few matters."

Liam and Cara sat down. "You're investigating what happened to Cara?" Liam asked.

"Tryin' to, though I can't say it's been easy. Miss Larson is a little bit of a mystery."

Liam smiled. "*Little* is not exactly the adjective I would use."

"I reckon you're right about that. Seems your gal is mixed up in a bit of trouble."

Liam turned to Cara with a question in his eyes. "We can talk freely, Liam. I told Andrew everything."

"Well, maybe not everythin'," the policeman said as he sipped his coffee. "But I'm purty good at readin' between the lines."

Liam's face turned serious. "What happened, Cara?"

"Peter happened, or at least I'm pretty sure it was Peter. His men attacked me yesterday afternoon. They were looking for Aerie. They took my hard drive and all my disks."

"How did he find you?"

"I imagine word of my whereabouts slipped out sometime after your conference—"

"Do you think Lauren told him?" Liam asked abruptly.

"That would be my guess."

"Damn."

"Liam, I don't think she meant me any harm, or even that she realized what Peter would do. I think she was trying to protect Windwear. Once you and I showed up in the same place, I think she was afraid Peter would think we were working together. She wants to make sure no one suspects Windwear has Aerie."

"So she wants to make you the suspect, instead. That's been her strategy from the beginning."

"Yes, which is why I need to leave."

"What do you mean, leave?" Liam asked, concern in his tone.

"I mean, get out of town, leave. Lauren is right, Liam. If Peter thinks we're working together, he'll go after both of us. He won't suspect you if he thinks we've argued and I suddenly leave again."

"But he'll go after you. I can't agree to that. Not now. Not after what he's done."

"Liam, it will be okay. There's a bus heading to San Francisco this evening. Andrew will run interference so I can leave without Peter's men seeing me."

He stared at Cara, then at the policeman. "Do you think this is a good idea, Andrew?"

"It's not Andrew's call, it's mine" Cara interrupted. "It's the best solution. For me and for you."

"What happens if Peter finds you?"

"I'll be careful."

"You were careful last time, Cara, and look what happened. One little slip-up, one little accident of fate, and Peter found you and attacked. The situation is no better now. In fact, it's worse. Peter's watching you. Do you recall the charade we went through a few minutes ago just so I could sneak in your back door? What happens if he finds you, and you're somewhere ... God knows where, alone?" He reached across the table and touched her cheek. "What will he do the next time, Cara? Kill you?"

She shook her head but couldn't deny the fear creeping through her. "Peter is not going to kill me. Peter is a slimy slug, but he's not a murderer."

"How can you tell? He's not exactly a model of restraint. He's already assaulted you. You can't predict what he'll try next." He paused. "Cara, you have every right to run, and I can't blame you for wanting to, but I don't want you to go. I don't want to lose you again, now that I finally found you."

Cara studied him silently for several moments. She wanted to ask him what those words meant, but his eyes gave nothing away. "I can't think of anything else," she said quietly.

"Well, you're in luck, Ms. Larson." His crooked grin brushed the moment away, along with her questions. "I have a plan to protect you and buy me the time I need to finish Aerie. But I'll need your help."

"Finish Aerie? What do you mean? Are you close?"

"We are. We're really close. A few more weeks, a month at most, and we'll be ready to roll Aerie out to the world."

Cara felt relief wash through her. "Liam, that's wonderful news. Congratulations."

"We couldn't have done it without you, Cara. With the information you gave Lauren, Paul made quick progress—"

"Does Lauren know? About your development effort?" Cara asked, unable to hide her concern.

He shook his head. "No. No one does, except Paul and me. And now you two." He eyed her ruefully. "When I thought you were developing Aerie, I was afraid you might find out what we were up to, so we went underground. I buried Aerie deep off-site. There is no connection, not even a whisper, between Aerie and Windwear, anywhere."

"You were smart. That probably saved you."

"We're not done yet. The next stage is critical. We need a little more time. With this plan, I think we can get that time and protect you too."

Cara threw a glance at Andrew. "Well, you'd better tell us, or Miss Cara is goin' to take off like a jackrabbit. Her bags are already packed, y'know. I barely stopped her from skippin' town last night."

Liam nodded. "All right. Here's the plan. It has a few moving parts, so bear with me." He took a deep breath. "I play the smitten lover." Cara gasped and Andrew laughed. Liam held up his hand. "Hear me out before you two start throwing rocks." He paused before starting again. "I play the smitten lover. Cara, you play the ice princess. You know the type, plays hard to get, drives a hard bargain, aloof as hell. I'm the sucker willing to do anything to win you over. Here's the story: I found you at the beach and I fell hard. You convinced me you don't have Aerie. I, in turn, convinced you to come to work for Windwear. You told me about your noncompete clause. I know you can't work on an Aerie-like project for another seven months, but I don't care. I'm smitten."

He glanced at her and caught the look of utter surprise on her face, which he ignored. "Now, this is the part we can do tomorrow night. There is a big gala downtown, a fundraiser for American Charities or some such organization. Both Pyramid and Windwear are sponsors. Peter is planning to attend. We'll make sure we visit with him and give him the whole story; that you don't have Aerie, that we are aware of your noncompete clause, and that we plan to wait it out before we start work on Aerie II. We'll make sure he understands I don't care about the delay, that I'm busy trying to … you know … get you in my bed, so to speak." He blushed before continuing. "I … I intend to hire you now and let you develop Aerie II once the noncompete lapses. Peter won't believe us, of course. He will proceed to do two things: first, he'll initiate an investigation into your activities; second, he'll demand you turn over Aerie. That's when I step in. I go from smitten lover to knight in shining armor—"

"Are you sure this isn't some type of fairy tale you cooked up because you've been away from Miss Cara for too long, son?"

"Just listen, Andrew." Liam turned to Cara and caught her trying to hide a smile. "Peter's been telling us for months he has Aerie but can't sell it to us because he can't find you. All of a sudden, we produce you. As you have assured us you don't possess Aerie, we get, as Mike would say, 'our knickers in a twist.' We accuse Peter of lying and demand that before he takes any action against you he produce Aerie."

"But he doesn't have Aerie." Cara's expression was troubled.

Liam nodded. "You're right. Which is exactly his problem. He won't be able to produce Aerie, because he doesn't have it. Being a proper knight in shining armor, I'll make a big stink about the whole thing and accuse him of making everything up, that Aerie is a figment of his imagination he concocted to punish you for disobeying him."

Cara stared at him in utter shock. "Liam, that's a complete lie—"

"Turnabout is fair play, Cara. If he is going to accuse you of stealing something, I'm going to make him prove that something exists before he is allowed to proceed. He can't. Aerie has been removed from the project files. There's no evidence Aerie ever even existed. As a result, there's no evidence you ever did anything wrong. He'll be prevented from taking any action at all."

"Oh. I see."

"Peter will be forced to back off and accept the fact he's lost the opportunity to make a $2 million contract."

Cara gave him a puzzled look. "Is that what you think this is about? A $2 million contract?"

"Of course. What else besides money would Peter care about?"

She closed her eyes. "So, Lauren didn't tell you."

"She told me you gave her the software, and that she made up the story about you developing Aerie."

"But she didn't tell you about Peter? About his plans?"

"What plans?" Liam went still. "What are you talking about?"

"Liam, Peter Whittington never intended to sell Aerie to you. Ever. Peter is a liar. From the top of his balding head to the soles of his shiny wingtips. He lied from the beginning. To all of us."

"What? I don't understand."

"Peter planned to develop Aerie in-house as Pyramid's newest product. Once he realized Mike and I figured out a workable design, he recognized its potential as a stand-alone product. He wasn't satisfied with the new business Pyramid would get from implementing the software, he wanted the whole thing." She sighed. "He realized Aerie was a goldmine. He told me to tap dance, to convince Fleet and Windwear Aerie was in scope when it was actually excluded."

"How the hell were you supposed to do that?"

"Who knows? I didn't even bother to think about it. I decided right away I wasn't willing to play along. I didn't realize his full plan at the time, though. I thought he only intended to squeeze you for a new contract—"

"When in reality he planned to steal Aerie. How did you figure it out?"

She smiled at him. "You told me."

"Me?" Liam said in surprise.

"Remember after the review, when you said you didn't understand why Peter would kill Aerie when it was such an obvious win-win for both of you?" Liam nodded. "I realized his plan then. Peter never throws money away. He had to be after something even more lucrative. What could be more lucrative than those implementation deals? Easy. The implementation deals *plus* the software."

"I can't believe this."

"You're not alone, Liam, but once you told me Windwear wouldn't be able to recover if you lost Aerie, I realized I had to do something. Lauren assured me you were the rightful owner, so ..."

"So, you gave the software to Lauren." Liam let out a slow whistle. "Now I understand why you needed to get the hell out of town." His head snapped up as he realized something else. "And as long as you stayed hidden, Peter thought you took the software. Which took the pressure off Windwear. That was the eight week favor."

"Right." She smiled. "I told Lauren at least a hundred times to tell you about Peter's plans. I don't understand why she didn't." She stared at Liam. "Do you know what Peter's doing? Is he going ahead with Aerie?"

He shook his head. "I'm not sure. I sent Mike over to Pyramid to quietly glean information."

Cara couldn't help but laugh. "Mike? You sent Mike? To glean quietly? Mr. Subtle himself?"

Liam's eyes held an answering smile. "I gave him strict instructions. There's hope for the boy yet."

"He's lulling you into a false sense of security."

"Probably."

"What did he find out?"

"Not much. There's a lot of activity going on at Pyramid, but no one is talking. Even Anna couldn't tell Mike anything."

"Anna didn't know anything? Amazing. She knows everything. Even Neal Coleman's email password."

"Who's Neal Coleman?" Liam asked.

"The head of Pyramid. He's the managing partner of the New York office."

"Hmm." Liam paused, as if remembering. "One unusual thing caught Mike's attention. Peter took the entire Aerie team off the FIT project and transferred them to Pyramid's Seattle office."

It was Cara's turn to whistle. "I'd say he's forging ahead. With or without the prototype, he's in the game."

"I was afraid so. I think we can conclude his efforts aren't going well."

"Why do you say that?" Cara asked.

"He came after you. He wouldn't have attacked you or tired to steal the software if his development effort was succeeding."

"True." Her eyes were clouded with concern. "I understand your plan, Liam, but I have one major concern."

"Oh? What's that?"

"I'm not sure you can put Peter off so easily. If you float this story, and he's convinced I don't have Aerie, what do you think Peter will do? Who do you think he will suspect of having Aerie?"

Liam thought for a moment. Cara could practically see the thoughts chasing through his brain. Then he gave her a crooked smile. "Fleet?"

She couldn't help but laugh. "Try again."

"All right, you make a good point, but Peter won't come after Windwear first. He'll come after you. We can delay him with the knight in shining armor routine. We won't let him get close to Windwear."

"Maybe. Even so, I think we need a Plan B. Peter doesn't give up easily, and he often lets his emotions get away from him. If he gets angry enough, he'll go after you, whether it's wise or not."

"We can put him off for a few weeks. All I need is a few weeks, Cara."

She shook her head. "No. I know Peter. He'll use every bit of leverage available to him. And unfortunately, you have a lot of leverage to be used."

Liam thought for a moment, then looked up quickly as understanding dawned. "The IPO."

Cara nodded. "He could screw up your IPO with the threat of a lawsuit. He'll force you to back off."

"Hmm, I hadn't considered that angle." Liam was silent for a moment. "Andrew, what would you need to arrest Peter for the attack on Cara?"

Andrew shrugged. "Well, evidence for one thing. I can question him, but without evidence, I can't hold him. Once we get the results from the lab, we can lean on the folks we picked up last night and see if they'll talk." He shook his head. "I can't promise anythin.' Even if we make an arrest, he'd probably make bail purty quick."

"How long could we hold him off? Can we use the fact he attacked Cara as some sort of roadblock to prevent him from investigating her?"

Cara shook her head. "That wouldn't stop him from going after Windwear. In fact, he'll probably be more motivated." She was silent for a moment, and then said quietly, "I have an idea."

"You do?" Liam asked. "Let's hear it."

She took a deep breath. "We start by following your plan. You play the smitten lover—"

"I like it," Liam said. "Let's do it."

Andrew laughed out loud.

"Don't be a smart aleck." Cara rolled her eyes, but she couldn't help the glow of ... what was this feeling seeping through her? She started again. "You play the smitten lover. I tell you I don't have Aerie, but I agree to come back to Windwear and build Aerie II after the noncompete lapses. If Peter buys the story, we follow your plan. If he doesn't, and he decides to go after Windwear, we follow Plan B."

"Which is?" Liam asked, his voice suddenly wary.

"I tell him I have the software."

"No," Liam said sharply. "That's a bad idea. We know what Peter is capable of. We can't risk it. Besides, that won't prevent him from coming after Windwear."

"Not by itself. I'll need to convince him."

"Convince him? How?"

"By telling him I'm using you. I'll tell him I've been working on Aerie all along, and I'm just er ... bedding you," it was Cara's turn to blush, "to determine how close you really are on Aerie."

"Bad ending to the fairy tale, young man," Andrew chuckled.

"Hmm," said Liam. "I am liking this plan less and less."

"But being a true knight in shining armor, you play the innocent. You don't believe I am capable of such treachery."

Liam blanched, and she laid her hand over his and squeezed it gently. "Then you proceed to get a good lawyer, and tie him up in knots. Peter won't know what to think. I'm busy cheating you, while you are busy protecting me. I think we can confuse him enough to keep him from going after you right away, especially if you make a big stink, as you say. All you need is a few weeks to get Aerie launched and the IPO completed. Once those events occur, his leverage disappears."

Liam was quiet for several moments. "What do you think?" he asked Andrew.

Andrew tilted his head, deep in thought. "Well, I think Miss Cara is right. This Peter fella isn't gonna be too easy to corral. The plan has risks, but I reckon it's a fair alternative. Between you and me, Liam, I hope to God we don't need to use it."

"I agree. I can't think of anything better at the moment. We could pull it off and still keep Cara safe. But I want to add a Plan C, just in case."

"Does this involve you bein' a smitten lover?" Andrew asked.

"Of course." Liam smiled, but then his face turned serious. "I admit, it's not much of plan, but it would ease my mind."

"What is it?" Andrew asked.

"Plan C. The failsafe." He pierced Cara with an intent stare. "If at any time things don't go the way we planned, if Plans A and B go to hell in a hurry, and you feel like you're in danger, I want you to run, Cara. Drop everything and run. Run back to Cannon Beach. Run back to Andrew. He'll protect you from Peter. Do you hear me? Don't stop. Don't wait. Don't think. Just run." He glanced at Andrew who nodded once.

Cara gazed at the two men staring intently at her. "All right. We'll add Plan C."

Chapter 39

Cara stopped Liam before they reached Windwear's headquarters. She faced him, touching her cheek. "Liam, do I look okay?"

He smiled. "Gorgeous."

"No, I mean … my face. I did the best I could with the industrial-strength makeup."

He stopped, inspected her forehead and cheek and eyes. "You can hardly tell." He paused. "You are … quite beautiful, Cara."

She rolled her eyes.

"Now, that's more like the Cara Larson I've come to know. The one who has no clue how beautiful she is." She opened her mouth to answer, but he put a finger to her lips. "Hush. Not a word. Now … are you ready?"

She nodded. "Plan A. Plan B. Ice Princess. I'm ready."

"Good." He took her hand as he opened the door. "Hi, Staci. Any messages for me?"

"Well, welcome back, stranger. Where have you be—" Staci stopped in surprise. "Cara!" Her gaze flew to Liam. Then back to Cara. Then back to Liam.

He smiled. "Close your mouth, Staci. September is fly season." Staci closed her mouth, but her expression remained puzzled. "Cara is here for a business meeting."

"Oh." Staci hurried around the desk to embrace Cara, but halted mid-stride when she noticed Cara's expression. Cara held out her hand. "It's a pleasure to see you again, Staci."

Staci took the hand warily. "Uh, yes. Well, it's ... nice to see you, too."

"Staci, did you finish the form I asked you to prepare?" Liam asked.

"Yes, it's on my desk." She stopped, as if she just put two pieces of a puzzle together. "Do ... do you want me to add Cara's name to it?"

"That would be great. I'll need it right away." Liam opened the door to his office. "Come in, Cara. I want to catch you up on where we are."

He glanced at his watch as he closed the door. "Two minutes is all we'll need for Staci to warn everyone you're coming to the staff meeting."

"Two minutes?" Cara began pacing in front of his desk.

Liam studied her thoughtfully. "You don't pace too often, Ms. Larson. If I didn't know better, I'd say you were nervous."

"I am nervous," she sighed. "I'm not sure I can pull this off. I'm not a very good liar."

Liam walked over, put his hands on her shoulders, and dropped a light kiss on her forehead. "That's why I like you."

She eyed him with mock severity. "I thought you were smitten with me."

His eyes gleamed. "I—"

At that moment the door to his office opened and Staci entered. "Here is the form— Oh, excuse me."

Liam released Cara leisurely and took the file from Staci's hands. "Thanks, Staci."

He opened the file as she left and skimmed through its contents. "All right, Ms. Larson, I'll need you to sign this form before we go to the meeting."

Cara walked over and took the papers from Liam. *Nondisclosure Agreement.* She read them carefully, then reached for a pen, and signed on the last page.

He replaced the signed form in the file. "No questions?"

She shook her head. "No."

"I like the way you operate, Ms. Larson." He checked his watch again. "Time to go. Time to observe Mr. Smitten at work." He tucked her hand inside his elbow. "Come on, ice princess."

Liam sat at the head of the table and gestured for Cara to take the seat to his right. She sat squarely, face set, hands still and calm as she waited for the Windwear executive staff to arrive. She tapped her foot against the table leg without realizing she was doing so. Liam smiled and laid a hand on her thigh. "Stop," he whispered, "or you'll drive us both crazy."

"Oops. Sorry. I told you I was nervous."

Lauren was the first to arrive. She stopped abruptly at the doorway.

"Come in and take a seat, Lauren," Liam said.

Lauren walked slowly to the table and stopped next to Cara. "You're in my seat."

Liam looked up with a faintly annoyed expression. "Lauren, you are no longer an adolescent. Find an unoccupied seat."

Her lips drew into a tight line as she sat down next to Cara. Cara held out her hand. "Hello, Lauren."

"What are you doing here?" Lauren asked suspiciously as she shook Cara's hand. The rest of the team arrived just then, crowding out the need for Cara to respond.

They were an angry group. The chief financial officer, Brad Keller scowled as he took his seat. The head of operations, Mark Prentice, seemed disgusted. Joe Jenkins, chief engineer, was silent, but his face was a deep red, as if he were holding his breath. Susan Mikelson, head of sales, shook her head in complete frustration. Staci was there. Her expression remained blank, but her eyes were watchful. Then there was Mike. Wide-eyed with surprise. Smiling. Relief evident in every gesture. Thank God for Mike.

Liam began the meeting. He barely uttered a sentence when Lauren could no longer contain herself. "What is she doing here?"

Liam raised an eyebrow. "I beg your pardon?"

"This woman has caused a lot of trouble for Windwear. I would like to know why she is back and why she is attending our staff meeting." The words spread through the room like the after-effects of lightning. Utterly quiet. Awaiting the thunder.

"Fair enough. Cara and I are in ... negotiations. She is considering coming to work for Windwear." A collective gasp filled the room. "Or perhaps becoming my partner. Later, after her noncompete agreement expires, she will work on a project based on the ideas we put forward for the Aerie project. She insists on seeing Windwear's operations before making a decision." Then, as if he made a regular habit of dropping bombshells on his executive staff, he smiled. "Now, catch me up on what's happened since our last meeting. Lauren? Why don't you start?"

"Work for Windwear?" Lauren asked incredulously. "Liam, have you taken leave of your senses?"

"Actually, I would say I've just regained my senses."

"Liam," Lauren began again, and then hesitated. Liam watched as she struggled with her dilemma, stuck between the truths she had recently revealed and the lies she had been spreading for months. "This woman—"

"Cara. Her name is Cara."

"All right, Cara," Lauren said reluctantly. "Cara shouldn't be here. We all know what she did at Pyramid and how her actions impacted Windwear. You should not allow her anywhere near this company."

Well played, Liam thought as he faced Lauren. "That's ancient history. Cara may have done some things I ... wasn't too happy about, but she has proven to be a formidable opponent. The truth is, she knows more about Aerie than anyone else on the planet." He shot a glance as Mike stirred in his seat. "Even you, Mike."

"Maybe." Mike grumbled and slouched in his chair.

Liam addressed the rest of the group. "I can't afford *not* to deal with her."

"What's her price?" Lauren's tone remained even, but her insinuation was all too clear.

Liam's eyes sparkled with suggestion "I'm not sure." He flashed an admiring smile on Cara. "We ... aren't done discussing *all* the terms yet."

Liam saw the confusion rage over Lauren's face. What was Cara doing here? Had she been working on Aerie after all? Had she and Liam been working together all this time? "What's the deal? What are you offering?"

Liam leaned back in his chair. "Sorry, Lauren. No can do. Terms of the deal are closed. Cara's here to examine our operations and decide if we're a good risk. Unfortunately, Windwear isn't the only dog in the fight. We're not even on the top of her list." He paused. "We're not in the software business. She wants to be sure this isn't a step backward in her career."

"A step backward? After the fiasco at Pyramid? Does she even *have* a career?" A quiet snicker flitted through the room.

Careful, Lauren," Liam said quietly.

"Who are the other dogs?" Mark Prentice interrupted.

"Cara hasn't mentioned any, but I can imagine the list. Pyramid, of course. Sidwell Parker, Cole Martin. Those would be the top three."

"I can't believe Pyramid would be in the running," Lauren almost sneered.

"You'd be surprised. Cara is one of the best systems analysts around, and technical expertise is always in demand. Even Pyramid is willing to overlook a few ... bad decisions. They know how much business she can bring in."

Lauren faced Cara. "With those kinds of players, why bother with Windwear?"

Cara, who had remained quiet during the entire conversation, gave Lauren a cool smile. "I keep my options open. Liam made me an attractive offer."

The words hung in the air. Liam raised one eyebrow and gazed at her. "A *very* attractive offer."

There was a moment when Cara and Liam gazed at each other, she cool and composed, and he confident and smoldering. The stillness was obliterated by a sharp gasp from Lauren. "This is a mistake, Liam. I'm not sure what this woman ... Cara, is up to, but it's not going to help Windwear. How can you be sure she's not using you to get a better deal somewhere else? She shouldn't be here at all."

Cara slowly moved her gaze from Lauren to Liam. "Liam, you didn't tell me Lauren makes your decisions for you. All this time, I've been dealing with the wrong person."

Liam's eyes never left Cara's face. "Enough, Lauren. You had your say. The negotiations will continue. Let's get on with your presentation."

But Lauren didn't stop. "This isn't a good idea. I need to discuss confidential information about the stock offering. Cara isn't on staff. I cannot discuss these things while she's here."

Liam passed the file containing the Nondisclosure Agreement to Lauren. "Cara signed a Non Disclosure Agreement. We're protected. Please proceed." Lauren opened the folder and examined the form.

She shook her head in disbelief. "You're making a big mistake. You don't—"

Anger flashed briefly in Liam's eyes. "Do you refuse to give me your report, Lauren?"

"Liam, you need to be careful—"

"Please hand me your report." Lauren stared at him defiantly, and then slid the report across the table. He didn't even glance at it. He turned to his CFO. "Go ahead, Brad."

The CFO seemed uncomfortable. "Liam, this is confidential financial information—"

"And Cara has signed a Nondisclosure Agreement."

"Still, I'm not sure this is a good idea ... you can't trust her, NDA or not. She ran away, she took Aerie—"

"I'll give my report," Mike suddenly announced.

Liam eyed the younger man. Thank God for Mike. "All right. Go ahead, Mike."

"I don't have a written status report, but I carry it in my head. We've completed the payroll and payables modules. We've ordered new invoices for Accounts Payable and new payroll check stock. We should finish the Receivable module by the end of October. Data conversion will take place the last two weeks in November. We'll run the systems concurrently in December, and go live at the beginning of the year."

"Great work. Thanks, Mike." He faced the group. "Any questions for Mike?" The room was silent. "Cara, any questions?"

"Not at this time."

Liam faced his CFO. "Brad?"

The word hung in the air for several moments. "Do you trust her?" Brad finally asked.

Liam nodded. "I do. More than you know."

The CFO sighed. "All right. That's good enough for me." He opened his report and proceeded to update the team on the company's latest financial results.

Suddenly, the tension was gone. Liam could practically feel the temperature in the room drop. Everyone seemed relieved. Except Lauren. She stood up angrily and gathered her files. "You're making a big mistake, Liam." Every pair of eyes followed her as she left the room.

When she had gone, Brad cleared his throat. "Let me continue."

The rest of the meeting proceeded without drama. When all the reports were given, Liam faced Cara. "Any questions?"

"Not now." She smiled at the group. "Thank you for allowing me to participate."

"That goes for me, too," Liam said. "Thanks, everyone." He paused as they rose to leave. "Mike. I'd like you to stay for a minute, if you would."

"Sure thing, boss."

Cara walked to the window and gazed out over the city. Liam walked up behind her, placed a hand on her shoulder, and turned her to face him. "You were magnificent, Cara. Remind me never to be your enemy."

She closed her eyes and turned back to the window. "Now I understand why you had to play the role of the smitten lover. It's the only plausible reason you would allow me to get anywhere near Windwear. I didn't realize how bad my reputation was."

"Unfortunately, Lauren did a thorough job in that department. It's not a hopeless cause, though. The team came around."

"They respect you."

"And they'll respect you again, too."

"Except for Lauren."

"Well, I don't think that should count against you. It might even be a badge of honor to be on her bad side."

She smiled quietly. "FDR said that. 'Judge me by the enemies I make.' Something like that."

"Wise man. Unfortunately, Lauren has made a few too many mistakes where you're concerned. I've decided to terminate her employment."

Cara's eyes widened in surprise. "You have?"

"Yes. I'll do it as soon as I can find the right time. She did a lot of good things at Windwear, but I can't trust her anymore. Not after what she did to you."

"What about the IPO?"

"That's my one concern. My outside lawyers are reviewing what extra hoops we'll need to jump through to clear a change of attorneys with the Feds. As soon as they get back to me, I'll work out the details for termination."

Cara was silent for a moment. "Why do you think she did it, Liam? Tell you that I, and not Peter, was developing Aerie. I made it so clear Peter was a threat, but she ended up protecting him."

"I don't think she was protecting Peter as much as she was protecting Windwear. Can you imagine how I would have reacted if I learned of Peter's true plan? I think Lauren was afraid I'd go after Peter. She wanted me to stay focused on Aerie and nothing else."

"Maybe, but it makes me nervous. Peter is dangerous. She should have told you."

"What's important is that we know now and we have a plan. Let's see how Peter responds tonight before we do any more worrying."

"You're right."

Liam touched his lips gently to her forehead before he turned around. "Hey Mike. Would you do me a favor?"

Mike hurried from his place at the conference table. "What do you need?"

"How about taking your former boss to an early lunch? I have a facilities meetings I can't miss."

Mike's eyes lit up. "That'll be awesome. Just like old times."

Cara rolled her eyes, and the ghost of a smile appeared on her face. "You don't know what you're asking, Liam."

He noted her quiet laugh. He loved that sound. Thank God for Mike. "Just bring her back in one piece, Mike."

"Hey, no guarantees buddy."

Liam started out the door. "Back by noon, no later. Do you hear me?"

"Sure, sure. No guarantees buddy." He smiled at Cara. "Ready, ex-boss?"

"No."

"Ha! Just like old times. Come on. I'm starved."

Chapter 40

It was just like old times. First, Mike took Cara to
Nordstrom and made her try on at least eight hats before he
was satisfied she had worked up an appetite. It wouldn't have
been so bad, except he chose the most outrageous hats that
took forever to put on and take off. And three salespeople
waited on them. And he acted like Bill Gates the way he
talked about buying all of them just for the hell of it. The
poor salespeople were salivating, and Cara became more and
more embarrassed. She realized Mike didn't plan to buy even
one, except, of course, she made him buy two. She made sure
the store shipped one to his mother in Atlanta and one to his
sister in Minneapolis. He whined and complained and
protested about wasting perfectly good money. She just
smiled and nodded and made sure he signed the check.

They arrived at the restaurant three blocks away,
laughing and breathless, because Mike insisted they cross
against the lights. That almost killed them more than once.
Horns blared and drivers swore, which made Mike enjoy the
adventure even more. He was genuinely disappointed they
didn't run into a policeman. He always enjoyed arguing with
policemen who thought it was their God given duty to meet
their revenue quota by handing out jaywalking tickets to
innocent citizens.

"Thank you," Cara said as they sat down to lunch. "I had
forgotten how ... easy you make life seem. I needed that."

"I'm glad. I missed you. No one will go out to lunch with
me any more."

"Really? I'm shocked."

Mike's face became serious and Cara suddenly glimpsed a side of him she had rarely seen before. "What's going on, Cara? I have a million questions and not a single answer that makes sense."

She smiled. Sweet Mike who believed in her when everyone else believed the worst. "Ask away. I'll tell you what I can."

He peppered her with questions. What did Peter do to start this whole mess? Why did she leave so secretly? Why didn't she tell him? Didn't she understand he was worried about her? What the hell was she doing at the beach? And what was with Liam, anyhow, showing up with her like some superhero from a comic book? Especially when he was so full of lies. "Cara, I know you're not coming to work for Windwear or anyone else. So why not cut the crap and tell me the truth."

"How do you know?"

"I know your Pyramid persona, Cara. Whenever you're anywhere near technology you put on your professional armor. You get all stiff and serious. You get so tight we can use you as the entire string section of an orchestra. But you aren't tight at all. In fact, you look like you've been on a two-month vacation." He shrugged. "Plus, I know Liam already has Aerie."

Her eyes widened in surprise. "What?"

Mike rolled his eyes. "Come on, Cara. Liam is a good guy, but he's not going to cut it as the poster boy for Technology World. Even if he does pull off a minor miracle with Aerie."

"What are you talking about? Does anyone else at Windwear know?"

He studied her worried face. "Relax. His secret is safe with me. He hasn't been outrageously obvious, but a few pieces just don't go together unless Aerie fills the gaps."

"Like?"

"One, Paul Davis's sudden disappearance after Liam returned from Taiwan. They had a big fight in Staci's office. Paul is too mild-mannered to have an argument with a mouse, much less his oldest friend. Two, Liam's erratic hours.

Sometimes he's only in the office three or four days a week. Three, all these special security features in our new accounting system that are completely unnecessary. Four, he spent some big bucks upgrading all our hardware and connecting Windwear to the Internet. We now have an IP address and are linked into the CIX network for commercial use and NSFNET for some of our research work. We're about ten years ahead of everyone else. Half the people in the company still don't have any idea what the Internet even is. That's what really convinced me."

"I see."

"Yeah, and one last thing. Liam came in a month or so ago and asked me out to lunch. Gave me this story loaded with horse hockey about needing to be up to speed with all his direct reports and wanting to take us out for one-on-one lunches every now and then. Funny thing, I was the only one to go to lunch with him. Me and Mark Prentice, the head of operations. He's definitely been staying away from Lauren." He eyed her sharply, but Cara kept her gaze impassive. "Anyway, we went out to lunch this one time, and Liam started asking me questions about some guy from CERN who made an announcement on alt-dot-hypertext."

"The Usenet newsgroup?"

"Yeah, that's the one. Well my guess is Paul is linked into the group and read this post by a guy named Tim Berners-Lee. Since Paul and Liam are supposed to be on the outs, he sent Liam to ask me about it. He asked all about a new network of shared documents called W3 or WorldWideWeb. He was throwing around terms like File Transfer Protocol and Domain Name System and Hypertext Transfer Protocol. Cara, I tell you, it was a howl. He pulled out this notebook and wrote down everything word for word. He was being so careful. I started speaking really ... slow ... so ... he ... wouldn't ... miss ... a ... word." Mike laughed at the memory. "He didn't even notice. He kept writing and writing and checking to make sure he had everything right."

"You told him the truth didn't you? You didn't pull the usual smoke and mirror act you use for ... what do you call them—"

"Arrogant techno-dweebs?" He laughed. "Nah. Not with Liam. Arrogant, occasionally. Dweeb, never." His expression turned serious. "I could tell in about three seconds this was about Aerie. Remember, you and I built the prototype. I understand all the development issues. I was straight with him."

Cara breathed a sigh of relief. "Good."

"Here's the thing, Cara. I think Liam is planning to make Aerie more than a series of one-to-one links using CIX."

"What do you mean?"

"I think he's planning to use this WorldWideWeb network instead."

"But it's so new. That was only announced a month ago. There is no infrastructure anywhere to support W3."

"That's not exactly true. A coherent commercial infrastructure isn't in place, but all the pieces exist. Based on the interest from the newsgroup, it won't be long before the network comes together. I read the post by Berners-Lee. He identified all the pieces needed to create a universal information sharing system, explained how to use them, and put a copy of the tools in one place. People are already starting to use what he's done to build their own hypertext documents, just like Liam is planning to do. It won't be long before W3 is the go-to network. I bet NSFNET will support it. I don't think they have a choice. W3 is going to be huge."

"Are you sure no one else at Windwear knows? Does Lauren?"

He laughed. "Oh, no. Not a chance. I took it upon myself to personally distract her." Cara eyed him in horror. "Ooh, Cara, disabuse yourself of that notion right now! You have a sick mind."

"Well, then, what did you do to … distract her?"

"Cara, you make me sound so evil. I was quite helpful. She is always pumping me with questions, so, I finally answered them. I gave her the information she asked for."

"What? Mike, how could you?"

"Relax, Cara. It's not what you think. Ever since she and Liam returned from Taiwan, she's been acting strangely. Very strangely, considering I figured you gave her Aerie on the day of the review." Cara's eyes widened, but she said nothing.

"I thought she knew all about Windwear's development effort, but after awhile, I got the distinct feeling she'd been left out of the loop. She began sniffing around all over the company, asking questions and trying to find out everything she could about Aerie. She even came to me. That's when I realized she was desperate. She doesn't particularly care for me. I'm not sure why. So, I tried to help by giving her a few leads."

Cara shook her head. "I never thought I'd see the day when I felt sorry for Lauren Janelle. What did you do, Mike?"

"It was all very innocent. I happened to mention to Staci while Lauren was within earshot that Liam had been discussing an eagle's nest—also known as an aerie— in which he was incredibly interested."

She closed her eyes and tried to keep the smile at bay. "Very sorry for Lauren. And where was this *aerie* located?"

"Cara, I behaved. I kept her in the Western Hemisphere." He lowered his voice. "Barely."

"Where, Mike?" Mike looked sheepish. He mumbled something under his breath. "Tell me where?"

He smiled. "Lauren took a little trip to Barrow, Alaska." His voice became deep and as well modulated as a tour guide's. "Beautiful Barrow, Alaska. Northernmost city in the United States of America. A mere 1,300 miles from the North Pole. One of Alaska's more beautiful cities, with a population a shade under 3,000, home to more eagles than people. Location of the Naval Arctic Research Lab—"

"You didn't."

Mike nodded. "I did. A five-hour plane ride to Anchorage. Then another four hours to Barrow, with a couple of long layovers at Fairbanks and Prudhoe Bay. Plus, it's really cold up there."

"It is a credit to Lauren's control you're still alive."

"Ha! When I heard she was coming back I left town for a week. I had to take the time unpaid, since I haven't accrued any vacation yet."

"You *must* have been scared."

Mike thrust out his chest. "Me? Scared? Nah. I just moved. And blocked my phone number. And bought a security system." Cara laughed out loud.

"I should have sent her to Antarctica, but I was worried she would scare the penguins." His expression turned serious. "Or to hell. I swear, I could wring her neck after she started all those rumors about you. After you did everything you could to help Windwear. Your reputation is pretty much shattered. She's been in the press a lot because Windwear is going public, and she hasn't missed an opportunity to trash your name. Not in the papers themselves, mind you, but privately, with all kinds of influential folks. She's done her bit on the social circuit, too. You're going to have a hard time coming back here and rebuilding your good name."

"It's all right, Mike. I'm not staying long anyway."

"But ... I thought you were back for good. I thought you and Liam—"

"Liam and I are running a diversion to stop Peter Whittington from taking any action against Windwear until the IPO is complete."

Mike gave her a puzzled look, started to say something, and then changed his mind. He squeezes her hand. "Screw the penguins. I should have sent her to Antarctica."

Cara sat back from the table as the busboy removed their dishes. She observed Mike as he spoke with the headwaiter. Maybe he was growing up, she mused. He actually showed some evidence of maturity during their conversation.

Her thoughts were interrupted by deafening noises coming from the kitchen; beating drums and shrieking whistles, and... those couldn't possibly be kazoos? She peered at Mike suspiciously, but he was still deep in discussion with the waiter. She shook her head. No, it couldn't be. Of course, it wasn't. No, he didn't. At that moment, all the noise stopped at their table, and the restaurant staff placed a cupcake with a lighted pink candle in front of her. Then the staff burst into a modern version of *Happy Birthday* that was a cross between a walrus playing the blues and Elvis with a cold. She dropped her head in defeat. Yes, he did. Forget growing up. An impossible thought. Mike would never, ever, ever, be more than twelve years old.

She sighed as she pasted a fake surprised smile on her face. She had known Mike for what, six months? She had been gone for two of those six months. That left four months. In those four months, this was the fifth time she had celebrated her twenty-eighth birthday. At different restaurants, of course. And her birthday wasn't even until next February. He leaned over, patted her hand, and gave her a little-boy smile. "Happy birthday, Cara. I knew you'd be surprised. Are you going to eat your cupcake?"

Chapter 41

At noon, Mike delivered Cara to Liam's office. "Have fun, you two?" Liam asked.

She shook her head. "Just like old times, Liam. I hope your insurance is up to date."

Mike shrugged his shoulders, gave Cara a hug, and headed for the doorway. "What's life without a few adventures? See you tonight?"

Liam nodded. "We'll be there." As Mike walked out, Liam took Cara's arm. "Come on, let's get going. We have an appointment."

"Where are we going?"

He smiled mysteriously. "You'll find out. Come on. We need to hurry."

For being in a hurry, they took their time. Liam seemed to stop everywhere. First, to the Windwear outlet store to find her some hiking boots. Then off to Crown Point, a granite observatory built in the 1930s, overlooking the Columbia Gorge. The afternoon sun made the colors jump from the sky. The steep granite walls of the gorge were covered with trees, but she could imagine how the mighty Columbia River had cut through the impenetrable rock, moment by moment, year by year, eon by eon, until now the river lay far below, like a jewel in the sunlight. So strong that rock, she thought, but still vulnerable to the ravages of the tiniest drop of water.

They drove along the Columbia River highway, surrounded by pine trees and ferns and waterfalls that seemed to drift down the rocks like angel's hair. They found their way to the tiny town of Troutdale. Liam stopped the car near a small cafe. They wandered down to the Sandy River and walked along its shore. At the south end of town, they took a shadowy walkway up from the riverbank to a dilapidated shack. Ol' Bob's Bait and Tackle Shop. Cara turned toward him. "Where are we going?"

"Almost there."

Understanding dawned. "Liam, should we be doing this? Is it ... safe?"

"I think we took enough twists and turns to throw anyone off the trail. Besides, I want you to see it."

Liam removed a key from his pocket, unlocked the back door. Inside, was a metal door, whose handle was protected by an electronic scanner. He placed his hand on the pad, and the red light above the scanner switched to green. He opened the door. After closing it securely behind them, they went upstairs. He repeated the procedure at the metal door at the top of the steps.

The room was surprisingly large. Four computers stood along the walls, each connected to a modem, printer, and cables that snaked upstairs and linked to a satellite dish on the roof. Binders and notebooks and slips of paper lay scattered about the tables on which each computer sat. A data model was pinned up on the wall, and Cara immediately noticed the original design had been altered to add a sophisticated security system, a user subscription system, and procedures for uploading and downloading data.

At the far end of the room, stretched out behind one of the computers like a driver strapped into a speeding car, sat Paul Davis, deep in concentration, pointing and clicking his mouse. He turned as they entered the room, then stood up, knocking his chair over, surprise and suspicion on in his face. "Liam? What's going on?"

Liam walked over, and a rapid conversation followed. Cara heard snippets from where she stood. "... are you sure?"

"... I screwed up royally, Paul."

"You were the one who insisted—"

"... everything has changed now."

Finally, Paul nodded and turned toward her. "Hello, Cara. Forgive me for my ... rude behavior. This has all been such a closely guarded secret—"

"Please, you don't need to explain. This ... is awkward for everyone."

Liam took her hand and led her to the wall. "Come and see what Paul's done."

They walked across the room, and Cara studied the model. The original design was still intact, but some of the fields were changed. Functionality had been added to halt access to a product for any reason. She and Mike hadn't thought of that. An option was now available to store the results of several queries at once, so a company could batch multiple searches together and download them all at once.

She turned toward them. "Paul, Liam, this is amazing. Really incredible. You've done a remarkable job." She paused, studying the model. "You changed the name of the inventory ID to 'Recipient ID'. What does that mean?" Suddenly, it seemed as if they picked up a conversation they started nine minutes ago, instead of nine weeks ago.

"Well," Paul replied, "we decided to use the ID of the product whose status is being searched. When we did the calculations, the processing time was faster." He pointed to a separate section of the model. "We've added the ability to cross-reference codes so no one needs to keep track of different numbering systems. The setup takes longer, but the transaction time is reduced."

Cara nodded. "How will you manage the subscription information? Mike and I envisioned a self-managed arrangement, where every customer dials directly into another's system. This looks different. You centralized the access. And the security. Clever. Safer, too." She peered more closely at the model. "In fact, you centralized most of the functionality. Everyone dials into a central location, is authorized, and then sends a specific request to the owner of the data for transfer. I understand the transaction is faster, but how about the central hub? Didn't the performance drop? How did you increase the speed?" Her mind was going a million miles an hour. Thoughts she hadn't entertained for weeks came pouring into her head. "What kind of volume can the network handle? What's your transfer rate? Any problems with security during transmission? How do you—" she stopped, remembering her discussion with Mike a few hours earlier. "I see now. You're going to use the Internet."

Paul raised his eyebrows in pleasant surprise "You're right, Cara. We leverage off the fact that data is only stored in one place. We've just built an extremely efficient mechanism for authorized parties to access that one place, regardless of its actual location."

She examined the model further. Of course, it was a perfect solution. Centralize all access and security in one location through the Internet, then create a mechanism for each participant to provide only the information to be shared upon request. Precise knowledge. Maximum safety. Minimum risk. "Paul, the technology is so new. Can you build this?"

"Well, the system is clunky right now, not user friendly at all. So, we kept the interface super easy. With this new WorldWideWeb network I've been reading about, we'll move to a graphical interface which will be much easier to use. We have no time now, though. Liam wants to announce Aerie in a few weeks."

"Is the Internet … safe? You know what happens with new technology. The first experts are always the hackers."

Paul laughed. "Luckily, we have one of the best hackers around working for us."

Her eyes widened. "No. You didn't."

Liam smiled. "We did."

"Not Mike?"

"Yes, Mike."

"You can't. You'll violate his noncompete clause."

"Not at all," Paul said. "Mike has been working on some interesting and highly specialized encryption programs to keep our in-house accounting system secure. It just so happens we might be able to use these programs … well, for all of Windwear's systems."

She shook her head. "The Internet. This is brilliant." She turned to Liam. "Do you think you can get people to take the leap? The Internet will require new software, new hardware, new infrastructure ..."

Liam nodded. "The world is already moving in this direction. We'd be crazy not to build for the future. We might suffer slower growth at the beginning while companies ramp up, but once they do, they won't want to be left behind. We'll help them through. Cole Martin is eager to help. They stand to gain a lot of new business."

Cara reviewed the model for several more moments. Suddenly, inexplicably, she felt hot tears behind her eyes. No, she thought. She hadn't missed this life, hadn't missed the pressures or the problems or the politics. Until this minute. She'd forgotten how it felt to make a system sing, had forgotten the satisfaction of making an elegant design come to life. Abruptly, she looked down and picked up a notebook lying on the table. She flipped through the pages, but the words were all blurry. Liam and Paul exchanged a glance, and Liam quietly shook his head.

After a minute, she turned to the two men. "You should be proud. A well-designed system is like a work of art. When done right, all the pieces fit together with such symmetry you can't imagine it any other way. This one is done right."

"Thank you, Cara," Liam smiled.

At that moment, they were interrupted by a knock on the door.

Paul went to open it. "Rick, come in." Rick Penner, the Fleet systems manager, entered the room.

"For weeks, I've been working in lonely isolation," Paul complained. "And now all at once I have three visitors. I feel almost human again."

"Cara!" Rick's smile was genuine as he stretched out his hand in greeting.

Cara was surprised at his warm reception. She was already training herself to expect the worst from anyone she met from her past. She held out her hand. "Hello, Rick. How are you? How is FIT going?"

Rick laughed and bypassed her hand for a hug. "Same old, Cara. The customer was always first in your book."

Cara blushed. "I'm not sure my ex-boss would agree with you."

"Yes, and Peter only recognizes a customer if he sees the checkbook attached."

She smiled, but thought better of a response. "How is FIT coming along, Rick?"

"Plodding along. We've been forced to extend the schedule and expand scope because things we thought were included in the contract were actually excluded. We've spent an extra million so far. And that's without Aerie."

"Oh."

"But then, you know all about Peter's methods, don't you? I wish I had listened to you more closely. Now I understand how you tried to help Fleet in the review." He paused. "And the price you paid. Cara, I'm sorry."

She shook her head. "This wasn't your fault. I made my choices with my eyes open. I knew what the fallout would be. Still, I'm sorry about FIT."

"It's been an experience. Thanks to you, we're much more careful now. The extra million could have been five million." He paused. "I didn't realize how easily we could agree to something in concept that turned out to be quite different in practice."

Cara nodded. "This isn't unusual in this business. Both business and technology are so complex that the two don't always coexist well. Technology companies like Pyramid are so afraid of losing a deal they promise the sky during a proposal knowing full well they can't meet the requirements. Once the customer is on the hook they either roll back the scope or change the definition of their commitment."

Rick nodded. "And we pay extra for any changes. Well, I can't say you didn't warn us."

"Rick, not everyone operates this way. Don't judge Pyramid based only on Peter Whittington. I'd like to believe he was the exception. Pyramid has a lot of good people."

"I'll try to remember, but I think they have one less, now that you left. I could always trust you, Cara."

"Thank you," she whispered and blinked hard.

Liam walked over to them. "I'm glad you're here, Rick. Cara has some questions about the subscription process."

"Oh? As a matter of fact, I brought several more agreements with me."

Liam nodded and led them over to a battered file cabinet. He pulled out a thick file folder. "Rick and I came up with a new structure to implement Aerie, Cara. We've created a new subsidiary, called Windlogic which is wholly owned by Windwear. Its sole purpose is to own and operate Aerie. Windlogic receives fees from each subscriber who wants to participate in the system. A subscriber signs this agreement to become a member."

Cara read the document. It was full of legal whys and wherefores but specified clearly the role of Windlogic and its members. Windlogic retained ownership of all versions of the Aerie software, the security systems, and the centralized technology for access control. Each member was allowed to purchase a software license for as many locations as needed. A secure link would connect each member to the central management module.

She perused the document. As the silence grew, Liam shifted impatiently. "Well, what do you think?"

A slow smile spread across her face. "You two are brilliant. This is perfect. You will annihilate Peter in the marketplace."

"Really? What makes you think so?" Liam asked, a pleased expression on his face.

"Simple. Peter thinks one dimensionally. To him, this is a technology problem software alone will solve. To you, this is a way for people to communicate more effectively. Peter will build the system as we envisioned, as a series of one-to-one links. He'll let his customers muddle through on their own. You are taking the opposite tactic. You are providing the structure to make the process easy so they can do their business and not worry about the technology underneath. The difference is huge."

Liam nodded. "That's exactly what we're trying to do. We figure the system's structure will determine its success. If all these companies are running around, trying to access each other's information without any coordination, the system will grind to a halt out of sheer confusion. I can just imagine our customers trying to fix their problems by rewriting the software. They'd mess things up so badly that by the time they call us for help, they'd be so confused and angry, we would end up with a bad reputation even though we weren't at fault. We decided the full-support approach was the best approach."

"Yes. A safe structure giving your subscribers security and order. Easy sign-up, fast delivery, full support." She smiled at him. "You're going to win, Liam. Win big. Aerie will take off like a rocket."

Liam and Rick exchanged a glance. "I hope you're right, Cara," Liam said. "We make the introduction in less than four weeks. I've risked Windwear's entire future on Aerie."

Chapter 42

It took another hour for Liam and Cara to return to
Portland. Once again Liam wandered circuitously back to
town. After a good two hours of driving, he pulled into a
sloping driveway in the West Hills. Cara found herself staring
at an old Victorian house, three stories tall, painted white
with dark blue shutters. A large stained glass oval window
was cut into the front door. She gasped at the verandah that
ran around three sides of the house. "Liam. It's beautiful."

He smiled. "Come on in." He pulled her suitcase from
the trunk, took her hand, and led her inside.

"Sam! Maggie! Are you here?" Liam bellowed. He set
her suitcase by the stairs and started toward the kitchen, then
stopped as an old man walked in, grumbling under his breath.

"Pipe down, William. Half the county can hear you."

William. No one ever called him William. Except Sam.
Even Maggie called him Liam. Sam and Maggie, the elderly
couple who lived next door. The sweet pair who had adopted
Liam as if he'd been a homeless stray. They met the weekend
he moved in. It didn't take them long to realize he needed a
little help keeping his life in order. The divorce had crushed
him. He didn't take care of himself. And he worked so many
hours at his little company that their neighborly concern grew
from worry into action. Maggie cooked and organized the
house. Sam tended the garden. He and Sam built a pathway
through the back hedge so they could come and go as they
pleased. They constructed a greenhouse so Liam could
experiment with his roses year-round. Somewhere, amidst all
that neighborly concern, Liam had healed. Now, he loved

these two as if they were his own parents. They were certainly as tough as parents. As wonderful as parents. And as peculiar. Sam was peculiar about his name. He believed in calling people by their given Christian names. So, William he became. "Sorry, Sam." He smiled. "I didn't know you were here."

Sam held a huge bouquet of lilacs in a vase. "These just came, William. Cost you a pretty penny, too. I don't understand why you needed them in such an all-fired hurry. You call me on Saturday and say you need them as soon as possible. I was calling every darn florist in the Southern Hemisphere. Finally found these in Argentina—" He stopped. His gaze moved from Liam to Cara. "Oh."

She stared at the lilacs as if mesmerized. Liam wondered if she remembered the last time they'd been together, when the scent of lilacs wafted between them, when he kissed her senseless only to leave her minutes later.

"They're beautiful," she said.

Sam walked over and put the vase in her hands "These must be for you."

"Thank you." She closed her eyes and breathed in the fragrant scent for several moments. Suddenly, her eyes flew open, and she stared at Liam as if she had never seen him before.

"Cara, what is it? Are you okay?" Liam asked in concern.

Slowly, she set the lilacs on the table. "Oh my God," she whispered almost to herself.

"Is everything all right?" Liam asked again.

She nodded. "Everything is … fine." But she gazed up at him with the strangest expression.

He gave her a piercing look. "You sure? Let me introduce you. Cara Larson. This is Sam Myers."

The older man shook her hand. "I'm happy to meet you, Ms. Larson."

Cara seemed to snap back to reality "Likewise, Mr. Myers. Thank you for the lilacs. They're my favorite flower."

Sam's eyebrows shot up. "I just this minute figured that out, Ms. Larson."

"Is Maggie around?" Liam asked. "We've been on the go all day, and Cara is probably hungry." At that moment, an older woman came from the kitchen.

"I thought I heard you, Liam. Welcome back." She stopped. "Who is this?" She eyed Cara speculatively.

Liam stepped over and kissed her on the cheek. "Maggie, this is Cara Larson."

"Welcome, Cara. So, you're the one who finally brought the light back to this boy's eyes."

Cara blushed but refused to meet Liam's sharp gaze. "Maggie, don't embarrass her," Liam said, but he noted with surprise that Cara didn't seem to mind the comment. And was this the first time in history she hadn't rolled her eyes? What was going on with Cara Larson, he asked himself.

Cara took the older woman's hand. "It's nice to meet you, Mrs. Myers."

"Please, call me Maggie." She put her arm around Cara and led her to the kitchen. "Now come in, I'll fix you something to eat." She looked back toward Liam. "You too, young man."

Sam picked up Cara's suitcase and started up the stairs. "Where should I put this suitcase, William?"

Liam hesitated for a fraction of a second. "In ... in the guest room, please."

Sam raised an eyebrow as he clucked noisily up the stairs. "That young fool doesn't have a lick of sense, if you ask me."

Cara closed the door of the guest room and leaned against it. Oh my God. How had she not realized this before? The lilacs did it. Their soft scent opened a door Cara had kept closed and locked for too long. Their sweet fragrance confused her past and present, and somehow brought everything into focus.

She remembered the first time she'd smelled lilacs. The memory was barely a fragment now. She had been only two years old. Her father was lifting her up to a massive lilac bush, his strong arms clutching her tightly as she thrust her face into a clump of purple blossoms. "You don't need to dive in, Cara baby." She remembered his laughter as he fished her out. It was the only memory she had of her father. He died only weeks later.

When Cara turned eight, she and her mother planted a lilac bush in the back yard. To honor her father. She still remembered the first time it bloomed. Her mother gathered a large bouquet and brought it into the house. From that large bouquet, she made a smaller one for her daughter. Cara had placed the flowers by her bedside, and that night, dreamed of her father. Every year after, she kept a bouquet of lilacs in her room whenever they were in season.

Then there was Liam. He brought her lilacs after her mother died. He could not have known how much they meant to her, but somehow, he found a way to tap into her hidden sorrows and heal them. When he kissed her, she could no more have resisted him than she could have stopped the sun from coming up. She should have realized the truth then. Should have understood then, but she had been blinded by too many worries and too much sadness.

Oh my God, she thought. Is this what Mama meant about peace? About happiness? To find the thing in life that meant more than anything else in the world? The thing so important a person would abandon everything else for it? She thought back over the time she had known Liam. And of course, it was right there for her to see. Liam Scofield was that thing. She had believed in his dreams. She had trusted him with her secrets. She had tossed her own career aside to save what rightfully belonged to him. And he had done the same for her, she realized suddenly. He had trusted her with his dreams. He had kept her secrets. And right now, he was risking the future of his company to keep her safe. He was a man she could believe in. A man she could respect. He was the one man in the world she could trust with her life. Mama called it peace, Cara thought. And it was peace, in a way. But Mary Larson's daughter would call it by a different name. "Oh my God," she said to the empty room. "I'm in love with Liam Scofield."

"Cara?" Liam's voice was soft as he knocked on her door. "May I come in?"

She opened the door. "How are you holding up? Just wanted to see if we need to call pacing patrol."

She smiled and tried to match his easy tone. "I think I'm too exhausted to even pace. It's been a … big day. The staff meeting. Seeing Aerie. My … my …"

"Your what?"

"Nothing." She smiled. "It's a lot to take in for one day."

"And the fun's only just beginning." He looked at his watch. "We have about a hundred headaches to face before this is all over. Starting with the gala in two hours."

Cara's eyes widened. "Oh my gosh, Liam. I just realized. I have nothing to wear to a gala."

He shook his head and gave her a crooked grin. "Check that." He studied his watch with exaggerated care. "The headaches begin … now." He smiled and took her arm. "Come on, Ms. Larson. Let's get moving. We need to find you something to wear to the gala."

Chapter 43

"Stop fidgeting, Cara. You're supposed to be the ice princess." They were riding the escalator up to the hotel ballroom from the parking garage below. "I suppose it's hard to pace on an escalator."

Cara took a deep breath. "Guilty as charged, Liam. I confess to being nervous."

"Relax." She was standing one step above him, and their heads were level. He touched his fingers to her chin. "All you need to do is remember six words."

"Six words?"

"Plan A. Plan B. Ice princess."

She laughed, and Liam let his eyes linger over her. "You really do look stunning, Cara. I understand now why you didn't show me the dress at the store."

Cara smiled in spite of her worries. She was wearing a deep green, one-shoulder satin dress that made her eyes look like emerald pools. "I wanted to make sure Mr. Smitten played his part."

"I think you succeeded." He leaned down and brushed his lips over her bare shoulder.

"I wouldn't do that if I were you." They both whirled around to find Mike standing below them, his brow furrowed. "Haven't you heard the stories? About people getting their toes caught in the top of the escalator and losing their lower extremities?" He shook his head. "Do you realize what's underneath us right now? Hundreds, perhaps thousands of loose toes and feet, forever lost to their original owners, all because people were not paying attention on the escalator."

Liam stepped Cara over the edge with exaggerated care. "Thanks for the tip, Mike." Cara didn't seem to hear Mike's banter. Liam watched as she gazed around the room. The ballroom was sparkling, the crowds were buzzing, and the woman at his side seemed suddenly the very opposite of an ice-princess.

"You go ahead, Mike. We'll catch up."

Mike glanced at Cara. "All right. I'll meet you inside, but I'm warning you, Liam, don't touch the supersized inner tube."

"What?" Liam asked in confusion.

Mike pulled out his auction sheet. "Here we go. Item number sixty-three. Don't bid on that puppy. It's mine."

Liam nodded knowingly. "You'll receive no competition from me, but Staci may give you trouble. She has two boys."

"Damn, maybe I can pay her off," Mike said, but he cast another troubled glance at Cara before he left.

Liam and Cara walked to the balcony overlooking the street and the tree-filled park. The night was warm and the breeze soft. The streetlights peeked out from beneath the massive elms. They took in the sight quietly. After a few minutes, Cara took a deep breath. "Plan A. Plan B. Ice Princess." She smiled at Liam. "I'm ready."

Hundreds of people were in attendance. Cara recognized many faces from Pyramid, Fleet, and Windwear. Liam placed a hand at her back and led her toward a group from Fleet. Stunned silence met them as he introduced her. People murmured cordial hellos to Liam, but they wouldn't meet Cara's eyes. Then, hurriedly, and not particularly politely, they departed to seek other conversations. He led her to another group. With similar results. Even Rick Penner, whom Cara knew harbored no resentment toward her, seemed uneasy when they met.

Liam and Cara were standing together, once again stranded, looking at the backs of several uncomfortable attendees, when Peter Whittington approached, his face suspicious, and his eyes watchful. Cara couldn't help but note his extra girth and the new lines around his eyes. These past two months had not been kind to Peter Whittington. He stopped so abruptly his wine spilled onto the hem of her dress. She gasped and jumped back as the dark liquid splashed over her. "Well, isn't this a surprise." Peter held out his hand to Liam. "Liam Scofield and Cara Larson together. I heard a rumor you were back in town, Cara."

"Hello, Peter." Liam extended his hand. "It's good to see you again."

"So, Scofield, you found Cara, after all. Why didn't you tell me?"

"I haven't had much of a chance. Cara and I ran into each other at the beach this past weekend. We've had a lot to catch up on." He gave Cara a smoldering glance and threw a possessive arm around her shoulders.

"Well, young man, I hate to throw cold water on your ... reunion, or whatever you think it is, but now that Cara's back, I'll be continuing my investigation."

"I understand. I told Cara all about your ... accusations. In fact, that was what convinced her to come back to Portland with me. She wants to clear her name."

"What?" Peter exclaimed. Cara watched the telltale purple creep up his face.

Liam gave Cara another lingering glance before turning to Peter. "You were wrong, Peter. Cara doesn't have Aerie. She says she gave the software to you as you instructed and didn't keep a copy. This has all been an unfortunate misunderstanding. She understands why you fired her for ... the announcement she made at the review, and she isn't angry about it any more. Are you Cara?" He smiled reassuringly at her, as if trying to coax her into agreement.

Cara gave him a slight nod, her assent grudging at best.

"This is a win-win for both of us, Peter. Now that we know Cara doesn't have Aerie, your investigation won't take long. Then we can proceed where we stalled out two months ago. You can finally sell Aerie to Windwear."

Peter's face turned a darker shade of purple. "Sell Aerie?"

"We're in no hurry, though. Since Paul is no longer with me, I'm short a decent systems expert. I think I've convinced

Cara to come to work at Windwear." He gave her another
smoldering glance. "I realize we'll need to wait until her
noncompete expires, but I wanted to make sure I told you, so
there wouldn't be any misunderstandings between us."

The silence stretched out as Peter absorbed Liam's
words. Cara felt Liam's arm tense as they waited for Peter's
reaction.

Peter pierced Liam with a steely glare. "Well, all I can
say, Scofield, is I hope the sex is good, because that's all
you're getting out of this deal. If you believe anything this
bitch tells you, you're a fool."

"Hold on a second, Pet—"

"No, you hold on. This bitch is a thief and a fraud, and
I'm going to pursue her with every resource at my disposal.
I'll give you a choice, Scofield. Either you work with me to
make sure justice is done, or I add you to my investigation as
Cara Larson's willing accomplice." He smiled, and the purple
receded from his face as he shook Liam's hand again. "You
think about that, son, and let me know how *you* want to
proceed. You two enjoy your evening."

Liam and Cara stood quietly as he walked away. "Well,"
Liam sighed, "at least he didn't leave any doubt about where
he stands."

Cara nodded. "No, he did not. So, we move to Plan B."

Liam looked at her intently. "We don't need to, Cara. We
can drag our feet on any action Peter takes. We can delay
long enough to get Aerie to market."

"And hurt your IPO in the meantime?" She shook her
head. "I'm willing if you're willing. You have everything to
gain if Plan B works, and if it doesn't, well, you aren't any
worse off than you are right now."

He gave her a long look, and then nodded. "Okay. Plan B
it is."

"Liam, I should go to the powder room. My dress needs
some repair, and … and …"

"And you need to shore up your Ice Princess armor? I
understand." He kissed her softly on the lips. "Do what you
need to do, Cara. I'll be waiting for you. Don't worry. I'll be
right behind you the whole time."

Cara reached up and kissed him in return. "Thank you, Liam. I ... I ..." He waited for her to finish. She blushed slightly, and gave him a small smile. "Thank you," she whispered as her lips brushed across his cheek.

"Go suit up, ice princess." He gave her a crooked grin. "We're down to four words."

Cara was still smiling at Liam's comment as she headed for the powder room. She didn't see Peter stroll over to Lauren as if he hadn't a care in the world. Nor did she see them stop at the hors d'oeuvres table and engage in tense conversation.

Cara leaned over the sink and rinsed her face. The icy briskness of the water refreshed her. She patted her face dry with a towel as she mentally rehearsed the story she would tell Peter. The door opened behind her, and Lauren Janelle, sheathed in scarlet silk, sauntered in to greet her. The lawyer leaned against the wall near the sink, her manicured hands folded across her chest. "Congratulations, Cara, you managed to put Peter in a vile mood. He's practically spitting nails. Do you affect all men this way?"

Cara looked up and slipped a cool mask over her face. "Lauren. What a pleasure."

"What the hell are you doing back in town? What game are you and Liam playing? Do you realize how much trouble you're causing Windwear?"

"I don't know what you're talking about. Liam explained why I'm here."

"Don't give me that pack of lies." Lauren reached into her purse, pulled out a sheaf of papers, and handed them to Cara. "This will be filed in district court first thing in the morning if you don't give Aerie to Peter tonight."

Cara's eyes widened in surprise. She took the papers from Lauren and unfolded them. She realized in an instant Peter's threat had not been idle. Or spontaneous. She was looking at a legal document. A complaint. The widely spaced words screamed in black and white. "Plaintiff: Pyramid Corporation. Defendant: Cara Larson." The charge must be here somewhere. She scanned the pages. There it was.

Violation of noncompete clause. The complaint demanded she halt any work related to her previous employment. Read Aerie. It asked the court to allow Pyramid to take possession of any work she had produced since the date of her termination.

This was what she expected. Right down the line. But she did not expect another name to be listed under hers. Another defendant. Windwear Corporation. She examined the document more closely. The plaintiff demanded Windwear turn over all documents related to Aerie. She looked up at Lauren. "This will never fly. Oh, the noncompete against me will take some time to fight, but there's no evidence Windwear has Aerie."

"Are you sure?"

"No one knows about Aerie but Liam and you—" Cara stopped. "No, Lauren, you didn't. You didn't tell Peter Windwear has Aerie? Tell me you didn't betray Liam."

Lauren scowled. "I didn't need to. You did the job all by yourself. You come waltzing in here, dangling the promise of Aerie in front of the whole world. How did you think Peter would react? This is all your fault, Cara. If you had stayed away, Peter never would have suspected Windwear of anything. Instead you come back with Liam hanging all over you like a lovesick puppy. Do you realize how many alarms went off when you showed up this morning? You've made a mess, and I need your help to repair the damage."

"My help? Why would I help you?"

"Think of it as helping Liam. You've done it before. As I recall, you paid a hefty price the last time. Do you want your sacrifice to go to waste? Do you want Peter to destroy Windwear now, after everything that's happened?"

"What's your plan?" she asked warily.

"Much better, Cara. Helping Windwear is the least you can do after the damage you've caused." She reached for the complaint and returned it to her purse. "You're going to tell Peter you'll deal, that you will give him Aerie."

"What!? News flash, Lauren. I don't have Aerie."

Lauren smiled. "I know that. You know that. But Peter doesn't know that. He's convinced you and Windwear are working together. He wants to take your place."

"You expect me to believe that? He wants to take my place and force Windwear out of the picture."

"Don't worry. I won't let him do that."

Cara closed her eyes and pressed her fingers against her forehead. "What happens when he finds out I don't have Aerie? How long do you think I can pull off the lie? Two days? Three? A week? Then what? Peter will pick up right where he left off and sue Windwear. He won't stop. He wouldn't stop if God himself gave the order."

Lauren nodded. "Two days might not be enough time. Three could work. Definitely a week. A week would be enough time."

"You're not listening to me, Lauren. Peter will not stop pursuing Windwear."

"I told you, I'll take care of Peter."

"How?"

"Never mind. That's my business."

"Oh no. You tell me, Lauren, or I don't cooperate."

"Then you'll be the reason Windwear goes down."

Cara shook her head. "Good try, Lauren. You can no more risk Peter suing Windwear at this stage than I can. It will kill the IPO. Tell me, or I don't cooperate."

Lauren stood silent, considering her options. "All right. Peter is known to have a few ... exploitable weaknesses."

"What kind of weaknesses?"

Lauren reached over and touched Cara's bruised face. "I happen to know he was responsible for this—"

Cara did her best to swallow her revulsion. "Of course you do. Because you told him I was in Cannon Beach, didn't you?"

"All's fair, Cara. Anyway, I think Peter will be opposed to having a felony charge leveled against him."

"So, extortion is part of your legal repertoire."

"If that doesn't work, I can always use his fondness for money."

"Bribery, too. Nice."

Suddenly, Lauren pushed Cara up hard against the edge of the wall. "Enough with the holier than thou shit, Cara. I am only undoing the damage you caused. Now you listen, and you listen carefully. Here's how this is going to play out ..."

Chapter 44

Cara leaned against the wall next to the sink and gathered her thoughts. Damn. This was far worse than she could have imagined. Not only was Plan A dead, but Plan B just went on life support. Peter knew Windwear had Aerie. Nothing would stop him from pursuing Windwear now, and killing the IPO in the process.

She bit her lip in apprehension. Lauren may think she could bribe and extort Peter, but she was mistaken. Lauren didn't know Peter the way Cara knew him. He would never stop pursuing Windwear now. What had she said to Lauren? Peter wouldn't stop if God himself gave the order.

Cara stopped. Of course! She couldn't convince God to step in, she thought, but the next best thing might do. She looked in the mirror. Her reflection slowly smiled back at her. Yes, indeed, the next best thing would do nicely. The next best thing to God. Neal Coleman.

Liam met her as she emerged from the powder room. "Cara, how are you doing?"

"Fine." She smiled. "My steel underwear is in place."

"That's what I like about you. Tough as nails." He searched the room for Peter. "Well, our target seems anxious to speak to you. Are you ready?"

She took a deep breath. "I'm ready."

"Care to dance, Cara?" Peter said as he approached them.

"That would be lovely. Would you excuse us, Liam?'

Liam frowned. "What are you doing, Cara? You don't mean ... you're not going to talk to Whittington, are you?

After all his threats and innuendo? You can't talk to him, we have a deal—"

"Correction, Liam." Her tone was cool. "We're still in negotiations, which is quite different from having a deal. I am free speak to whomever I want, whenever I want."

Liam's lips tightened. "You can't be serious. After all that's happened between us—"

"Please excuse us." She turned away from him and faced Peter.

Peter led her to the dance floor. "Lauren tells me you've seen the light. She says you have Aerie and that you are willing to … cooperate. At last."

Cara hesitated for a fraction of a second. "That's right."

"Excellent. Here are my terms. You give me Aerie tonight, and I won't bring charges against you."

She faltered slightly. "That's it? Those are your terms?"

"I think they're generous."

She shook her head. "No deal."

Peter glared down at her. "I beg your pardon? I don't believe you have a choice in the matter."

"On the contrary. I have Aerie."

He danced her around for a few moments. "What do you want?" he finally asked.

She gazed up at him. "These are my terms. I give you a copy of Aerie in three days. The handoff will happen midnight on Thursday. You will meet me at my house in Cannon Beach." She paused. "You know where I live, right?"

He stared at her in surprise. "Don't act so shocked, Peter. I'm quite aware your men were the ones who paid me a visit last weekend. Do you think I'd be so stupid as to leave Aerie lying around for you to steal? God, you must think I'm a fool."

"Go on."

"You will cancel the noncompete agreements for Mike and me, effective from the dates we left Pyramid. You will drop any lawsuits related to Windwear. In exchange, I will give you 10 percent of Aerie's revenues."

"Are you out of your mind? I won't agree to any of these terms."

"Let me remind you again. I have Aerie."

"I'll get Aerie one way or another, Cara. From you or from Windwear. I know Scofield has a copy, too. What were you thinking, giving the software to him?"

Cara forced down her sense of disquiet. Damn. Had Lauren told Peter everything? "Go ahead, knock yourself out, Peter, but you're fighting the wrong enemy. Your problem isn't me or Windwear. Your problem is time. Or lack thereof. Both Liam and I are so far ahead of you that no matter how hard you try, you're going to lose. You want in? I'll cut you in, but you deal on my terms."

He grasped her hands tightly as they made their way around the dance floor. "Fifty percent."

Cara shook her head. "Fifty? No way. Twenty. Max."

His eyes were hard. "You don't realize how miserable I can make your life. Fifty."

"You don't realize how good I can make yours. I'm close, Peter. Why do you think I'm even here? Do you have any idea where Windwear is on Aerie?" She paused noting his angry expression. "I didn't think so. What do you think I've asked Mike to do these last two months?" Peter's eyebrows shot up. "Windwear is only inching along. Oh, they've made an effort, but they're not even close. I'm ready to go. I've convinced Liam to back off—"

"I knew you were working with him. I didn't believe that horseshit about waiting until the noncompete lapsed."

"What do you think will happen to my efforts to market Aerie if you threaten to sue? No one will touch Aerie if Pyramid is waving lawsuits in every direction."

Peter was quiet again, but he stopped squeezing her hand so tightly. "Okay. I can agree with your other terms, but I want 50 percent."

"Thirty. That's the highest I'll go." She frowned at him. "Such an interesting dilemma for you, Peter. Vengeance or greed. You'd like nothing more than to punish me and Windwear for taking what you think is yours—"

"Aerie is mine."

"Right. We'll agree to disagree on the point. Even so, there's a lot of money sitting on the table, just waiting for you. Vengeance or greed. Which is more important, Peter? Thirty percent."

"You're right, that is a tough choice. And I hate compromise." He ran a finger down her bruised face. "Fifty."

She willed herself not to cringe at his touch. "All right, Peter. You win. Fifty percent."

He smiled. "Excellent. Now, I have one more condition. I want the software tonight."

She shook her head. "Impossible. Aerie's in a safe place. I told you, I need a few days to get it."

He paused, mulling over her words. "All right, Cara. Here's what we'll do. You see those two gentlemen standing at the entrance?" She turned her head and spotted two men in dark suits. "They're my ... er ... associates. When we're done here, you will allow them to accompany you wherever you go for the next three days. Until I get the software. Do you understand?" He smiled and ran a finger down her face again. "I'll instruct them not to hurt you. As long as you cooperate."

Cara felt icy fear crawl up her body. Damn. What was she going to do now? She pretended to consider his words while she searched the ballroom. Liam was at the far end of the room, watching her intently. His words popped into her head. Plan C. *"Drop everything and run ... Do you hear me, Cara? Don't stop. Don't wait. Don't think. Run."* Her gaze flitted around the room as she tried to quell her growing panic. She spied Mike next to the buffet table. And behind the buffet table ... she turned to Peter, and hoped he didn't catch the look of relief in her eyes. "That's fair, Peter. I don't like it, but I understand your point."

"You ran before. I'm not taking any chances, this time."

She nodded. "All right, but I need to talk to Mike first."

"Oh no. I'm not letting you out of my sight."

She gave an exasperated sigh. "Have it your way, Peter, but you won't get Aerie unless I speak to Mike. Alone. He built an impenetrable encryption program for Aerie, and he needs me, or more precisely, certain information only I can provide, to access it."

"Okay, we take him with us. He'll keep you company for a few days."

"No. The protocol doesn't work that way. If the steps aren't precisely followed, the software goes underground." Damn, she thought. She was making this all up on the fly. She hoped she didn't say anything so completely stupid that Peter realized she was full of more shit than a horse. "You can keep me under wraps for a few days, but not Mike. If he doesn't show up at a certain place within a very short time frame and with specific information from me, Aerie is gone. For good."

Peter hesitated. "Three minutes."

"Five. You can watch from here." She stepped from his grasp and hurried over to Mike. She grabbed his arm and led him behind the buffet table. "We need to talk. Quickly."

"Hey, hold on. I was just getting to the lobster. Can you believe it, Cara? Lobster!"

"Hush, Mike." She took a breath and tried to calm down. "Please listen carefully to me. Our plan's gone sideways. Liam is in huge trouble. I need you to help me and not ask any questions." She took his plate and set it on the table. "Now, I want you to do exactly as I say."

"Okay." His words were agreeable, but his tone was uncertain.

"Good. Act like you're arguing with me."

"How do I do that?"

"I don't know. Gesture. Flail. Yell a little."

He raised his voice. "What are you talking about? You have got to be kidding me!"

Cara responded loudly. "Mike, listen …" Then she began to whisper quietly. "Good, now get out your key card to the office."

"What? Why?"

"Just do as I ask." Then she said more loudly, "I don't have much time."

He pulled out the card, and she elaborately rolled her thumb across the back. She took out a tissue, carefully wrapped it around the key card, and handed it back to him. "Act like this is the Hope Diamond."

Mike nodded and held the tissue-wrapped key card gently in his hands. "All right. What's next?" He placed the card in his wallet.

Cara saw Liam from the corner of her eye. He was still at the far end of the room, watching them. "Put your arms around me."

Mike gasped. "What?"

"Please, Mike, or everything Liam's been working for is gone." As he wrapped his arms around her, she started again. "Okay, here's the plan ..."

After several moments, she leaned away from him. "Do you understand, Mike?"

"You're crazy. It'll never work."

"We need to make sure it works, because Liam is on his way over here. If we're not convincing, he'll skin us both alive before we can explain."

Mike shook his head. "I hope you know what you're doing."

"I can't think of anything else on such short notice."

He sighed. "Okay, let's do it." Slowly, and almost gracefully, Mike switched directions. And his tone of voice. He bearing became stiff and formal. "Roger, one-niner, target is approaching north by northwest of our present location. Weeee are presently canoodling in the eye of the intended target at a level of 5.6 on the Masters and Johnson amatory scale—"

"Stop, Mike. I'm trying to concentrate. Here comes Liam." Mike's voice had faltered anyway. He was beginning to panic. "Time to get to work. Stay calm. Now, relax and do as I say. Now, hold me a little tighter."

"Cara! Stop. This is hard enough without you giving me step-by-step instructions."

"Dammit, Mike." He tightened his grip on her. "Don't you know anything? Relax your hands and hold me." She leaned into his body and put her arms around his waist. She rubbed against him sensuously.

"Cara, stop that! Cara!" She nestled again, and Mike tried to relax his arms and hold her like he had at least one clue about what he was doing.

"Now, run your hands up and down my back."

He was blushing furiously. "Cara—"

"Do it, Mike."

"I'm not sure this is such a good ide—"

She laughed despite the tension. "I don't believe this. I finally found the great Mike Taylor's weakness. The boy genius is stumped. Bewildered. Overwhelmed. And it was so easy. I will never forget your Achilles' heel."

"Neither will I." Then he began inching his hands over her buttocks.

Mike sneaked a peek sideways. "Liam's coming. He looks mad."

"Good. He's supposed to be. When he gets about ten feet away, bend your head and start kissing me. Do not stop until Liam gets here, do you hear me? Mike?"

Mike turned pale. "Cara, I can't kiss you like that." He cringed. "You're like a sister."

"And you're like a brother, but if you don't do this right now, I'm going to slap you upside the head. Do you understand?"

Mike frowned. "He's coming closer. Okay, Cara. Get ready. Five ... Oh my God ... Four ... I hope this works ... Three ... He's mad as hell ... Two ... I hope he kills you first ... One ... Here we go ..." He bent his head and kissed her.

It was like kissing a piece of fuzzy cardboard. Cara reached up around his neck, pressed closely into him, and tried not to think about what she was doing. He lifted his head slightly and hissed at her. "Stop doing that." She pulled his neck lower and kept on kissing him. This wouldn't take long. And then it happened. Right on time.

Liam tapped Mike on the shoulder. "Hey, Mike. What's going on?"

Suddenly Mike turned and bull rushed into Liam with all his might. The breath came out of Liam in a sharp whoosh as he and Mike tumbled into the table. There was a loud crash as plates and silverware and trays of lobster and bowls of salad scattered to the ground. Then Mike was on top of him, wrapping him in a bear hug as he held his face close to Liam's. "Abort," he whispered. "Cara says to abort." Liam squirmed to get out of Mike's grasp, but Mike held him tight. "Do you understand, Liam? Cara says Plan B is dead, and Plan C is in effect. Now stand up and hit me. And make it look real."

Cara ran as soon as Mike released her. She hurried to the door behind the buffet table. Oh God, she hoped she hadn't run into a dead end. She pulled the door shut and found herself in a darkened room. Her eyes needed a few seconds to adjust to the dim light. She looked around. She was in another ballroom, this one empty. She spied double doors at the far end of the room and edged around the wall as swiftly as she could.

As she opened the door to the corridor, a crack of light spilled into the room from the door she had just exited. Then she didn't waste time looking any more. She ran down the escalator to the first floor, turned left, and hurried onto Broadway. She kicked off her shoes, hiked up her dress, and sprinted as fast as she could away from the hotel. She ran for six blocks before she slowed down to catch a cab. She opened the door as the taxi came to a stop and folded herself into the seat. "I need to get to the airport. Quickly."

The cabbie stared at her. "Dressed like that?"

She closed her eyes. "Trouble with a date."

The cabbie's eyebrows shot up. "Must be a real son of a bitch."

Chapter 45

Liam stood quietly and watched the rain roll off the windows. No one was on the river today. No paddleboats taking tourists out for a leisurely lunch on the Willamette. No dragon boaters. Just the yachts moored in the marina, and a few Coast Guard boats piled up next to the dock, abandoned for the moment. It was early for the winter rains to come. He pressed his fingers over his eyes. God, he needed to get hold of himself. He had so much to do, so many things to attend to, but he just couldn't seem to get to them. He couldn't move beyond this deep worry.

Abort, Mike had said. Abort. Cara had cancelled the plan. Then disappeared. She didn't go to Cannon Beach. He had called Andrew as soon as he'd managed to extricate himself from the crowds and the security force and that nervous hotel manager. Andrew said Cara never showed up. He'd been calling the policeman every few hours. Still not a word. Where did she go? Was she in trouble?

What about Mike? They had been separated after their 'fight,' and Liam hadn't been able to ask him a single question. Now, Mike had disappeared too. He picked up the phone and dialed Mike's number once more. Still no answer. Was he with Cara? Was he in trouble too? Should he worry about Mike? He scowled as he remembered the young man's hands all over Cara, his head bent, kissing the woman he planned to marry. He had half a mind to hit him again just thinking about it. He smiled wryly in spite of his worries. Maybe Mike wasn't so stupid to keep his distance for a while.

He walked to his desk and sat down. He opened the folder containing the facilities plans and scanned the report. Everything was on schedule. They were only waiting for the money to come in from the stock offering before they broke ground. He closed the folder and opened another. The first deliveries from Hsin were small, but of good quality. Mark Prentice was pleased. He suggested they try Hsin with something more complex, like the running flashlight he'd designed. A hazy memory of green eyes and a soft smile hit Liam. He closed the folder. He picked up the phone to call Jared Dafoe, and then replaced it in frustration. How could he instruct Jared to start Cara's defense when he didn't know where she was or what Peter had said? The last thing he wanted to do was jump too soon and create more trouble for Cara. Damn. Where was she?

Lauren walked into the trendy restaurant at the corner of Fourth and Salmon at exactly noon. She glanced around as her eyes adjusted to the dim interior. He was already here. In the booth in back. The fellow with the purple face. She grimaced. He was drinking lunch. This was not going to be easy. Somehow, she needed to get Peter to delay this lawsuit. It would really screw things up if he insisted on suing Windwear. She sighed. As if matters weren't totally screwed up, anyway. It wouldn't make a hell of a lot of difference what Peter did if she didn't find Aerie soon.

The consortium was getting nervous and ratcheting up the pressure. Something had to break soon, and she hoped it wouldn't be her kneecaps. The IPO was scheduled to go in nine days. If she didn't get her hands on Aerie, Streeter threatened to cancel the IPO. The gall of Carl Streeter to demand proof. He accused her of making Aerie up, of concocting the existence of the software as an expedient lie to stoke investor interest in Windwear. He demanded proof the software actually existed before he allowed the IPO go forward. How dare he not trust her?

The damned software had to be somewhere. She had looked everywhere. In one way or another, she had pressured everyone at Windwear about Aerie. She scowled. And if she ever found herself alone with that little twerp Mike Taylor, she would kill him. Slowly and with pleasure. Barrow, Alaska! The little shit. She lost a solid week alone on that wild goose chase.

She was running out of options. She thought she might shake Aerie loose with Peter's help. Despite what she told Cara at the gala, she had indeed informed Peter that Liam had Aerie. She hoped Peter's threats would force Liam to run to Lauren for help. After all, she was his attorney. But Cara screwed up her plan, just as Cara seemed to screw up every plan Lauren had ever made. Somehow, the bitch managed to remove suspicion from Liam and elude Peter with one swift move. Lauren scowled in frustration. She still had no idea of Aerie's whereabouts. She looked at Peter, now starting on his second drink. It was down to this. Grape face was her last chance. Damn.

She slid into the seat across from him. "Hello, Peter."

"Hmmmph."

"Are you ready to file the lawsuit?"

Peter leveled a belligerent gaze her way. "Yes, goddammit. I want you to file. Do everything you can to find that bitch and bring her back here."

"All … all right. I'll file first thing in the morning."

"Now, dammit. I want you to file now."

She took a deep breath. "Well, I'd like to, but I need to make a few changes to the document."

"What changes?"

"Well, now that you've added Windwear to the complaint, *I* can't file the document. I'm the attorney for Windwear. I now have a conflict of interest. Unless of course, you want to remove Windwear from the lawsuit. Then I can file for you."

Peter took a sip of his bourbon. "No, I want to take them both down."

Lauren closed her eyes. Damn. "Then you'll need to have another attorney file."

He slammed his fist on the table. Several patrons nearby turned to stare. "Goddamn that bitch." He stared at his drink as if it were an enemy and said almost to himself, "First Scofield, now me. Maybe she's not as stupid as I thought."

"What do you want to do, Peter?"

"Okay, okay. Take Windwear off the lawsuit. File only against the bitch."

Lauren willed herself not to show any sign of relief. "All right. I'll need some time to make the changes. I can file in the morning." At that moment, the waiter came by and she ordered an iced tea. "You know," she said after the waiter left, "a lawsuit against Cara could have some unintended consequences. It could hamper your own efforts to take Aerie to market."

"What the hell does that matter if the bitch beats me to the punch? First things first. I need to stop Cara Larson." Peter glowered into his drink. "One more thing. Get me a meeting with Scofield. Maybe that bitch had a good idea, after all. Maybe I should make a deal with Windwear."

Lauren froze. "A deal with Windwear?" With Liam? Was he kidding?

"Yes, dammit. We're in a goddamned race now. Cara is going to eat our lunch if I don't do something quick." He smiled for the first time since Lauren sat down. "Yes, indeed. Tell Scofield I'll buy whatever he's done so far. Maybe the two of us together can stop that bitch. If I go after Cara on the noncompete, we don't even need to mention Aerie. That will hold her up while Scofield and I forge ahead. What do you think?"

She nodded guardedly. "What … a brilliant idea."

Peter sat up straight, his eyes suddenly glowing. "I want a meeting. Today."

Lauren opened her calendar and made an elaborate production of checking her schedule. "I can't meet today. My next opening is … tomorrow, at 3:00 p.m."

"Tomorrow at three? Anything earlier?" He frowned. "You don't need to be in the meeting. I need to see Scofield, not you."

Lauren bit back her angry retort. "Let me go back to the office and check Liam's schedule." She paused. "Perhaps we should stick with this time. Liam is not exactly … er … fond of you, Peter. Let me use the extra day to warm him up to the idea of a meeting."

"What's this crap about fond?" He glared at her. "To hell with *fond*. This is business. Get me a meeting ASAP."

"Trust me, Peter. Let me soften him up first."

"All right." He scowled again. "Three o'clock tomorrow. I'll go to Windwear."

Lauren stood up and kept her steps smooth and steady as she walked out of the restaurant. "Dammit all to hell," she muttered under her breath. Could this get any worse?

Lauren tapped on Liam's door. "Come in, Staci."

Lauren smiled. She had no trouble getting rid of Staci for a few minutes. These days, important legal documents requiring the secretary's signature were often being delivered downstairs. "It's not Staci."

Liam looked up with a heavy frown. "Please leave. I'm busy."

His desk was empty his feet were up, and he was staring into space. "I can see that." She gave him her most engaging smile. "I came to ask you a few questions about the IPO. I won't take much time." She paused and gave him another smile. "Then you can throw me out and continue being busy."

"What do you want?"

"I have a better idea. Why don't we talk over dinner tonight?"

"No."

She gave him a sympathetic look. "I know you're worried about Cara—"

"What do you want, Lauren?"

"Well," she said, choosing her words carefully, "I have something important to discuss with you, but I don't think we should talk at the office." She hesitated, as if spies lurked around every corner. "It's about the IPO. And Aerie."

"What do you know about Aerie?"

"Only what you tell me. Which isn't much. I know you're working on it. The word is out Cara is working on it too."

"Where did you hear that?"

"Only from everybody. The guys in manufacturing started a pool. Finance is about ready to explode. Peter Whittington said—"

"Oh that's rich. Peter Whittington. I would certainly believe anything Peter Whittington has to say."

"Liam, we have a real problem on our hands. This business with Aerie has the potential to hurt the IPO. We need to discuss the matter but not at the office. Let's go to dinner. What do you think? Pazzo's? It might do you some good to get out."

Liam seemed to be turning something heavy over in his mind. "What time?"

"Seven."

He nodded. "I'll meet you there." He dismissed her with a wave.

Chapter 46

The phone rang in Mike's apartment late on Tuesday afternoon. "Yo. Taylor shop. We keep you in stitches."

"Cute, Mike."

"Hold for one minute, please," Mike said. Abruptly, the phone went dead.

Cara stared at the phone in her hand, the dial tone practically screaming at her. She was standing in the middle of O'Hare International Airport. The hum of thousands of travelers echoed around her, but all she heard was that buzzing dial tone. Slowly she hung up. Eight seconds later the phone rang.

"Cara? Is that you?"

"Mike. What happened?"

"Good, I'm glad you're still there. I ran as fast as I could."

"Where are you?
I'm calling from a neighbor's apartment."

"Is everything okay?"

"Of course. I'm just hot, right now. I'm sexy too, but that's another story altogether." Cara rolled here eyes. "Ha, I bet you just rolled your eyes, Cara, didn't you? I can always tell."

"Mike, what's happening?"

He sighed. "I'm looking out the corner of my neighbor's window. Two guys have been sitting outside in a gray car for the last nineteen hours." He paused. "I wonder how they take bathroom breaks. Did you ever think about that?"

"Mike ..."

"They tapped my phone. I can hear the hiss on the line."

She let out a sharp gasp. "Oh, Mike. I'm sorry I dragged you into this mess."

"Don't be." He chuckled eagerly. "I think this will be an opportunity for me to learn a few new skills."

She sighed. "Well, I hate to say this, but you're probably going to need them."

"Excellent." She heard the smile in his voice.

"Are you ready to go?" she asked.

"Yep."

"Can you get to Cannon Beach without your friends in the gray car seeing you?"

"Are you kidding? Piece of cake. Do you want to know how?"

"Probably not."

He ignored her. "I've discovered those onboard computers in cars are super easy to hack."

"Mike, please don't rack up too many felonies."

"Now, now, Cara. They're only felonies if you get caught. Don't worry. I can reverse my ... er ... work when I'm done. I happen to be an excellent de-hacker as well."

"Okay. I'll call Andrew next. Then we'll be ready to set the trap."

A short silence fell between them. "I hope you know what you're doing, Cara."

"I do. With you and Andrew to help, we'll make this thing work." She paused. "Mike?"

"Yeah?"

"Have you been able to talk to Liam?"

"I'm afraid not, other than during our fight, which was awesome, by the way. Unfortunately, Liam's going to get the bill for our little fracas. I should have thought of that before I ran him into the lobster."

"Mike ..."

"I told him about Plan C, Cara. That was all I could get out before the security goons grabbed me."

"Do you ... how is he? Is he okay?"

"Sure, I didn't hurt him. I'm not that big."

"I mean—"

"I know what you mean. No, I don't have any idea. I haven't been able to talk to him, and I don't want to call him. If they bugged my phone, they probably did the same to his. I did talk to Staci, though. At home, not at the office. I tried to bribe her into giving him a message. I even offered to give her kids a ride on the supersize inner tube, but no go. She's really mad at me."

"Why?"

"She went ape-shit over the whole kissing thing. Personally, I think she's jealous."

Cara closed her eyes. "Liam may still skin us alive."

"I'm going to let you go first. That would be the gentlemanly thing to do, right?" He paused. "Hey, when does your plane get in?"

"Around eight o'clock."

"Run by his house, Cara. No one will see you. No one even knows where you are. Go and talk to him. You'll still have plenty of time to get to Cannon Beach."

She sighed. "I'm not sure that's a good idea. Liam will ask a million questions, and he needs complete deniability in case this thing doesn't work out."

"Ooh, Cara, you sound like you're working on a felony of your own."

"No way. That's your department. I'm staying on the right side of the line."

He sighed. "Too bad. But have a little mercy on the man. Staci says he's sick with worry over you. Her words, not mine. I would never say anything so sappy."

"All right, I'll think about it." She paused. "Mike?"

"Yeah?"

"How did you ever get the inner tube thingy? All hell broke loose before the auction even started."

"Are you kidding? Where money is concerned, chaos cannot rule for long. Anna said after Liam and I were kicked out, they cleaned up the mess and proceeded as if nothing happened."

"But how did you—"

"You didn't think I'd let that little puppy get away, did you? Anna bid for me."

"Anna bid on the jumbo inner tube? Super-put-together-trend-a-day-Anna?"

"Yeah. She paid a thousand bucks for it, too. Man, I couldn't believe it. I told her to get it at all costs, but I didn't mean a thousand bucks!"

Cara laughed. "It was for a good cause."

"I'll take you for a ride when you get back in town. It's awesome."

"You bet." She looked at her watch. "I need to go, Mike. See you at eleven."

"That sounds like a teaser for the news," he said, but she didn't hear him. She had already hung up the phone and was dialing again.

"Peter Whittington, here."

"Peter, this is Cara Larson."

The explosion was immediate. "What the hell are you doing calling me? Where are you? When I find you, I'm going to—"

"Save your threats, Peter. I have the software. I'm ready to hand it over to you. As we agreed."

Silence filled the line. "Did I hear you right?" he finally asked.

She rolled her eyes. "If you heard me say I'm ready to do the deal, then yes."

"Why now?" Suspicion practically dripped from his words.

"I told you I needed a few of days to get it."

"And you knew my terms. You were supposed to be under my ... control until the handoff."

"Yes, I understood your terms, Peter. And when was the last time you actually listened to someone while you were busy telling them what to do? I told you the protocol to get the software was very specific. I couldn't risk Mike screwing it up. He's smart, but he's young. There's too much at risk."

"So you gave me the slip. What else have you been doing since you took off?"

"This is getting old, Peter. Either you do the deal or you don't. I have the software. Do you want to go ahead or not?"

"When do we meet?"

"As we originally planned. My house. Cannon Beach. Midnight tonight."

"So cloak and dagger all of the sudden, Cara."

"That's because I don't trust you."

"Hmmph. You're learning."

"Also, call your dogs off Mike. I need him with me to decrypt the program."

He drew in a breath. "What are you talking about? I don't—"

"Save the lies, Peter. They can follow him. They just can't touch him. I need him to get to the beach unharmed. If anything happens to him, I won't be able to give you the software."

"All right."

"The rest of the terms remain as we discussed."

"I want 60 percent."

She rolled her eyes again. What a slug. "No. The terms remain as we discussed."

There was a short pause on the line. "All right, Cara. Midnight."

Cara hung up the phone as travelers rushed by. The trap was set. She glanced at her watch. She'd better hurry; her plane would be boarding soon.

Cara held her breath as she rang the doorbell. Maggie answered the door with a gasp of surprise. "Cara! What are you doing here?"

"Hello, Maggie. I came to see Liam. Is he in?"

"I'm afraid he's out. With—" She stopped abruptly.

Cara sighed. Too much had happened to phase her anymore. She was immune to bad news. "With?" She gave Maggie a tired smile. "A woman?"

Maggie frowned. "I guess you could say that. He's out with that witch woman."

"Oh, Lauren." Wrong. Cara felt a sharp jab of pain.

"That's right. I can never remember her name."

"Well, that's okay. Would you tell him I came by?"

"Would you like to wait?"

Cara shook her head. "I don't think so. Please tell him I stopped by."

Maggie eyed at the clock on the wall. "He shouldn't be long."

"No, Maggie, I need to be on my way." She turned to leave, then stopped. "Actually, I should pick up my bag. I left it here the other day."

Maggie nodded. "Sure. Go right up. You remember where your room is. Second door on the right." Cara walked up the stairs. Did she remember? She sighed as she recalled how she stood against the door and realized she was in love with Liam. Now, he was out with Lauren.

She pushed the door open. The room was neat and tidy. There was no evidence she'd ever been here, except for the black bag sitting in the corner. A few hardy lilacs still stood in the vase by the table. She crossed the room and picked up the bag.

She turned, took one last look at the room, and caught the heady scent of the lilacs. She walked over to the table and breathed in their scent. She hesitated for a moment, then pulled a sprig from the vase and wiped its stalk dry against her jacket. She walked next door to Liam's room and laid the sprig on his pillow. Tomorrow, she told herself as she turned the light out. Tomorrow, this will all be over.

Chapter 47

"Ms. Janelle, there's a phone call for you. I was told to tell you the matter is important."

Lauren peered at the maître d' in surprise. "Thank you." She smiled at her dinner companion. "Please excuse me, Liam."

She hurried to the phone. "Hello?"

"Call it off." It was Peter Whittington.

"Peter. How did you know I was here?"

"I called your office. Your girl told me."

"My girl?" Lauren asked in confusion.

"Well, Liam's girl. Traci or Stella—"

"You mean Staci."

"That's the one. She told me you and Scofield were here. I figured this was the 'soften up' dinner. I called to save you the trouble. I want to cancel the lawsuit."

"What?"

"You heard me. Call off the lawsuit and cancel the meeting with Scofield. Cara just called me. I'm getting the software tonight."

"What brought about this turn of events?"

"I'm not sure the events ever turned in the first place. Cara had a special procedure for getting the software. She needed to take care of it herself."

I'll bet she had a special procedure, Lauren thought. She wasn't sure what Cara was up to, but she didn't care. That annoying bitch just bought her some unexpected and desperately needed breathing room. "Okay, I'll cancel the filing and the meeting."

"On second thought, keep the meeting with Scofield. Once I have the software, I want to scare the living shit out of him so he drops his development effort."

She closed her eyes. "Okay, the lawsuit is off, and the meeting is on. Anything else?"

"No, that's all. See you tomorrow. At three."

Lauren hung up the phone. What was Cara Larson up to? Cara no more had Aerie in her possession than she did. Never mind. Peter Whittington could fend for himself. He had not come through as she hoped, and he was no longer of any use. From here on out, he would receive no more help from her. Besides, she had more important things to do, like finding Aerie and saving her kneecaps.

"I'm sorry for the interruption." Lauren sat down across from Liam.

"Everything okay?"

"Yes. An easy fix, unlike our problem with Aerie."

"Well, you're certainly not wasting any time." Liam put down his menu. "What's going on?"

Lauren reached into her purse and pulled out the complaint, the very complaint Peter just asked her to cancel. "This is going on." She laid the pages on the table. "Peter Whittington called and asked me to meet him today. He gave me this. He's planning to file in the morning."

Liam picked up the papers and read through them. "He thinks we have Aerie."

"Yes."

"And why does he think that?"

She saw the accusation in his eyes. "Well, I suppose you told him," she said calmly.

"Me?" Liam asked pointedly.

"Yes, you. What did you think you were doing, traipsing all over town with Cara Larson? Are you surprised Peter thinks you've been working together all this time?"

"We haven't been working together all this time."

She shook her head. "Do you think that nuance makes any difference to Peter?"

"It's not exactly a nuance, Lauren."

"Whatever. It doesn't matter. By the end of the week, he'll have subpoenaed every scrap of paper related to Aerie. We'll be piling up legal fees left and right, and the publicity will kill the IPO."

He sat back. "Don't worry about it. I'll take care of it."

Her jaw dropped in surprise. "That's all you have to say? 'Don't worry about it?'"

"Yes."

Lauren took a deep breath. "Liam, I know I made a mistake when I gave you Aerie and made up the story about Cara. I know you don't trust me, now—"

"You're right, I don't."

"I accept that I'm on … probation." She could barely spit the word out. "I know I must earn back your trust. You gave me one job and one job only, to take care of the IPO. All I ask is you tell me enough so I can do the job you've asked me to do. I need to understand enough about what is happening with Aerie to respond to this." She waved the complaint in the air.

"That's not necessary. I know how to respond without compromising the IPO. All I need is a little more time."

She looked at her watch. "Okay. Well, you have about fourteen hours until this is filed. Then the IPO will be toast." Liam remained quiet. "At least tell me what you're planning to do. Maybe I can mitigate the effects on the IPO if I know what you have in mind."

Liam paused, weighing her words. "Fair enough. Jared Dafoe is preparing a complaint on behalf of Windwear. We will demand Peter stop any action against Cara or Windwear, until he shows reasonable justification. As part of the demand, we'll ask him to produce Aerie."

"What? He doesn't have Aerie."

"No, he doesn't. Nor does he have any evidence Aerie ever existed. When the court discovers he has no grounds for taking any action, his case will be thrown out."

Damn, Lauren thought. If Liam pursued this strategy she would never get her hands on Aerie. "I see where you're going with this, Liam. Unfortunately, it won't stop Peter from filing in the first place or prevent the publicity that will follow. In fact, the exposure will likely increase once you challenge him."

"Only for a day or two. When Peter doesn't produce Aerie, the case will be over. Besides, I think we can make the publicity work in our favor. I plan to use the media to spread the word that Windwear is the legal owner of Aerie. "

Lauren shook her head. "I think it's too risky. You can never predict how the media will play a story like this. They are just as likely to play up the conflict between you and Peter if they think it will sell more papers." She paused. "Then again, the Cara Larson angle might capture their attention."

"What do you mean?" Liam asked sharply.

"Well, if you stop Peter, he will redouble his efforts against Cara. Once you start pushing back against any effort that hurts the IPO, he'll lay off. Cara will become the easier target. He thinks she has the software."

Liam closed his eyes. Damn, he thought. Plan B. Of course, Peter thinks Cara has the software. She told him she did.

"Actually, Liam, that is the perfect diversion. Everyone thinks Cara has the software, anyway. Let Peter go after her. If we play up that side of the story, the media will forget all about Windwear."

Liam rubbed his fingers across his forehead. "Damn."

Lauren patted his hand. "Cara's a big girl. She can handle Peter. God knows she deserves some blowback after coming back and stirring up this hornet's nest of trouble."

"No, she does not deserve this."

Lauren studied him with apprehension. She needed to goad him into action, but she didn't want to push him so far he went all superhero on her. "Maybe there's another way. Maybe we can reduce Windwear's exposure without any publicity at all."

His eyes shot up to meet hers. "Oh? What do you suggest?"

"Instead of attacking Peter overtly by demanding he produce Aerie, we could strike first. We could draft a complaint, stating we are working on an unspecified, but potentially lucrative product that Peter is attempting to appropriate without any legal right to do so. We tell the court that if Peter is allowed to proceed, he will wrongfully threaten Windwear's future and inhibit its competitive advantage. Due to the confidential nature of the matter, we ask the court to shield all documents related to the case, at least until the IPO is complete."

"Hmm. Do you think the court would agree?"

"I'm not sure. The courts generally favor openness, which works against us in this instance. We would need to convince them of the merits of our case by providing as much supporting documentation as possible." She gave him a careful look. "This is where Aerie comes in. We must show the courts all the documentation Cara originally gave to you plus everything you've done since. We would show Aerie was your original idea, that you worked with Pyramid for a time on a preliminary design, but the majority of the work was done outside of Pyramid's control. We would prove you created a saleable product substantially from your own efforts."

Liam sat quietly, considering the idea. "The court would keep the information confidential?"

"Yes, as long as we can convince the court we own the product and our rights are being wrongfully threatened. We don't need to spell out what the product is. Given Windwear's business, people can speculate on all kinds of products and never guess the subject of debate is a piece of software. We will also argue Pyramid's name and legal actions must be shielded, as they would lead to speculation on the nature of our product."

"And you can protect Cara?"

"Not perfectly, but to be honest, it's better than any other option. With this move you are asserting your rights to the software. If the court rules for you, Peter will have no legal right to the software. He can't go after Cara for stealing something he doesn't own. He can still go after her for violating her noncompete or any other employment rules she's broken, but he won't get her on anything criminal."

Liam closed his eyes, indecision warring within. He rested his elbow on the table and scraped his chin with his thumb and forefinger. "You can file this before Peter files his complaint?"

"Yes, but I must move fast, and I must to be thorough. If we're going to succeed, you must tell me everything about Aerie. The more detail I disclose, the more convinced the court will be."

Liam remained quiet for a long moment, considering his options. "All right, Lauren," he said at last. Then he told her everything she needed to know about Aerie.

Lauren's eyes were shining as they finished coffee. She glanced at her watch. Ten o'clock. "I'd better get home, Liam. I should get to work on this tonight. I'll hand it off to Adam Johnson at 7:00 a.m. sharp. He'll file as soon as the court opens its doors."

"Wait a minute. Aren't you going to file?"

"No, I'll be on an early flight tomorrow. Don't worry. Adam is quite good. He's a legal courier from SwiftMen, and I trust him with all my filings."

"Where are you off to?"

"Boston." She smiled. "I need to meet with Richard Bancroft to finalize the details on the IPO. I'll only be gone a day or two."

Liam nodded, but she saw the mistrust in his eyes. "Don't worry, Liam." She laid her hand over his. "I'll take care of everything. You can trust me."

Liam's eyes met hers. "Thank you, Lauren."

What a difference a day makes, Lauren thought, as she let herself into her office. Yesterday, all her dreams of fame and fortune seemed like a prelude to disaster. But with just the right amount of leverage on Liam's emotions, the floodgates had opened, and she was now swimming in an ocean of information about Aerie. She was once again on track to save the IPO and entertain dreams of fabulous wealth. Liam Scofield was nothing but a lovesick puppy.

She sat at her desk and booted up her computer. She typed in her password and opened the document she'd been working on for several weeks. *Sales Agreement.* It was the document transferring ownership of Aerie to the Cyclops consortium. This document would save her. After the fiasco in Taiwan, she'd been in big trouble with Carl Streeter. She hadn't been able to deliver a low-cost producer as she promised. Liam had screwed those plans up. Instead of investing in a joint venture with Wangchao, he committed his capital to production facilities stateside and made only nominal, short term purchase contracts with Hsin, which, of course, was a high-cost producer. What a fool. Carl practically exploded when she'd told him the news. He demanded Aerie as compensation.

With this agreement, she would prove to Carl Streeter Aerie was real. She could hardly believe what Liam had accomplished. Aerie was going to be far more profitable than she'd ever imagined. But Liam Scofield would not enjoy the fruits of his labors, because as soon as the IPO was complete, Windwear's new management would sell Aerie to Cyclops. All the profits from the software would go not to Windwear, as Liam planned, but directly to the consortium members. Streeter considered it a fair trade for the low returns the consortium would be forced to accept, now that Liam had committed the company to the Portland facilities. Unless she managed to kill Windwear's expansion plans. That would take time, and she had no time right now. She needed to deal with the most immediate issues first, and at the top of her list were the sale of Aerie and the rescue of her butt, which had been sitting precariously in a sling for the last several weeks.

What happened, she wondered, to halt Peter's lawsuit? Peter said Cara had agreed to give him Aerie. But Cara didn't have Aerie. She shook her head. Never mind. Whatever that bitch was up to, it was to Lauren's advantage. Intentional or not, Cara had pushed Peter out of the picture. Now the IPO could go forward without a problem. Lauren smiled. Cara had also unwittingly cleared the way for Lauren to steal Aerie right from under Liam's nose. This was almost easy. First Liam, then Cara. She was another lovesick sap. God, she hoped it wasn't something in the water that made people this way.

"Maggie, what are you still doing here?" Liam glanced at his watch. "It's almost eleven o'clock."

"I can tell time, Liam. I was waiting for you."

He smiled wearily. "No need, Maggie. I'm a big boy."

Maggie harrumphed a little and set down the cup of tea she'd been drinking. Still turning the pages of her magazine, she said casually, "Cara came by."

The moon fell into the sea. The world stopped turning. The sun went out. Maggie could have said any of these things, and he would have a better chance of believing her. "What did you say?"

"I said Cara stopped by. Cara Larson. You remember, don't you? The young lady you're in love with?"

He sat down abruptly in the chair opposite Maggie. "Cara? That's impossible. She left ... She—"

"She was here, but no longer. I told her you were out with that witch woman—"

"Lauren."

"Yes. I told Cara you were out with her. She picked up her bag and left."

Liam slumped in his chair. Cara, here! What the hell was she doing here? And gone again. Without a word. He let out a deep sigh. "What did she want?"

Maggie shrugged. "Didn't say."

"How did she look?"

"About the same as you. Tired, worried, sad." Liam didn't say anything.

Maggie closed the magazine. "Well, I'd better get home." He stood up, reached for Maggie's sweater, and draped it over her shoulders. He walked her through the arch in the bushes and made sure she reached her house safely. He retuned to the house, flipped off the lights, and trudged up the stairs to his room.

He stopped at the guest room. Her bag was gone, just as Maggie said. He couldn't believe how empty the room felt with that one little change. He went to his bedroom, brushed his teeth, and washed his face. He stripped off his clothes and threw them in the corner. Then he turned on the lamp by his bed and reached for the covers.

The scent of lilac hit him first. The pungent odor made him think of things that hurt too much to think about. He lifted the sprig, now drying and wilted, from the pillow. He closed his eyes and breathed in the scent. A message without words. Dammit. She should've left him a note. Told him what she wanted to say in words he could understand, because right now, his brain wasn't working. There'd been too many twists and turns these past few days, and he wasn't sure which way was up anymore. And all at once, he was so tired of it. He lay the sprig down on the table and turned out the light.

But for the first time in months, Liam Scofield slept soundly.

Chapter 48

Cara stopped in the doorway of the Cannon Beach police station and stared at the man standing in the middle of the room. "Hello, Andrew."

Andrew Carson walked over to her. "Well, Miss Cara, I'm sure glad to see you again. You had us all worried for a spell." He gave her a warm hug. "I'm glad you're safe."

"Thank you, Andrew."

He held her away from him. "Have you seen Liam?"

She shook her head. "I tried. He wasn't in. How … how is he?"

"Been better, I'd say. He's been callin' every few hours since you pulled the disappearin' act. You were supposed to come here, Miss Cara."

"I know. I needed to do something first."

"That sounds a little ominous, especially now I've been acquainted with you for a bit of time. Does this somethin' have the word 'technically' attached to it anywhere?"

She smiled despite her tension. "No. I needed to get an insurance policy."

He raised one eyebrow. "Sounds like you moved a notch higher up than 'technically' on the trouble scale, Miss Cara. An insurance policy against what?"

"Peter. Plan B was a bust, Andrew. Peter is going after Windwear. He is far more dangerous than I thought."

"So, you bought an insurance policy against Peter. You think that was necessary, given our plans for tonight?"

"Especially given our plans for tonight. If things go wrong, and Peter gets any opportunity at all, he's going to strike at Windwear and strike hard."

"So you scrapped Plan B and ignored Plan C. Did you happen to tell Liam about this ... Plan D?"

Her eyes widened in alarm. "No! Andrew, I couldn't. Peter has a long reach. There's still a good chance this whole thing will crater. If that happens, the only protection Windwear will have is if Liam can honestly say he didn't know anything." She sighed. "This is all such a mess. You know as well as I do Liam would have been better off if he had just let me leave, at least until Aerie went to market and his IPO was complete."

"Miss Cara, you know as well as I do Liam never would have allowed such a thing."

She nodded. "Now, he's put his whole company at risk."

"Well, I get what you're sayin' but I don't think Liam sees things the same way as you."

"What do you mean?"

"Well, I don't think his ol' company comes close to winnin' any contest with you. I think he'd just as soon dump the whole thing if he thought you were in danger. He didn't tell me so in words, mind you, but I got the gist after his first seven phone calls."

"Andrew, I don't want to be the reason Liam loses Windwear. I can't let it happen. That's why I needed to go. Do you understand?"

He nodded. "I think so, but if you don't mind my sayin', I think you're tellin' this to the wrong fella."

She smiled. "You may be right. After tonight, I might actually get a chance to tell the right fella."

"Sounds like a mighty fine idea. I reckon Liam Scofield wouldn't mind playin' out his fairy tale, busted and bent up as it might be."

Cara looked up at him sharply, but Andrew didn't notice. He had turned away and reached for something on the desk. When he turned back, his eyes were serious. "Now we got that matter all squared up, we need to get ready for our little meetin' tonight."

"Right." Cara took a deep breath. "Time to spring the trap."

Cara arrived at her house at 10:15 p.m. The night was cool and cloudy but not rainy. It was high tide, but the cloud cover made the waves sound muffled and far away. She flicked on the kitchen light and walked to the back door. She checked the window where the pane had been cut out. All fixed and good as new. Andrew was on top of things. She unlocked the door and ran upstairs to change her clothes.

Mike arrived shortly after eleven. He practically knocked down the front door with his banging. "Cara!" he yelled. "Cara, I'm here. Open up!"

She opened the door and threw her arms around him. "Oh, Mike. Thank God you're okay. I'm so sorry to mix you up in this mess."

For once, Mike didn't even cringe at her affection. "Cara, you scared the hell out of all of us. Please, don't ever run away again."

"I'm sorry, Mike. This is all going to be over soon. By tomorrow, this will all be behind us, and Liam will have nothing but clear sailing when Windwear goes public."

"I hope so. Are you ready?"

She pointed to the coffee table where a wooden box sat.

"Mmm. The cherry wood version. Very sophisticated."

Cara laughed. Thank God for Mike.

The knock came at two minutes past midnight. Cara and Mike exchanged a glance. He gave her a thumbs-up. She nodded, stood up, and walked to the door.

"Cara," Peter Whittington said harshly, as if he could barely stand to get the words out. He was followed in by the two men who had broken into her house four days earlier.

"Hello, Peter." She pointed to the couch. "Sit down. Did you bring your computer? I want to make sure you test the software before you leave. I don't want you coming back at me for any reason."

He held up his briefcase. "Yes. Do you think I'd trust your word? I'm not stupid."

"Of course." She tried hard not to roll her eyes.

"Is Aerie in there?" Peter stared at the box.

"Yes."

He hurried over to the coffee table. Mike stood and planted himself in front of the table, blocking Peter's way. "Hold on," Cara said. "Before you test the software, I need you to sign the agreement."

She pulled out a folded sheet of paper from her pocket. "These are the terms we agreed on."

Peter took the paper and studied the contents. "This seems to be in order."

"Good. Now read it out loud."

"What?"

"This is part of the protocol. I need Mike to hear the terms before he does the final step in the decryption process."

Mike nodded. "That's the deal, buddy. Cara told me the terms. I need you to read them aloud. If the terms don't match, I won't unlock the software."

Peter closed his eyes. "Of all the …"

"Read," Mike ordered.

Slowly, Peter read through the entire document. When he was done, he looked up at Mike. "Satisfied?"

Mike shrugged. "Except you mispronounced one thing. The word is not *sequel*; it's not part two of anything. It's pronounced *S-Q-L*. You ought to know better."

"Okay Mike, we can live with that," Cara interrupted. "Anything else?"

"No. I'm ready to proceed."

"All right." She nodded to Peter. "Go ahead and sign the document. I'll follow."

Peter reached into his pocket, took out a pen, and began to sign. Then Cara took the pen and signed. She leaned back against the couch. "Okay, Peter. Go ahead."

He leaned over the coffee table and unlatched the box. Suddenly there was a noise from the kitchen, and a muffled din filled the room. Six policemen, their guns drawn and pointed at Peter, stood in a line. "Stop right there, Peter Whittington," Andrew called out. "You are under arrest."

Peter drew his hands back in surprise. "What ... what's going on?"

Cara leaned over and opened the lid of the box. Up popped a clown's head connected to a spring. She turned to Peter. "Surprise. I lied."

Chapter 49

Liam stepped into his office with a smile and a bouquet of roses for Staci. "Staci, I'm sorry, I've been unbearable. Forgive me."

Quietly, Staci took the flowers and set them down. She walked around the desk and hugged Liam. "Will you be all right? I've been so worried."

He returned her hug. "I'm not sure I know anything more than I did yesterday, but I plan to find out. Would you try Mike again? I need to talk to him."

Staci tilted her head toward the door. "Er ... Liam?"

"Yes?"

Liam looked over. "Well, speak of the devil. Mike!" He hurried over and shook his hand. "How are you, Mike?"

"You aren't going to hit me?" Mike half cowered as Liam approached.

"I should. You were probably smart not to answer your phone yesterday. Where's Cara? Is she all right? Tell me, what's going on."

"She's still at the beach—"

"The beach? But I've been calling Andrew nonstop—"

"It's a complicated story, Liam. Cara needs to explain. She sent me ahead to tell you she's all right and not to worry. She'll be here by noon."

"Mike, what—"

"Patience, Liam. Everything is okay."

Just then, Staci's phone rang, and she hurried to answer. "Liam." She poked her head into his office. "Richard Bancroft is on line one."

Liam nodded. He hadn't spoken to his longtime friend and banker since the early days of the IPO negotiations way back in July. He gave Mike a pointed look, and Mike shrugged. "Okay, I gotcha. I'm gone."

"Thanks." He smiled and waved. "Back at noon, Mike. With Cara." He picked up the phone. "Richard, how are you?"

"Fine, Liam. Are you surviving the flood of paperwork that comes with a public offering?"

"Actually, the process has been relatively painless. Lauren has been handling the details. I've been focused on our operational changes, but she's kept me in the loop on the IPO. How can I help you?"

Richard laughed. "You must be busy. I've tried to call you several times, but you're a hard man to reach. Always away from the office or in a meeting."

"I apologize, Richard. We have a lot going on here. I hope Lauren is doing a better job of keeping in touch."

"Yes, she's been great. In fact, I had a few questions for her, but your secretary said she was away from the office. Can I risk going all the way to the top of the food chain and talk to you?"

Liam laughed. "You can always talk to me, but I'm confused. Isn't Lauren there? She told me last night she was meeting with you today."

"Who? Lauren? Here? In Boston?"

Liam glanced at this watch. "Oh, it's only 11:30 your time. Maybe she hasn't arrived yet. What time are you supposed to meet?"

Richard sounded confused. "Hmm, I must have missed something." Liam heard the pages flipping in his notebook. "I'm not scheduled to meet with Lauren today." More pages flipped. "Or all week, as a matter of fact."

"I could have sworn she said she was meeting with you today. Let me find out where she is. Would you hold for a second?"

"Sure."

Liam punched the hold button. "Staci?" When she appeared at the door, he asked, "Would you check Lauren's itinerary and find out where she was heading? I thought she said Boston, but I must have misunderstood."

"No problem."

He pressed the hold button again. "I'm back, Richard. I'm trying to locate her. In the meantime, what's going on? Maybe I can answer your questions."

"No need. I'll follow up with Lauren. But now I have you on the line, I want you to know I've changed my mind."

"Changed your mind about what?"

"About including Windwear's voting shares as part of the offering. At first, I didn't like the idea, but the more I thought about—"

"What are you talking about? I didn't place the voting shares up for sale." There was strained silence at the other end of the phone. Liam felt an odd twinge run down his spine. "Richard, the stock sale is for common nonvoting shares only." Silence echoed over the line. He was aware of a sudden sinking feeling, as if he were falling. "Richard? What's going on?"

"Why don't *you* tell me what's going on?" Richard responded. "You signed the agreement. Initialed each page. We all saw your signature. You sold 51 percent of the voting stock to the Cyclops Consortium. For ten million dollars and their firm commitment to buy two million shares at sixteen dollars a share."

"WHAT!?!" Liam shouted in disbelief. "I did not agree to such a thing." He pulled open a file sitting on his desk and riffled through its contents. "I'm looking at the agreement right now. I see absolutely no mention of the voting stock being sold to anyone. No mention at all."

Liam heard a rustling of pages on the other end of the line. Richard's voice was puzzled. "Liam, I have the agreement right in front of me. Page five, paragraph six. I quote, 'The shares for sale will consist of the following: six million shares of common nonvoting shares, convertible to voting status five years from date of issuance—"

"Right, I follow."

Richard continued as if Liam hadn't spoken. "And 510 shares of preferred voting stock to be sold to the Cyclops Group, consisting of—"

"What? That is *not* written on my agreement. I swear to you." He paused. "What's the date of your agreement?"

"July eleventh. You were back in Portland at the time. You had that family emergency. Lauren said she express mailed the agreement to you for signature. We all signed on the twelfth, at the Cyclops office, in front of her."

"Richard, would you fax me your agreement, please? Right now?"

"Are you telling me you didn't authorize this agreement?"

"That's right. I never authorized the sale of the voting shares, and I never signed such a document."

"But Lauren—"

The dam broke inside Liam's head. Lauren. Lauren sold his company out from under him. "I want to kill this deal, Richard. I want to cancel the whole thing. Now."

Richard took in a sharp breath. "Wait a minute. You can't do that. You signed this agreement, filed forms with the government—"

"I didn't sign the agreement. The agreement you have is a fake. That's not my signature."

"But Liam, it is. It's in blue ink. We checked the signature against our records here. It's standard procedure if a signer isn't present. It's a perfect match."

"Hold on, the fax is coming through." Liam put down the phone and hurried to the fax machine. The machine clicked and whirred as he picked up each piece of paper, scanned the contents, and threw it on the ground. Until he reached page five. There it was, in black and white. His company. Gone. For ten million dollars. He closed his eyes. Somewhere, the thought ran through his head the price was considerably higher than thirty pieces of silver.

He pawed over the papers. The last one was coming across now. There was his signature. *His* signature. And the date. July eleventh. The date was correct. He had signed the agreement on that day, had Staci notarize it, and then express mailed it back to Lauren. He examined the page more closely and drew in a sharp breath. Such a simple difference. Who ever looks at the notary stamp? Until now. The signature page didn't show Staci's notary stamp, but Lauren's. How was that possible? He thought back to the only papers he signed in Lauren's presence that had Carl Streeter's name on them too. They had been at the airport, in the car, in a hurry. He had signed the Nondisclosure Agreement. He stopped. Check that. He had signed two Nondisclosure Agreements. And he had signed two lines in her notary book.

"Richard?" Liam said. "I understand what happened. Lauren switched the signature pages of the document. This is out and out fraud. I do not intend to sell the voting shares of my company. I need to void this agreement and cancel the IPO."

"What? But how?"

"She used the signature page from a completely different agreement and attached it to the Broker Agreement."

"Well," Richard said quietly. "This is ... I'm having a hard time believing this."

"You're not the only one. I'll figure out what to do about Lauren, but first I must stop the sale."

"Stop the sale?" Richard said, his voice troubled. "Liam, this situation isn't so clear cut."

"Of course it is. Lauren committed fraud. I'm not bound by her actions."

"Liam, Lauren didn't sign the document. You did. Obviously, you can sue her, but you can't keep the consortium from demanding you fulfill your part of the agreement you signed."

"Then I'll change the agreement. I'm not opposed to selling the nonvoting shares. I just don't want to sell the voting shares."

Richard was quiet for a few moments. Liam once again heard the pages flipping over the line. "It would be difficult to cancel one part of the sale without the other. The agreement ties both stock sales together. The consortium buys the voting shares and agrees to buy two million common shares at sixteen dollars if the market won't carry. Canceling the voting share portion of the agreement will impact the remaining stock sale for both the consortium and the public, especially if the price falls below sixteen dollars."

"I'm not giving up management control of my company."

"Liam, this situation may not be quite as bad as you think. That's what I was trying to tell you when I first called."

What do you mean? This agreement says I give up 51 percent of my voting shares, which means I don't control my own company. That's pretty bad in my book."

"On the surface, yes. However, I think you should consider going ahead with the sale, anyway."

"No."

"Liam, hear me out." The silence on the line lengthened. Richard continued, his voice now calm, as if he were recovering from his shock. "You know, when Lauren first presented this agreement, I thought it was a mistake—"

"Not a mistake, fraud."

"Just listen. I know how you feel about Windwear, and, frankly, I couldn't believe you had agreed."

"I didn't—"

"I know. But the more I thought about it, the more I'm inclined to think this is a pretty shrewd move on your part."

"How do you figure?" Liam's tone was wary.

"Liam, your original proposal was undesirable from an investment standpoint. Low returns in the short term, conservative growth, risky expansion. No one was going to invest in your company given those terms. When Lauren presented your alternate projections—"

"What alternate projections? We didn't have any alternate projections. We only had one deal." Richard remained quiet. "Damn, I'm afraid to ask."

"Lauren presented a rosy picture," Richard continued. "High returns from foreign investments and limited manufacturing facilities here." Wangchao, Liam thought. No wonder she'd been so insistent Windwear sign with those snakes. No wonder she'd been so angry when he returned with a completely different strategy. He forced his attention back to Richard. "... and Aerie and—"

"Aerie. What about Aerie?"

"The discussion was vague. Lauren didn't share all the details. She described Aerie as an additional source of revenue, something to assist in achieving higher profits."

"Well, at least she told the truth about something."

"The point is, your original proposal would never have raised the capital you're now going to get from the stock sale. Streeter was on his way out the door when Lauren presented the new numbers. I reviewed your updated capital plans. They're different from the ones Lauren presented. They're even more capital intensive, much more risky than what she presented to us. You tripled the investment in manufacturing facilities in Portland and added a research and development department. Frankly, I'm surprised Streeter didn't put up more of a fuss. Given the new numbers, your P/E ratio is too high. I thought he might walk from the deal; he's not known for paying top dollar. Word on the street is that Windwear must be a good company to keep Streeter interested."

"Well, that's because the agreement was based on a bunch of lies."

"That was true at one time, but the plans are fully disclosed now, and Streeter hasn't budged. You have the opportunity to get sixteen dollars a share and keep your expansion plans intact—"

"And allow someone to look over my shoulder and second guess every decision I make."

"What do you think will happen if you cancel the offering?" Richard asked. "You won't be able to go forward with any of your plans without the money from the stock sale. You're committed to those new facilities. You could be facing serious financial problems if you back out now."

"I could borrow the money."

Richard laughed, but the sound was hollow. "I suppose so, but we're talking about $40 million. I can extend credit, but only for a fraction of that amount. It will look mighty fishy if you publicly cancel a stock offering and then turn around and immediately try to borrow from the financial community. Besides, Carl Streeter is very influential. He doesn't like to be outmaneuvered. He'd do his best to prevent you from getting other funding if you bail on this deal."

"I understand what you're saying, but do you understand the risk I run trying to implement my plans when 51 percent of the voting stockholders are working at cross purposes?"

"Listen to me, Liam. If you don't let 51 percent of your company go, you might end up destroying 100 percent of it. Is that what you want? Do you want all those years of hard work to go to waste? I admit, this is a hell of a situation to be in, but you need to play the game with the hand you're dealt. You must decide what's most important. Do you want Windwear to survive with a different management structure, or let everything you built die because you insisted on retaining control? I don't envy your decision, son, and I don't know what I'd do if I were standing in your shoes—"

Just then, Staci poked her head in the door. "Hold on a second, Richard."

"Sorry I took so long. Lauren didn't leave an itinerary. I needed to call the airline. She flew into New York early this morning."

Liam's eyes widened as he took in her words. He nodded his thanks to Staci as she left. "Richard? I'm back. I—"

"I want you to consider something else, too, Liam," Richard cut in.

"What's that?"

"You're not giving up complete control of Windwear. Under the agreement, I own 10 percent of the voting stock."

Liam's voice was quiet. "Are you willing to sell your shares back to me? Or at least ..." He checked the agreement. "Eleven shares? That would give me a majority."

Richard paused. "I would need approval to sell any of my shares. I'll call Carl and put the matter on the agenda for the first management meeting."

"Do you think the consortium would agree?"

"Well, I'll talk to Carl. He owns 306 shares, which is 60 percent of the consortium's 510 total shares. I'd need his approval. He's a tough old bird. He'll probably angle to get a steep price and a few other concessions, but I imagine we can convince him to deal."

"After the offering, I'll have about $40 million. I'm sure I can meet his price."

Richard's voice was reassuring. "Until then, I hold a 10 percent stake in your company. I can't promise I'll agree with every move you make, but I do promise to give you an open hearing at all times."

Liam closed his eyes. "I appreciate your support, Richard, but it's not enough. We've fought too many times over our conflicting responsibilities. I can recite your speeches verbatim. You have responsibilities to your management and your depositors at the bank. 'How long would I last if I didn't maximize revenues for my customers?'" Liam parroted Richard's deep baritone. "You've turned down more than one of my proposals for conservative paybacks and low profitability. You've pushed me into decisions I didn't like because of your loan terms. I can't afford that kind of conflict. My expansion plans are subject to too much uncertainty. I need total control of Windwear to handle the problems that will inevitably come. I can't shoulder Windwear's responsibilities and your profit requirements at the same time."

Richard sighed. "Well, I'll talk to Carl right away. At least consider what I'm saying before canceling the whole offering."

"All right. Oh, by the way, don't expect Lauren in Boston. I just found out she flew to New York."

"Hmm. Do you think she's meeting with the consortium?"

"Probably."

Richard was quiet for a few moments. "I need to take some of the blame for this, Liam. Lauren made a very effective presentation. I tried to call you before we signed, but I couldn't get hold of you. She said you were busy with your family emergency and couldn't be reached. When I saw your signature, I just assumed you changed your mind as Lauren explained. I had no idea you hadn't agreed to it."

"This is not your fault, Richard. This is on me, Richard. I trusted Lauren."

"Did you have any idea this was coming? Any clue whatsoever?"

"No. Not ... not last July, when she did this. I had no idea at all. Up until a few days ago, I thought she was an exemplary employee."

"Well, this is a hell of a thing, son. Let me know if I can help. I'll call Carl right away."

"Richard, hold off on talking to Carl. I want to think about this before I take action. If Carl was this intent on getting management control of Windwear, I don't want to telegraph my plans until I'm sure about what I'm going to do."

"Good point. I'll wait to hear from you."

"Richard, thanks for letting me know. I appreciate it. I know it may not seem like it, but I do."

"This is a hell of a situation, son, but think about going ahead with the IPO."

"I will."

"Good luck, son."

Liam hung up the phone, closed his eyes, and dropped his head to his chest. "Fuuuuuuck," he whispered quietly.

Chapter 50

"Staci, please call Abrams, Williams and Dafoe. I need to get an appointment with Jared Dafoe immediately." She nodded. "Oh, and check on an Adam Johnson at, what was the company called, SwiftGuys, or something like that. A courier company. Find out if he filed a complaint in District Court on behalf of Windwear this morning."

"All right. Liam, what's going on?" Worry was written all over her face.

"Not now, Staci."

He walked down the hall to Lauren's office. He sat down at her desk and examined the few folders stacked in her inbox. A worker's comp claim. He set the file down. A couple of contracts for some new suppliers. He set that folder on top of the first. A new sexual harassment policy. He raised an eyebrow at that, and then placed it with the others. That was all. He tried the drawers. Locked. He reached over and flipped on her computer and waited, chin resting in his hand, while the machine hummed to life. The monitor blinked on: "*Password*," the screen mutely requested. Liam punched in a few combinations of numbers and letters. Nothing. He'd never get in at this rate. He picked up the phone and dialed the extension to Staci's desk. "Staci? Please send Mike over to Lauren's office. Thanks."

Liam stood up and paced around the office. He stopped in front of the file cabinet. He tried the drawers. Locked. Of course. He bent to inspect the cabinet. The brand was the same as the file cabinet in his office. He pulled his keys from his pocket. He learned long ago file cabinet manufacturers only made a few different keys for file cabinets of the same brand. He often wondered how they managed to get away with that. Then he remembered how many times he'd been able to get into Staci's files when she wasn't around. He inserted the key. The lock turned, but not all the way. The drawer wouldn't open. Hmm. Strange. He shook the cabinet a little as he rattled the key in the lock. It was heavy. Much heavier than a normal file cabinet.

He left the office and walked down the hall to the manufacturing floor. He reached the maintenance room and pulled out the biggest crowbar he could find, and then grabbed a heavy, long-handled hammer. He made his way back through the manufacturing area, heedless of the questioning stares of his employees.

When he reached Lauren's office, he went right to work. He inserted the crowbar between the rim of the cabinet frame and the top of the first drawer. With swift strokes he banged it in as far as possible. He pushed the crowbar back and forced out the metal face of the drawer. The drawer didn't move much, but it bent back a little. He moved the crowbar along the drawer and repeated the procedure. *Bang*! *Bang*! *Bang*! *Screech*. And again. *Bang*! *Bang*! *Bang*! *Screech*. Before long, the drawer, scratched and bent, looked like a figure in a carnival mirror.

Liam didn't stop. He didn't stop when Mike walked in and took in the sight. Or when his hand slipped on one of the sharp edges of the now ruined cabinet and began to bleed. Or when he caught a glimpse of several folders in the top drawer. He was focused completely on his task. After a few more blows, he extended his hand though the narrow opening.

He grasped as many files as he could reach and pulled them out. He opened the folders and studied the papers, blood seeping from his hand. There was the original agreement he'd "signed." A totally different version than the copy Lauren had given him. And the alternate projections she had presented. And the correspondence between Lauren and Carl Streeter about ... he rustled through more pages ... about joint ventures with Wangchao and eliminating manufacturing in Portland in favor of overseas production.

"Liam?" Mike was standing at the entrance to Lauren's office. "Is everything okay?"

Liam looked up from the documents in his hand. "Mike, I need you to get into Lauren's computer. I can't get by her password."

Mike's eyes lit up. "Authorized breaking and entering? This will be fun!" His smile fled as he saw Liam's expression.

"Bring me everything you find. I'll be in my office." Then he left the room, the skewed mass of papers clutched in his bleeding hands.

Mike sat down at Lauren's computer. He needed only a few minutes to discover her password. A long time ago, in his wild and uninhibited youth, he had written a program to decipher almost any password. He was lucky he'd never been arrested for some of the computers he'd hacked. He shrugged. Those were the days of his impetuous youth. He had matured. He didn't do things like that anymore. Unless his boss asked him to.

Mike examined the files one by one. Most of them contained legal mumbo jumbo he could ignore out of hand, but located deep inside several layers of directories sat a hidden password-protected directory. Aha! In a few minutes, he was examining a set of documents he could scarcely believe. "Holy scumbags!" he whistled. An hour later he had reviewed all the files and printed them out. After he finished, he shut off the computer and headed to Liam's office.

Liam stood at the door, shaking hands with a short, middle-aged man wearing a very expensive suit. "Thanks for your help, Jared."

"I'm sorry the news isn't better. If this were a falsified signature, you might have a chance to nullify the agreement. Because the signature is genuine, the consortium can legally hold you to its terms. You can break the agreement itself, but the clause specifying these huge cancellation fees will hurt financially. You might be better off negotiating a change in terms rather than cancelling."

Liam sighed. "I understand. That's what I needed to know."

"Liam, did you have a problem with the way I did the Windlogic work?"

Liam shook his head. "No, that was separate from anything we did at Windwear. Why?"

"I thought that's why you didn't call me earlier about this matter. We haven't been involved much in the IPO."

"No, Jared. I didn't know I even had a problem until an hour ago. I hired Lauren to handle Windwear's legal work in-house. She was to call you when she needed advice." Liam sighed. "I understand now why she didn't call you on this."

"Why did she do this?" Jared asked, puzzlement in his tone. "Do you have any idea?"

"My best guess?" Liam asked. "She wanted to jump the stock price. We disagreed on the purpose of the IPO from the beginning. She was frustrated at my approach. I think she found an opportunity to do things her way, and she took it."

"We can take action against her."

"We'll need to, but first I need to deal with the IPO." He shook the attorney's hand. "Thanks for dropping everything and coming by. And thanks again for your work on Windlogic. Aerie, at least, is protected." He stopped suddenly, remembering the dinner he shared with Lauren last night. He closed his eyes. He had told her every single detail about Aerie. And Windlogic. Now, she was on her way to New York.

Jared shook his hand. "Call me if you need anything else."

"Liam?" Staci said as the attorney left. "I found out about Adam Johnson from SwiftMen."

"Let me guess. He didn't file anything in District Court."

She nodded. "You're right. I checked a little further. There are no filings at all related to Windwear, as either plaintiff or defendant."

Liam smiled ruefully. "Believe it or not, Staci, that is a glimmer of good news. Thanks for checking."

Just then Mike entered the reception area. "What's wrong?" Staci asked when she saw his face.

"I need to talk to Liam. Don't bother us for a few minutes. Okay, Staci?"

She nodded as she watched Mike knock softly on the door. Mike. Knocking. Softly. Not barging in as if he owned the place. She bit her lip in apprehension.

"Liam?" Mike halted just inside the office.

Liam looked up from the pile of papers on his desk. "Did you get into her system?"

"Yes." Mike walked further inside.

"What did you find?"

Wordlessly, Mike held out a sheaf of documents.

Liam stared at the younger man as he reached for the papers. He'd never seen Mike Taylor so uncharacteristically quiet.

He studied the first document: *Sales Agreement*. He read it quietly. The only sound in the room was the slow crackling of the pages as he turned them, each one like an explosion in a tunnel.

When he finished reading, Liam laid the documents on his desk and went to stand by the window. Over, he thought. Dead. Finished. Gone. It was the final blow. One he could not possibly survive. Lauren had taken Aerie too. And all the money Aerie would generate to finance his new investments. It was the end of Windwear. The consortium would win. He would be forced to renege on all his plans. His company might survive the blow, but in such a form as to be unrecognizable. He closed his eyes and leaned his head against the window.

"Liam?" Mike's voice was worried.

Liam didn't even turn around. "Please leave, Mike." Quietly, Mike backed out of the room and closed the door.

Chapter 51

"Mike!" Cara threw her arms around him with a happy smile as he walked into the reception area.

Mike greeted Cara without a smile or a joke. "I'm glad you're here."

His tone set off alarms inside her head. "Mike, what's wrong?"

"You need to talk to Liam, Cara. Right now."

"What's happened?" She couldn't keep the sudden panic from her voice.

"It's about the IPO. It's bad. Real bad. Go. He'll tell you." Cara hesitated. "Go," he ordered.

Liam stood silhouetted against the window, the energy drained from him, defeat apparent in the slump of his shoulders. Cara loved him more in that minute than she ever had before. She walked over and placed a hand on his arm. "Liam?"

His eyes flew open and he stared in stunned surprise at the woman in front of him. Then he folded his arms around her. "Cara," he whispered. "You're back. You're safe. God damn, I was worried sick about you."

"I'm okay. I'm sorry I didn't tell you." She said nothing else for a long time.

When he finally let her go, she gazed up at him, her eyes troubled. "What's happened?"

Liam turned again to stare out the window, his arm resting on her shoulders. "Not the best day in the annals of

Windwear history, Cara. I'm going to lose control of my company. And of Aerie."

"What!?"

He took her hand and led her to the desk. He swept his arm above the documents strewn across the table. "It's all here. The whole story."

They talked for hours. He explained what happened, detail by sordid detail. Cara stared, as stunned as Liam was, by the depth and duration of Lauren's deception. As she listened, she picked up a small envelope lying amidst the array of papers. Its very plainness caught her attention. She opened the envelope and pulled out a small card. It contained a number. A long number. Twelve digits. Nothing else. She turned over the card. The other side was blank. "What do you think?" Liam was asking, his voice cutting into her thoughts.

Cara dropped the card on the desk. "Liam, I am so sorry. You don't deserve this. You, of all people. You are the most honest person I've ever known. First Peter, now Lauren. I don't even know what to say."

"Well, I guess in a way this is a backhanded compliment." He gave her a crooked grin that was almost convincing. "Both Windwear and Aerie must have something going for them to garner such attention."

She smiled at his words. He would be all right. He was even more resilient than she had imagined. He would not let this blow destroy him. It would hobble him, hurt him, weaken him, but never destroy him. They walked to the window and stared at the rainy streets below. "What are you going to do?"

"Well, the way I see it, I have three possible options."

Yes, he would be all right, she thought. He was already thinking about his next move. "Which are?"

"The first is easy. I could take the money and run. It's awfully tempting, Cara. Quit and run away. I own half the common stock. At the IPO price, I'm worth almost $50 million. Not exactly pocket change. I could leave Windwear's problems behind for the consortium to deal with. I could head to the beach and start a new life, like you did. Of course, I'll be worth exactly zero when the geniuses at Cyclops proceed to screw up the company and bankrupt it within a year."

She smiled. Yes, he would be okay. "What's your second choice?"

"Not much better than the first, I'm afraid. I could cancel the IPO and take my chances running the company as I have for the last seven years."

"Why not do that? You're successful. Windwear makes great products, and you enjoy an excellent reputation. Nothing has happened to change that."

"On the contrary, everything has happened to change that. The world has happened. Windwear is now a player, or more precisely, a potential player. By entering the public arena, we are now subject to its expectations. The financial community now has license to pass judgment on our every move, even if we aren't a public company yet. Windwear is now subject to the whims and fancies of the financial community in a way we were completely insulated from before. Hell, if they don't like the color of my next hiking boot, they can skewer us in the press and cause business to tank. I can't go back and take the knowledge of our existence away from them. The best I can do now is try to take their reaction into account before I commit Windwear to a specific move."

Liam ran his hand through his hair. "Worse, cancelling the IPO would force me to halt my expansion plans. And I'll never get a chance to pursue them again. Richard Bancroft made sure to tell me the financial community will deem cancellation as a failure, not a conscious choice to delay. The pipeline of money will be cut off for good." He rubbed his eyes with tired fingers. "What's frustrating is that Windwear is ready for this step, ready for growth. How can I tell these people who've been with me for seven hard years that we're going to languish in this limbo of almost. Almost big enough, almost a player, almost a leader. I would feel like I betrayed them."

"I hear what you're saying, Liam, but you know as well as I do 'forever' in the financial world lasts about two years. The financial community will forget you ever existed after a short time. Then you'll be free to start over. Especially if you make a success of your company in the meantime. You can go public later. Your past history will be just a blurb to make your story more interesting. With a colorful history, you might even get more attention and a better stock price."

"If we could survive until then. Without Aerie to fund us, I'm not sure I can keep the company afloat."

"So, you're down to the third choice."

Liam sighed. "Third and last. Stay. Fight. Beat my head against a wall battling a bunch of financial geniuses who can't distinguish a hiking boot from a glass slipper. And probably lose anyway. The expansion plans will fall by the wayside if the consortium takes Aerie. I planned on using the revenue from Aerie to finance our operations until the new lines were up and running." Liam's shoulders slumped. "God, if I had Aerie, I would at least have a fighting chance. I would raise so much hell I would get my way at least some of the time. Now, I don't know. I don't know if I can pull it off."

They stood quietly, staring out the window, immersed in their own thoughts. After a few moments he turned to her. "What would you do, Cara? If you were in my shoes?"

She shook her head. "That's not a fair question, Liam. I'm not you."

"That's beside the point. What would you do?"

She gave him a quiet smile. "You already know the answer."

He paused for a moment, thinking, and then his face lit up with a smile. "You chose door number one. You went to the beach."

"Correct on the first try. I took the money and ran, in a manner of speaking. I started a new life at the beach. But Liam, you aren't me. You don't get to sing my song. You have to sing your own. My mother used to say that." She tapped his chest gently. "You love Windwear. Windwear is where your heart is. Where your life is. If you ran away, you would be tearing out a part of yourself. I'm not sure you could live with the fallout. Oh, maybe for a while, a month or two or six. Sooner or later, you'll wake up and regret you didn't stay and fight.

"Me, I'm different. Pyramid was never my life. It never held my heart as Windwear does yours. Otherwise, I wouldn't have been able to leave so easily. The beach is where I belong. With Bill Martinson and his tomatoes. Sue and her music. Sam and his surfboards. These things, simple as they are, these things touch my heart. Do you understand what I'm saying?"

Liam wrapped his arms around her. "How do you know me so well, Cara?"

She held onto him tightly. "You're not so hard to figure out, Liam Scofield. Your river runs deep, but it flows right through everything you do." She closed her eyes and sighed against him. "You'll work this out. It will be hard, but you can make things happen just by being in the mix. You may not win every management decision, you may not win any of them, but you'll be the one to implement the decisions, to put them in place in a way that's best for your company. If anyone can keep the spirit of Windwear alive, you can."

"God, I want to believe you, Cara, but I can't help but think I'm fighting a losing battle. Without Aerie, Windwear will never be what I dreamed it would be."

"Didn't you say Richard holds a 10 percent stake? Surely he won't let Aerie get away if you disapprove so strongly."

Liam shook his head. "Unfortunately, I blew all Lauren's financial projections to hell with my expansion plans. Richard made promises to his investors based on those projections. If he gives away Aerie, his investors will earn a far lower return than he promised. How do you think they will react? Believe me, I've been around and around with Richard over these types of issues before. He'll be forced to agree to the transfer of Aerie just to satisfy his investors and keep his job."

"Maybe there's a way to keep Aerie."

"I wish there was, but I saw Lauren's plans. Aerie is as good as gone."

Cara's gaze flitted about the room before settling uncertainly on his face. "Maybe not, Liam—"

At that moment, Staci knocked on the door. "I'm sorry to interrupt, but you have a three o'clock with Peter Whittington." She tapped her watch. "Ten minutes."

Liam closed his eyes. He'd forgotten all about the meeting with Peter.

There was a commotion outside the office. Cara heard several voices, and Mike poked his head through the door. "Cara, Andrew's here. Can we come in?"

She nodded. "Come in, Mike." She turned to Liam "I don't think you need to worry about your three o'clock meeting."

"What do you mean?" Just then, Mike walked in with Andrew Carson right behind him. Cara walked over, gave Andrew a hug. "Did everything go okay?"

The policeman nodded. "Right perfect, Miss Cara. The wire recorded everythin' clear as a bell."

Liam looked from Andrew to Cara. "What's going on?"

Andrew walked over and shook Liam's hand. "You're lucky to have this purty woman on your side, Liam."

Liam smiled. "I know that."

"No, I don't think you know half that. You see, Cara helped us arrest Peter Whittington last night. For conspiracy to commit robbery and assault."

Liam's eyes widened in surprise as he turned toward Cara. "Is that where you've been these last few days?"

She nodded. "Among other places."

He stared at the three faces in front of him. "Would any of you care to tell me what's going on?" He paused. "Please?"

Mike and Andrew both nodded toward Cara.

Cara leaned against Liam's desk. "I suppose I'd better start at the beginning." Then she told him the whole story. When she finished, Liam was quiet. "I guess I *am* glad I didn't know the plan, or else I might be sitting in the jail cell next to Peter."

"Yep." Andrew smiled. "Just as well. Our jail is purty small."

"Cara, why didn't you go straight to Cannon Beach?" Liam asked.

"I needed to go to Chicago first."

"Chicago? Why? What's in Chicago?"

"Plan D is in Chicago," Andrew offered.

Cara ignored the policeman. "I met with Charlie Schmidt, the managing partner of Pyramid's Chicago office. He's probably the only person at Pyramid I trust."

"Pyramid? You met with someone from Pyramid?" Liam's expression was suddenly wary. "Why would you do such a thing?"

"To stop Peter."

"I don't understand. You stopped Peter. He's in jail."

"For now. Peter will make bail in a few days, and then he is going to come after Windwear. Probably with even more ... er ... enthusiasm than before. I know Peter. He won't stop."

"Unless you went to Chicago and talked to Charlie Whosists? What did you do, ask him nicely to tell Peter to stop?"

Cara smiled despite Liam's growing discomfort. "No, I asked him nicely to arrange a meeting with Neal Coleman, the president of Pyramid."

"Wow, the top of the Pyramid!" Mike exclaimed. "You met with Coleman?"

"No." She shook her head. "That will be Liam's job. I only arranged the meeting."

"And what am I supposed to meet with Mr. Coleman about?"

"About distributing Aerie in the Eastern United States."

Liam's mouth tightened into a grim line. "You want Pyramid to distribute Aerie? After what Peter's done—"

"Liam, please listen. I know this is counterintuitive, but you were the one who taught me to think creatively."

Liam stopped, and Cara caught the glimmer of a smile at the corner of his mouth. "All right. You've piqued my interest."

"First of all, I didn't tell Charlie anything about Aerie itself. I mentioned a software distribution deal in very vague terms. I told him that if you decide to approach Pyramid about a deal, it would be in Pyramid's best interest to listen."

"I'd have a hard time trusting Pyramid in any kind of deal, Cara."

"I understand, Liam, but this is not just any deal. It's the perfect deal. Pyramid would get training and customization revenue, exclusive distribution rights in the East, and a percentage of every copy of Aerie it sells. In exchange, Pyramid would stop Peter's activities. Not only his development effort, but his legal attacks on Windwear. It's not wise to sue the company that's poised to make you a ton of money. Pyramid would also void our noncompete clauses and drop any employment lawsuits I might have racked up in the last few months. Windwear ends up with a market presence in the East to match Cole Martin's presence in the West, which should bring in twice the revenue to keep your expansion plans alive."

As Liam considered the implications of her words, a slow smile spread across his face. "Cara, you're brilliant. The old Trojan Horse concept. Come to the enemy bearing gifts. With a New Age twist. We both win." He laughed. "Machiavelli, be damned! Do you think Pyramid will listen?"

"Charlie Schmidt was receptive. He's a decent man. I worked with him quite a bit when I was in Chicago. He is probably the closest thing I have to a father. He wields a lot of clout, and he has Neal Coleman's ear. He agreed to get you an audience with Coleman in New York. You'll need to make the sale."

Liam nodded. His mind was already turning with new ideas. Cara walked across the room to where she'd dropped her purse and briefcase. She opened the case, pulled out a file. "I mapped out some of the terms you might want to include in an agreement. To get you started. That is, if you think you want to ... " She stopped. "I'm sorry, Liam. I'm pushing, aren't I?" She gave him an embarrassed smile. "I didn't mean to be presumptuous, to bulldoze you with all this."

Liam walked swiftly to her side and took the file from her hands. It was thick. He opened the file and studied the contents. Several scenarios were listed, each identifying different distribution rights, revenue sharing options, upgrade responsibilities, even the potential purchase of the software after a specific time period. "You did all this, Cara? In two days?"

She smiled. "It's a long flight."

"You did all this for me?"

She nodded again.

"Why?"

"Because I couldn't think of any other way to stop Peter." She hesitated for a moment. "And because Aerie is yours. You, and no one else, should decide its fate."

"Thank you, Cara." He smiled. "You are quite brilliant. And you're right. This is the perfect solution."

"Unfortunately, it doesn't solve the problem at hand." She sighed in frustration.

Liam shook his head. "No. In fact, given the circumstances, this will provide even more incentive for the consortium to pursue Aerie. The profit potential is huge." He frowned. "This is ironic. If we execute your plan, Pyramid will halt Peter's activities and support Windwear's ownership rights. And the very fact that Windwear holds clear ownership to Aerie will be its downfall. If I go through with the IPO, everything Windwear owns, Aerie included, will be subject to control by the consortium."

He clenched his jaw in frustration. "There must be a solution to this problem. If I could just pick up Aerie and—" Liam stopped abruptly. Cara caught the glimmer of a smile light up his eyes. She recognized that look. She had seen it before. It was the same look she'd seen when he sat in her office and pitched the idea of Aerie forever-and-a-half ago. It was the same look he wore when he kissed her the first time, in the conference room not a hundred feet away from where she now stood. And it was the same look he showed when he hatched Plan A in the kitchen of her Cannon Beach cottage.

Cara felt hope leap through her. An idea. Liam Scofield had an idea.

Chapter 52

Liam swept Cara into his arms with a loud laugh. "You are brilliant, Cara Larson." With an arm still draped over her shoulders, he faced Andrew and Mike. "I have an idea, but I need to sort out a few details before I can explain. Would you three go to the conference room and wait for me?"

Andrew, Cara, and Mike exchanged a glance. "Sure, why not," Mike said.

Liam followed them out. "Staci, would you call Rick Penner at Fleet and ask him nicely to drop everything he's doing and come right over."

Staci nodded. "Should I give him a reason?"

"Yes. Tell him the chick fell from the nest."

"Ohhhh-kay." Her voice oozed with doubt as she reached for the phone.

"He'll understand. Oh, I'll need Windlogic's incorporation papers from the safe. And would you please ask Cara to catch Rick up on what's happening when he gets here? I might be a while on this call."

"Liam?" There were at least a hundred questions in Staci's tone.

Liam smiled. "Everything is going to be okay, Staci."

He walked into his office and picked up the phone. A few seconds later, a familiar voice came on the other end of the line. "Hello, Liam."

"Paul. We have a problem."

Liam walked into the conference room. "Thanks for waiting, everyone. Rick, good to see you. Thanks for coming on … no notice."

"No problem. Cara just finished telling me the details. She says you have a plan."

He nodded. "Yes. I just talked to Paul. We've worked out the basic strategy. Everybody, take a seat. Let me tell you what we're thinking about."

They all sat around the conference table. "There are a couple of parts to the plan, so bear with me. First, we're going to push Aerie's schedule forward. We want to announce availability to the public before the IPO. Which means we have eight days to finish, instead of thirty, as we originally planned. Paul thinks he can do it, with the help of Cara and Mike. While they finish development, Rick and I and the folks at Cole Martin will start selling Aerie in earnest."

A flurry of noise erupted. Liam smiled and held up his hand. "I thought you might have a few questions. Let's go one at a time. Cara, you first."

"What about the noncompete? If Mike and I work on Aerie, we violate the terms of our noncompete clause. Pyramid can come after you."

"Not if we follow your plan. We'll pursue a deal with Pyramid to distribute Aerie in the East. Part of the deal will be to drop the noncompete requirements."

"What if they don't agree and we've already been working on Aerie?"

"We'll just need to formulate terms so sweet they can't say no. From the brief look I took at your projections, that shouldn't be a problem. Both parties will win big on the deal."

Cara nodded. "All right. It's a risk, but I agree that's the best way to handle Pyramid."

"Good. Would you call your contact in Chicago and schedule a meeting? Preferably for the day before the IPO." She nodded.

Liam smiled. "Thanks. Okay, next. Mike."

"I don't understand why you need to finish Aerie. You said Lauren is planning to transfer Aerie to the consortium, right? Won't we just be helping the consortium by finishing Aerie?"

"You're right. This is a backup plan in case my first plan doesn't work out. Let me explain my reasoning. The consortium agreed to buy two million shares for a base price of sixteen dollars per share. If the stock trades higher, the requirement disappears, and the shares will be sold on the open market instead.

"I looked through the filing documents. Lauren didn't disclose any information about Aerie. That in and of itself was not improper. We are not obligated to disclose operational details. But because the investors don't have full knowledge of Aerie, the stock is artificially underpriced. If we announce the availability of Aerie before the IPO, chances are good the stock price will go up past the sixteen-dollar mark. If that happens, the consortium won't be required to buy the stock. That, in turn, means the consortium members are only on the hook to buy the management shares. I might have an easier time buying eleven management shares from a consortium member who hasn't invested too much money and doesn't want to mess with me when I start causing trouble.

"Now, if we don't finish Aerie, and existence of the software remains undisclosed, the stock price will be artificially low. The consortium will be forced to buy the two million shares at sixteen dollars. Once the IPO is complete, and the consortium announces Aerie, what do you think will happen to the stock?"

"The price goes sky high," Mike answered. "And the consortium will make a huge profit as the stock rises and they dump the shares they bought at sixteen. The rats."

"Right. So—"

"Again," Mike interrupted, "I don't mean to be a pain in the butt, Liam, but who cares? The problem still remains. If we finish Aerie, the consortium will take all its profits. Windwear is still left without the money from Aerie."

"But now the stock price is higher. Remember I will own a lot of Windwear stock after the IPO. If the price goes high enough, maybe I can fund the expansion plans without the need for Aerie."

"But you lose Aerie," Mike said.

"Yes, under this scenario. That's why it's the fallback plan. In case the other plan doesn't work."

"What is the other plan?" Rick Penner asked.

"I can't take credit for it. Cara gave me the idea."

"Me?" Cara said in surprise.

Liam smiled and turned to face Cara. "Cara, how would you like to be the new owner of Windlogic?"

Cara's eyes widened. For a moment, she was shocked into silence.

"You're dumping Aerie?" Mike said. He closed his eyes, and Cara saw him working out how the pieces fit together.

Liam smiled. "If Windwear doesn't own Aerie, how can Windwear get the funds produced by Aerie? Is that your question, Mike?"

"Exactly," Mike said. "You can't play it both ways. Either Windwear gets the money from Aerie's operations, which means the consortium gets it because the consortium controls Windwear, or ..." He turned toward Cara. "Or Cara gets the funds from Aerie. Either way, Windwear gets nothing."

"Right. Unless we make the terms of the sale of Windlogic to Ms. Larson not in dollars per se, but in other, more concrete terms. And I mean, literally, concrete terms, as in, a new manufacturing facility."

"You mean, Cara would pay for Windlogic by buying you a new building?" Mike asked.

"And new equipment for the R and D Department. Among other things. The point is, we tie the terms of the sale of Windlogic to Windwear's operations. As the money from Aerie comes in to Cara, she pays off her 'debt' to us by buying us a building and by buying new R and D equipment, things the consortium can't possibly convert to cash for their own purposes."

A long silence filled the room as Liam's words sunk in.

"Liam," Mike finally said. "I like it."

"Me too," Rick said. He turned to Cara. "Well, Cara? What do you think?"

"I ... I am not sure what to think."

"What's bothering you, Cara?" Liam asked. "What am I not thinking of? Am I missing something?"

"Liam," Cara said, "May I speak to you for a minute? In your office?"

"Sure."

"Ha, I know that look." Mike laughed. "Watch out, Liam. She's in negotiating mode. She's going to squeeze every last dime out of you. Be care—"

Liam closed the door behind him as he and Cara left the room. "That kid. Too smart for his own good."

Chapter 53

Cara closed the door to his office. "Liam, do you realize what you're doing?"

"Yes."

"You can't just give away Aerie. After everything you've been through. You and Paul have sweated over Aerie from the beginning. You can't—"

"I'm not giving Aerie away. I'm selling it."

"For no cash and a promise to pay in the future. That's not a smart deal."

"You're right. It's not smart. It's brilliant." She rolled her eyes, and Liam smiled. "Cara, look who's on the other end of the deal? You are."

"And what is preventing me from reneging on every one of those promises and taking Aerie for myself? I could be on a plane to Las Vegas tomorrow, with Aerie in hand, and you would be left with nothing."

He shook his head. "That's not going to happen, Cara. At least not the Las Vegas part. You're more the Paris type. I can picture you drinking espresso in a Parisian café, visiting the Louvre ..."

"Liam, don't make fun. You trusted Lauren, and look what she did. You can't blindly trust people with the most important things in your life—"

"The answer is nothing."

She stopped in mid-protest. "Nothing, what?"

He smiled at her. "Nothing is preventing you from taking Aerie and reneging on every promise you make."

She stared at him in exasperation. "And that's okay with you?"

"With you leaving town with Aerie? No, but you can if you want. I won't stop you." His voice became quiet. "Is that what you want to do, Cara?"

She rolled her eyes again. "Of course not, but Liam, you can't—"

"I know. I can't blindly trust people with the most important things in my life." He put a finger on her lips and stopped her words from rushing out. "Please, Cara, hush for a minute. I have three reasons for giving you Aerie. I think they're good ones. Let me explain. If you still don't agree after I finish, we'll think of something else. I promise."

She slowly removed his finger from her lips. "All right. I'm listening."

He led her to the table in the corner. "Have a seat. This might take a while." They sat down, and he was silent for a moment, rehearsing what he planned to say. "All right. Here we go. The three reasons why I want to give you Aerie. Reason number one. You've earned the right to own Aerie. You are an incredibly talented designer, Cara. I learned that when I worked with you, and Paul has said the same more times than I can count. He's been truly impressed by the work you did on the prototype. Aerie is as much your child as it is mine."

He covered her hand lightly with his. "I know you went to the beach and were happy there. But I can't help but think you were driven away by a truly unfortunate experience with Peter at a particularly hard time in your life. I caught your expression when you saw Aerie again the other day. A part of you misses what you gave up. Personally, I couldn't put Aerie in better hands. You know the software. You understand the customers. You grasp how the business should be run. Frankly, I don't know why I didn't think of this from the beginning.

"The only thing I ask is that you honor the commitments I've made up to this point. First to Paul. He would like to stay on and help run Windlogic. To Rick Penner and Fleet. They've been more than helpful, and all they've asked is we give them priority during implementation and fair compensation for their work. And to Windwear. I told you what Windwear needs. Other than these commitments, Windlogic would be entirely in your control. You will be free to run the company the way you see fit." He squeezed her hand lightly. "The beach will always be there if you want to go back, but Windlogic is here for you right now."

Cara looked up at Liam with a soft smile. "Liam, you have no idea how kind you are; how your words ease my mind."

"I'm just telling you the truth, Cara. Do you doubt me?"

She sighed. "I doubted almost everything when I worked for Peter. Before returning to Portland, I had been at Pyramid for five years. I was beginning to think I wasn't ... half bad at my job, but I lost my confidence after working for Peter for only a few months. He was so ... harsh. I couldn't do anything right. I was demoralized. To be honest, I was relieved when I resigned."

"Cara, what happened with Peter should never have happened. No one deserves to be treated the way Peter treated you. Your experience wasn't a reflection on you, but on him, on his character. Having Aerie would be an opportunity for you to try again, but this time without anyone like Peter in the way."

"I admit I'm tempted."

"Then you'll take it?"

"Hmm. Maybe." She smiled almost shyly. "I'd like to hear your other two reasons."

"Damn." He gave her a crooked grin. "Mike was right. You're going to drive a hard bargain, aren't you?"

"I'm more curious than anything else. I'm always amazed at what springs up in that creative mind of yours."

"Well. This may be one time where curiosity works in my favor." He smiled mysteriously. "Okay, reason number two, coming up. You said I shouldn't trust people with the most important things in my life. I say you're wrong."

"Liam—"

"I trust you, Cara," he interrupted before she could say more. "I trust you with Aerie. I trust you with ... a lot of things."

"But—"

"Let me speak, Cara," he said quietly. Something in his tone made her stop. "I was going to tell you this sooner or later, but now seems to be the right time." He took a deep breath. "Cara, I've been married before."

Her eyes widened in surprise. "Liam, I didn't know."

"It happened a long time ago. She ... she left me. It was ... difficult. I loved Jennifer. I trusted her with my life, with everything, and she . . well, things didn't work out. For a long time after she left, I was bitter. Angry. I didn't trust anyone at all. I threw myself into building Windwear mostly to forget about Jennifer.

"But a strange thing happened as I struggled trying to put my life back together. I found people who trusted me, who believed in me and what I was doing. Sam and Maggie. They practically dragged me back from the dead. Paul Davis. God, that guy has worked so hard. Mark Prentice and Brad Keller, and all the people at Windwear. They trusted me and believed in my vision, and worked damned hard to make it a reality. In time, I learned to trust them, too. And I have to say, it's been the best experience of my life.

"It took me a few years, but I finally realized it wasn't my fault Jennifer left me. She didn't leave me because I loved her too much or trusted her too much. She left me because ... she chose to. Because she didn't love me. It was that simple."

"I find that hard to believe," Cara whispered.

He smiled. "Do you think I trusted her too much? That trust opens the door to ... manipulation and betrayal?"

"No! I just can't believe any woman wouldn't ..." Her voice trailed off.

"Wouldn't what?"

"Never mind. I'm interrupting."

"Yes, you are Ms. Larson, and you're throwing me off track." He gave her another crooked grin. "Now, where was I?"

"Jennifer who wasn't in love with you."

"Right. Jennifer. I trusted Jennifer, and things turned out badly. In the short term, at least. In the long term, I don't think things turned out badly at all. Which brings us to today and to Lauren. Lauren who has just committed the worst betrayal I could imagine. I admit to being blindsided by her actions, Cara. There wasn't one thing in Lauren's past to hint that she would commit such deceit. Her resume was spotless. Her references checked out. Her work here at Windwear has been exemplary. Up until a week ago, she did nothing but reinforce my belief I could trust her without question."

He shook his head sadly. "It's not as if I made things easy for her. I can see now she planned this all along. She committed fraud, Cara. She created a broker agreement I never would have accepted, switched the signature pages with legitimate documents I signed, then covered her tracks by sending me a fake agreement. She didn't do these things because I trusted her. She did them because she chose to do them. She wanted to do them. She planned to do them.

"Lauren is clever and careful, and she nearly succeeded with her plan. But she didn't. At least not yet. I don't have time to regret that I trusted her. I need to deal with her actions. I need to save my company. There are a half dozen people sitting in the conference room right now, willing to do everything they can to help Windwear. They trust me. I trust them. And I have no doubt we'll succeed." He paused. "Cara, trust is a double edged sword. It causes nothing but trouble when it's betrayed, no question. But when you have real trust in your life, there is nothing better. For me, that's what makes life more worth living."

"God knows, I've made my share of mistakes in life, but I can tell you with utter certainty that the biggest mistakes have come not because I trusted people, but because I didn't trust them." Cara's gaze flew up to meet his. "I can tell you know what I'm talking about."

His expression was sad as he faced her. "You say I shouldn't trust you, that you might take Aerie and run away. I say you're wrong. I know you, Cara. I understand how your mind thinks and your heart works. Greed and selfishness just aren't in you. Hell, if you told me right now you were wanted to take Aerie and head to Las Vegas and bet the whole thing on 'Red,' well, I'd let you go. Because I know you, Cara, and I know you wouldn't do it unless you had a damned good reason for doing so."

His smile was laced with sorrow. "Once upon a time I didn't trust you, and that was the biggest mistake of my life. I believed the 'facts' I was given by Peter and Lauren. I believed their lies when everything in my gut told me not to. I believed their lies when you stood in front of me and told me nothing but the truth. And you called me out. Do you remember? I don't recall the exact words, but you said something like, 'Damn you for believing the worst in me, for not trusting me the way I trusted you'."

"I shouldn't have said that. I was angry. I was wrong," Cara whispered.

"No, you were right." He held up his hand, his finger and thumb an inch apart. "I was this close to losing you, Cara. When you left the Inn that night, I was so angry I never wanted to lay eyes on you again. Thank God for Mike. If he wouldn't have made me talk to you, I would have lost you forever. All because I refused to trust the one person my gut told me to trust, the one person who risked everything for me." He looked at her, his gaze somber. "Never again, Cara. I will never mistrust you again as long as I live."

Sadness was etched in her face when she met his gaze. "Liam, you didn't do anything wrong. You had no way of knowing Lauren and Peter were lying to you. And my history is not exactly … a shining example of trustworthiness."

"Are you kidding? You—"

"Please, Liam. I need to tell you this. I don't want you to make a mistake with Aerie. You've worked to hard for it. I'm not sure you should give it up so easily. And even if you do decide to give it up, I might not be the best person to have it." She gazed up at him quietly. "You're a good man, Liam. You see the world in such a positive light. You work to make the world a better place. You're amazing. But I'm not the person you think I am. I'm not worthy of your trust. I may have tried to do the right thing, tried to make my world a better place.

But I haven't been as successful as you. All I ever did was make things worse."

"No way, Cara. You're wrong."

"Then you aren't seeing the truth about me, Liam. I've made mistakes. I've used poor judgment. I've been unfair. Look at what happened with my mother. While I was out earning money to make her life easier, she got sick. And she died, Liam." Cara stopped for a moment, holding back her tears. "My mother died because I wasn't home. She never spent a dime of the money I earned for her. Not a single dime. That's pretty strong evidence I did the wrong thing, and not just one time, but for years and years and years."

"Cara—"

"No, Liam. I need to tell you this. I want you to understand."

He nodded. "Okay. Go on."

"My next major mess-up: my job with Pyramid. Do you have any idea how many rules I broke? Peter has every right to investigate me and press charges and do whatever else he plans to do. I'm guilty. In the worst case, I'll end up with a felony record. In the best, I'll have so many black marks against my name that I'll never get a real job again. How's that for doing the right thing?

"Then there's Aerie. And you. God, I tried to do the right thing by giving you Aerie, but I screwed that effort up royally. I hit you, Liam, when all you were trying to do was solve your problem. My God, I never struck anyone in my life, least of all a man who didn't deserve it. Then you put your company at risk by trying to protect me. That just made everything worse—"

"Whoa, Cara," Liam cut in. "I've listened to you, and I even understand what you're trying to tell me. I'm going to say this as nicely as I can. You're wrong. Actually, you're totally, completely, 100 percent wrong, but I'm not going to be too hard on you, because you're doing a damned good job of being too hard on yourself."

"No, it's the truth." She sighed as she stabbed at her eyes, trying to wipe the tears away.

"Cara, you're not being fair. You're not seeing things objectively. You didn't just do the right thing; you did the right thing in the most difficult of circumstances. Let me tell you how I see things. First, your mother—"

She let out a sharp gasp, and Liam covered his hand with hers. "Your mother knew you felt guilty. She understood you blamed yourself for her illness."

Cara started in surprise. "How do you—"

"She told me, among other things, in her letter to me. She asked me to tell you, when the time was right, that it wasn't your fault, that it wasn't anyone's fault, that death is ... as natural as the sky is blue or the grass is green. Those were her words." He stopped for a moment, having trouble with the words himself. "Cara, you didn't do the easy thing. You could have continued on with your career in Chicago, and let Jeanine take care of your mother. But you came back. You helped your mother. You were with her when she needed you most. You cared for her. You didn't lay your guilt at her feet. You made her last months happy ones. Nothing you did can be construed as wrong or bad. Nothing.

"And your job? I've thought about what happened the day of the review a thousand times. You could have done the easy thing at Pyramid, too. You could have stayed quiet during the review. You could have given Aerie to Peter. You could have kept your job and your successful career. You didn't need to give Aerie to me, but you did, even when you realized how steep the cost would be.

"Last but not least there is me, and my stellar performance at the beach. All I can say is, knowing what I know now, you let me off easy. You should have pummeled me, not just slapped me. God, I was an idiot." He brushed his fingers back and forth across the top of her hand. "No, Cara, you're wrong. You deserve every single ounce of my trust. You are the most trustworthy person I've ever met. I wouldn't give Aerie to anyone but you."

Liam watched as the tears welled in her eyes. She had a habit of brushing them away, as if they were unwelcome intruders. He hated that he knew so much about her tears. He reached into his pocket, pulled out a handkerchief, and handed it to her. "Please don't cry, Cara. I still have one more reason to go."

She gave him in puzzled stare as she grasped the handkerchief. She wiped her eyes and smiled as if he had handed her a buoy in a stormy sea. "You surprise me, Liam. No one carries handkerchiefs anymore. Especially not mad cool CEOs of soon-to-be public corporations."

"Blame my mother." He flashed her a grin. "Drilled the habit into me early on. Believe me, it comes in more handy than you'd think."

"Because you're in the habit of making girls cry?"

"Well, I do seem to be in the habit of making one girl cry."

She gave him a weak smile. "I don't think that's your fault. I'm … not myself lately."

"Well, what a surprise. Getting yanked from your quiet life at the beach. Being pulled one way by Lauren, and the other by Peter. Running halfway across the country to set up a high-stakes meeting with the president of Pyramid. Wearing a wire to arrest a white-collar crook. I'm shocked, shocked, you aren't ready to climb Mt. Everest this weekend, Cara."

She wiped her eyes and smiled again. "How do you do that, Liam?"

"Do what?"

"Find a way to make me laugh when I think I'll never laugh again."

"I'm glad I can do that," he said quietly.

Silence hung between them for several moments. "Liam?"

"Yes?"

"You still owe me one more reason."

He nodded. "I do. Indeed I do." He took a deep breath. "Reason number three for giving you Aerie." He hesitated for a fraction of a second. "Reason number three is … I'm in love with you."

"What?!" Cara gasped and started to stand up.

He took her hand and guided her back to her seat. "Please, Cara, let me say this, now I've come this far. I'm in love with you, Cara. I have been for a long time. These past few days, when you were gone, I was beside myself with worry. I couldn't think about anything else. I wanted nothing more than for you to be safe and ... with me."

He smiled ruefully. "You know I love Windwear. I won't deny it. And you know I love Aerie. I won't deny that either. But Cara, neither of them can come close to competing with you. Giving you Aerie is nothing, nothing compared to how I feel about you. I want you to have it, because maybe it will show you, maybe it will express ... maybe it will make you understand in some small way what I'm having a hell of a time trying to put into words. I love you, Cara. There is no one on this earth I trust more, believe in more, or want to be with more than you. No one." He looked at her, a smile lighting his dark eyes. "I want to marry you, Cara Larson."

Cara looked at him in utter surprise. She stared at him for the longest time, but no words came out of her mouth.

"Cara, you can say something now, because if you don't, I'm going to start getting nervous."

She blinked rapidly. "Liam, I didn't expect this. I'm so surprised—"

"Are you?" He smiled gently. "I can hardly believe that. Everyone else knows. It took Sam and Maggie about twelve seconds to figure it out. Andrew realized it after about fifteen minutes. Paul caught on after our first meeting at Windwear. Mike has known from the very beginning—"

"Mike!"

"Yes, Mike. Personally, I think he set the two of us up from the start. All his blather about you being a badass Genghis Khan. He knew I'd bite." He smiled. "That kid is smart."

"I can't believe it."

"Cara, I think everyone knew but you. Even Lauren figured out. Especially after Taiwan."

"What happened in Taiwan?"

He raised an eyebrow. "Not my best moment, Cara. I promise to tell you sometime, but today isn't the day." He paused and peered at her closely. "Cara, are you doing that thing again?"

"What thing?"

"The one where you avoid my question by talking a lot of nonsense? If you are, I'll know for sure this proposal isn't going well."

She smiled and put her hand in his. "Oh, Liam. I thought when I came to this moment, it would be so easy to say the words, to tell you …"

"What are you saying, Cara? That you don't …" He felt a sudden sinking sensation. "Then just tell me, and be done with it."

She shook her head. "No, no." She gazed up at him with a curious expression. "Liam, my heart is too full. I don't have any words to explain how I feel. All the words I know are too small. They can't express what I want to say to you. They can't explain how important you are to me, how much a part of me you've become, how whole I am now compared to how empty I was before. It's too … hard to describe to myself, let alone to you. I just know it's true. And it will take at least a lifetime for me to show you how I feel."

Relief washed through Liam, followed by crazy, unspeakable joy. He leaned over, brushed a tear from her eye, and pressed his lips gently to hers. "I love you, Cara." His lips caressed hers. "Let me help you. Here's what you do," he whispered softly, his lips brushing hers with every word. "Repeat after me. Ready?"

He felt her smile beneath his lips. "Yes."

"Say, 'I love you, Liam. Yes, I'll marry you'."

Her smile grew broader. Her laugh bubbled up as his lips caressed hers. "I love you, Liam Scofield," she whispered, her lips brushing against his. "So much it hurts sometimes. Of course, I'll marry you."

His kiss deepened, and after a long moment, he lifted his head and looked into her eyes. One look, he thought through the haze. One look was all he needed. And there it was, right in front of his eyes. The truth. Cara Larson was indeed in love with Liam Scofield. Then he stopped thinking. He stood up, gathered her in his arms, and kissed her as if there were no Windwear and no Aerie and no IPO coming in nine days. And the heavy weight that had settled on him a lifetime ago, suddenly lifted.

After a long time, Liam let out a whoop, picked her up in his arms, and whirled her around in a circle. Suddenly they were laughing as if they were children. "Cara Larson, you've made me the happiest man in the world."

At that moment, the door to the office opened, and Staci poked her head in. "Er ... excuse me." She stopped. "Once again, I prove my knack for perfect timing."

Liam halted in mid-twirl. "It's okay, Staci. Come on in. What's up?"

"Richard Bancroft just phoned. Lauren is on her way back from New York. Her flight gets in at nine. If she decides to come to the office, she'll be here by ten."

He sighed and set Cara back on her feet. "Back to the real world." He smiled at Cara. "Well, future Mrs. Scofield, what's the verdict on Windlogic?"

"I'll take it." She smiled. "Sold for the price of one manufacturing facility."

"Plus R and D equipment to be named later."

"Thank you, Liam. I ... I appreciate it more than you will ever know."

"I mean what I said. You've earned it, and you deserve it. Besides, it's is a win-win, Cara. The best kind of deal to make." He nodded at his secretary. "Thanks, Staci."

Staci nodded. "You can get back to your ... negotiations, now." She smiled as she closed the door.

Liam gave Cara a knowing smile. "Staci knew too."

Chapter 54

Liam and Andrew sat quietly in Lauren's darkened office. Liam glanced at his watch. "Well, if Lauren plans to come to the office tonight, she'll be here soon."

Andrew nodded. "If she doesn't, I'll head over to her house." He opened the papers in his hand. "I have her address right here on the warrant."

"Good. I realize you won't be able to hold her long, but can you arrange for her bail to be high and her movements limited? She's definitely a flight risk."

"You make a good case. I'll add that request to the bail application."

"One more thing. Will you ask the court to permit you to accompany her to New York? Given our new plan, I can't afford to change attorneys now. I'll need her signatures on the final IPO filings and stock certificates. I'll be happy to reimburse the city for your trip. I wouldn't dream of asking the good taxpayers of Cannon Beach to pay for my problems."

"I'll add that to the bail application, too. If nothin' else, it'll raise a few eyebrows over at City Hall."

Liam and Andrew went still as the door to the office opened, and the neon light sputtered on.

"Hello, Lauren," Liam said quietly.

"What the hell?" Lauren pasted a smile on her face. "Liam. Hello. What are you doing in here? And in the dark." She looked at the policeman. "Who is this?"

"Officer Andrew Carson, ma'am. Cannon Beach police."

Lauren went utterly still. "What's going on?"

"Andrew, would you please excuse us for a few minutes? Lauren and I need to speak privately."

"Sure enough." The policeman left the office, closing the door behind him.

"Where have you been all day?" Liam asked quietly.

"I told you. Boston. My ... my meeting finished early, so I caught a late flight. I ... I thought I would catch up on some paperwork."

"I see. I spoke to Richard Bancroft today. He says you never quite made it to Boston for the meeting you never scheduled. Your itinerary indicates you went to New York, instead. What were you doing, Lauren? Were you finalizing the sale of Aerie to the consortium? That's what the paperwork we found seems to imply."

Lauren glanced over to the corner where the file cabinet had been. It was gone. As was her computer. In fact, her office was stripped bare of everything but her desk and chair. Her gaze flickered for just an instant, but Liam caught it. She was trying to gauge what he knew, was trying to work out a story. "What's going on, Liam?"

"That's exactly what I want to ask you, Lauren. I'd say the game is up."

"What game? I have no idea what you're talking about."

"The game where you sell the majority of my voting shares to a bunch of crooks."

She sat down at her desk and dropped her briefcase on the floor. "They aren't crooks. They are a respectable group of Wall Street investors."

"A semantic difference, I would say."

"What exactly did I do wrong, Liam? *I* didn't sell anything. *You* signed the agreement, not me. *You* signed the forms with the SEC, not me. I'm just your lawyer doing your bidding." She smiled with saccharine sweetness. "Any reasonable person will assess the facts and realize that you, and you alone, sold your company down the river."

"Except for the fact you committed fraud along the way. You created your own version of the agreement, switched the signature pages from the NDA, and led the consortium to believe I agreed to the new figures. I have the evidence."

Lauren laughed out loud. "Go ahead, knock yourself out, Liam. You're too late. You can go after me. You might even get the courts to slap my hand for being a little overzealous at my job, but you can't stop the stock sale. You're boxed in. You can't stop the consortium from getting your precious software, either. Carl Streeter has the agreement; he knows what to do. Aerie is as good as gone."

"Why are doing this, Lauren?"

"This was your own damned fault. I'll never forgive you for what you did in Taiwan."

"You mean … when I rejected your advances?"

"Spare me your overgrown ego, Liam. You should never have ignored my advice about Wangchao. You should have signed a joint venture agreement with them. If you had listened to me, Carl Streeter would have been satisfied, and he never would have considered taking Aerie. Instead, you pull the 'long-term wealth of the shareholder' crap that's so naive it makes me want to throw up, and you shot my plans to hell. Streeter was livid. He demanded Aerie after that."

"And you were happy to oblige. Even though you will ruin Windwear."

"I had no choice. Besides, it won't hurt me. When Windwear starts to fail, I'll convince the consortium Windwear needs a change in day-to-day management. You'll be out in a matter of months, and I will become president and CEO of Windwear. I'll run the company the way it ought to be run."

The muscle in Liam's left cheek flickered. "You mean run it into the ground. You don't know the first thing about hiking boots or outerwear or camping gear."

"But I do know about profits and growth and market share. I don't care what the products are. I'll find someone a little more cooperative than you to run things the way I want them run, and I'll be wildly successful."

"And if you aren't?"

"It's a fact, Liam, not a supposition. I can't lose. I'll run Windwear until I've used it up. When I'm ready to move on,

I'll leave with lucrative stock options, generous perks, and an enormous golden parachute. I'll use my success at Windwear to garner another position where—"

"Where you'll repeat your methods with yet another up and coming company? Is that your plan, Lauren?"

"You know, that's what bothers me the most about you, Liam. This reverse snobbery act. You think you're so much better than everyone else because you're not part of the establishment. God, you're such a fool. I'm going to take everything you own." She paused and gave him a thoughtful look. "For what it's worth, you were a fair opponent. Much more tenacious than I first thought when I targeted Windwear. You had me worried for a while, when you locked Aerie up so tight. I thought my whole plan might come apart. But you didn't disappoint me. The way you spilled your guts about Aerie the other night was priceless. You made it so easy. A wholly owned subsidiary. So neat and tidy. Clear boundaries with everything in one package. A simple transfer of shares."

Liam nodded. "Yes, that was a fortunate piece of luck."

"What do you mean?" she asked, a wary note creeping into her voice.

"You'll find out in due time. In the meantime, I'll turn this discussion over to Andrew. Before I do, I need to inform you of one more detail. From now on, you are relieved of all duties except those administrative duties necessary to complete the IPO. All those activities will be done in the presence of an attorney from Abrams, Williams and Dafoe. You are not to be alone at any time while you are conducting Windwear business. Two security guards will accompany you home this evening to remove and return any Windwear files you might be holding off site."

"How dare you—"

"If you agree to these terms," he interrupted as if she hadn't spoken, "I will grant you a limited number of stock options. Not nearly the number we originally planned, but it's fair to compensate you for the work you've already done on the IPO, tainted though it may be."

"And if I quit?"

"Go ahead. I'll be happy to make the call to Carl Streeter and tell him the news. Oh, in that case, you'll get no stock options."

"If I quit, the stock sale will be delayed."

"True, but I can live with a delay. I'll make sure the press understands you were the one who betrayed the company and got yourself fired and caused the whole IPO to be stopped in its tracks. That should stand out on your resume. You might even get disbarred. Plus, I would gain more time to get Aerie back. Which I will do."

"You're too late. You can't stop what's coming—"

"I can stop you, Lauren. I'll start there."

She closed her eyes and was silent for several moments. "All right. I agree."

"Good." He tilted his head toward the door. "Andrew," he called.

The door opened, and Andrew returned. "She's all yours."

"Thank you." The policeman walked across the office and stood in front of Lauren. "Miss Lauren Janelle, you are under arrest—"

"What the hell?" She stood up, her face angry. "You can't arrest me—"

"For conspiracy to commit burglary and assault."

She glared at Andrew, then at Liam. "I didn't—"

"Excuse me, ma'am," Andrew interrupted. "Please let me finish. Before you say anythin' else, I think you should know we arrested Peter Whittington last night on these same charges. For the attack on Miss Cara Larson."

Lauren's mouth dropped open in surprise. She sat down abruptly. "Now I see you get my point, ma'am. Quiet might be a good strategy, right about now." He laid the arrest warrant in front of her. "You have the right to remain silent. Anything you say can and will be used against you in a court of law ..."

Chapter 55

Cara, Mike, and Paul were crowded into Ol' Bob's Bait and Tackle Shop. They had been there eighteen hours a day since the meeting in the conference room. The hours had flown by as they had squeezed thirty days' work into a single week. Surprisingly, Aerie was nearly complete.

Cara's mind flew over the past week. Mike and Paul completed several versions of Aerie to run on all the most popular platforms. She performed the testing to make sure each program operated as designed. They were now working to fail-safe security. Rick, Liam, and the Cole Martin teams were in the field, selling Aerie to anyone who could breathe, trying to establish a solid customer base that would dazzle any potential distributor. When she wasn't testing, Cara sat between the two teams, acting as troubleshooter.

So far, the work had gone remarkably well. They found some bugs, which they were able to fix. They discovered a few flaws in the design. Paul widened the sort order options when multiple products were retrieved. However, they wouldn't be able to redesign the cross-reference table linking customer and supplier inventory codes. The change affected the underlying data structure too significantly and would need to wait for the first upgrade. So far, the delay wasn't a deal breaker. When the sales teams explained the situation, most customers indicated they were willing to live with the current design in the short term.

Cara let her mind drift to thoughts of her fiancé. She may not have been able to be with Liam, but she'd been able to talk to him. He was in his element, pushing a product he believed in, showing customers how they would improve their decision-making capabilities. She heard the enthusiasm in his voice when she participated in teleconference presentations. She saw it in the fuzzy satellite images when they conducted videoconference demos. But she missed him. Much more than she ever realized. The separation was worthwhile, though. Liam's vision was rock solid. The orders were pouring in. Aerie was indeed proving to be a goldmine. Which was why the information staring back at her on the screen worried her so much.

"Cara, have you finished loading the test data into the tables, yet? I need to check the security of the data transfer." Mike looked up from his workstation and took in her faraway gaze.

"Hello, Cara, I need the test data."

Cara snapped to attention. "Sorry. I loaded it an hour ago. The tape is on your desk." She stared at the mass of papers and disks covering his desk. "Somewhere." She frowned and turned back to the screen.

Mike raised an eyebrow at her expression. "Hey, Cara. Are you okay?"

She nodded. "I'm tired, that's all."

"We're all tired, but you seem to have added a few extra cellos to the orchestra. What's up?"

"Nothing." Her eyes met his briefly, then slid away, and fixed once more on the screen in front of her.

"Cara, you are and will forever be, the worst liar on the face of this earth. What's going on?"

She gazed up at him with a troubled expression. "Mike, I have to go to Liam's office. Would you come with me and let me in? I have his office key, but I don't have a card key to get into the building."

He was immediately wary. "Why? What's in Liam's office?"

"Lauren's documents. I want to go through them again."

Mike shook his head. "Uh-oh. What's going on in that orchestra pit head of yours?"

"I'm … I'm not sure."

"But you want to go through the documents to find ... what?" Cara was quiet. "Cara, I'm not taking you unless you tell me."

She brightened. "Will you take me if I tell you?"

Mike closed his eyes. "I believe I've just been snookered. Okay. I'll take you."

"I think we might have a legal problem with Liam selling Windlogic to me."

"Why? Windwear owns Windlogic. Liam owns Windwear. He can do whatever he wants with it. Can't he?"

"Normally, yes, but from what I'm reading here, he can't, and I quote, '*sell, lease, or transfer a substantial part of the applicant's business or assets*' before an IPO."

"Who cares? Aerie was never disclosed, remember? No one knows it exists."

"True, but that's irrelevant. What matters is the nature of the asset. You've seen the orders Liam and Rick are bringing in. Aerie definitely qualifies as a substantial asset. The consortium won't lie down when they find out the software's been sold out from under them." She clicked down the screen in front of her. "The remedies are broad. They can give Aerie back to the company, which means the consortium will end up with it. Or they can let the sale stand and then return the profits. Or ... several other options are listed here. None of them are good for Liam."

Mike let out a sigh. "Okay, you win. You convinced me. Get your coat. We're going to Windwear."

The offending documents still lay on Liam's desk, untouched since the day Liam sat in this very room and proposed to her. She didn't want to think about that now, because then she would miss him even more. She sat down and picked up the first document in the pile. The Broker Agreement. Underneath lay a copy of the Registration Statement filed with the SEC. She reread the section outlining the percentage ownership in the voting stock. The consortium owned 51 percent, leaving Liam with 49 percent. Maybe this wasn't so bad, she thought. All Liam needed to do was convince one consortium member holding at least 1.1 percent of the voting shares to see things his way. How hard could that be? Then she remembered what Liam said about Richard Bancroft. There were too many pressures to ever be sure a longer-term, lower-return option would win out over a short-term, higher-profit one. Unless Liam somehow gained permanent possession of eleven shares. With eleven shares, he would retain control of Windwear. "Mike, I think I have a solution. All we need to do is find one consortium member to sell eleven shares to Liam."

Mike came over and Cara showed him the page. "You're right. Why not Richard?"

Cara smiled. "Of course." She felt the tension begin to leave her body. "Richard would do that for Liam. Especially after what Lauren did."

Mike did not return her smile. "Houston, we have a problem."

"What?"

"Right here, below the percentages. This states that the transfer of voting stock held by the consortium members can only be made by majority vote of the consortium."

"What does that mean?"

"It means Liam doesn't control what the consortium does with its shares. The consortium alone decides. Which will make transferring eleven shares to anyone pretty much impossible without," Mike pointed to the name at the top of the list, "... this guy's approval. Carl Streeter. This Streeter guy owns 60 percent of the consortium's stock. His vote swamps everyone else's. Which means he alone determines who can own the consortium shares."

Cara read the agreement more carefully. "You're right."

"And if Mr. Streeter really wants to control Windwear, he's not going to let even one share out of his control."

"What makes you think Streeter wants to control Windwear?"

"This." Mike rustled around the desk among the disheveled papers. He held up a printout of an e-mail from Lauren to Carl Streeter. Lauren had attached a copy of the sales agreement with a cryptic message: "*At last. Windwear is yours. All yours.*"

Cara felt her stomach tighten once again. "In that case, we need to convince Mr. Streeter to sell eleven shares of his stock to Liam."

"Cara, you're not listening. He's not going to do that."

"Probably not." She sighed. "Mike, I think we should research every consortium member anyway. Maybe we can find something that would make one of them receptive to a pitch by Liam."

"But—"

"I realize it's a long shot," she interrupted, "but I think we should try."

"All right." Mike frowned. "But first, let me go over here and beat my head against the wall. Just to get in the mood."

Cara wasn't listening. There must be a way, she thought. She started through the pile of documents once more. How, she asked herself, would a person convince Carl Streeter to give up eleven shares of stock?

She had just finished reviewing the documents a second time. She sighed and began to straighten them into a neat stack when a plain white card fell out from the middle of the pile. She picked it up. She remembered seeing this before. The strange card containing a single number. "Mike, what do you think this is?"

Mike walked over and held out his hand for the card. He inspected it, and then shrugged. "No clue. A Social Security number?"

She shook her head. "Too many digits."

"Could be anything, I guess. An insurance number, a customer account number, a credit card number."

"Not a credit card number. Not enough digits." She studied the pile of documents splayed over the desk. "This card must be linked to this business somehow, or Lauren wouldn't have kept it with all these other documents."

"Probably an account number to Witches Anonymous."

"Mike, can we go back and check Lauren's computer files again? Maybe we missed something."

"Cara, I've been through all those files." He noted her worried expression. "All right, Ms. String Quartet. One more look can't hurt."

They walked into Mike's office. Mike had stored Lauren's computer there after he removed it from her office. Cara flipped on the machine. "Can you get me in?"

Mike leaned over her shoulder and typed in Lauren's password.

Cara searched the files. "What are you looking for?"

She shook her head, her brow furrowed in concentration. "I'm not exactly sure."

"I've been through all this stuff before, Cara. All the incriminating files are already in Liam's office."

"I know." When they reached Lauren's secure directory, she stopped. "Do you know this password too?"

Mike grinned. "Sure thing. Same as her other one. Broke the first rule of system security."

Cara nodded. "Always create a different password for everything."

He bent over and typed in the password. The directory opened and they began to search through the files. An hour went by before they finished. She leaned back in the chair and closed her eyes. "Damn. I thought we'd find something here." She fingered the card she had brought with her from Liam's office. "Mike, could you write a program to check the contents of Lauren's files for this number?"

"I could. But why?"

"This card seems out of place with everything else here. It must be connected somehow."

"Could be a wild goose chase."

"We can't be any worse off than we are now, which is nowhere."

"Okay, okay." Mike sat at the computer and connected to the company network. He accessed the operating software and began writing code. Before long, he built a rudimentary program that opened each file, scanned the contents for the designated number, and closed it again if it wasn't found.

"Make sure you check several versions of the number. With dashes, with spaces, with slashes, without anything. And subsets. We should search for parts of the number—"

"I know, I know, I know. Don't tell me how to program this little puppy."

"Sorry. I get a little carried away."

"Tell me something I don't know." He worked for several more minutes, testing to make sure the program ran properly on several test files. "Okay, let's give this a go."

They watched as the program began to run, then grimaced as it crashed when opening a file that didn't contain a three-character extension code. "Damn." Mike reopened the program, made a few changes, saved it, and closed it again. "Let's try this."

Again, they watched as the program began to run. The messages slid by on the screen. *Opening file. Examining file. Closing file. !1 files examined. No matches found. !2 files examined. No matches found. !3 files examined. No matches found.* Cara smiled. "It's working! Good job, Mike."

His eyes were intent on the results. "Let's see if we get anything."

They were nearing the end of the disk. Only the system and communications directories were left. Cara felt hope slip away. She stood up and paced the room in frustration. Suddenly, Mike let out a whoop and waved his fist in the air. "We have a hit! We have a hit! In the communications directory. Hoo boy! In the cache files! Why the hell didn't I think to look there before?"

She rushed over to his side. He was already typing frantically. "Here we go." He clicked on the file name, and a gray and red and black image appeared on the screen. At the top was displayed in large red letters: "*Welcome to RLM AG, Switzerland's Most Trusted Bank.*"

Cara studied the screen. "What is this, Mike?"

"It's an image preserved as a cache file." He lowered his voice into its most official tone. "When one accesses other files over a communication network, each individual screen or part of a screen that's been accessed is saved on the hard drive as a separate file, known as a cache file. Whenever possible, the communication program will read the cache file instead of retrieving the entire screen from the network. This saves time and reduces traffic over the communication lines. Cache files are stored on the hard drive until they are intentionally deleted or until they fill up their allotted space and the communication program itself deletes them. Most users don't even realize they exist—"

Cara patted his arm. "Mike, you're forgetting. I'm in the business too. I know what a cache file is. What I want to know is, what is this place on the screen?"

He studied the contents of the screen. "Ah, Mon Cherie, I think we have found ze Achilles heel of Meez Lauren Janelle. Zees eez a Sveez bank account."

Her eyes widened in stunned surprise. "A Swiss bank ..." She stared at Mike, then back at the screen.

"You see, there? Zat eez her Swiss bank account num-behr."

They stared at each other for several moments, neither of them able to speak. "Mike, can you get into this account?"

"Not here, but we can log onto the outside network and try to access the bank directly."

"Well, what are you waiting for?"

Mike let out another whoop as he dialed in. He tapped his foot impatiently as the dual-toned modem hummed to life. "First, I need to find its domain name." He accessed the Domain Name System registry, and typed in several characters. "Aha, here we go." A few more clicks and they were staring at the same screen they had been looking at earlier. Mike typed in the account number. The screen blinked and displayed one word: *"Password?"* Mike and Cara looked at each other. He smiled and took a deep breath. "Well, here goes nothing." He typed in the password Lauren used for her system and secret directory. They heard the whirring as the hard disk saved a cache file. Then they were looking at an account with a balance of just over one million dollars. "Eureka! We're in! Cara, I think Lauren Janelle just dropped below rodent level."

Cara studied the screen. One million dollars. "When was the account opened? When was the deposit made? Can you tell where the money came from?" Her mind was working quickly. "Scroll up, I want to see the top of the screen."

"Calm down, Cara. One thing at a time. The money was deposited, hmm ... two deposits are listed. A sum of

$250,000 was deposited on the ninth of July, and $750,000 on the eleventh. The account was opened ... July ninth."

Cara frowned. Two days before the agreement between Windwear and the consortium was signed. "Who gave her the money? Can you tell who gave her the money?"

"Hold your horses, I'm checking." Mike double-clicked on the two transactions. "There's not much here. Both deposits were wired in from the First Bank of New York. Nothing else is recorded here." He glanced up from his screen. "This is enough, Cara. Lauren clearly took a bribe. Plus the attack on you. I wonder how many years she'll get."

Cara was still studying the screen. "Would you print that out, Mike? With the transaction note open, just like that. Four copies please."

"Are you going to call the police? Or Andrew?"

She shook her head. "Not yet. I want to think about this."

"What's up? I thought you'd be overjoyed by this. We can sue Lauren six ways to Sunday with this information." Cara didn't answer. "Cara?"

Cara jumped. "I'm sorry. What?"

"I said, we can put Lauren away with this."

She stared at Mike, but she wasn't really seeing him. "Yes, we can put Lauren away."

Mike raised an eyebrow. "Uh-oh. I was afraid of this. What's going on up there?" He tapped the side of her head.

"What?" She smiled vacantly. "Oh, nothing. Absolutely nothing."

Mike rolled his eyes. "You are such an incredibly bad liar, Cara. What are you planning?"

Cara gathered the printouts and folded them neatly. "Come on, Mike. We'd better get back and save Paul from rewriting the entire security system."

She was halfway out the door before Mike logged off the network and powered down the computer. He shut off the light and followed her down the dark corridor. "I hope this plan doesn't involve Liam hitting me again."

Chapter 56

Cara was packed and ready to go by 6:00 a.m. She carried her bags from the guest room downstairs to the kitchen. It was strange to be a guest in Liam's house when Liam wasn't there. Sam and Maggie didn't seem to mind. They welcomed her as if she were their own daughter. She thought back to when Liam called them after the meeting in the conference room had broken up, after he had proposed, after he had signed Windlogic over to her. "She needs a place to stay for awhile," he told Sam. That was all Sam needed to hear. He gave her the keys to Liam's car and made sure she knew how to get to the tackle shop. At night, Maggie was always waiting, no matter how late she returned, with a smile and a warm plate of food.

She placed her bags by the back door and reached for the phone in the kitchen. Maggie wouldn't be here until seven. She had one hour to make her calls.

"First Bank of New York."

"Records department, please."

"One moment." There was a slight buzz and a click on the line.

"Records."

Cara forced her voice into a high rush. "Oh hi! My name is Susan Whitfield and I run a small accounting firm here in New York. There's been a big mix-up with a couple of my clients, and I wonder if you might help me."

"What do you need, ma'am?" The voice on the other end sounded young and bored.

"Well, one of my clients transferred some funds to RLM AG on July the eleventh, and I lost the copy of the transaction. Do you believe that? I'm so embarrassed. I mean, to lose a copy of a receipt for $750,000! Mr. Streeter and Mr. Bancroft are coming back from vacation today, and they'll have my head if I don't book the transaction to the right company. Do you think you could tell me which company made the transfer? I know the amount, and the date, and the bank of deposit. I'm not sure if it was done by Mr. Streeter's company or Mr. Bancroft's. Or Mr. Wehrli's. Or Mr.—"

"Normally we don't do this kind of thing, ma'am. All you need to do is use the bank statement as proof."

"Oh, and normally I would, but all the records are filed at their offices, and I can't get there before Mr. Streeter and Mr. Bancroft return, and they want a report right away. They're going to be so angry. Would you make an exception this once? Please? This is the first time I've had real paying clients, and I—"

"Just a moment." There was a bored sigh on the other end, and Cara heard the clicking of keys in the background. "Yes, here is the entry, as you said. The $750,000 was deposited on July 11 to RLM AG. What did you say the name was?"

Cara held her breath. "Streeter or Bancroft?"

"No. None of those names match. This deposit was made by a Renssalear Corporation."

"Oh, that's Mr. Streeter's company," Cara improvised. "Perfect. She paused. "Do you see another deposit on July ninth? For $250,000?" She smiled into the phone. "I'm a little worried I messed up all these transactions."

"Yes, right here. Made by the same company."

"Would you fax those pages to me? For my records?"

"Sure, I guess."

"You're so kind. Thank you so much. You just saved my career. Here's the number." Cara rattled off the number, said another quick thanks, and hung up before the clerk could ask about the strange area code. In a minute, the fax machine in Liam's office began to hum.

Cara returned to the kitchen and dialed directory assistance for the state of New York. "Yes, the number for the corporations department please?" She wrote down the number, hung up, then lifted the receiver, and dialed again.

"State Division of Corporations."

Cara straightened herself as she sat at the kitchen table. She tightened her voice and surprised herself by how official she sounded. "Yes, I am calling from the First Bank of New York. I need to verify a corporate officer for a New York corporation."

"Let me transfer you." Three transfers later, she reached a voice with some information attached.

"Yes. I am processing a loan application for a Mr. Carl Streeter. He indicates he is the president and CEO of a Renssalear Corporation, which was incorporated in ..." Cara made a wild guess as she rustled papers in front of her, "1986. I just need a simple yes or no, so I can check the box on the form."

The clerk was silent while she checked the system. "One minute, ma'am. Mr. Carl Streeter is the sole owner and officer of Renssalear Corporation. It was incorporated in ... 1988, not 1986."

"Well, that's why we call. Those few years can make a big difference when we process a loan application. Thank you very much."

Cara hung up. Bingo! She closed her eyes, and the plan that she had been formulating all night began to take shape. She felt the nausea build in her stomach, but she forced it down. She picked up the phone again and dialed the number to Ol' Bob's Bait and Tackle Shop. "Mike?"

"Cara? Where are you? Why aren't you here?"

"I need to go to New York. I'm leaving in a few minutes."

"Cara, you can't. Liam will kill me when he finds out you're gone. He told me—"

"I know what he told you. I just wanted to let you know I won't be back until the IPO is completed on Wednesday." She paused for a moment. "Mike? I need a favor."

"You'd better tell me what you're up to. I promised Liam I would keep an eye on you."

"Mike ..." She paused again. "I might need your help with something ..."

He laughed aloud. "Ooh, I recognize that tone. Something ... challenging. What? Do you have another system to hack?"

"Not exactly. This ... this might be more along the lines of a felony ..."

"Mmm mmm, you know how to get my attention, Cara. I've told you before. It's only a felony if you get caught." He lowered his voice. "Now, what do you need?"

Cara pulled her brand new cellular phone from her purse as she stared down at the streets of New York sixty stories below. "Yes, this is Cara Larson from Windlogic. Is Liam Scofield available, please?"

"Mr. Scofield is in a presentation with the management team at the moment. Should I interrupt?"

"Oh, no. Would you ask him to return my call? Here's the number."

He called five minutes later. "Hey beautiful. How are you?"

She laughed. God, it was the most wonderful thing in the world to hear the smile in his voice. "Good. I wanted to call you and tell you ... I've had a slight change in plans. I needed to go to New York a day early. Do you think you could change your flight to come here tonight?"

"Why are you in New York, Cara?"

She heard the sudden tension in his tone, and she could imagine the thoughts running through his mind. Lauren's betrayal had shaken him badly, despite his determination to overcome it. Now, here she was, the sole owner of Windlogic, the key to his corporate survival, in New York, where all the big investors were gathering for the IPO on Wednesday. His question practically screamed through the silence. "I need to get you a wedding gift."

She heard the sharp release of his breath. "Cara, Portland may not be as big as New York, but it does have stores."

She giggled. "Of course it does, but I wanted to get you something special. Portland doesn't have a Bloomingdale's."

"Cara, I'm not a Bloomingdale's sort of guy."

She sighed. "Okay. I'd better take it back."

"Take what back?"

"I'm not telling. Especially if I have to take it back." She paused for a minute trying to read his silence. "Well? Can you come to New York tonight? We might need some time to go over everything once more before the meeting tomorrow."

"I'm sorry, I can't get away. We scheduled another demo for late this afternoon. If I take the red-eye, I'll be lucky to arrive just in time for the meeting."

"Oh. Okay. I understand. I'll see you tomorrow, then."

"All right. Cara?"

"Yes?"

"Is everything all right?"

"Yes. I just miss you." She paused. "I love you, Liam."

"And I love you. I'll see you in the morning, sweetheart." Liam hung up the phone and studied the receiver for a moment. Hmm, he thought. I wonder what she's up to.

Cara switched off her phone and stared out the window. "Mr. Streeter will see you now." Mrs. Bosun, Carl Streeter's secretary, stood erect as she leveled a cold glare at Cara. Cara ignored the look as she followed her into the office. She walked over to the man who was in the process of stealing her fiancé's company. "Mr. Streeter?"

Carl Streeter held up the documents he'd removed from the envelope Cara had given his secretary twenty minutes earlier. His face was gray. A copy of the bank log she'd received from First Bank of New York fluttered to the ground. "What's the meaning of this?"

Cara stood in front of him. "You and I have some business to conduct, Mr. Streeter. You are going to sell me eleven shares of Windwear stock."

Chapter 57

It was nearly 9:30 a.m. when Liam arrived at the Pyramid lobby. Cara spotted him from the far end of the foyer. She ran across the floor, her heels clicking on the tiles, and threw her arms around him. "Liam!" He held her tightly. Whatever she was up to, he thought, it was okay. Her eyes always said everything. And right now, they said she was glad to see him. Very glad.

"I reckon that's them." Liam and Cara turned as Andrew and Lauren approached.

Liam reached out to shake Andrew's hand. "Andrew, you made it. Did you two have a good trip?"

Andrew shook Liam's hand. "Reckon we did. I've never been out this way before. New York's a right interestin' place." Lauren snorted in disgust and refused to meet Liam's gaze.

"Let's sit down for a minute." Liam gestured to a group of sofas nearby. "Lauren did you get my fax yesterday?"

"Yes."

"Are the terms clear?"

"Yes."

"Nothing ambiguous to trip us up?"

Lauren glared at him belligerently. "I don't know why you're asking me these questions, Liam. You know there is nothing legally wrong with the agreement. I don't understand why I'm even here. Why isn't Jared Dafoe here? He wrote it. He's the one who—"

"Unfortunately, Jared Dafoe is not Windwear's attorney of record. You are, and as such you are required to sign any legal documents committing Windwear to action."

She shook her head dismissively. "This is a wasted effort, Liam. Do you think the consortium is going to allow a distribution deal with Pyramid? As soon as Carl Streeter gets control of the company, he's going to void this deal."

"I don't think so. The penalties for cancellation are harsh. The consortium will lose a lot of money if it tries to kill the deal."

"Maybe, maybe not. Even if the consortium decides to honor the deal, Windwear won't get a penny of the proceeds. They have no intention of going forward with your expansion plans. The income from Aerie will go into their pockets. The consortium will get its money one way or another."

Liam shrugged. "Well, we'll cross that bridge when we get to it."

"You fool. There is no bridge. You don't even have a boat. You're a drowning man, only you don't know it yet—"

"Enough, Lauren." He turned to Andrew and Cara. "Are we ready? Let's go."

"Cara!" A tall man with silver hair was walking across the lobby toward them.

Cara turned. "Charlie!" She rushed towards him, and he enveloped her in a warm embrace. "How was the flight from Chicago?"

"Fine. Fine. How are you, young lady?" He held her away from him. "You look … good. Much better than when we last met."

"Thank you. A lot has happened." She grasped his hand and tugged him forward. "Come on, Charlie, I want you to meet Liam."

As they approached, Cara saw Liam lean over and whisper something to Andrew. Then Andrew and Lauren walked to the elevator. Liam held out his hand as Cara introduced them. "Liam, this is Charlie Schmidt. He's the managing partner of Pyramid's Chicago office. He is the one who wrangled the meeting with Neal Coleman. Charlie, meet my fiancé, Liam Scofield."

Charlie almost choked at her words. "Fiancé? Cara, you didn't tell me you were engaged the last time we met."

She blushed. "That's because I wasn't. It … happened rather suddenly."

"So, romance blossoms over late nights developing a new product—"

Cara rolled her eyes. "Please, Charlie, you're embarrassing me. You're much worse than a real father could ever be."

His face appeared hurt, but his eyes danced. "Who, me?" He grinned wickedly and turned toward Liam. "You're a lucky man, Mr. Scofield. I never thought I'd see the day when Cara gave in. She used to drive the guys wild with her rejections. They would sit at lunch, shaking their heads, comparing notes about how she blew them off—"

"Charlie that's enough …"

Liam laughed outright. "We need to have a drink sometime soon. Cara hasn't let me in on many of the sordid details of her past."

"The only sordid detail you two need to discuss concerns Aerie," she cut in as she glanced at her watch. "We don't have much time. We're scheduled to meet with Coleman in a few minutes."

Liam and Charlie and Cara chatted like old friends who hadn't seen each other in years. To anyone walking by, they seemed innocent. To anyone close enough to hear, the discussion was anything but innocent. In the space of ten minutes, every term, condition, and nuance of the deal was discussed, stretched, twisted, pondered, and questioned with a minimum of words. Until finally the two men stood facing each other, nodded, and shook hands.

Liam and Cara were ushered into Neal Coleman's elegant suite. Red damask curtains hung from the windows, and three deep red sofas were situated around a glass-inlaid coffee table that was bigger than Cara's old kitchen back home. Andrew elected to wait outside in the reception area.

Lauren was already seated on one of the red sofas. Liam and Cara were shown to the sofa adjacent to an antique wing chair that looked suspiciously like a throne. Charlie sat opposite them on the other side of the throne.

They waited. Five minutes. Ten minutes. Fifteen. Cara rolled her eyes. She had heard about this when she worked at Pyramid. It was part of Neal Coleman's mystique. He kept everyone waiting. It was a sign of his power. And the people who wanted to do business with him had to take it, because he owned the technology, and he owned the people who understood the technology. And they needed him. And he would make them beg. It was said he liked to see them beg even more than he liked taking their money. Her colleagues had spoken of his manner with awe, as if they desired one day to aspire to such heights. She grimaced. Peter Whittington had been a living example of that aspiration. Now, she would observe for herself whether the rumors were true. She glanced at Liam. His face was perfectly blank.

Neal Coleman strode into the office with his Armani suit shimmering in the gray light. He raised bored eyes to his guests before spying his subordinate. "Charlie, good to see you." He walked over to Charlie and shook his hand, his back to his guests. "I'm sorry I'm late. Had a videoconference with Jack over in London regarding the British Airways deal. That bloke can't nail down a deal on his own if it came with a hammer. You sure you don't want to go to London for a couple of years, old boy? I need someone to straighten that office out."

Several minutes passed before Neal Coleman ended his one-sided conversation and Charlie was able to urge his boss to greet his visitors. Liam, Cara, and Lauren stood up. Neal's expression turned bored again as he walked toward them. He studied Liam contemptuously, assessing the quality of his suit, trying to determine the mettle of the man in front of him. They stood almost the same height, but Liam was thinner, darker, more chiseled, and probably fifteen years younger. Neal Coleman had icy blue eyes and dark, thinning hair. His face was smooth, all curves to Liam's sharp angles. He had a circular head and a rounded chin, but he had a long, aquiline nose he used to look down on the younger man. No Armani suit, his expression seemed to say, as he shook Liam's hand. "Mr. Scofield. From Windsong, is it?"

Charlie, standing by his side, quickly corrected him. "Windwear, Neal."

"Oh, yes. Windwear."

Liam met his gaze steadily. He even smiled politely. But Cara noted how the muscle flickered in his left cheek. She forced herself to relax. Liam was perfectly capable of handling the situation. Besides, she wanted to watch the great Neal Coleman in action.

Neal turned to Cara. "Ms. Larson, Charlie tells me you recently left Pyramid."

Cara kept her face passive, but her mind whirred. So, he'd done his homework. "That's right."

"May I ask why?"

She smiled. "If you know I left, I'm sure you're aware of the reason."

"Reasons, I would say. There are several ... documents in your file. It appears you were not quite prepared for the responsibilities of management." Cara and Liam exchanged a glance, as she let out a quiet sigh. "A shame," Neal said as Cara turned toward him again. "Peter Whittington is one of our best managers, one of my protégés, as a matter of fact. You could learn a lot from him."

"Oh, I did," Cara said politely, "I learned quite a lot. But I found I wasn't able to meet Peter's standards." Liam stifled a laugh.

"Couldn't swim in the deep end, eh, young lady? Well, don't you worry. Not everyone is cut out to work with the best technology company in the world." He paused, and Cara barely kept her eyes from rolling. "You resigned a few months ago. What have you been doing since then? Are you working for ... Windsong?"

Cara let the insult hang in the air. Liam didn't move a muscle. He was being very patient. "I'm running my own business, now."

"Ah. Some competition. Should I be worried?" He looked at her indulgently, his patronizing manner half hidden by a smile.

"I don't think so, but I hope we will work together someday soon."

"Really." He smiled, but his expression said otherwise, that perhaps pigs would make regular takeoffs from LaGuardia before such an event occurred.

Abruptly, Neal dismissed Cara and turned to Lauren. Her face was belligerent, and she didn't even try to smile or shake his hand. Neal was immediately intrigued. "Ms. Janelle. I understand you hail from Harvard. Good school if you like that sort of thing. Me? I never finished high school."

Lauren gave him a disgusted glare. "It's all right with me if you want to be an uneducated twit."

Neal's head snapped back in surprise. Hurriedly, Charlie ushered Neal to his seat. "Why don't we get down to business?"

Neal strolled to the throne, unbuttoned the jacket of his Armani suit, and crossed one long leg over the other. "So, tell me, Scofield, you're here to make me an offer."

Liam unbuttoned his non-Armani suit jacket. "That's right. It appears our companies are in direct competition with each other over a piece of software."

Neal raised his eyebrows. "Ah, yes. Aerie. The software owned by your subsidiary, what is its name, Charlie? Wind … something?"

"Windlogic," Charlie sighed.

"Right. Windlogic. Charlie filled me in on the situation."

"Windlogic is prepared to offer you exclusive distribution rights to Aerie for all territory east of the Mississippi."

"In exchange for?"

"For Pyramid dropping its development effort. Windlogic and Pyramid will divide all revenue from the sale and distribution of Aerie in your territory, seventy-five to twenty-five respectively, during the first year. Every year thereafter, Pyramid's share will increase 5 percent and Windlogic's will decrease 5 percent, providing Pyramid meets the agreed-upon volume targets. Windlogic retains the right to hire additional distributors if you do not meet such targets. At the end of five years, if both parties have fulfilled the terms of the agreement, Pyramid will receive an exclusive option to buy Aerie from Windlogic at a price negotiated at that time. In addition, you'll receive 100 percent of all ancillary business you contract while distributing Aerie."

Neal was silent for a minute. "An attractive offer. Too attractive, I'd say. Are you afraid of a little good old-fashioned competition, Scofield?"

Liam's smile didn't come near his eyes. "Not at all."

"Your offer is generous. Not the type of offer someone would make if he were confident in his product. Or of their advantage over the competition."

"I have no concerns about the quality of my product."

"Then you're worried about Pyramid?"

Liam tilted his head for a moment, as if considering. "No, I have no concerns about the quality of your product."

Neal's eyes flared in anger, but his voice was careful. "What's the catch?"

"I have some additional conditions you will need to accept if you agree to this proposal."

"Ah. I figured as much. Go on."

"First, we ask you to void the noncompete clauses in place for Cara and Mike Taylor, who now works for Windwear. And we ask that you cancel the current lawsuit Pyramid has against Cara and Windwear. Your company is suing Cara for violating her noncompete clause and my company for its efforts to develop Aerie. I don't want any confusion about the legal status of Aerie, especially when we can make so much money by working together."

Neal seemed puzzled. "Do we have a lawsuit pending, Charlie?"

Charlie shrugged. "I don't know."

"Call Nate Thomason. Get him up here right away."

Charlie rose to use the phone located near the door. Liam opened his briefcase and removed a folder. He opened the folder, picked up a document, and handed it to Neal. "This is my copy of the complaint."

Neal read the complaint with interest and studied the signature at the bottom. "This wasn't prepared by a Pyramid lawyer. This is not our approved format."

"No. Unfortunately, this was prepared by my lawyer. Without my knowledge."

Neal's eyes widened as he read the document. He turned toward Lauren, who stared defiantly at him. "Really?"

Lauren lifted her chin higher. "I did what I needed to do to save Windwear. Peter thought—"

"Enough, Lauren," Liam interrupted. "Mr. Coleman can read."

She snapped her mouth shut, but her eyes flashed. "Hmm." Neal inspected the complaint. "Fine. I can stop this without any trouble." He nodded. "I agree with condition number one. Your second condition?"

"Peter Whittington never touches Aerie while he is employed at Pyramid."

Neal leaned forward with a scowl. "Now, just a damned minute. No one dictates personnel policy to me. No one."

"I'm not dictating anything. It's a condition of the agreement."

"Peter's a good man. I taught him everything he knows. I'm grooming him for great things. Why do you want him out of the picture?"

"I just don't want him in Aerie's picture. There's a provision to review Peter's work on a monthly basis to make sure he's not involved with Aerie in any way. The minute we find he is, the deal is off. No revenue sharing, no option to buy, nothing."

Neal leaned back and laughed. "Well, it's a point for negotiation."

Liam shook his head. "I don't think you understand." Liam looked at his watch, then handed Neal a copy of the proposal. "The terms of this proposal are not negotiable, and the offer is good for exactly thirty minutes."

Neal stared at him in disbelief, and then dismissed him. "Then the answer is no. No one rushes me. No one corners me into a decision without due deliberation."

"Fine. No problem." Liam turned to Cara. "Why don't you give Infogence a call, Cara, and let them know we can fit them in, after all." She nodded, opened her purse, and pulled out her cellular phone. He turned back to Neal. "Well, Mr. Coleman, thank you for your time. I need to get to my next appointment. I really hate to keep people waiting." He smiled and stood up. Lauren and Cara stood up as well. "Thanks for arranging the meeting, Charlie. I'm sorry we couldn't do business."

Charlie stood up with a troubled expression. "Yes. A shame. A real shame."

Neal eyed him angrily. "We'll bury you when our version of Aerie goes live, Scofield."

Chapter 58

Liam reached the door and turned around. "Oh, about that. Here are a couple of things you may want to keep in mind, Mr. Coleman. Windlogic holds the patent to Aerie. If you do *happen* to finish your development effort any time this century and you do *happen* to pursue its marketing and distribution, I will not hesitate to sue the living hell out of you."

Neal laughed scornfully. "Your tiny company sue Pyramid? That's a picture, Scofield. You'd be buried in paperwork before you filed the first complaint."

"We won't be small for long. Not with this software. We've already booked advanced sales of five million dollars, and maintenance contracts worth another five. I won't have any trouble matching you legal dollar for legal dollar if that's the way you want to play it. Too bad. The only people who ever win that game are the lawyers."

Liam glanced at his watch. "Well, we need to run. We need to prepare for the festivities. We're holding a press conference in a few hours to announce the immediate availability of Aerie. Cole Martin, our distributor in the West, will attend. As will several of our key customers." He ticked off their names one by one. Big names. Huge names. Some of them current Pyramid customers. "We would have liked you to attend as well, as our Eastern distributor, but I understand your concerns." He smiled brightly and opened the door. "Good-bye gentlemen."

"Wait just a damned minute." Neal snarled at Liam's back before he took another step.

Slowly, Liam turned to view the havoc he created. The room was tense and silent. Lauren's jaw gaped open in surprise. Neal's eyes were narrowed in anger. "Charlie?" he rasped, without taking his eyes from Liam. "What is the status of our version of Aerie?"

Charlie frowned. "I spoke to Whittington yesterday. He's going through a second run at conceptual design. Apparently, his team rushed through the first time, and the design didn't stand up in programming. No one on the team understood its business purpose, and they got lost in the details." Cara, standing by Liam's side, stared straight ahead and willed herself not to react. So, Peter biffed it big time in a rush to write code. She supposed she shouldn't have been surprised.

"What's the completion date?"

She focused her attention back on Charlie. "Unsure right now. A couple of weeks ago, he said his team was on the verge of completing a prototype, but nothing ever came of it. Said he ran into some unexpected difficulties. There were conflicting reports from the team. Some team members complained they'd never been assigned to work on a prototype. Peter was quite unhappy." Cara gasped as Charlie's words hit home. She touched her face gingerly as she recalled Peter's unexpected "difficulties." From the corner of her eye, she saw a red tinge climb up Liam's face.

Stunned, Neal turned to Liam. "Give us thirty minutes to discuss this, Scofield. Charlie, make sure Nate Thomason is on the way."

Liam looked at his watch. "You're down to twenty-five." Without another word, he walked out the door, gently guiding Cara ahead of him.

Lauren and Charlie followed them out. "Whew, you forgot to mention the detail about the press conference when we talked earlier," Charlie said.

Liam's eyes were empty of expression. "Did I? Hmm."

Charlie shook his head. "I need to get Nate. I'll be back in a few minutes."

The time passed slowly. Liam and Cara waited quietly in the reception area. Andrew brought them coffee, which they drank without tasting. Charlie left and then returned, ushering a gray-headed man with rimless spectacles into Neal's office. Lauren left immediately to use a telephone in a nearby conference room. Cara peered worriedly at Liam when Lauren asked the receptionist for permission to use it, but Liam shook his head, dismissing Lauren's actions as if they were of no consequence.

The minutes seemed to stretch into hours. Cara looked at her watch for the twenty-third time. Twenty-three minutes had passed. "I wonder why he's taking so long."

Liam shrugged. "Patience. We need to wait him out."

"You gave him so much, Liam. If I knew Peter was so far behind, I wouldn't have offered half what you did."

"I would have offered twice what I did if I thought I needed to. The offer needed to be attractive enough for Coleman to commit, given the short time frame. The only thing he understands is money."

"But Liam, an option to buy—"

"I'm getting a bargain, Cara." He touched her cheek, now healed and smooth. "Peace of mind is sometimes expensive but always worth the price. I learned that lesson from you."

"Why don't you come in?" Charlie stepped out of the office and motioned toward them. "Where is Lauren?"

Andrew jumped to attention. "I'll get her."

Liam and Cara entered the room. "There you are." Neal came striding over, beaming from ear to ear. He shook Liam's hand effusively. "Call me Neal, Scofield. Meet my attorney, Nate Thomason. He reviewed the agreement and found it satisfactory." Liam cast a quick glance toward the attorney. The older man was shaking his head in puzzlement, as if the terms were too clear. Not a single labyrinthine turn or sneaky twist to decipher. Bah, what a waste of his skills. Neal led them to a small glass table where the pages were laid out for signatures. "Take a seat, Scofield." He gazed around the room. "Where is your attorney?"

"I'm right here." Lauren strode in and took a place at the table next to Liam. Liam glanced at Lauren, then over at Cara, who was still standing in the middle of the room.

"Come on, Cara, you and I get to sit in the spectator section." Charlie guided her by the elbow to two chairs situated several feet from the table.

She smiled at Charlie. "Of course."

Pyramid's lawyer faced Liam eagerly. "I've read the agreement and want to make a few clarifications before we sign."

"All right," Liam said.

"First of all, what is this payment of $500,000? I don't understand. Windlogic is paying Pyramid this money?"

Liam nodded. "That's right. When Cara was on the FIT project, her team worked with Windwear to build the prototype. There was a problem during development, and Peter removed Aerie from FIT's scope—"

"What?" Neal exclaimed. "He pulled Aerie from the project scope?"

"It's a long story, but suffice to say Pyramid was never properly compensated for the work Cara's team did on the prototype. This payment corrects the situation."

"You didn't have to do this, Scofield," Neal said. "Given the amount of money to be made on this deal, I would not have demanded payment."

"I understand, but I believe it's necessary. I need to make sure Windlogic's claim to Aerie is rock solid, and as such, I want a clean paper trail showing we properly paid for Pyramid's services." He smiled. "Despite what your files say about Cara's management skills, she and her team did an excellent job on the prototype. Her work deserves both compensation and recognition."

"Hmm." Neal looked up at Charlie. "Schedule a meeting with Whittington for next week, would you Charlie?" Then he glanced at his attorney. "Any other questions?"

Nate Thomason nodded. "Yes. I'm not clear on the procedures if Pyramid fails to make the targeted revenue numbers. Do you expect an annual audit? Semiannual? Something else? Who pays for it? Does Pyramid get a warning first?" The attorney droned on, and Liam cast a quick glance at his future wife. He smiled to himself. The expression on her face alone was worth the half million dollars.

They wrangled through the issues and clarified the procedures. At last, Nate Thomason looked up. "I'm satisfied, Neal. We'll attach the detailed review procedures in a rider. Go ahead and sign."

"Liam hasn't told you everything, Mr. Coleman," Lauren said as Neal picked up his pen. Throughout the entire discussion, Lauren hadn't uttered a single word. Now, her declaration fairly shouted for attention.

Neal turned his icy gaze on her. "What hasn't he told me, Ms. Janelle?"

"He hasn't told you Windwear will be under new management tomorrow." She paused to let her words sink in. "Windwear's new management is not going to like this deal. In fact, I just spoke with them. They will do everything they can to void this deal once they take control tomorrow."

Neal's confusion grew into a roar of protest. "What the hell are you talking about? Who is this new management? What is going on here?"

Lauren glared at Liam. "Do you want to explain?"

Liam shook his head. "Why don't you go ahead and enlighten us, Lauren."

She looked at him uncertainly, as if she had expected him to panic. "Windwear is going public tomorrow," she said, as if the words explained everything.

Neal nodded impatiently. "Of course. It's been in the newspapers for weeks. Tell me something I don't know."

"The offering consists of two parts. The first is for common nonvoting stock. Windwear is issuing three million shares of common stock at sixteen dollars per share."

"And?"

"The second part of the offering is not as well understood by the general public. The Cyclops consortium is committed to purchase two million shares at that price. In exchange, they will receive 51 percent of the preferred voting stock of Windwear. By tomorrow, Liam will not be the majority owner of Windwear. That honor will go to the Cyclops consortium, which is headed up by Carl Streeter."

"Carl Streeter?" Neal said with delight. "Great guy. Sharp guy. I've done business with him for many years. He's on the Board at Pyramid, you know."

Lauren nodded. "Yes, he is the best in the business at growing small companies into large ones in short time horizons. He is looking forward to the challenge of Windwear." Her smile faded. "Unfortunately, due to some ... er ... unforeseen circumstances, the consortium will not be able to honor this agreement." She turned a pointed glance toward Liam. Liam's expression remained impassive.

Neal's expression was anything but impassive. "Why the hell not? This is an outstanding deal! We'll all be rolling in money. Your consortium would be stupid not to pursue this."

"Cyclops has ... other plans for Aerie."

"Other plans? What other plans?" He was incredulous as he turned toward Liam. "What is the meaning of this? Why the hell would you make an agreement your own management will turn around and cancel? And why is your own lawyer advising me against it?"

Liam shrugged. "Lauren is incredibly disloyal. She has repeatedly placed her own interests above those of my company."

"Disloyal?" Lauren shot back. "My God, I'm the only person at your company with the guts to stand up to you and do what needs to be done. It takes a strong person to do what's right, and that is what I've done. I've saved your company from its worst enemy, which has always been you."

Liam continued as if she hadn't spoken. "In this case, Lauren is wrong."

"Wrong?" she exclaimed. "How can you say I'm wrong when—"

"Are you telling me your company is not undergoing a change of management?" Neal interrupted, trying to assess the truth amidst the confusion.

"Oh, no. Lauren is perfectly accurate regarding Windwear's management changes."

"Then what the hell are you talking about?"

"It happens to be completely irrelevant to our agreement."

"I don't understand." Neal's frustration was rising.

"The terms of the agreement are clear. If either party cancels, the other is entitled to 50 percent of revenues earned from Aerie. If the consortium cancels, Pyramid stands to earn more than if the agreement was in place. Cyclops isn't going to give away half its revenues out of spite. Even a non-Harvard graduate who doesn't know what's right," he paused and glanced at Lauren, "can figure that out. Besides, the consortium doesn't have a clue as to how to market Aerie. When they realize how much money they'll earn from this deal, they'll be dancing in the streets. From what Lauren is saying, they're only interested in skimming cash off the top anyway. With this deal, they won't even need to worry about all the details that go along with marketing the software. Isn't that right, Lauren?"

Lauren hesitated for a moment. "We might be able to get more if we sold the software outright."

Liam laughed harshly. "Unproved and untried and without the support of the people who built it? I guarantee if the consortium takes Aerie, the people who built it will turn their backs on it. The consortium won't know how to make Aerie a success, but Mr. Coleman will. He's built an empire on that kind of knowledge." Liam glanced at his watch. "I'm nearly out of time, Mr. Coleman. Sign the agreement or don't, it doesn't matter to me."

Neal eyed Liam, jaw set, eyes hard and unyielding. Then he glanced at Lauren, slightly uncertain, hands trembling as they rested on the table. He turned toward his lawyer.

"Sign," Nate Thomason said.

Neal clicked open the pen and signed. He handed the pen to his lawyer, who placed a flourishing scrawl across the paper. The lawyer handed the pen and the agreement to Lauren.

Sullenly she picked up the pen and located the place on the document for her signature. "Hold on a second, Lauren." Liam's voice was quiet.

"What now?" she scowled.

"I don't believe you're required to sign the document."

She hissed her frustration at him. "What the hell are you talking about, Liam?"

"This agreement is between Windlogic and Pyramid. You're not the attorney for Windlogic."

Lauren snorted in disgust. "What do you mean? I'm the attorney for Windwear, and Windlogic is a wholly owned subsidiary of Windwear."

Liam nodded thoughtfully. "That was true at one time, but not now. All the shares of Windlogic have been transferred. Windlogic is no longer owned by Windwear."

"You're losing me. What are you saying?"

Liam reached in his briefcase and pulled out an official-looking document. "We received the official paperwork yesterday. Jared Dafoe is the attorney of record for Windlogic. Since he couldn't be here today, he granted me power of attorney to sign this agreement."

Lauren was puzzled. "But ... if you don't own Windlogic, who does?"

Liam turned around to where Cara and Charlie were watching the exchange. "Cara why don't you come over and sign the papers now. As your attorney for the day, I would say they meet all your requirements."

Lauren stared at Liam as Cara approached the table. "You sold Windlogic to her? After everything she's done?" She shook her head in disbelief. Then the implication hit her. "You think you can shelter the income from Aerie by transferring it to her? The consortium will never allow it. They'll take you to court so fast, your head will spin. You can't divest your assets during a pending stock offering. The courts will void this transfer in a minute."

"I'm not so sure, Lauren. I reviewed all the registration information we filed with the SEC. Aerie is not mentioned anywhere. All those auditors. All those reviews. And not a single word about Aerie. According to the documents, Aerie doesn't even exist."

"Don't start trying to play lawyer, now, Liam. Normal business operations are not required to be disclosed."

"But these aren't normal business operations, are they? Aerie was never part of our core business. I wonder what the courts will say when they find out the only people who knew about Aerie were the members of the consortium. The average Joe Investor on the street doesn't have any idea about Aerie. The courts might say you created two classes of investors, one with a distinct advantage over the other. Especially when the first order of business after the IPO is to sell Aerie to one of those classes. No, that's not going to seem suspicious at all. If I were a common shareholder, I might be upset. I might even try to sue. I might even try to void the IPO altogether." He smiled pleasantly. "So, you go right ahead, Lauren. I want to see what the courts say about this matter. I would say we have at least a fighting chance of getting Cyclops thrown out on its eye."

"You think you're clever, maybe too clever for your own good. If Windwear doesn't own Windlogic, that means your company doesn't get the money coming from Aerie, either."

Liam signed the document. He handed the pen to Cara. "Go ahead and sign, Cara."

"You are absolutely right, Lauren," Liam said as Cara signed. "Windwear has no access whatsoever to Windlogic's funds." He placed his hand on Cara's back and caressed it gently. "But maybe I can convince my future wife to work a deal with me."

Liam stood up and reached across the table to shake Neal's hand. "The press conference is at 2:30 p.m. in the lobby of the Waldorf, Neal. I hope you will attend." He gathered the papers and placed them in his briefcase. "I'll deliver copies of the signed agreement to you as soon as I can."

"Oh, one more thing." Liam turned to Lauren. "When you talk to Carl Streeter again, make sure to let him know that if he insists on going after Aerie, he will not only have to go up against Windwear, he'll also have to take on the big dogs at Pyramid. Would you make sure he gets the message?"

Neal nodded. "I sure would hate to go up against Carl Streeter." He stopped. "On the other hand, that might prove to be … satisfying."

Lauren closed her eyes and leaned her head down on the cold glass-topped table.

Nate Thomason leaned over and patted her arm. "Let me give you a little advice, Ms. Janelle. Rule number one in the legal field. Never, ever, ever bite the hand that pays you."

Lauren looked up, her face angry. She stared at Pyramid's lawyer, then at Pyramid's leader. Neal Coleman shook his head as he stood up. "Too true. A shame, Ms. Janelle. I'm sure it would have been quite interesting to work with you. If only you could be trusted."

Liam put his hand at Cara's back as they turned toward the door. "After you, Ms. Larson."

Chapter 59

The elevator opened onto the forty-fourth floor of the shiny New York office building. Cara and Liam examined the directory to find the offices of Marshall, Longham and Fray Investment Bankers, Carl Streeter's employer. Carl Streeter's legitimate employer, Cara corrected herself. "Well, are you ready for the big day?"

They both turned to see Richard Bancroft standing in front of them. For a day of celebration, the banker seemed unusually subdued. "Liam?" He shook the younger man's hand. "You're doing the right thing, son. It will be rough, but you're doing the right thing."

Liam's smile held no conviction. He nodded as he shook the banker's hand. Cara realized he didn't trust himself to say anything. She sighed. This day was going to be much harder on him than she ever imagined.

Richard seemed to understand. He glanced at Cara. "Are you planning to introduce me, Liam, or should we just fend for ourselves?"

"Oh. Sorry, Richard. Meet my fiancée, Cara Larson."

"So, this is the new owner of Windlogic." He shook her hand.

"A pleasure to meet you, Mr. Bancroft. Liam's told me a lot about you."

Richard smiled. "You two made all the newspapers yesterday. And the six o'clock business news. Quite a splash, I must say."

Liam raised an eyebrow. "We weren't exactly prepared for the reception we received. It was a little … surprising."

Surprising wasn't the word, Cara thought. Shocking. Stunning. Overwhelming. They had planned a simple announcement with Cole Martin and a few major customers. Just a quick message to let the world know Aerie was available through Windlogic, and that Windwear would serve as its primary implementation partner. A little publicity to enhance awareness of Windwear on the eve of the IPO, and to nudge the stock price up when the opening curtain was raised on Windwear's shares in the morning.

The plan changed the minute Neal Coleman walked in the door with two TV cameramen and a dozen reporters. What a dog and pony show the event turned out to be. Neal strutted and boasted and spouted plans and promises as if he alone had conceived of Aerie. Neal introduced Cara as the owner of Windlogic, and she was surprised by the flash of cameras and the crush of questions hurled at her. She managed a polite wave as she leaned toward Liam and whispered, "I'm not quite ready to go solo." Then he smiled and stepped up next to her into the spotlight.

They answered every question thrown at them. Cara took the technical ones, and Liam took the business ones. They posed for pictures. They announced the company's plans. At one point they glanced at each other in silent amazement. Cara was thinking of the day when Liam first walked into her office with the idea for the software, more blue sky than solid earth. Had Aerie truly become a reality?

The rest of the day was a blur of activity. Neal Coleman insisted they attend a reception to honor a political candidate he was supporting. They met more important people in one evening than they had met in their whole lives. Welcome opportunities aside, Cara saw how Liam became increasingly subdued as the night wore on. He dropped her at the door of her suite with a light kiss and troubled eyes. "I need to prepare some paperwork for tomorrow."

She wanted so badly to invite him in, to comfort him, to make love to him. But his eyes said more than his words could. Not now, they said. Not until this is over. So, she let him go with a smile and a light kiss of her own.

Now, here they were, with the final challenge left. And this one made the events of yesterday seem like child's play.

They opened the door to the conference room and a kaleidoscope of images blurred around Liam. The consortium members gathered in small groups, exchanging important words. Lauren, in a vivid red dress, flitting between them, her face serious, her eyes intense. A closed-circuit television monitor tuned to the trading floor, buzzing in the background. The voting stock certificates spread out on the table, waiting for the appointed time to be signed and transferred to their new owners. Carl Streeter approached them. He greeted Liam and Richard but pointedly ignored Cara.

At 9:30 a.m., a hush came over the crowd. Everyone turned to face the screen at the far end of the room. As if on cue, the bell on the trading floor clanged, and where relative quiet prevailed before, a flurry of activity erupted. One of the consortium members sat at the computer terminal in the corner of the room and studied the display. "Excellent! Seventeen dollars and climbing. We're going to make a bundle."

The price of Windwear stock seesawed for the first few moments, then settled into a more sedate pace. When the price held at $19.675 for five minutes, the members grew bored, and Carl Streeter called everyone together. "It's time to sign the papers, gentlemen."

Liam walked to the table and took a seat next to Lauren. "After we sign, we'll conduct the first meeting of the new management team." Liam looked up sharply at Carl's words. No one told him about this. His mouth tightened into a hard line, but he nodded his agreement. Streeter's lawyer handed him the stock certificates. Each certificate specified the type and number of shares as well as the name of the new owner. The words hammered at him. *Windwear Corporation. Preferred Voting Shares,* followed by a line specifying the actual number of shares, and then, *held in joint ownership by,* and another line specifying the member's name, *a member of the Cyclops consortium.* A summary page displayed the number of shares being transferred: 510. Fifty-one percent of his company.

Liam inspected the first certificate. Then the next. Then the next. Twenty-five shares here. Forty-four shares there. Eleven more. He kept his face blank as he faced each one. He didn't really see them. All he could think of was how he couldn't, just couldn't lose his cool now. It was bad enough to lose his company; he didn't want to lose his pride too. He glanced up at Cara. She appeared as unsettled as he did. Was this as difficult for her as it was for him? Did she hurt like he did over this? He sighed. Then signed away his company in the gray silence of the New York morning.

"We're at twenty dollars and climbing! We're going to be rich!" someone yelled from the rear of the room. The sudden whoop of joy brought all heads back to the television monitor. Liam blinked and stepped away from the table. In the commotion that followed, he and Cara silently left the room.

"Are you all right?" she asked.

He nodded. "It's done. We just have to take whatever comes, now."

"Yes."

"Cara, I need to take care of some business with Lauren and sit in on this management meeting." He paused, as if reluctant to leave. "I don't know how long I'll be."

"Do what you need to do, Liam. I'll be here when you're done."

He nodded. Suddenly his eyes brimmed with tears, and he hugged her close, buried his head in her hair, and held her as if he would never let go.

She gripped him tightly. "Everything will be all right. Don't worry. Everything will be all right."

He nodded again, gave her a tight smile, and returned to the conference room.

Cara waited until he was out of sight before hurrying down the hall to the stairwell. Moments later, she opened the door to Carl Streeter's office. Mrs. Bosun, Carl's secretary, was waiting for her. She showed Cara into Carl's inner sanctum. "Mr. Streeter will join you in a moment."

"May I speak to you for a minute, Lauren?"

Lauren whirled around at Liam's words. "No, I'm busy."

"I only need a minute. It's important. It's business. You do still work for me, you know."

Lauren eyed him warily. Reluctantly she moved away from the crowd of consortium members he'd interrupted. "Make it quick. I need to prepare for the management meeting."

Liam swallowed and held onto his temper. "Let's go out here." They walked from the conference room and into the hallway, away from the door. "This is for you. Long overdue, I'm afraid."

"What is this?" She eyed the thick packet suspiciously.

"Your walking papers, Lauren. You are officially fired, effective immediately. You will find your termination papers, final check, and severance benefits, as well as the reduced number of stock options we agreed to."

She stared at him openmouthed. "You can't do this, Liam. I'm too valuable to Windwear. The consortium is counting on me to—"

"Then the consortium can hire you."

"You don't understand. I told them everything. They're already putting together a lawsuit challenging Cara's claim to Windlogic. That was a stupid move. Selling Windlogic right before the IPO. It won't stand up in court."

"That's a battle I'm willing to fight. Tooth and nail. I made up my mind. I will fight the consortium with everything I've got."

"Big words, Liam, but you gave away the store a few minutes ago. You may want to fight, but you won't be able to. You have nothing left to fight with."

The muscle ticked in his jaw. "Then the next time we meet will be in court."

"Are you Lauren Janelle?" Liam and Lauren turned to find a man wearing blue jeans and a tan windbreaker staring at them. He seemed out of place in the roomful of suits.

"Yes." Lauren looked up expectantly.

"This is for you." He handed her an official-looking, brown envelope.

"Thank you." She grasped the envelope and eagerly unclasped the flap.

"No problem." He paused for a beat, as if to make sure she opened the envelope. "You've been served," the man said as she examined the document. He turned quickly and walked away.

"What?" Lauren stared down at the papers and then at the retreating figure.

"Hmm. Jared Dafoe must have finished the paperwork on our lawsuit against you." Liam gazed quietly at Lauren. "I guess I will see you in court. Soon."

Liam walked toward the conference room. He went slowly. He needed to stay focused. He needed to stop the quiet dread growing inside him, needed to calm the worries threatening to smother him. Because Lauren had said the words he'd been unwilling to say to himself; that as much as he'd planned and maneuvered and tried, the truth was right behind that door. He had lost control of his company. He wanted to fight. God, he wanted to fight so badly, but he didn't have any weapons to fight with. He had only words and loyalty to this company he'd built, and they were no match against the power held by the people behind that door.

He walked in and took a seat next to Richard. Carl smiled smugly. "Let's get started."

One of the consortium members in the back spoke up. "Streeter, what the hell should we do about Aerie? You said we'd be able take ownership immediately after the stock transfer. What the hell is all this about Aerie and Windlogic not belonging to Windwear?"

Streeter glared at Liam. His voice was slow and measured. "This has all been a misunderstanding, hasn't it Scofield? You transferred Windlogic to your fiancée to keep it from your new partners. That was a big mistake. One I'm sure you didn't intend to make."

"No, that was not a mistake."

Carl's smile was smooth. "Come now, Scofield. We're partners now. We need to work together in the best interest of our stockholders."

"I am."

Carl frowned as he faced the consortium members. "We're drawing up a lawsuit to void the sale of Windlogic to Scofield's fiancée. Lauren says the procedure shouldn't take long. She says this is a clear case of asset divestiture. As soon as the matter is resolved, we will assess whether or not to cancel the distribution deal with Pyramid."

Liam didn't say a word.

"In the meantime, I want to review the operational plans for Windwear for the next three months." Carl gazed around. "Where is Lauren?"

"She's not here," Liam said. "I fired her."

The room broke out into gasps. Carl held up his hand to quiet the outburst. "You can't do that, Scofield."

"On the contrary. I can, and I did."

Streeter turned to one of his lieutenants. "Find her right now. Bring her back. We'll rehire her." One of the members left the room.

"Not on Windwear's payroll. I am still the president and CEO of Windwear. I make the hiring and firing decisions. As long as I run the company, I will continue to make those decisions. I fired Lauren and she will remain fired."

Streeter's eyes narrowed in rage. "I'm afraid that's not acceptable. It's time we set things straight. Let's vote right now. Someone move we fire Liam Scofield as president and CEO of Windwear."

Liam hid the jolt of shock that rocked him. It was happening already. No small skirmishes. No preparatory battles. War.

A lieutenant at the far end of the table piped up. "I so move."

"Second." Another voice spoke from the around the table.

"Wait just a damned minute, Carl. Are you crazy?" The room grew silent as Richard Bancroft's deep baritone reverberated in the tense silence. The older man eyed his colleague of many years. He swung his head toward the monitor, whose screen was still flashing, but whose volume was muted when the meeting started. "What's the stock up to, Joe?"

Joe leaned over and studied the monitor. "Twenty-two and a half. And still rising!"

Richard looked slowly around the table and settled his gaze back on the consortium leader. "What gives, Carl? I've never known you to be so impulsive." Carl began to interrupt, but Richard held up his hand to stop him. "Are you really willing to harm Windwear because this young man went against your wishes? How much money have you made from Windwear in the last hour? A million dollars? Two? Ten? The stock has already risen over 35 percent from your purchase price. What do you think will happen when you fire the man who not only built the company but steered it so successfully into the public arena?" Richard gave a long, slow whistle imitating a falling bomb. "Good-bye millions. Good-bye Windwear. Is that what you want? Is that what all of you want?"

"We'll put on a positive spin. Management changes happen all the time. Especially if we install a strong replacement."

"Not on the day of the offering. Unless ..." Richard paused and eyed Carl warily. "Unless you already have someone in mind. Have you been planning this move all along, Carl?"

Carl smiled smoothly. Too smoothly. "The idea has crossed my mind." He paused, making sure he had Liam's attention before he continued. "I believe Lauren Janelle would make a fine president of Windwear."

Liam remained still as stone. He willed himself to show no reaction. But the visions roaring through his brain tormented him. Lauren sitting at his desk. Lauren gutting the plans for his new manufacturing line. Lauren putting Windwear's name on that crap produced by Wangchao. Lauren flushing every goddamned thing he ever believed in down the toilet for a few more dollars. Good thing she wasn't in the room. It was bad enough to see the supercilious smirk on Carl's face. If he saw the matching one on hers, he might not be able to control himself. As it was, he sat still, tense, waiting.

Once again, Richard's voice filled the silence. He removed his glasses, rubbed his eyes, and shook his head in disappointment. "Come on, Carl. You must be joking. This is not the time to make drastic decisions. You'll frighten the shareholders out of their wits, and we'll all lose millions."

Carl's voice was stiff. "I don't work with people who won't work with me. We have a lot to do if we're going to grow Windwear. We all need to be on the same team. I don't want any opposition."

"This is not a question of opposition. It's a question of common sense—"

"You had your say. Lauren will provide the continuity the investors need. I will not discuss it further. Let's vote."

Richard straightened in his chair and stared at the man at the head of the table. "You're a fool, Carl. Your nose is out of joint because Scofield had the nerve to think for himself and do what he felt was best for his company. If your positions were reversed, you would do the same. Why don't we hear Liam out—"

"No, goddammit! I'm done with this discussion. Scofield," he spat out the name, "lied and cheated me out of Aerie. I want him out."

Richard shook his head. "Well, I won't vote with you on this one. Especially not on the day the company goes public."

Carl glared at the man sitting next to him, but a dangerous smile spread across his face. "Vote any way you please. It won't make any difference."

Richard frowned. "It makes plenty of difference. I own 102 shares. That's 10 percent of Windwear. With Liam's shares, we can block you."

Carl couldn't resist showing a triumphant grin. "Not exactly, Richard." The room fell silent.

Both Richard and Liam turned stared at Carl in confusion. "What do you mean?" Liam asked. He faced his friend and mentor. "Richard, what's Carl talking about?"

"I'm afraid Richard has misunderstood the mathematics of the arrangement." Carl seemed to be savoring the moment. "Take a good look at those shares you purchased, Richard. You don't own 102 shares at all. You own 102 shares of a 510-share block held jointly by this consortium. That's a 20 percent vote in any decision made by Cyclops." He leaned back in his chair, the grin now widening into full victory. "Since I own 306 shares of the 510-share block, I am the majority owner of Cyclops." He leaned back further, placed his hands behind his head, and let out a satisfied sigh. "As such, I am the new owner of Windwear."

Liam's eyes flew up in surprise. His mind raced in a thousand directions at once. Not Lauren in his chair, but Carl. It wasn't possible. He had misheard. He had missed something somewhere. But the images slamming into his brain told him he hadn't misunderstood at all. The smug grin on Carl's face couldn't be denied. Nor the incredulous look on Richard's face as he scoured the agreement Carl handed him. The frail hope he had of standing up to the consortium crashed headlong into despair as Richard's somber gaze met his. Richard passed the document to him.

There it was. In black and white. The sly taking. One word. Jointly. The one word that twisted the world onto a different plane. A plane where deception was a way of life and fairness the exception, where a lie was the truth and the truth a lie. A twisted world he thought he had learned to live in and still maintain his balance. He had been wrong. The depth of this deceit was incomprehensible. And now, it had defeated him.

He raised his head and saw the truth mirrored in Richard's face. Lauren fooled them all. From the beginning. He checked the date of the agreement. July eleventh. It was ironic that on the day he went to help Cara in her time of need, he had given Lauren the opportunity to steal his company. He sighed in defeat. Lauren had won. She had taken Windwear right in front of his eyes. In fact, right in front of the whole world's eyes.

Carl turned a self-satisfied stare toward his vanquished opponent. "Now, let's have that vote. It's just a formality, I know, but I want to do everything by the book." He turned to the man on his left. "Todd, please record each vote." He faced the room. "As Todd reads your name, cast your vote." His voice rose as he announced clearly, "All in favor of removing Liam Scofield as president and CEO of Windwear."

Chapter 60

Cara checked her watch. Twelve minutes had gone by, and Carl still hadn't shown up. She paced the room. Where was he? He was supposed to have met her here immediately after the stock transfer. The clock ticked off another minute. Where the hell was he? The truth suddenly hit her. "That liar!" She tore out the door and collided with Mrs. Bosun.

The secretary held her arm. "I'm sorry, Ms. Larson. I'm not permitted to let you leave." Mrs. Bosun was no match for Cara in size or strength. Cara tore her arm from the older woman's grasp and ran from the office. "Wait, wait!" the secretary called. She ran to the phone to call security before chasing after the younger woman.

Cara flew down the stairs and stopped at the closed conference room. She heard Carl's voice through the door. "All in favor of removing Liam Scofield as president and CEO of Windwear."

She burst into the room in a panic. "No! Stop! You can't do this." Every head turned to stare at her.

For a moment, Carl's eyes were tight with alarm. Quickly, he emptied all expression from his face. "You are not permitted to be in here, Ms. Larson. This is a closed meeting."

Cara ignored him. "Liam?" She took in Liam's ashen face and stricken eyes. "Richard? You can't let them do this. Together your shares outweigh theirs."

Richard shook his head. "I'm afraid that isn't so, Cara." He struggled with the words. "Carl holds the voting majority in Windwear."

Surprised, she turned back to Carl. He watched her carefully. "That's right, Ms. Larson. For all intents and purposes, I am the new owner of Windwear."

She faced Richard. "How can this be?"

"I should have read the agreement more closely. It's so clear now." Richard sighed. "The consortium didn't buy the shares severally, Cara."

"Speak English, Richard. What does that mean?"

"We bought them jointly. The agreement written by Lauren specifies joint ownership. That means the consortium votes as a block. By majority rule. And Carl is the majority owner of the consortium."

This was Liam's worst nightmare. She looked at him again. It was as if the light had gone out of him. He sat so still, completely shell-shocked. Everything he had strived for, now destroyed. After he'd worked so hard and against so many odds. He had pitted his incredible creativity against treachery and greed, and lost.

"You asked for me, Carl?" Lauren stood at the doorway, a question in her eyes.

Carl's gaze moved from Cara to Lauren. "Lauren, come in, come in. I have some exciting news for you." He strode over, put his arm around her shoulders, and walked with her to the head of the table. "We just placed a motion in front of the committee to make you president and CEO of Windwear."

Lauren's eyes widened, and then her face broke into a smile. She flashed a victorious gaze toward Liam. The room was brittle with silence. Liam's eyes narrowed, his anger evident in his taut posture. Richard put a calming hand on his arm, as Liam stared fixedly at Lauren. Lauren's smile wavered slightly as she faced Carl. "I'm honored. Truly honored."

Cara couldn't believe what she was hearing. She stepped out of the way as Lauren took a seat next to Carl, as if she were a queen accepting the accolades of royalty.

Maybe the smattering of applause from Carl's cronies was what sent Cara over the edge. Or Carl's obnoxious condescension. Or Lauren's triumphant sneer. Whatever the reason, the feeling hit her hard. Anger washed through her like a flood in winter, icy and furious and dark. To hell with them, she fumed. To hell with Lauren. To hell with Carl. To hell with all the rest of these crooks. She had the power to right this wrong, and right it she would. She waited for the applause to end before she spoke. With a calmness she was far from feeling, she turned to Carl. "A perfect idea, Carl. An absolutely perfect idea." The room stilled to a puzzled silence.

She saw the sudden alarm in Carl's eyes as she walked toward Lauren. With slow deliberation, she opened her purse and removed the papers. Carl gasped. He clenched his hands by his sides, and Cara turned and stared at him. She sensed his fears as if he'd shouted them out loud. She faced Lauren. "In fact, as the owner of Windlogic, I have many matters to discuss with you, Lauren." She unfolded the documents from the bank and laid them in front of the dark-haired woman.

Cara wanted to stop the moment in time, the moment when justice turned the corner. She wanted to savor the look of shock on Lauren's face. She wanted to make Lauren suffer as she had made Liam suffer. She wanted to feel Lauren's hatred directed at her. The hairs on Cara's arms started to tingle, and her heart raced with the sharp edge of revenge.

But it was not to be. Just as she laid the documents down, just as Lauren cast her eyes on them with suspicion, Carl leaped from his seat, grabbed the papers, and crumpled them into a tight wad. "I told you to get the hell out of here." The words hissed from his throat in a guttural rage.

"Not until Lauren and I have talked," Cara snapped.

"No! I said leave, you bitch!" Carl gave her a hard shove toward the door. Cara stumbled and fell to the ground, letting out a gasp as she hit the floor.

Liam bolted from his chair. He rushed around the table, leaned over Cara, and helped her up. "Are you okay?" he asked quietly. She nodded. Liam turned to face Carl in the hushed silence of the room. In a blinding flash of movement, he flew at the older man, knocked him down, and straddled him. Enraged, he raised his fist and swung down with all his might. There was a harsh thud as Liam's fist hit Carl's jaw.

Oh, God, Cara thought. He's going to kill that sorry excuse of a human being without an ounce of regret. As Liam raised his fist to hit Carl again, two burly security guards grabbed his shoulders and dragged him from the older man.

Liam thrashed like a madman. "Let me go!" he cried in rage. "I'll kill him. I swear I'll kill him." He struggled free and lunged after Carl, who was still wincing in pain on the floor. The guards were too quick, and they dragged Liam, twisting and writhing in fury, from the conference room.

The ruckus that followed Liam's forced departure was a mass of images and voices and sounds. Everyone rushed around in a panic, talking, yelling, exclaiming. Cara heard Lauren yell, "Someone call the police." Richard reached down and helped Carl to a sitting position. Cara hurried over to them.

She pushed in front of Richard and faced Carl. Her words were quiet and tense. "What will it be, Carl? Do we deal? Or do I make the call?"

Still dazed, Carl stared at her. Richard tried to make sense of Cara's words. "So help me God, Carl." She straightened and searched the room. "Where the hell is my phone?"

Carl attempted to rise, but Richard placed a restraining hand on his shoulder as he helped him up. "Hold on a minute, Carl." Cara fumbled with her purse and grasped her phone with shaking hands. She came back and stood in front of them. Richard held Carl's arm as he struggled to maintain his balance. She handed Carl a business card and then watched as the color drained from his face. Agent Raymond Farley, the card said. Federal Bureau of Investigation. "All right," he said haltingly. "Let's go to my office."

The three of them left the noisy room and moved toward the stairway. Behind them, they heard Liam shouting as the security guards restrained him. "The police are on their way," Mrs. Bosun called as they entered the stairwell.

"Get your lawyer up here, now," Cara ordered as they reached Carl's suite. Richard raised an eyebrow at her tone. Carl picked up the phone, dialed an extension, spoke a few words, and hung up.

Cara turned toward the banker. "Richard, would you please wait outside? But stay close, in case I need you."

"What's going on, Cara?"

She walked over and opened the door for Richard. "No questions, Richard. Not yet."

Richard stepped out as Carl's lawyer stepped in. Cara closed the door and turned toward the two men. Carl sighed. "Get the certificate out, Johnson." Tight-lipped, the lawyer pulled out the recently signed certificates from his briefcase. He thumbed through the papers until he reached the one he was looking for. With narrow, angry eyes, the attorney glared at Cara, signed the certificate, and handed it to Carl. Carl added his signature, and then gave it to her.

Cara examined the document. "Cross this out, and add the word ..." What did Richard say? Severally? That was the word he used. "Cross out the word *jointly* and add *severally*. And initial it. You too, Mr. Johnson. Carl glared at her furiously but didn't move. She shook her head in disgust. So, she thought, he planned to outmaneuver her the same way he had Liam and Richard. "I'm out of patience, Carl. Make the change." Still, he refused to sign.

Sighing, she pulled out her phone and dialed the number she had long since memorized. "FBI? Yes, this is Cara Larson. I'd like to speak to Agent Farley. Agent Raymond Farley." She paused. "Yes, he's expecting my call."

Carl and his lawyer shared a panicky glance. Cara stared at them icily. "I'll end this call if you initial the certifica—" She turned away. "Yes, I'm still here. Thank you. I'll wait." Fifteen seconds passed in tense silence. Cara stared straight at the two men. Another fifteen seconds. "Ray, hello. This is Cara Larson. I'm ready to tell you that story, now. Where should I start? With fraud? Or bribery?"

There was a frantic bustle as Carl's lawyer picked up the pen, made the changes she'd requested, and initialed them. Just as quickly, Carl added his initials. "Just a second, Ray.

Will you hang on for a minute?" She stood in front of the two men and inspected the document. "Now, notarize it." Carl nodded, and the lawyer walked to his briefcase, took out his notary stamp, and clamped the paper between its inky jaws. Cara picked up the document, studied it, and then spoke into the phone again. "I won't need to speak to you after all, Ray." She smiled into the phone. "You bet. I'll be sure to keep in touch. Thank you. Good-bye."

Cara hung up, examined the document, and then faced the two men. She opened her mouth to say the words she'd longed to say since discovering their deception. There was so much she wanted to say. So much contempt she wanted to heap on them. Instead, she snapped her mouth shut and left the room.

On the other end of the line, Mike Taylor held the phone away from his ear in stunned amazement. A slow smile spread across his face. "Cara Larson. You are such a conniving bitch!" He doubled over and fell to the floor in laughter.

Richard and Cara walked down the stairs in silence. When they reached the hallway, she went directly to the ladies room. After a few minutes she returned, her hair combed and makeup repaired, looking like she had nothing more on her mind than the color of her lipstick. She put on a smile. "Do I look normal?" She twirled round. She would need to hide her hands. They were still shaking.

Richard eyed her warily. "Cara, what happened upstairs?"

She stopped in mid-turn. "Absolutely nothing. After the fiasco in the conference room, you escorted me to the ladies room where I had a chance to pull myself together."

"What did you—"

"Nothing."

"All right, I won't ask. At least, for now."

"Excellent." She smiled at him. "Come on, Richard, let's go rescue Liam." He raised an eyebrow as he offered his arm to Cara. She took it, and together they walked toward the conference room.

Liam stood alone at the window near the far end of the reception area, staring down on the street below. Ten feet away, the two security guards eyed him closely. The area still buzzed with activity. Consortium members hovered, Lauren spoke on the phone, and the police questioned Mrs. Bosun. The secretary sounded puzzled. "I don't understand, officers, but Mr. Streeter just called and said he doesn't want to press charges. He wants to forget this whole unfortunate incident ever happened. Now, if you'll excuse me, I should clean up the conference room and reschedule the next management meeting with the consortium members before they leave."

Richard gave Cara a sharp look. "Hmm," was all she said as she returned his stare.

Cara approached her fiancé. "Liam? Are you okay?"

Startled from his reverie, Liam turned to find Cara staring up at him. "We need to leave, Cara. I need to call Jared Dafoe right away and figure out how to fight this."

They rode the elevator in silence. Out on the street, Richard shook their hands. "I need to get back to Boston, this afternoon. Liam, I'll call you tomorrow." Cara gave him a nervous glance. "I'm sorry about all this, young man. Truly sorry."

Liam nodded. Cara realized that he couldn't answer, couldn't get any words out. She held his arm and faced the banker. "We'll be in touch, Richard."

"Good-bye." Richard turned back to Liam once more. "You have a good woman, young man."

"I know," Liam smiled bleakly. "It's the kind of man *she* has that's worrying me, right now." He failed at his smile. "Good-bye, Richard." Liam started slowly along the sidewalk.

Richard peered at Cara. "If there's anything I can do—"

"Later, Richard. Liam will need you later."

He hugged her. "Take care of him."

Cara nodded. "I will."

Chapter 61

Cara had to hurry to catch up with Liam. Neither of them spoke until they reached the hotel. They entered her suite in silence. "Liam, would you come in, please?"

Liam shook his head. "I need to go to my room and start packing. You should too, Cara. We need to get back to Portland right away. I thought we'd have a little time before Streeter attacked, but I was wrong. I need Jared to review the agreement right away. I may be too late already. I may be out of Windwear in a matter of days, not months."

"Just for a minute. Then we can pack."

"Okay." He followed her in, walked to the window, and stared out at the city below. She stood beside him and wrapped her arms around his waist.

"Well, that didn't go exactly the way I planned." He gave her a rueful smile and threw an arm over her shoulder.

"No." They were quiet for several moments. "Liam." She turned to face him. "I need to tell you something. Something important."

"What?" He looked down at her as if he hadn't seen her in a long time. "Are you okay?"

"I'm fine." She smiled despite her tension. "Please, Liam. Come and sit down."

He followed her into the room and sat in a high backed wingchair. Cara walked over to the nightstand where the flat gift box she purchased yesterday rested. She slipped the certificate from her purse into the box. She walked across the room to Liam, leaned down, and kissed him softly. "This is for you."

He held the box uncertainly. "What is it?"

"It's my wedding present to you."

"Cara, we're not married."

"True, but you gave me Windlogic before we were married. It's only fair."

He examined the box suspiciously. He turned it over, shook it. "It's not from Bloomingdale's."

"No. You told me you weren't a Bloomindale's sort of guy."

"Is this what you came to New York early to get?"

She took a deep breath. "Yes, but it's not really a New York thing. It's ..." Her voice trailed off.

"It's ... what, Cara?"

She stroked the lapel of his suit. "You belong anywhere you are, Liam ... New York, Taiwan, Portland ... anywhere, but you will always be the Northwest to me. So, I decided to get you something very Northwest. I hope you like it."

He frowned. "It's not very big."

"No."

"Or heavy."

"No."

"What is it?"

She rolled her eyes. "Open it and find out."

Liam lifted the top edge and removed the cover. It was just a piece of paper. Innocent, really. Innocuous. It couldn't have weighed more than six ounces. It probably started out as a pine tree in western Oregon; was chopped, stripped, sliced, bleached, and finally ended up here, three thousand miles away, where its sole purpose was to shock the living hell out of Liam Scofield. Which it did. Because the words written on the silvery green-trimmed paper hit him like an explosion. WINDWEAR CORPORATION was emblazoned across the top in large bold letters he could not mistake. Precisely in the middle were the words ELEVEN SHARES. At the bottom was the signature he had numbly affixed to it not two hours earlier. He stared at her in confusion. "Cara?" It was all he could manage to say.

She smiled a little uncertainly. "I call it Windwear in a box. Do you like it?" He just sat there. "Liam?" Her smile turned to alarm. "Please, say something."

Liam's face had gone completely white. He looked at the paper. It was the same document he signed this morning. Eleven shares. With the words scribbled across the description: "*Severally owned.*" Eleven independent shares. Just enough. With the 490 shares he already possessed, this little piece of paper gave him 501 shares. Exactly 50.1 percent. Majority ownership. Management control. Of his company. He stared at Cara in astonishment. Windwear was his company once again. "Cara? Is this real?"

"Yes."

For a minute, he closed his eyes, and Cara saw the relief flood through him. "This is amazing." He smiled. "Did you get this from Richard? Did he ... No, he couldn't have." He flipped over the paper and read the words. "*I hereby transfer these eleven severally owned shares of Windwear Corporation voting stock to Ms. Cara Larson.*" But it was not Richard Bancroft's signature affixed to the bottom, but Carl Streeter's. "Cara, how did you get this?"

She knew that would be the first question he asked. She took a deep breath. "First, tell me if you like it."

"Don't play games. What did you do to get this? Is it real? Is this some kind of joke?"

She shook her head. "No, I wouldn't joke about something like this. All I need to do is sign these shares over to you, and Windwear is yours."

"How ... how did you get them? Streeter would never give these up." He peered at her with troubled eyes. "What did you give to Streeter to get these? Did you give him Windlogic? Something else? What, Cara? Please, tell me."

She sat in the chair next to his. "I didn't even think about giving him Windlogic." She paused. "We ... made a different deal."

"What kind of deal?"

"Well," she said slowly, "he agreed to give me these eleven shares. And I agreed not to expose to the world he bribed Lauren and committed fraud while he colluded with her to take Windwear away from you."

Liam's jaw dropped. "Bribed ..." He paused as her words sunk in. "You blackmailed him? You blackmailed Carl Streeter?"

"I believe extortion is the proper term."

He closed his eyes. "Oh my God. What have you done?"

"I've only done what Carl does every day, I'm afraid."

Liam closed his eyes. "Okay, Cara, I will concede right off the top you are the gutsiest person I've ever known in my life. But even with that concession, I can't agree to accept these shares. Do you have any idea what Streeter can do to you?"

"Yes. I'm clear on the risks of my strategy."

"The risks of your strategy? This isn't a board game, Cara. You can't extort people like Carl Streeter without serious consequences."

"I guess that's probably why no one has gone after him before. The snake."

Liam shook his head and handed the box back to her. "I can't take these shares. I would be putting you in too much jeopardy."

"I see." But she refused to take the box.

"No, you do not see. Don't you realize how important you are to me? Don't you realize that even Windwear, which has been the most important thing in my life for years, is a poor second compared to you? I love you, Cara. Do you think I could let anyone or anything hurt you?"

She touched his cheek gently. "I understand, Liam. And I love you. That's why I didn't tell you." She smiled. "You've done that before, you know. Come to my rescue. Protect me at the expense of your company. But you don't understand. I refuse to be the reason you lose Windwear. We both know what Carl will do if he owns these shares. He'll destroy your company. Do you think he cares about Windwear or its customers or its products? Do you think he cares about hiking boots or running lights or camping gear? Carl Streeter cares about one thing. Money. And with Lauren's help, Windwear became another easy target for him to make a lot of it."

"We'll fight him, Cara. If you have proof Carl committed bribery and fraud, we'll fight him the right way. In court."

"How long will that take?" She sat back and crossed her legs. "Liam, do you have any idea how much Carl Streeter is worth? Upwards of three billion dollars, the last time I checked. How long do you think he can tie you up in court while you contest the provisions of the registration statement *you* signed? And what happens to Windwear in the meantime? He'll lose no time in stripping the company bare of every last dollar."

"We don't get the choice, Cara. We have to fight within the bounds of the law—"

"Like Carl did?" She shook her head. "He had no trouble working outside the bounds of the law. I thought about going to the feds, Liam, I did, but I decided I needed to fight him on his own turf."

Liam shook his head. "If what you say is true, the last thing you want to do is take on a guy like Carl Streeter, especially on his turf. He's not a guy you want to piss off. I saw him at work today. He doesn't take too kindly to people trying to cheat him, or worse … extort him. He's worth three billion dollars. My guess is he'll spend a good chunk of it coming after you."

"I don't think so. He has too much to lose."

"No. Carl Streeter can afford to lose more than you and I will ever have."

"On this point we disagree, Mr. Scofield." She rested her arms on the wings of the chair. "Actually, I think I would enjoy facing Carl Streeter in court. Alas, I will never get the chance. Carl's a coward. He always takes the easy path. And he just discovered today that you're not worth the trouble. He won't risk it."

"I don't think *we* can risk it."

"Liam, the only thing more important in Carl Streeter's life than his greed is his ego. And that's where he runs into a big problem." She smiled as if she didn't have a care in the world. "Do you know Carl is on the board of several museums? And the opera? And the symphony? Not to mention some of the biggest corporations in the country, including Pyramid. He is one influential man. Which is precisely why he won't come after me." She leaned back in her chair. "If we go to trial, I will expose the fact he used bribery and fraud to make the deal with Windwear. And if I get a good lawyer who can do some decent research, I bet we'll find out Windwear isn't his first victim. Then everyone will know the truth about Carl Streeter. He wouldn't be able to handle that."

"Truth? What are you talking about?"

"Carl Streeter takes great pride in the fact that he's a financial genius. He's sold the whole world on the idea he is successful because he's smarter than everyone else. If he goes to trial, everyone will know he's just a common cheater, no better than a two-bit loan shark on East Burnside Street. And once the word is out, poof! There goes the symphony and the opera and all those lucrative board seats that do nothing more than feed his giant ego. No, he'd never risk letting the secret out. He'd rather let Windwear go."

Liam shook his head. "You're risking an awful lot on a supposition. He'll find a way to sue you without ever allowing a court to hear any testimony."

"Not if I get a good lawyer. And there's always the press. I think the media would enjoy having some fun with Carl Streeter. After all, those folks are driven by money, too. The sordid story of Carl Streeter bribing his way into the ownership position of small companies so he can rob them blind might sell a few papers." She shrugged. "But let's say you're right. Worst case, I figure I'll get a couple of years in jail."

Liam choked. "A couple of years. Cara, are you listening to yourself? You've actually thought about this?"

"Of course. It's always best to identify the worst case scenario before—"

"Before you extort a guy worth three billion dollars?"

"I was going to say, 'before taking any action,' but you make a good point."

He closed his eyes. "I can't believe I'm hearing this."

"Liam, think about this. What's the worst that could happen? I have a clean record. I've never been in any trouble.

For me to be convicted, I have to go to trial. If there's a trial, the story comes out. My lawyer will paint the picture that I was merely trying to right a terrible wrong committed against my fiancé's company. Do you think the SEC will allow Streeter to take control of Windwear? Or make you give Aerie to him after the whole story comes out? No way. They will let you keep Windwear. You'll probably get off with a fine for not properly disclosing Aerie from the beginning. And I'll get, what, a couple years in a minimum-security facility? As a first-time offender with no previous record, and with a proper show of remorse, I might get as little as six months. I admit though, the remorse part will be tough to do."

"Oh God."

"I'm willing to take the risk."

"Well, I'm not."

"It's too late. I've already done the deed."

"Why didn't you talk to me about this?"

"Because you would have tried to talk me out of it. And because this way you have complete deniability. You can freely testify you knew nothing about my plans. It's kind of brilliant, if you think about it."

He rubbed his fingers across his forehead. "Yes, it's brilliant. It's also dangerous. Cara, you shouldn't have done this."

"It's done, Liam. All that's left is for you to accept my gift. Take the shares. Run your company. Move on. Live your life."

"And wait every day for the police to come and take away the most important thing in my life?"

"What do you want me to do, Liam? Do you want me to give the eleven shares back to Carl?"

He shook his head. "I'm not sure. I need to think about it. I can't let you risk your future this way."

"My future? You are such an optimist, Liam. That's what I love about you. The world is a good place to you. You see me as ... good, but if you saw me the way the rest of the world does, you would get a different picture. Then you would realize the only one taking any risk is Carl."

"What do you mean? How does the rest of the world see you, besides amazing and brilliant?" he asked in puzzlement.

"You are sweet, Liam." She gave him a sad smile. "The objective view looks something like this: I recently lost my mother. I have no family left. I lost my job. My professional reputation is ruined. I rent a house on the beach and do odd jobs for the locals. I don't even own a car." She gave him a rueful smile. "What can Carl Streeter possibly take from me that I haven't already lost?"

"What about me?" he asked quietly. "You have me to lose. And Windlogic."

"Yes, I do. I do have you." She shook her head. "But I won't lose you over this. No, I know you too well, Liam Scofield. Windlogic will be okay. I'll transfer Windlogic back to you, and as long as you control the company, it will be safe. And the whole jail thing? I know you'll wait for me while I serve my time. In fact, I bet you'll be the first one in line each week on visiting day. You'll probably bring roses, too. And Maggie will make a care package big enough to feed everyone on my cellblock."

A reluctant smile spread across his face. "That is probably true."

"No, I won't lose you because I go to jail, Liam. But I'll tell you how I would lose you. I would lose you if every day you had to wake up and live with the fact that Carl Streeter and Lauren Janelle stole your company. They didn't play fair like you did. They didn't follow the rules. They didn't stay within the bounds of the law. I understand why they targeted you. They thought you were weak because you are decent and honest. You pay a reasonable price for the things you buy, you make transparent deals that give a fair return, you go for the win-win instead of the win-lose. Facing the fact that Lauren and Carl cheated you, and will now cheat others using Windwear as their weapon, well, that will kill you a little every day, Liam. Sooner or later, the damage will be so great that I would lose you as surely as if they'd up and stabbed you in the heart from the very start."

Cara searched his face. "Don't you see, Liam? I told you your river runs deep, but what you don't seem to understand, is that your river runs through me. I can't separate you from me any more than I can separate east from west. Seeing you hurt and doing nothing about it, is like hurting myself. I was in the position to prevent Carl from taking the ... second most important thing in your life, and I did it. Happily. And I would do it again in a heartbeat."

Liam was quiet for a long time. After several minutes, he rose, took Cara's hands in his, and pulled her up next to him. He wrapped his arms tightly around her, kissed her, and smiled into her eyes. "Thank you, Cara. Thank you for being on my side and risking everything you think you don't have." He sighed. "All right. I'll take the shares. I'll get you the best lawyer money can buy. And I'll make Windwear such a success Carl Streeter will have no reason to come after you."

She threw her arms around him. "Thank you, Liam."

"I don't like it, Cara, but I'll do it. For you. Because I am not willing to let your generous, unselfish, badass bravery go to waste. And because I love you like crazy."

"You won't change your mind?" She searched his face.

"No, I won't change my mind, but in the future, promise me you won't do anything like this again without talking to me first. No more Joan-of-Arc, tie-me-to-the-stake, go-out-on-a-limb, heroics until you at least discuss your plans with me first. Is that fair?"

She leaned into him and placed her head against his chest. "That's fair." She paused. "Thank you, Liam."

"No, I'm the one who needs to thank you." They stood together for a long time, quiet, still, soaking in each other's warmth.

"Liam, I need to tell you something else."

"What?" he asked lazily as he began to kiss her.

She smiled as her lips met his. "I ... I've decided to pursue another career."

His head snapped up sharply. "Another career? Instead of Windlogic? Do you want to change your mind about owning Windlogic, now that I have control of Windwear again?"

"Oh no. I want to keep Windlogic, if that's still okay. But... I've decided to add another line to my resume."

"What is it? You didn't you tell me about this before."

"I thought you knew. It's been in the works for a while, now ..."

He closed his eyes. What now? What bombshell was she going to drop this time? He should not be surprised. This was badass Cara Larson.

"Anyway, I probably shouldn't tell you too many of my plans."

"I thought we just finished agreeing we would talk to each other before—"

"I shouldn't tell you because I will be in direct competition with Windwear."

"In competition with Windwear?" His eyebrows shot up in surprise. "What are you planning, Cara?"

She placed a gentle finger on his lips. "Relax, Liam. I'll come clean." She rolled her finger down his cheek. "From now on, I'll be spending a considerable amount of time and energy as the wife of the handsome and sophisticated CEO of Windwear. My goal is to lure him into my bed, my heart, and my life. I don't want any distractions to keep me from this important position. He's an intense man. A rich man. A man who is far too busy for his own good. A man who has no time to go to the beach or count the stars or dance in the waves. It's going to take all my expertise to make this new endeavor successful."

Liam closed his eyes and let the relief surge through him. He gave her a crooked smile as he raised his head in challenge. "You will never be able to manage it, Ms. Larson. I'm much too focused on business to let any distractions distract me."

Cara's eyes danced. "Oh, really? Hmm. My first assignment." She placed her hands on the sides of his face and began to kiss him.

Liam gently grasped her wrists and held them at a distance. "Nope. No effect whatsoever. You will need to try much harder than that if you are to successfully lure this executive out of the boardroom and into the bedroom."

"Hmm. If you insist." She wriggled her hands from his grasp, removed his jacket, and threw it on the bed. His tie came next, then his shirt. She rained soft kisses down on his chest.

He stifled a groan. "Sorry. No go, Cara. This … is … not … working."

"You are proving more of a challenge than I thought." She let her hands slide down to his stomach, then lower …

Liam pulled her hands away and trapped them with his own. "Just one second, Ms. Larson. It has just occurred to me you can't start your new career unless I start one, too. You need a husband if you plan to be a wife. And I have a few conditions of my own before I agree to take on the role."

She raised an eyebrow as he held her hands in his, her body warm against his. "What might those be?"

"First, a big wedding."

Her mouth dropped open in surprise. "Liam, I don't need a big wedding."

"Of course you don't. It was your mother's request."

Cara stopped. "My mother's—"

"Mary told me in her letter. The one Jeanine gave me. She knew I was in love with you, Cara."

"She did?" Cara whispered.

"I told you everyone knew. Even your mother. She asked me to give you a big wedding even though she said you would probably prefer to elope—"

"That's true. I don't need any wedding froofery—"

"And she wants you to carry lilacs and roses, even though I believe that will violate every floral arrangement rule in the universe."

She removed her hands from his grasp and wrapped her arms around him. "Then I'll do it for sure. If I'm forced to endure a big wedding, I may as well have some fun and break a few rules."

"You sound like Mike."

"I do, don't I?" She laughed. God, it felt good to laugh again. "I love you, Liam Scofield," she whispered as she snuggled against him. "Thank you. Thank you for being so kind to my mother during her final days."

"You're welcome." He kissed her gently.

"Now, where were we?" Once again she spread her fingers across his chest.

"Uh-uh. Nice try, Ms. Larson. You can't distract me from this negotiation. I have one more condition."

"What? One more? You're already asking a lot with the big wedding and all. What is it?"

"A promise." He smiled, but his eyes turned serious.

"What kind of promise?" she asked, curiosity getting the best of her.

"Your promise that if things ever go haywire with our careers, that if Windlogic and Windwear get to be too much for Mr. and Mrs. Scofield to handle, you and I will drop everything and run to the beach. And we will hide out, count stars, dig clams, dance in the moonlight, and talk until the two of us decide what to do. Together."

She closed her eyes as if considering. "Well, Mr. Scofield, you are not at all as tough a negotiator as I anticipated. I think I can agree to your demands."

"Of course, you can, Ms. Larson. It's a win-win." He kissed her deeply as he began to remove her clothes. "The best kind of deal to make."

About The Author

Anne Riley lives in Hillsboro, Oregon with her husband and better half, Tim. They are the parents of three children, Jim, Celeste, and Erin, all of whom have grown up and left the nest. They make their parents proud with their interesting and uniquely suitable lives.

Aerie is Anne's second book and first work of fiction. She surrendered to the writing bug in 2012 when she published her first book, a non-fiction work entitled *Elusive Little Sucker, My Entirely Too Long and Totally Circuitous Search for Happiness*. It is the completely true, and occasionally embarrassing, story of how she struggled with and finally found happiness.

Anne's true love is writing fiction. She will continue to write rich and interesting stories that allow readers the chance to enjoy a delightful ride into the lives of characters who are forced to deal with complicated problems that exist all around us in this complicated world.

Follow Anne at:

Website:	www.AnneRileyAuthor.com
Facebook:	http://www.facebook.com/pages/Anne-Riley/447831115284513
Twitter:	https://twitter.com/AnneRileyAuthor
Goodreads:	http://www.goodreads.com/author/show/6927877.Anne_Riley
LinkedIn:	https://www.linkedin.com/profile/view?id=296989625

12198208R00286

Made in the USA
San Bernardino, CA
12 June 2014